To Merry Hahn—
a precious sister and kindred spirit.
There is so much I could say,
but for once in my life I'll be brief.
I love you.

Acknowledgments

I never dreamed this book would be so long in the making, but at last it's here. I'm not the same person I was when the idea was conceived. Thankfully, God never gives up, but keeps honing and changing me for His service. I would like to thank the people who have aided in that process.

Roxane Carley. When I told you the short story about a woman's visit to see her brother in Hawaii, you told me it should be a full book. Thank you for your wisdom. It's been a wonderful journey to that end.

Pam Jeffcott and Joy Inafuku. I didn't get to Hawaii as I planned, so your technical support was wonderful. Thank you for taking the time to talk with me. I hope you can forgive me in the areas where I guessed. The Hawaii I wrote about might not really exist, but I still hope and pray that you enjoy the book.

Connie Handel. Thank you for the medical facts and info. It's so nice having someone with your expertise and willingness to help right up the street. You are dear to me.

Pastor Mark Cymbalak. Thank you, Mark, for helping me to see how personal God's Word is, and how seriously He takes grumbling and complaining.

Cathy Yasick. You are so precious to me, Cathy. Thank you for your wonderful, warm spirit, encouraging attitude, and your determination to keep on. You have taught me so much. I love you, dear friend.

The children in my fourth, fifth, and sixth grade Sunday school class. Thank you for the laughter and fun. Thank you for good questions and using the great minds God has given you. I'm learning so much from you and pray that your hearts are being changed forever as we look into God's Word.

Randy Vesperman. I need to thank you for sharing Mary with me and supporting the work we're doing. But mostly, Randy, I want to thank you for your wonderful sense of humor and your kind friendship through the years.

Phil Caminiti. Thank you for the song on page 147, and for being one of the most perspicacious persons I know.

My son, Timothy. There are no words to describe my joy in you. I would have been weak. I would have given up. Thank you for playing hard and keeping on. I love you.

And always, my Bob. You're a part of every romance I write. When the male lead is strong, patient, humorous, and working hard to be God's man for the job, I just have to look to you for an example. Thank you for being my very own to keep.

Foreword

December 25
Dear Father,

It's late here, and busy as my day was, my thoughts have turned fully to you and Lily. You were in my mind all day, but without deep joy, and I have finally understood the cause. My work for the next year makes it impossible for me to come to you. I know you understand that, and I know it's difficult for you to leave Lhasa, but there is no reason that Lily cannot come to visit me in Hawaii. Please consider how special this would be for both of us. She hasn't been out of Kashien since she was five.

Jefferson Walsh sat back now, knowing he would have to choose his words carefully. After a moment he knew what he needed to say.

It would be a great learning experience for Lily. We would not be idle. And I need to tell you that I'm thinking of an extended visit—hopefully six months, three months at the very least. If Lily is going to experience and learn from this culture, it could be no less.

Again Jeff sat back and studied the letter. His father was not always the most predictable of men, and he so wanted to persuade him to at least consider this visit.

I know you'll be fair in your consideration of this. I'm enclosing a letter to Lily telling her of my idea, knowing that she will take her cue from you.
I hope this Christmas was a blessed one for you. The gifts you sent were great. I miss you as always and pray that we'll see each other soon.

Love always,
Jeff

~

February 2
Dear Jefferson,

*I'm glad your Christmas was fine. We enjoyed your gifts
as well. Your sister and I spent Christmas Day with Lee
Chen and his family, and had…*

Jeff swiftly scanned the entire contents of the letter and sat
back with a disappointed sigh. His father had completely ignored
his request for Lily to visit. There was also a letter from his sister
in the envelope, but he knew she would say nothing of a visit
without first gaining permission from their father. However, Jeff
was not deterred. He immediately took out paper and started a
letter back, one that immediately addressed the subject on his
mind.

Dear Father,

*I'm disappointed that you did not reply to my request to
have Lily visit. If both of you can come, you know I would
be overjoyed, but please don't make Lily stay because you
are too busy to join her. I want to see you both, but Lily's
work in the village will not suffer if she is with me for six
months.*

Jeff hesitated now, gauging how bold he should be. He opted
to tell his father just the way he felt.

*I want Lily to come. You write and tell me how proud
you are of my work and that you understand I am not free
to come to you. Please put actions behind your words. Do
not keep my sister from me. It's been three years since I
was in Kashien. I don't have to ask Lily to know she would
be willing. I know travel plans would need to be worked
out, but if you are willing, it would be the greatest gift you
could give me, not to mention Lily. Please do not ignore my*

voice from so many miles away. Please respond to my request so that we may at least speak of this.

Love always,
Jeff

〜

February 26
Dear Jefferson,
 I am leaving to meet with a troubled man. I have no time to discuss this with you just now, but I will consider your request to have Lily visit. I will address it in my next letter.

Love,
Father

Jeff received and read this letter in the middle of March, his heart filled with delight that his father would consider the matter. He had been praying fervently for Lily to visit once the idea came to him, and knowing the door was still open was so wonderful that for a moment he could only sit at his small kitchen table and smile.

Chapter One

~

Lhasa, Kashien
May

Taking her usual shortcut through the trees, Lily Walsh slipped across the pathway on swift, silent feet. She wasn't in a hurry, but her long legs covered the ground in easy strides, and at the moment there was no reason to dawdle.

Ling-lei Chen's house was in sight just a moment later, and in less then a minute she was knocking on her door. Ling was like family, so Lily didn't wait to enter but slipped inside. She had just shut the door when a toddler and two older children came flying at her. Lily had hugs for five-year-old Hope and six-year-old Faith, but two-year-old Charity had lifted her arms into the air, begging to be held. Not able to resist, Lily pulled her into her arms.

"Hello," the children's mother greeted Lily as she came forward with Charity on her hip. The two women hugged.

"How are you?" Lily asked, knowing her friend was not feeling well during the early stages of her fourth pregnancy.

"I'm all right for the moment, but I'll probably eat the whole time you're here."

Lily only smiled, thinking that Ling could use every calorie. She was a minuscule woman with three active girls.

"Lily," Ling now asked, "has your father given any hints about Hawaii?"

"Not a one. I'm beginning to think he's told my brother no."

"Are you disappointed?"

Lily had to think about this.

"Now that you ask, I guess I don't actually believe he's told Jeff no." The women's eyes met. "When he does, I'll be very disappointed."

"So you think he will?"

"In my heart I do. I'm trying not to get my hopes up, but it's hard not to."

Ling desperately wanted to give her friend some hope.

"If it is no, maybe Jeff will come."

"Maybe," Lily said with a smile. This had crossed her mind, but she didn't think it likely. "Let's get started," she said in an attempt to take her mind from her own worries.

Lily was teaching Ling-lei to read. Ling had married young and started a family within ten months of her wedding date, and unlike most village families, time had not been made for her education.

"Girls," their mother said, and the children who had been playing on the floor at the women's feet stood in a line to face her.

"Lily and I are going to the table to work now. You keep quiet."

Little heads bobbed, even that of Charity, who was still little more than a baby. She naturally took her cue from her sisters.

After Ling had set tea out for both her and her guest—and a small bowl of thin crackers for her own unsettled stomach—they sat down with the book between them. *Stuart Little* was not what most people would have used to teach reading, but Lily knew that Ling would love the story and not find the words overwhelming. They picked up at chapter 12 where Stuart sets out on his journey. Ling smiled at the drawing of him in the tiny car after he was hired to be a substitute teacher.

"I'll have to tell the children about this."

"Read it to them," Lily encouraged her.

Ling frowned. "I don't do as well when you're not listening."

"Ling," Lily said with a hand to her friend's arm, "Faith is only six. None of the children will miss a wrong word now and again."

"I could read them the entire book," Ling said. "From the beginning."

"I think you should."

Footsteps from without caused the women to stop, eyes lowered, as Lee Chen, Ling's husband, came in the door.

"I wondered if I would find you two together," he teased. Both women smiled. "How is the reading? Will you be much longer?"

Ling answered, although both women continued to keep their eyes lowered.

"We just started, but we can finish if you need something."

"Actually, I just saw Pastor Owen. He's looking for you, Lily."

Lily's eyes came briefly to her friend's, and the two women smiled.

"Thank you, Lee Chen," Lily said as she moved to bid the children goodbye. Usually she had time to play with them, and for a moment they looked confused at her departure.

"Is there bad news?" Ling asked of her husband when they were alone.

"I don't think so, but with Pastor Owen it's hard to say."

The Kashienese man looked at his wife.

"Look at me, Ling," he commanded quietly.

Ling did so without hesitation.

"Is she still hoping for word on visiting Jeff?"

Ling smiled into her husband's eyes before asking, "What do you think?"

Lee smiled back before the children headed their way. Ling once again lowered her eyes—out of habit, but also as an example to her daughters—and for the moment the subject of Lily's trip was dropped.

With its close proximity to Chinese, Japanese, and Taiwanese neighbors, Kashien was a small country whose existence had been battled over many times in the past. Since 1936, however, it had been free and independent. Some areas, mostly in the mountains, were utterly behind the times, while others, like Capital City, were thriving, bustling places, full of modern conveniences and ways.

Lily Walsh had only heard about the past wars and unrest. Her life in the village had been one of tranquillity and peace, something she took for granted as she left the Chen home and made her way along the river toward the small house she shared with her father. The village of Lhasa, which sat high in the Katoose Mountains, was spread out on acres of terraced land. Lily gave sights that she'd seen since birth little notice as she thought about what her father might want. His looking for her in the middle of the morning meant neither good news nor bad, but it meant something.

"Lily," another friend called to her as she passed her field, "come for tea."

"My father is looking for me, Rika. Thank you, anyway."

Rika waved her off in understanding, and Lily kept on her way. Just a few more minutes passed till her house came into view, and Lily entered as she always did, eyes down with respect in case her father was at home. He was.

"Come in," he told her, his voice giving nothing away.

"Lee Chen told me you were looking for me."

"I was, yes. Were you and Ling having your lesson?"

"Yes," Lily spoke as she took the seat across the small living room from him. "She's over halfway through the book. We'll be going onto something more difficult very soon."

"Good."

Lily nodded, her eyes still lowered.

Owen Walsh was from Chicago, but since his wife, Cathleen, had died almost 12 years earlier, he had taken on more and more traits of those who lived in the village. Having been born there and only away from Kashien for six months as a little girl, Lily thought nothing of it.

"Don't be afraid to introduce her to something more challenging, Lily. Ling is a quick study."

"Yes, she is," Lily was swift to agree. "Although I think she's still working to understand that. Just today she figured out she could read *Stuart Little* to the girls. I was going to mention it to her a few weeks back, but I'm glad she came to it on her own."

"I've decided that you're going to visit Jeff."

Lily was so shocked by this announcement that she forgot herself. Her lids flew up so she could see her father's face. It was not a happy one.

Brow lowered in offense, Owen snapped his fingers loudly as Lily dropped her eyes.

"You forget yourself, Lily Cathleen," he said, a distinct chill in his tone.

"I'm sorry."

The room was quiet for a moment. Lily's joy over the news had been greatly dampened by her father's disapproval. She knew he would not cancel the trip. He wasn't spiteful, but he was a fanatic when it came to propriety in the village.

"Look at me, Lily," he commanded, his voice still a bit stern.

Lily would never have disobeyed such an order, but only years of training in keeping emotions from her face hid the turmoil inside.

"I know you are excited, but that is no excuse. There will be many exciting things in the months to come, but you must not forget yourself. You must not shame me. This is not a pleasure trip, Lily, but an educational one. I expect you to return to me full of knowledge and report on the things you learned. If this is not the plan, there is no reason for you to go."

Lily did not agree but kept her opinion to herself. She would work hard and learn a lot, of this she was certain, but she would mostly enjoy time with her brother and being a part of his world. Had she not made her father angry, she would have asked when she could go and for how long, but such questions would need to wait.

"Why don't you head to your room now and take some time to think on what your mindset needs to be when you go."

"Yes, Father."

Lily rose and left on nearly silent feet. She slipped into her own bedroom, the cloth door covering falling back in place behind her. Her bed was a low wooden structure, just a foot off the floor, but Lily was used to sinking down to lie or sit on the village-made mattress. She sat on it now. She stared out the small window across from her and tried to be repentant. It didn't work. Knowing that her father took some things much too seriously, Lily grabbed her pillow so she could scream into it. She was going to see her brother! It was almost too good to be true.

I didn't dare to hope, Lord. I wanted to but... Lily couldn't go on. She had asked the Lord to let her go. She had petitioned Him many times, all the while working to accept whatever His will for her might be. A trip to Hawaii to be with Jeff sounded wonderful, but in truth, she wasn't God. She didn't know what might be awaiting her. As much as she wanted to see her only sibling, she didn't want to be in Hawaii unless God wanted her to be.

Lily suddenly came to her feet. She hadn't been in her room long at all. She found her father at the kitchen table and approached him as she would at any other time.

"I'm going for a run."

Owen looked at her. He had meant what he said. He wanted her to think on this upcoming trip and to take it seriously. But looking into her face, even with her eyes down, he was reminded of what a wonderful daughter she was.

"Will you be back for lunch?"

"If I'm not, everything is ready in the cupboard."

"Very good."

Lily left silently, starting to run almost as soon as she was out the door. Her stride was smooth and graceful. Lily loved to run with all of her heart. It helped to clear her head, and often she prayed. She also slept better at night if she ran at some point during the day.

Her normal route took her up a small rise, and as she bent a little with plans to sprint to the top, she did what she always did:

thought of Jeff. She wondered if he might be running too. Had she stopped to think about the time difference, she might have had her answer. But even if her brother was asleep, Lily was talking to him.

I'm coming, Jefferson. I don't know when and I don't know for how long, but Father said YES!

~

"I made him cross, so he didn't tell me the details until evening prayer time, but I'm going as soon as I can book the flight."

"And for how long?" Ling-lei asked next.

"Three months. Jeff wanted me for six, but Father said three was enough."

Ling bit her lip in excitement and asked, "You'll write to me?"

"Yes, and after I do, you'll know my address and write back."

Ling looked at her.

"I'll miss you, but I wouldn't want you to stay."

"Thank you, Ling."

As the women embraced, the children came over, and for a time the five of them talked about Hawaii. Lily told them all she knew, and realized it wasn't much. She knew the facts and figures about the fiftieth state and even the layout of Jeff's apartment, but not much else. It didn't bother her, though. It was just a matter of time until she would have more to tell than she could imagine.

~

August 31

The trip to Capital City from Lhasa had been long and hard enough, but nothing at all compared to what Lily's journey would be once she started flying. According to her itinerary, the flight from Capital City to Tokyo would take three hours and 15 minutes. She then had an unavoidable seven-hour layover. After that, the flight from Tokyo to Honolulu would take seven hours and 15 minutes. To top it off, the flight crossed the international date line, bringing even more confusion into the matter. Her body would be telling her that twenty-four hours had passed, but the calendar and clock would show only 35 minutes elapsing.

Owen and Lily arrived in plenty of time to have something to eat and spend some time alone. Owen had been quiet for most of the time, and his daughter wondered if this trip was bothering him more than he let on. He hadn't even noticed that Lily had been carrying her own bag until they were inside the terminal.

"I can get it," Lily assured him when he tried to take it, but Owen took it from her anyway.

Not prepared for the weight, his entire right side sank down as he took the handle in his grasp. He looked at Lily to find her standing quite still. He set the bag down at his side and faced her squarely.

"Look at me, Lily," he said quietly.

She would have given anything to disobey. If she had to leave Kashien after one of her father's scowls, she didn't know what she would do. Always a little unpredictable, his mood swings had been off the chart since he had given her permission to leave: laughing and joking with her one day and utterly quiet the next.

Knowing she had no choice, Lily looked up.

"What's in this bag?"

"My books," she whispered.

Owen melted his daughter's heart by giving her a small, tender smile.

"So like your mother."

"Well, the flight from Tokyo is very long," she felt free to tell him, "and so is the layover. I can pick something up in Hawaii for the trip back, but I thought I needed plenty now."

"So these are just books to read on your trip there?" he asked, a slight tease in his voice.

Lily smiled. "Plus a few of my favorites."

Owen gave her an indulgent look, lifted her bag, and started down the corridor of the terminal. Lily easily kept pace with him and followed as he found the gate for her to check in. That done, he led them to seats in the waiting area. Lily glanced around at the busy terminal, but Owen took out his newspaper and began to read.

From her place across from him, Lily took the opportunity to covertly study her father. He was not a young man. He had not met and married her mother—who had been much younger—until he was nearing his mid-forties. Jeff had been born to them when Owen was 45; Lily, four years later. Lily had just turned 24, making Owen 73. He didn't look or act old, but the sagging flesh around his face and neck and the full head of white hair did make him look more like her grandfather than her father.

While Lily was still thinking about her patriarch, Owen put the paper aside and tapped the seat next to him. Lily moved and, with her face in profile to him, began to listen to his instructions. Much of what he was saying—urging her to work hard and learn a greal deal—he had said before, but his voice sounded tense now. Lily wished she could look into his eyes, but she didn't dare. She didn't know if she felt rescued or cheated when they called her flight, effectively cutting her father off.

Lily stood, feeling the separation for the first time and not knowing quite how to handle it. She stole a peek at her father, but he was looking stern, so Lily dropped her eyes.

"Thank you for bringing me, Father."

This said, Lily lifted her own bag and moved into line. Her face was as calm and serene as though she were home resting in the village, but inside she was suddenly afraid. What if she never saw him again? What if he never wanted her to leave but couldn't find the way to tell her?

Lily's tumultuous thoughts halted when she realized he had come to the line with her. Even risking his wrath, she stole a look at his face. For the first time in years their eyes held.

"Take care of yourself," he said quietly, speaking to her for the first time in English. "Give Jeff my love."

Lily smiled up at him with such relief that Owen hugged her.

"Come back to me, Lily," he whispered into her ear.

"I will, Papa," she whispered back and watched as he slipped away into the crowd.

Heart pounding again, she turned back to see that only 20 people stood between her and the portal that led to the plane. She held her boarding pass outside her bag and noticed that it shook a little. She remembered little about her only other flight and honestly didn't know what to expect this time.

A glance behind her brought no sign of her father, so she assumed he had gone on his way. Lily felt slightly let down over this, but thought it might be best. At the moment she was having second thoughts.

Suddenly it was time to hand over her boarding pass. Lily did so, not aware that the kind smile of the airline worker stemmed from what she saw on Lily's pale face. Lily walked aboard, found her seat, and settled in. Before she was ready, the plane was taxiing down the runway and lifting into the air. It occurred to her as the aircraft jetted into the sky—with a good deal of noise and movement—that she didn't really want to do this. However, it was much too late to turn back.

～

Honolulu, Hawaii

In the morning bustle of the airport, Jefferson Walsh watched passengers emerge from the customs area, his eyes scanning each one. He thought it odd that Lily had not appeared. He knew she would pack light and could only hope there was no problem with her passport.

He was getting ready to ask the security guard at the door about going in to have a look around when he spotted her. Standing out of the flow of traffic, eyes down, bag at her feet, she did not look up as Jeff approached.

"Excuse me," he began, "I'm looking for a slim woman with dark hair and green eyes. Have you seen anyone like that?"

"Oh, Jeff," she whispered just before his arms came around her.

Not given to tears, Lily was amazed at how much she wanted to cry. Having slept little in 24 hours probably didn't help, but seeing her brother for the first time in three years was also a major factor.

"How are you?" Jeff asked and watched her keep her eyes down as she answered.

"I'm all right. The flight was long."

"Look at me, Lily."

His voice was so like her father's that it startled her.

Jeff waited until her eyes came to his and then shook his head. Her eyes, nearly black with fatigue, stood out all the more against her pale features. Jeff lifted her bag, put a hand to her upper arm, and started to lead her down the corridor.

"We have a number of things to work on, the first being that you're not going to lower your eyes for the next three months. But before we do that, you need some sleep."

Jeff glanced down to see Lily nod, but as he expected, her lids were down so she would not meet the eyes of any man. Jeff could only shake his head. It might take awhile, but before he was done, his sister would be stuck having to completely retrain herself when she got back to Kashien.

Lily woke slowly, her head fuzzy and disoriented. The pillow was soft against her cheek, and the mattress was so comfortable that she never wanted to move. She lay facing the wall, her gaze taking in a white blur. The sound of something mechanical suddenly came to her ears, and a cool breeze blew over her.

Lily's eyes opened fully, and she smiled as she rolled to her back.

"This is your bedroom" had been Jeff's words when he had brought her into his second-floor apartment and directly to the room where he told her she could sleep as long as she liked. It wasn't fancy, but Lily didn't have painted walls at home, so reaching out and touching their smooth white surface was a delight.

Lily was still touching the wall and trying to make herself move when she heard the door open. Jeff peeked in and then swung the door open wide.

"I wondered if you were ever going to get up," he teased.

"How long have I been asleep?"

"Almost six hours."

"Oh, my," Lily said as she tried to sit up. Her back was stiff, and she couldn't get one foot out of the sheet.

Her brother laughed at her and turned away.

"I've got something for you to eat when you feel like it."

"Thank you. Jeff?"

"Yeah?"

"Where is the bathroom?"

"Out your door and to the left."

"In the apartment or out?"

"In."

"Okay."

Lily hurried that way but came to a complete stop when she got there. Having gone to Capital City with her father over the years, she had certainly seen indoor bathrooms with flush toilets, showers, and tubs in them, but this was Jeff's. It was clean and white and shiny with dark green towels that looked soft, but it was more than that. It was her brother's bathroom, and he was family. She could use it all she wanted for the next three months.

"Are you all right?" Jeff had come to the door that Lily hadn't even bothered to shut.

She turned to him and smiled, her eyes meeting his for only a moment.

Knowing that her pleasure would be hard to explain, Lily said only, "I'm just fine," before she shut the door to make use of the facility.

Chapter Two

"What is this?" Lily asked for the umpteenth time, and this time Jeff patiently explained how the CD player worked. As with most things, she had read or heard about them but not seen them. The remote control for the TV fascinated her, as did the garbage disposal. She also took a long time inspecting the thermostat in the hallway and the way it would give cold air or hot, and the slight rumble in the apartment when it kicked in.

Jeff stood back and let her lead, well remembering the countless times he had made a fool of himself when, at 18, he had left Lhasa to attend school in the United States. He wished someone had been there for him to ask questions of and let him explore.

"Does this chain actually hold people outside, Jeff?" Lily now asked from the front door.

"Not if they really want in, but it is still a security measure. Why don't you come and eat?"

"Okay. Did you need me to fix something?"

"No, I've got a sandwich here for you and some tea."

"Thank you," Lily said gratefully as she took a seat. "You're not eating?"

"I ate while you were asleep."

Lily nodded and bowed for a moment in prayer. She took a small bite of sandwich, looking distracted until she got it in her mouth.

Watching her, Jeff smiled as her attention went completely to the food.

"What kind of fish is this?" Lily asked.

"Tuna."

"And what is the white sauce covering it?"

"Mayonnaise."

"It's good, isn't it?"

"Very."

Lily caught the teasing tone in his voice and ducked her head a little.

"I'm sorry to be such a pest."

"Look at me."

Lily obeyed.

"We're going to talk now, and you're going to start...Look at me, Lily," he put in gently, waiting until she complied. "You're going to start practicing not lowering your eyes. Understood?"

Lily nodded, automatically dropping her eyes, remembering, and then swiftly looking back up at her brother.

"How was the flight?" he asked as if he hadn't noticed.

"It was fine. The layover in Tokyo was long. I couldn't get comfortable, and I was getting tired." Lily glanced down at her plate in embarrassment. "I dropped the book I was reading twice when I nodded off in the middle of a page."

"So what did you do?"

Lily remembered to look at him before saying, "I took a little walk and that helped." Lily took another bite from her sandwich and then a drink of tea. She noticed the ice cubes for the first time and fished one out to have a look.

"Why are they half circles?"

"Because the ice maker in the freezer makes them that way."

As he knew she would, she dropped the sandwich and crossed the room to explore the freezer. She had her head buried inside that appliance when the phone in the kitchen rang, nearly scaring her out of her wits. Jeff reached for it, his eyes brimming with merriment as Lily's hand came to her pounding heart.

"Hello," Lily heard Jeff say. She listened to his side of the conversation. "Yep, no problem. Thanks for praying. Sunday? Sure. What time? Okay, we'll see you then. 'Bye."

Jeff was still laughing at Lily when he hung up, and she shook her head at him.

"Don't tease me, Jefferson. I couldn't believe how loud that was."

"I'm going deaf in my old age."

Lily only chuckled.

"Are you going to eat any more?"

"Not right now. Is that all right?"

"No, it's not. Come and eat every bite," he said with mild sarcasm even as he cleared the table. "How about a run? Are you up to it?"

"I would love it."

"Okay, but before we go, I have some things to show you."

Telling herself she could explore the thin plastic her brother had wrapped around her sandwich later, Lily followed Jeff back into her bedroom and watched while he opened the closet door. He then opened two drawers in the dresser and stood back.

"I shopped for you so you would have plenty to wear."

Lily's mouth opened.

"You bought me clothing? I mean, more than these shorts and T-shirt?" she asked, referring to the things he had given her to sleep in.

"Here," Jeff motioned her close. "How did I do on sizes and such?"

Lily came forward slowly. She was overwhelmed. Her father had given her a little American currency, and she had decided to buy one outfit, but the cost of flying to Honolulu had been significant. She never expected this.

"Oh, Jefferson," was all Lily could say for a time.

Jeff didn't say anything, but anyone who knew him would have seen that he was pleased by his sister's response.

"This is so pretty," she said of a navy and teal dress she found hanging in the closet, realizing with a start there was a skirt and blouse next to it.

"Look down too," Jeff suggested.

Lily shook her head in amazement when she saw the shoes. Three pair! Sandals, running shoes, and low-heeled navy pumps. Lily once again exclaimed, "Oh, Jefferson," and spent another few moments admiring his selections. They finally left the Kona Loni Apartments to run to the beach and back. It was only a mile away, easy for both of them, but Jeff knew that Lily would still be feeling the effects of flying.

"So, how is Father?" Jeff asked when they ended up walking the beach so Lily could look her fill.

"He sends his love," she said quietly.

"I appreciate that, but it doesn't answer my question."

Lily was glad she didn't have to look at him. She could feel her brother glancing at her from time to time, but she kept her eyes on the beach in front of them. Not a hard thing to do, considering the beauty of it all.

"I think he had a hard time with my leaving." Lily found that it felt good to admit this out loud. "As you know, he's been more moody in the last few years, and it was even worse once he gave me permission to visit you. I think he feels things that he doesn't know how to share."

"What do you think he was feeling?"

"Maybe that he was losing me like he lost you and mom."

Jeff could only nod, but it was without guilt. His mother had died when he was 16. Long before he had become a teenager, he had told his parents of his desire to go to college in the United States. They had never had trouble with the idea, but once his mother died, his father assumed he would cancel his plans. When he finished his schooling in the village and still left at 18, his father had been devastated. Jeff knew this was the reason his father had educated Lily himself once she turned 18, sending for any and all textbooks he could lay his hands on and teaching her at home.

Jeff knew his sister had vast knowledge in both world history and physics. He was certain she could pass any exam given in her area of expertise in any college or university in the English-speaking world. Her letters to him had often sent him back to his own books or friends to respond intelligently to questions she asked. Along with the intense Bible training she had been given, she was one of the most educated persons Jeff had ever known.

Even though he knew how difficult his leaving had been for his father, Jeff had no regrets. A whole new world had been opened up to him at the university in southern California, and that education had led to the job in the research department of Lang Chemical, a position he loved. It had taken a few years, but in time his father had come to see that his son had made the right decision. Jeff had continued to grow as a person and in his faith. He and his father were actually closer through the mail than they had been when he was growing up.

"So will his mood ruin your time here?" Jeff suddenly asked.

"What do you mean?"

"I mean, will his lack of full approval make you feel you shouldn't have come?"

"No, and I don't mean to mislead you, Jeff. I know he was glad for me. He hugged me right in the airport, but it was still hard. And he's not a young man. He still works as hard as he did when he was in his fifties and sixties. There are many men in the church now, and so many are changing and growing, but Father still does a lot of traveling to the needy in outlying places. The hungry—those who are thirsting after righteousness—energize him as they always have, but the unrepentant take their toll. I can see it in him a little more every year."

"And what about Father's own areas of unrepentance? Is he still hard to talk to? Does he still think you're Kashienese?"

Lily laughed a little, but she knew Jeff was serious. She was too. At times like this, she asked herself if she was as blind to her own sins as her father sometimes seemed to be to his.

"I figured something out, Jeff."

"What's that?"

"Papa is a maverick. If he was only as accountable to someone else—the way everyone is to him—I don't think he would be so stiff-necked on some issues. And, Jeff!" Lily exclaimed, having warmed to her subject. "The things he holds onto so tightly are not biblically based! They are just preference issues, like our prayer time in the evening and my subservient stance with him."

"Maybe I could write him once you go back."

Lily nodded. "You mean, tell him the things I've shared with you?"

"Yes. Maybe your having spoken through me, a man, would go a long way with him."

"And you wouldn't mind doing that?"

"No. We'll talk more about it, and you can tell me what you would like me to speak to him about."

"Thank you," Lily said quietly.

"Are you ready to head back?"

"Yes. Is it far?"

"No. Come on. Let's run awhile."

Lily fell into pace beside her brother, a full smile coming to her face—one that showed how glad her heart was that she had come.

～

"Your brother has been quite excited," Mrs. Crowley whispered, and Lily smiled at her.

This was the fifth elderly lady Lily had meet in Jeff's apartment building. Evidently everyone knew that his sister was coming for a visit and had been eager to meet her.

"I still have to work, you know," Jeff had explained before they had left to make the rounds. "This way you'll have someone to visit with when I'm gone."

"But you have all of this week off, right?"

"Yes. And I've taken occasional days off for the next three months to give us some three-day weekends."

Lily had nodded with pleasure, and now having seen how nice everyone was, she was not worried in the least. It would be great if Jeff could be off more, but she had learned that the library was within walking distance, and now she knew some of her neighbors. Lily could not see a single cloud on the horizon.

"Was the trip long, dear?" Mrs. Crowley asked.

"Very. The time in the air was quite lengthy and made worse by a long layover."

"Where was your layover?"

"Tokyo."

"How did you get along with the language?"

"I speak enough Japanese to get by, and almost everyone speaks English."

Mrs. Crowley turned to Jeff.

"Do you speak Japanese, Jeff?"

"Yes, ma'am, I do."

"I don't think I knew that. Does Mrs. Kondo know that?"

"Um-hm. We speak quite often. Especially in the laundry room."

"Mrs. Kondo is a stickler for clean clothes," Mrs. Crowley told Lily. "I had a stain on my blouse one day—I don't know what it was—but she got it right out."

Lily smiled at her again, but inside she ached for some of the women in Lhasa. In a heartbeat she thought she must be homesick or in need of some additional rest.

Jeff noticed her face, more specifically her eyes, and closed things off fairly soon. But his sister surprised him as they headed back to his apartment.

"Did you notice her clock?" she asked.

"I'm not sure I did."

"It was a cat. And the eyes and tail both moved as it ticked."

Jeff laughed. "I've seen those."

"How does it work?"

Jeff explained as best he could but then said, "You aren't as tired as I thought you looked at Mrs. Crowley's."

"Is that why we left?"

"Yes. You looked as though you might cry."

Not accustomed to having her face read so easily, Lily was reminded that this was her brother; he knew her very well.

"We didn't have to leave."

"You're not looking at me again."

"We didn't have to leave," she told him, her eyes obediently raised up.

"Yes, we did. I'm tired."

For some reason this gave Lily a case of the giggles. At that point Jeff knew she was tired. And he was right. When they arrived back in his living room, she wanted to watch television, but long before Jeff was ready to turn in, Lily's lids were drooping. She gave up before 9:00 rolled around, and even with the strange bed and sounds, slept hard all night long.

～

Jeff and Lily planned to spend Lily's first full day seeing the sights, but before they left to take Oahu by storm, they ate breakfast and shared the newspaper.

"Listen to this," Lily said about halfway through the news. "A man, angry with the way his employer had spoken to him, left work in a rage. He later returned with a gun, shooting and killing six fellow employees."

"You're kidding," Jeff said in surprise.

Lily could not stop the shock she felt from showing on her face.

Jeff needed no time in understanding.

"I'm sorry, Lily," he said with a brief touch to her arm. "That's a bad habit that many of us have."

"But you thought I was kidding."

"Not at all. It's only a thoughtless expression, but I want you to be warned that you'll hear it again, and probably other expressions that sound just as foolish to you."

Lily nodded, her face thoughtful. Finding cat clocks interesting or wanting to understand the workings of the thermostat weren't in the same ballpark as hearing phrases that were foreign and trying to understand the way people thought.

"Why do people say that, Jeff?"

Jeff had gone back to his paper.

"Jeff?"

"Yeah?"

"Where does the phrase come from?"

"I don't know. I don't think people know what else to say when they're shocked or hurt."

"Why must they say anything?"

"Because silence, for the most part, is uncomfortable."

This Lily could understand, and she relaxed a bit. Cultures were certainly varied, but people were alike the world over.

Thursday morning started early for Jeff, earlier than he had planned. The day before had been full of sightseeing and hiking, and he was ready to sleep in, but those plans were interrupted. Just before 5:00, he slipped into Lily's room and woke her.

"My boss just called and needs to see me. I'll be back as soon as I can. I'll have my cell phone if you need me. The number will be on the table in the kitchen."

"Okay. Is there something I can do?"

"No, it's all right. Maybe you can go back to sleep."

Lily wasn't able to sleep again, but she stayed in bed until she was fully awake. After a long, hot shower—an indulgence she was still getting the hang of—she studied her Bible. She read the paper when it arrived and then started a letter to her father, all the while hoping that Jeff would return soon.

～

A little before 8:00 Jeff drove slowly into the parking place and put his Honda into park. He climbed from the car on legs that felt stiff and approached the building that said OFFICE.

He stepped inside to the tinkling of a soft chime and found the resort office empty. A moment later, coming from the inner office, Jeff was greeted by his closest friend, Gabriel Kapaia.

"Well, Jeff! What brings you out so early? Is Lily with you?"

"I've got to talk to you, Gabe."

For the first time Gabe saw his friend's face. Jeff's features were strained, his mouth a tense line.

"Sit down, Jeff," Gabe invited once they had gone into Gabe's personal office.

"Randolf sent for me early this morning," Jeff said, referring to his superior at work. "I've got to leave for the mainland on Sunday."

"This Sunday?"

Jeff nodded, his face telling of his shock. "I'll be gone for eight weeks on a project that's so secret I can't even tell Lily where I'll be."

Gabe was utterly silent. He stared at Jeff, who stared right back.

"She just got here, Gabe." Jeff's voice was hoarse. "I haven't seen her for three years, and now this." Jeff shook his head a little, trying to deal with a disappointment he never anticipated. "There was so much we were going to do. I was going to teach her to swim and play tennis."

"Why now?" Gabe asked. "Why does this project have to be worked on now and by you?"

"I was always the one slotted for this job; it has to do with a merger we're involved in. But no one, not even top-level management, knew it would come together before the first of the year. In fact, most thought it would be next summer."

"But now that it has come together, you have to go."

The men stared at each other until Jeff leaned forward, his elbows on his knees, and buried his face in his hands. He couldn't remember the last time he wanted to cry, but right now he thought he could sob his eyes out. Just thinking he had to tell Lily she was headed home was enough to choke him.

"Bring her here," Gabe said quietly into Jeff's tortured thoughts.

"What?"

"Bring Lily here. We'll take care of her."

Jeff stared at him.

"You just started your slow season, Gabe. I can't do that."

"But don't you see? It's perfect. We don't have guests to work with right now, and she can just hang with us. We'll teach her to swim, play golf, and cover all the learning experiences your father wanted for her, and when you get back for the last weeks of her visit, you can just relax."

Jeff stood and went to the window. The small resort that Gabe and his family owned and operated was right on the beach. From the office window he could see the pounding surf and endless miles of sea—a sight he never grew weary of. And already Lily loved it. He knew she did. How in the world could he leave her here alone? But then, would she be alone? Hadn't Gabe just offered to take her in?

"I would tell you I need to think about it," Jeff said to Gabe as he turned back, "but I'm out of time."

"It's all settled then. I know my family will be fine with it, and I'm sure that when Lily gets to know us a little, she'll have a great time."

Jeff did not look convinced.

"Maybe you should discuss it with them, Gabe. Especially Evan and Bailey."

"They'll be fine with it. I'm certain. You've talked to us about Lily for years. We feel as though we already know her."

"You're sure?"

"Yes. Now give me the details again. You leave when?"

"This Sunday."

"Will you be at church?"

Jeff had to think a moment.

"Yes. I don't fly until 3:00, so Lily and I will come to church, and then I'll bring her here a little while before I have to head to the airport. I hope you'll understand if we don't come for lunch like we had planned."

"Of course, Jeff, that's fine. But will you want to leave your car at the airport the entire time?"

"No, I won't, actually. So I'll leave time to go home and take a cab." Before Gabe could ask, Jeff added, "I don't want Lily to see me off."

"Okay," Gabe said with great understanding. "I have one more question. How will we contact you if Lily needs you?"

"I have a number I can give you. You state who you are and who you need to speak to. They'll get word to me."

Gabe, a very organized man, was taking notes all the while, nodding in confidence and choosing not to comment on the way Jeff's life had just been turned upside down, not to mention Lily's.

"I'd better get home," Jeff said, moving for the door. "Thanks, Gabe."

"You're welcome, and you know I mean that."

The two men embraced. Gabe ached for his friend but still remained quiet. Jeff didn't notice the pain on the other man's face. He was already thinking about a phone call he needed to make before he saw his sister.

Chapter Three

"Hey, Peter," Gabe called to his five-year-old nephew the moment he was in the kitchen door. "Where are your folks?"

"Mama's in the kitchen, and Daddy is somewhere."

Gabe smiled and touched his head. "Okay, buddy. Thank you."

Having already reached his brother, Ashton, to tell him he needed to see the whole family, Gabe headed toward the kitchen, where he found his sister, Bailey Markham. His three-year-old niece, Celia, was playing on the floor.

Set on the north side of Oahu, the Kapaia Resort was a special place. Started by Liho Kapaia and handed down from father to son for three generations, the restaurant, office, gift shop, large swimming pool, tennis courts, and 13 beach cottages were now owned and operated by Bailey, who was the oldest, her husband, Evan, their two children, and her two brothers. On top of all that, the six of them lived together in one large home.

The cottages had guests for ten months of the year, but the family took September and October off to rest and rejuvenate for the coming season. The phone still rang, but a secretary in the office usually handled that and other minor office duties. The restaurant was open year-round, but as with the office, they had a competent and faithful staff. This morning Gabe had told the secretary, Mollee, where he would be, and he now attempted to gather the family and explain Jeff's predicament.

"Hey, Bailey, is Evan available?"

"Yes." She looked up from the list she was making. "He's in the yard. What's up?"

"Jeff was just here to see me. I need to tell all of you about it."

"Okay. Should I get the children busy doing something?"

"No. It's not private. In fact, it involves all of us."

Bailey's curiosity was roused enough that she went for Evan herself. By the time she found him and they held the door from the kitchen to the main part of the house so Celia could join them, both of Bailey's brothers were waiting in the living room. Peter had made himself comfortable in Ashton's lap.

"What's up?" Evan wasted no time, speaking as soon as he and Bailey had taken a seat.

"Jeff has been called away. He has to leave on Sunday. He'll be gone for eight weeks."

"But Lily just arrived," 24-year-old Ashton said; he was the youngest of the family.

"Yes, she did, that's why I've told Jeff that Lily can stay with us."

"Good," Evan said, and then remembered to look at his wife. She was also nodding her head but still had questions.

"How does Lily feel about that?"

"Jeff was headed home to tell her. He came here first because he was so upset."

"Tell us the whole story."

Gabe did just that, and for a moment they all sat and thought about the horrible disappointment. Jeff was like family. They all knew how excited he was when his father had finally given Lily permission to come to him. They also knew that this had to come as quite a shock.

"So, what's the plan?" Ashton asked.

"Jeff will bring Lily over on Sunday afternoon. I think he'll stay a little while to see that she's settled and then head to the airport."

"And how many weeks are we talking about?" Bailey asked.

"About eight. I think there's a possibility that things could wrap up sooner for Jeff, but I don't think he is counting on that."

"Could it take longer?" This came from Bailey again, and all Gabe could do was shrug. Jeff's finishing early had been more of a hunch on his part, so he kept his mouth shut.

"Is the guest room made up, Ash?" Evan wondered aloud. Ashton had been the last one to have company—a friend visiting from college—and that made the room his responsibility.

"The bed is fresh, but I don't know if it needs vacuuming or dusting. I can check that today."

"Thank you," Evan said as he turned back to Gabe. "Is she allergic to anything—foods and such?"

"Not that Jeff has ever mentioned. I can ask him."

With that settled, the meeting broke up, and each person went his or her own way.

"Come here," Bailey invited her son, and Peter moved close; Celia had been in her lap for the whole meeting.

"Did you understand all of that?"

"I think so. Is Jeff coming to stay?"

"Not Jeff—his sister, Lily."

"Oh. How come?"

Bailey looked into his huge black eyes and melted a little over his sweetness.

"Well, Jeff has to work out of town, and she needs someone to be with her."

"What's her name?"

"Lily."

The little boy nodded, and Bailey was filled with a fierce protectiveness. She asked him to bring several books from the loaded shelf in the living room and decided to stay right where she was and read to her children.

Lily moved around the corner of the kitchen wall when she heard the front door open. Trying not to drop her eyes, she found herself smiling, so glad was she to see her brother. She had not wanted to call him, but he had been gone for hours, and she had started to wonder if something was wrong.

Forcing her eyes up, she saw from his face that something was wrong. Feeling compelled to ask but knowing she must not, Lily remained quiet, wanting to drop her eyes in the worst way.

"It smells good in here. Have you been baking?"

"I made cookies," Lily said simply, not going into detail about all she had learned in the process. "I hope I didn't use something you need."

"I'm sure not. Have you got some coming out now?"

"No. They're done."

"Good. Come in here and sit down. I've got news that neither one of us will like."

Lily did as she was told and sat in stunned silence as her dream trip fell to pieces around her feet. This was Thursday, which meant they would only have a few more days. Lily hated the thought of getting back on that plane so soon. If they had had the whole three months, at least she could have left with a heart full of memories. It was too soon, much too soon, unless…

"I'll just go with you."

"You can't. I can't even tell you where I'm going."

Lily nodded and began to second-guess making the trip in the first place.

"Should I call the airport about my ticket?" Lily asked. It would do no good to cry. That would only make Jeff feel worse and not change a thing.

"Do you remember all the times I've written you and Father about Gabe and his family?"

Lily nodded.

"Well, I've just come from seeing Gabe, and they want you to come and stay with them."

Lily nodded, her face serene, but in truth she was experiencing her second shock of the day.

"They'll teach you to swim and do all the educational things that Father wanted, and then when I get back—I've already called my boss and confirmed it with him—I'll take off work for the rest of your visit. We'll have time to just relax."

Lily smiled in his direction, not wanting him to be upset, but also aware that a deep sadness was mirrored in her eyes.

"All right," she said, thinking she should voice her agreement and not expect him to see it in her smile. "I'll go stay with Gabe and his family."

"Are you sure you're okay with that, Lil?"

"If that's what you want me to do, I will."

What you want me to do.

Jeff had cried in the car on his way home. He thought he could again. Lily had been raised to be subservient to authority, especially to men, and flexible in all situations. At times he struggled with these aspects of her upbringing, but never as much as now. Right now he hated it.

"Is that what you want me to do, Jefferson?" Lily asked again, not sure what the look on his face meant.

What I want you to do, Lily, is not be the sweetest person I've ever known. What I want you to do is to get angry at me and make it easy to leave. What I want you to do is explain to me what God's plan is for this, because I feel as though my heart has been ripped out of my chest.

"Listen to me, Lily. I was so upset about this that I went to see Gabe before coming home. It wasn't that I was afraid to face you, but I'm more upset about this than I guess I'm letting on."

Lily nodded. This she understood, since she was trying to hide her pain and planning to cry all the way back to Kashien.

"So when I went to Gabe, he suggested you stay with them. I love these people—you know that from my letters. I wouldn't think of leaving you with anyone else. They will take great care of you, and even though your stay won't look the way I've been imagining it, we will still have four weeks together in November."

Lily nodded, telling herself to be brave. Jeff was being brave. Why should she demand any less from herself?

"That's fine. What day will I go there?"

"Not until Sunday," he said, knowing he would have to take her at her word. "You and I have a lot to do in the next few days."

"Like what?"

"Well, first we're headed to Honolulu to do a little shopping."

"For what?"

"Your swimsuit."

Lily made an "oh" with her mouth, even though no sound escaped. Jeff had not eaten breakfast, so after he wolfed down a bowl of cereal, the two hit the road. Had Lily known what she was in for, she would have been tempted to defy him and stay home.

Evan Markham came back into the house just ten minutes after the meeting broke up, the thought in the back of his mind still niggling enough that he wasn't going to ignore it. He found his wife and children almost as he had left them and knew just what he must do.

Making a trip to the bookshelf for two books, Evan approached the threesome. He waited for his wife to finish the sentence she was reading and look up at him. Evan's eyes, however, were on Celia.

"You there, with the face," he pointed at her playfully. "You sit right here."

Celia, in her adorable, pudgy way, crawled from her mother's lap and into the chair her father indicated.

"Okay, CeCe," Evan said as he put the book in her lap. "You sit in this chair and look at this book."

"'Kay."

"Now, Pete," he continued, turning to his son, "this is your chair and your book. I think this is the one with bears."

"If I finish this, can I get another?"

"Yes, but then get right back into your chair."

"Okay."

Evan saw the second child settled before turning to his wife.

"And you," he said, pointing to Bailey, "head upstairs to our room."

This was far from the first time he had done this, so Bailey went wordlessly to the stairs and started up.

"All right, you two," he addressed his children one more time, "you stay in your own seats. No wrestling. We'll just be a little while."

Evan took the stairs two at a time and ended up just a step behind his spouse. As soon as he followed her into their bedroom and shut the door, he spoke.

"All right. What's going on?"

Bailey hated being so transparent to her husband but still said, "I don't know what you mean."

Evan heard the playfulness in her tone and kept his light too.

"Come on now. Out with it."

Bailey turned to look at the man she had been married to for almost seven years. She adored him and knew the feeling was mutual.

"I thought wives were supposed to be creatures of mystery."

Evan shook his head. "You're going to have to work harder to pull that off with me."

Bailey stared at him and didn't answer, but Evan still knew what was on her mind.

"If you didn't want Lily to come, you should have said so."

"Then Gabe and Ash would have wanted a reason."

"What is the reason?"

"Do you really not know?" Bailey looked crushed.

"Tell me; don't just get upset with me."

"Evan, we've been waiting to get pregnant, thinking that when you slow down, it will happen. Now I'll have another woman in the house to take care of, and I'll be the busy one. I thought we both wanted another baby."

"We do, but I don't think Lily is going to be any extra work for you—not if she's anything like Jeff has described."

Bailey looked thoughtful as she mentally agreed with him. Lily was a grown woman, not a child who would need looking after.

"And you're doing God's planning for Him again, Bailey. Leave it to Him. You know your job, and that's all you're expected to do." Evan added, "You just attack me every night at bedtime, and we'll leave the rest to the Lord."

Bailey's light laughter filled the bedroom, and Evan came to take her in his arms. He held her close, and Bailey sighed when her head rested against his chest.

She realized then that she had had her mind on herself to the point that she hadn't even prayed for Lily and Jeff. She knew right now they needed it more than she did.

Lily came from the first dressing room, her face a dull red, her eyes down.

"How was it?" Jeff asked, trying not to laugh at the horror on her face.

"I can't do this," she said, her voice so low that he had to bend to catch it.

"Lily," he tried, but the laughter in his voice made him stop and start again. "Tell me how it looked."

"A lot of me showed."

Again Jeff wanted to chuckle.

"Well," he began, trying to be pragmatic and wishing he had asked Bailey about this, just as he had when he bought Lily's clothes, "was the suit cut high on the leg?"

"Yes!"

"Show me here on the side of your pants."

Lily indicated the top of her thigh, by no means the high-cut area.

"You thought that was high?"

"My whole leg showed!" she whispered in panic, and Jeff had to cover his mouth and take a moment to recover.

He had picked out a very modest suit, a swimmer's suit with a high front and comfortable back, not having many exposed areas that would make it immodest.

"How about the neckline—how high did it go?"

Lily's hand went almost to her collarbone.

"And the back?"

"I don't think I looked."

"Go put the suit back on and come show it to me."

She looked as though he had suggested she undress on the spot.

"I don't think I can do that, Jeff."

"It's all right. Hardly anyone is in here right now, and you won't be swimming on the beaches of Waikiki."

"That makes a difference?"

"I'm just saying that even if the suit turns out to be all wrong, we don't know anyone in here, and you'll just pop out, show me, and pop right back. There's no reason to be embarrassed."

He could see she wanted to argue but did not. He watched as she moved wordlessly back to the dressing room and wondered if she would ever come out again.

～

"Gabe, it's Jeff."

"Hey, what's up?"

"I'm sorry to call so late, but I had to wait until Lily was in bed."

"That's fine. I was still up."

"There's something I forgot to tell you."

"Okay."

"Lily won't look at you."

"What do you mean?"

"I mean, she won't look at men. It's the way my father raised us. Women are not to raise their eyes in a man's presence."

"And she does that even here?" His voice sounded as amazed as he felt.

"Yes, it's all she's ever known. You're going to have to tell her to look at you, or she won't."

There was complete silence on the phone.

"Gabe?"

"Yes, I'm here. I'm just thinking. Does she really not look up at men?"

"Right."

"Is she afraid?"

"No, just showing respect the way she was taught. She's been getting better with me, but she'll have to start all over with the three of you. Added to that is the fact that she doesn't know any of you."

"Well, Jeff," Gabe responded, his voice returning to normal, "whatever it is, we'll work it out. We do know each other through you, so I'm sure that given a little time, we'll all do fine."

They talked for a few minutes before Jeff was able to hang up in peace. His friend was not just cheerleading. He honestly believed things would work out fine. Gabe was like that. And although Jeff was tempted to worry, he was working hard not to.

That phone call made, Jeff pulled out his briefcase and went to work at the kitchen table. He had much to do before he got on that plane Sunday afternoon. But if he had to work all night in order to sightsee with his sister all day, it would be worth the effort.

～

"You wrote to Father?" Lily asked on Saturday afternoon. They had just 24 more hours.

"Yes."

"What did you say?"

"I just explained the situation. I don't suppose he'll go all the way down to Hankuo to use the phone, but I even enclosed the number in case he feels a need to contact me. I also gave him the resort phone number and the address."

"What is the resort like?" Lily suddenly asked.

"Oh, we can go by there. In fact, maybe we should so you can meet everyone now."

"That's all right," she was a little too swift to say. "I think tomorrow will be fine."

Jeff didn't have the heart to tell her to look at him. Eyes averted, she was doing her best not to twist her fingers together, and he knew she was scared to death about the whole affair. There was so much he could say, but he didn't know where to begin.

"Do you remember the family names?"

"I think so. Gabriel Kapaia is your good friend. His brother is Ashton, and his sister is Bailey. Her husband is Ian…"

"Evan."

"That's right! Evan. And their children are Peter and Celia."

"Wow, you do remember. Now about the resort. There are 13 guest cottages on the beach, but you'll be staying in the main house with the family."

"They all live together?"

"Yes. They'll have to tell you how it works, but it does. I know that Evan has someone come in and help Bailey clean up a bit two mornings a week, but I think they always eat together."

"Okay."

"And do you know what I just remembered?"

"What?"

"I've got to do some laundry before I pack."

"Okay."

"Gather anything you need to have washed, and I'll teach you how to use a washing machine and dryer. And bring a book, or it's like watching paint dry."

Lily's laugh did much for his heart. Doing laundry on their last night was not exactly memorable, but Jeff thought it might be best to stay as "normal" as possible.

Chapter Four

Lily enjoyed Sunday school and the church service, but all the while her brother's departure was in the back of her mind.

I need to confess my anxiety to You, Father, she prayed even as they drove to the Kapaia Resort. *I missed most of the sermon because things haven't gone my way. I don't know if I'm afraid of this new situation or angry at You that You would dare to interfere with my plans, but even if I can't figure this out, Lord, I'm sorry. I have no right to play God.*

Jeff prayed for that very thing over breakfast, so I know he's struggling with the same issues. This is all so confusing, but You're not surprised. Thank You for whatever Your plan is, and help me not to fight You anymore. Help me to contribute to this home for the next eight weeks—not just survive and be in the way, but be a help and an encourager.

"Are you all right?"

"I'm getting there. I had a good deal of confessing to do."

"You too?"

"I'm afraid so," Lily said with a sigh. "I get so sick of my sin, Jeff. I don't know how God stands me."

"Grace."

"Yes, and more love than I can imagine."

On those words, Jeff pulled off the main street and under an archway that read Aloha and Welcome to Kapaia Resort. Everything was lush and green—an amazing difference from what they'd seen along the road, where many of the fields were dry and brown.

"They must water everything."

"Yes, they do. That's typical of the resorts at this time of the year. When the rains don't take care of it, they have no choice but to water to keep the grounds looking beautiful."

Up the road, signs directed cars to several driveways, and Jeff took the one that said Private Drive. The others had said Resort Office and Gift Shop, Little Bay Restaurant, and Deliveries. Jeff's light-blue Honda scooted past thick palms and dense bushes until it rounded a circular driveway that put the car parallel to a large two-story home.

"Here we are," he said unnecessarily.

Lily climbed out silently and reached for her bag in the backseat. Jeff had also given her a thin garment bag to hold the things he had purchased, and he took that in his hands. Lily felt her heart pound but tried not to show her fear.

"Should I have brought them a gift, Jeff?"

"No, Lily, nothing like that is expected, I assure you."

Lily's face was a picture of serenity, but Jeff could see she was pale. He suspected that she was trying to be brave for him. He almost laughed, thinking that's what he had been doing for her. He was so near exhaustion from lack of sleep and emotional disappointment that he thought he might sleep all the way to the mainland.

"Hey, Jeff and Lily! Welcome," Evan called as the front door of the house opened. None of the family had met Lily that morning in an attempt to give other people in their church a chance to get to know her.

"Hi, Evan," Jeff called in return.

"Come on up," Evan invited, and Lily climbed the eight steps to a deep, covered porch. "Evan Markham," he said by way of introduction, but Lily's eyes were already down, even as she shook the hand he offered her.

"It's nice to meet you, Evan," she said, and he stared in wonder at the way she kept her lids lowered. His brother-in-law had warned the family about this, but it was one thing to hear about it and another to see it.

"Come in," Evan invited, and Lily and Jeff entered to find the family waiting inside. Jeff introduced everyone, and before Lily knew it, Bailey was leading her upstairs to a bedroom, her brother following with her things.

"Right in here," Bailey said, and Lily glanced up long enough to smile at her.

"This is nice," Lily offered as she took in the white painted walls with the matching bedspread and curtains. The two night-stands, headboard, and a large dresser with a mirror were a light teak.

"This dresser is empty, Lily," Bailey said, "and so is the closet. So please make yourself at home."

"Thank you."

Bailey slipped out, and Lily knew that Jeff was watching her. She turned with a smile.

"I didn't think I would have a room to myself. I thought I might be in with the children."

"It's a big house."

Lily could only nod.

Jeff was not overly pressed for time, but he could see that it would be best to keep this short.

"If you need something, Lily, just tell them."

"I will."

"And look the men in the eye. It's perfectly normal here."

She nodded, even as she forced her gaze to stay up. The habit of dropping one's eyes did not disappear in five days. Five days! That's all the time they had had.

"I'd better go," Jeff said quietly, feeling as though he was deserting a child. His sister was a smart and capable woman, but Hawaii was not home. The culture she lived in was like night and day from his.

"Walk me down, okay, Lil?"

Still working not to panic, Lily only said, "Certainly."

～

The house was always a surprise to newcomers. The living room and dining area were wide open to each other, with the kitchen behind a closed swinging door. The stairway rose from the center of this large living/dining area to an open hallway that led to a master bedroom and bath, five other bedrooms, and two baths. There were no rooms over what the family called the "big room," giving a spectacular ocean view from 20-foot floor-to-ceiling windows.

The family was sitting in the living room, not exactly sure if they should join Jeff and Lily. But as soon as the two came down, Jeff rescued them.

"Thank you for everything," he said as he went from the last step straight ahead to where the sofas and chairs were gathered in a circle. In one corner were two more sofas and a television, but the center grouping was for conversation.

"You're welcome," Gabe said with a smile. "Did you settle in, Lily?"

"I thought I might do that after Jeff leaves."

"Good idea."

As Evan had, Gabe stared in fascination with the way she kept her gaze lowered.

"I'd better get going," Jeff said just before all the family came forward to hug him. Lily had known her brother was affectionate, but she hadn't expected it from everyone. Letting her mind stray to this caused her to forget how quickly he was leaving. Before she was ready, they were alone on the front porch.

It was on the tip of her tongue to tell Jeff she wanted to go home, but she knew that wasn't fair. She hadn't even given this family a chance, and deep in her heart she knew her brother would never do anything to harm her. Nevertheless, even the long plane ride back to Kashien would have been a relief compared to watching her brother depart.

"You've got to ask them the questions you ask me, Lily. They won't laugh at you."

"Okay."

"And work at looking at them."

Lily's gaze came up when she realized she had fallen back into her habit.

Jeff smiled at her, and Lily thought she would die when she saw the tears standing in his eyes.

"I won't do anything to make you ashamed of me, Jefferson."

A sob broke in the man's throat.

"Oh, Lily, I would never be ashamed of you." Even as he said it, he knew where her statement had come from. This would have been what his father had said to her in order to make her work hard and think seriously. He had to get out of there quickly, or he knew he wouldn't make it. Stepping forward, Jeff hugged his sister and Lily hugged him back. He told her he would call her as soon as he got settled, and then he moved down the front steps.

Lily followed him and smiled as she waved him off. She stood until the car was out of sight, even moving to gain a last glimpse of his bumper as the car slipped around the curve and was gone.

The sun beating down on her was hot, but Lily felt chilled to the bone. She crossed her arms over her chest and glanced around. She felt as though she was just emerging from a strange dream.

From the window next to the front door, the Kapaias stood and watched her. Bailey felt as though her heart were melting inside of her.

"Maybe she should have gone home, Gabe."

"Maybe" was all he could say, feeling as hurt by the scene as his sister.

It was obvious to all of them that she was in agony. They watched as she looked around a bit, not spotting them because of the sun in her face, and then sat on the bottom step, just staring in the direction Jeff had exited.

"Well, when she does come in," Ashton put in, "she really shouldn't find us standing here gawking at her."

"That's true," Evan agreed, but it took a few more minutes before they all went on their way. Each one wanted to do something but wasn't sure what.

Evan looked at the pain in his wife's face and could only shake his head. When he had said Lily would be no trouble, he hadn't counted on emotional toil. He couldn't help but wonder what they were all in for in the weeks to follow.

～

Lily rushed up the porch steps and to the front door where she paused in indecision, her heart beating rapidly. She didn't know what had come over her to be so rude as to sit outside all that time. She had no idea how long she had been out there, but such manners were inexcusable.

Not wanting to knock or be presumptuous about walking in, Lily opted to slip in quietly to cause as little disruption as possible. From the front door she couldn't see anyone. She moved forward out of the shadows to see that the adults who had been sitting in a circle were all gone.

"Do you like Winnie the Pooh videos?"

Lily's head turned to the sound of Peter's voice. He was sitting over by the television.

"I don't know. I've never watched Winnie the Pooh videos."

Peter waved her over with one hand, and Lily went.

"You can sit here," he told her.

"That's mine," Celia informed Lily in a nearly intelligible three-year-old way.

"No, it's not, CeCe. She's having a grumpy day," Peter explained to Lily, who sat down on the far right cushion on the sofa, the seat Peter had indicated. Peter sat to the far left, and Celia was between them.

Celia gave Lily one impersonal, cross look, brow lowered and disgruntled, before popping her thumb into her mouth and going back to the video. Peter had gone back to it too. Lily watched the antics of the animated characters as well, but her eyes often strayed to the children. They were beautiful. They had inherited their mother's black hair and eyes. Their skin looked so soft that Lily wanted to touch them.

Lily hadn't been sitting with them for more than five minutes when Celia suddenly shifted and crawled into her lap. Lily took it in stride, figuring she had been mistaken for the little girl's mother, but Celia looked up into her face before putting the thumb back into her mouth and leaning against her. She was looking drowsy and relaxed as a cat when Bailey joined them.

"Well, Celia didn't take much time."

"She was grumpy," Peter informed his mother absently.

"We'll talk about it later. Lily, I wanted to let you know how things work."

"Okay."

Bailey was having to ignore the change in her guest. With only the children and her present, Lily was looking up in complete normalcy.

"We eat breakfast and dinner together. Breakfast is about 7:15 and dinner is 6:00. For lunch we fend for ourselves, and if you miss breakfast or dinner, you also fend for yourself. We each clean our own rooms, but I have help with the kitchen and here in the big room. We also see to our own laundry. Does that all make sense?"

"Yes, thank you. Will I have some jobs to do in the house?"

"Well, nothing specific, but if you want to help at meals, that would be great."

"I'll plan on that."

"Thank you. Did you get settled in?"

"Not yet. Peter asked me to join him."

Bailey smiled at her, and Lily smiled back. She was nothing like Bailey imagined. Jeff had told them how highly educated she was, but there was nothing "bookish" about her. She was soft and unassuming, and her hold on Celia, who had fallen asleep, was very gentle.

"Do you want me to take her?"

"Only if you want to."

"She might wake if I do."

Lily smiled to reassure her, but at that moment, Ashton could be heard coming their way. Bailey watched as Lily's eyes dropped, her face losing all expression.

"Hey, buddy," Ashton said to Peter as he dropped onto the other sofa. "How much longer on your tape?"

"It's almost done."

"Okay, I'll just wait to see the game."

"Football?"

"Yeah."

"You can see it now. That's okay. I'll finish the tape later."

"You'd better go ahead and finish now, Pete, because the game will probably go until it's time to leave for church."

"That's okay."

Peter got down, popped the tape out, and gave the remote control to his uncle. His mother had been on the floor next to him, but she now moved to his seat and cuddled him close when he came back.

"Thanks, buddy," Ashton said to him, and Peter smiled when he winked.

Ashton glanced at Lily then and found her eyes down.

"Have you watched much football, Lily?"

"No, I haven't."

Bailey stared at her again. Lily's voice had sounded completely normal, not embarrassed or subservient, but she had not looked at Ashton. Bailey was thoroughly captivated.

And Lily stayed that way. With the sound of the game moving through the house, Gabe and Evan were not long in joining them, and although questions were directed to Lily, she kept her eyes down.

"So you don't have television in Kashien, Lily?" Evan finally asked her.

"We have television in the larger cities, but not in the village where I live."

"Look at me, Lily," Evan ordered, and Lily obeyed.

"So how much television have you seen?"

"Well, we go to Capital City every few years, and sometimes I'll see it in a hotel."

She lowered her eyes again, but Gabe went next.

"And since you've been here? Have you and Jeff watched much?"

"Mostly the news in the evening."

"Look at me, Lily."

It was Evan again. He seemed the most comfortable telling her. Bailey thought Lily might be blushing just a little, but again her voice was normal when she answered his question.

Is it really that easy for her? Bailey found herself asking. *Evan tells Lily to look up, and she does it?*

Bailey was bothered by it so much that she planned to tell Evan that he was putting Lily on the spot. The older woman glanced again at their guest, and that's when she saw a small drop of moisture at Lily's temple. The air-conditioning was on. No one else was hot, but then no one else had a three-year-old in her lap.

"Here, Lily, let me take her. I can see she's out cold."

"Oh, thank you."

They made the transfer easily, but Bailey was not done.

"Why don't you head up and unpack, Lily?"

"You don't mind?"

"Not at all."

"What time do you want me ready for church?"

"We leave about 5:30."

Lily nodded, excused herself, and came around the end of the sofa to move toward the stairs.

"Tell her it's casual, Bailey," Gabe put in quietly.

"Hey, Lily."

The other woman stopped and looked at her briefly.

"We just go in shorts on Sunday nights. It's very casual."

"Oh, all right. Thank you, Mrs. Markham."

Lily went on her way, and Bailey turned back, her eyes going to the window. The spectacular view, however, was somewhat lost on her. She could feel her husband's gaze on her, Gabe's too, but she couldn't bring herself to look at them.

How could Jeff leave her here like this, Lord? I know the alternative is sending her all the way back to Kashien, but she doesn't fit in here. How painful is this going to be? And is it worth it for a few weeks with her brother in November?

Because Bailey asked the questions in her heart, no one answered. She was left to think it through on her own and to wonder what their newest houseguest was thinking and doing right then.

∼

Lily was so tense that her skin hurt. Trying not to think about having to be at the resort for the next eight weeks, she put her clothing away and then put the suitcase and garment bag on the top shelf of the closet. A stack of her books sat on the bed, and Lily knew if she let herself look at them, she would cry. They reminded her too much of home; they even smelled like home.

Simply keeping her mind on the business at hand, Lily put them on top of the dresser, not even bothering to straighten them. She had passed a bathroom down the hall and now left her room to use it, her movements wooden and stiff.

She had meant what she said to Jeff. She would not shame him. If she had to pretend to be happy for the next eight weeks so that his friends would not have a poor impression of her, that's what she was prepared to do.

∼

Evan and Bailey had a minivan. Prior to going to church, Lily had never ridden in one. She thought it smelled nice inside and found the seat comfortable. And there was so much room!

Lily set her Bible on the seat beside her—they were done at church and headed home now—and was glad that once again no one said anything about moving the children to the very last seat so she could sit further up. She didn't want the children to be inconvenienced by her visit either.

Once the children were seat-belted inside, Evan shut the door, and Lily wondered again why Gabe and Ashton would take a separate vehicle. Had she but known it, they usually did ride with the rest of the family on Sunday nights. Gabe was nearly 6'1" and about 200 pounds. Ashton was slightly larger. If they had known Lily better, it wouldn't have been much of an issue, but as it was, the rear seat was more comfortable if Lily or the two men were on their own.

They had barely left the church parking lot when Lily found herself in a conversation with the Lord nearly identical to the one she had had that morning. As with that morning, she had heard little of the message because her brother had been on her mind again. She confessed this and then had a little pep talk with herself.

You wanted to be a part of this family and not just survive, and that means you're going to have to make an effort. That decided, Lily told herself to do just what Bailey had told her: fend for herself if she missed a meal. It was already 7:45, and she could tell that the dinner hour had come and gone.

Unlike the ride away from the house at 5:30, Evan took the van all the way to the garage, which gave Lily a chance to see a little more of the resort. She spotted a swimming pool and some tennis courts in the distance. She thought she might even have seen one of the guest cottages that Jeff had told her about.

She followed the family back to the house, going in by way of one of the sliding doors that looked out over the ocean. After taking her Bible to her room, she made herself find Bailey. That proved to be easy—she was still in the living room.

"Mrs. Markham?"

"Why don't you call me Bailey?"

"Oh, all right. Would it be okay if I fixed a little something to eat?"

"Absolutely. We all snacked, but that must have been when you went up to unpack, so go make the kitchen your own."

"Thank you."

Lily went toward the only logical door, and when she got close enough to see through the round window on that door, she realized she had indeed found the kitchen. The sun was headed toward the horizon and filling the room with light, so Lily didn't bother to look for a light switch. It was a wonderful kitchen, all decorated in navy blue and yellow, and large enough to work in comfortably. There were many feet of countertop.

The counter space was Lily's downfall, or rather the contents of the counters. She didn't know that many appliances existed. Starting with what appeared to be a small grinder, Lily began to investigate. She lifted the lid and smelled coffee.

"I wonder why Jeff doesn't grind his own beans," she whispered absently. "It smells so good."

With the lid back in place, she hit the button and started at how fast the little blade turned. She monkeyed with the grinder for a time and then moved to the coffeepot itself. It was similar to but not exactly like Jeff's, and Lily gave it a good going over.

She had just gotten to a machine that she suspected made a loaf of bread when the kitchen door opened. Lily dropped her eyes and turned from the counter.

"Is everything all right, Lily?" Bailey asked.

Lily looked up with eagerness that was not feigned.

"May I ask you a question, Bailey?"

"Certainly."

"Does this machine make loaves of bread?"

"Yes, it does."

"How?"

Out of habit, Bailey hit the switch which turned on the over-head fluorescent lights, came over to the counter, and showed Lily every aspect of the machine.

"And these little bars turn and do the kneading too, not just the mixing?"

"Yes."

Lily's intelligent green eyes came back to her. "But how does the bread rise?"

Bailey took the pan out and showed her the heating element.

"The coils warm things up enough to cause the bread to rise, and then they get very hot to bake it."

"How long does it take?"

"About three and a half hours."

Lily shook her head in wonder, and Bailey started to laugh.

"I'm sorry." Lily was immediately apologetic.

"No, don't be sorry, Lily. You've just made my day."

"How did I do that?"

"Well, for a little while there, I was worried about you. But if you can get this excited over a bread machine, you're going to do just fine."

Lily now laughed a little too, hoping as she did that Bailey's prediction would turn out to be true.

Chapter Five

"So have you eaten anything?"

"Actually, I haven't."

Taking pity on Lily, Bailey began to make her a sandwich but soon found out she was not easily distracted.

"Is this some of the bread from the machine?" Lily asked when Bailey set a ham-and-cheese sandwich, chips, and a sliced apple in front of her.

"That's the stuff."

Lily examined the bread on her sandwich as though she were conducting an experiment. Bailey watched her, knowing she had to be hungry, and now understanding why the younger woman was so thin.

Lily, completely unaware of her scrutiny, finally picked up the sandwich and started to eat.

"Oh, this is good."

"Thank you. How about something to drink?"

"Oh, yes, please. Anything will be fine."

Bailey, who had taken a place at the small kitchen table with Lily, stood and got her a large glass of milk. She had just set the milk on the table when the door opened. It was Evan.

"I have a little boy here who wants to bid you ladies good night."

Peter ran to his mother's arms, and Bailey cuddled him close.

"Good night, Mama."

"Good night, sweetheart. I love you."

"I love you too."

Lily's eyes were down, so she knew the exact moment that Peter came to her. She smiled into his eyes, and he smiled back.

"Good night, Lily."

"Good night, Peter, and thank you for inviting me to watch Winnie the Pooh videos with you."

"We can watch more tomorrow."

"I would like that."

Peter surprised Lily by reaching up to give her a hug too, but she recovered swiftly enough to hug him back and then watched as he went out the door.

"He's precious," she said to Bailey as soon as they were alone.

The mother laughed a little and admitted, "I certainly think so."

"Will Celia not come to say good night?"

"She's already down. She was grouchy and unthankful today, and as part of her punishment she was sent to bed early."

Lily smiled as she remembered the little girl telling her not to sit on the sofa. Sin was never funny, but Celia was so cute that Lily couldn't contain herself.

"You're laughing at something," Bailey said. She had continued to watch Lily.

"Celia didn't want me to sit next to her on the sofa today. It's so hard not to smile at her. She's so cute, even when she's cross."

"Yes, she is," Bailey agreed and then shook her head. "We're trying to break the strong attachment she has to her thumb. We let her suck it if she's sleepy, but not if she's upset with us or crabby about something. You'll see as you get to know her that she knows exactly when she can have her thumb. When she knows she *can't* have it, and we're in the room, she puts her other hand over her mouth to try to cover up what she's doing. It's hysterical, but we can't laugh at her."

Lily laughed at the demonstration Bailey gave. She could just imagine Celia doing that, and Lily was certain the other woman was right: She was going to want to laugh.

"How are you doing?" Bailey surprised her by suddenly asking.

"I'm all right, thank you."

Bailey leaned a little closer. "How are you *really* doing, Lily?"

Lily fiddled with one of the chips on her plate and then picked up an apple slice. At last she looked back to Bailey.

"I told Jefferson I wanted him to be proud of me, but I'm not sure he would be."

"Why is that?"

Lily sighed. "I can't bring myself to look up at the men, and I feel lost and alone." Lily's hand came suddenly to her mouth. "What a rude thing to say. You've offered me your home and been hospitable, and then I say that. I'm so sorry."

Bailey put a hand on Lily's arm.

"Don't be sorry. Of course you feel lost and alone. For a moment I was so angry at Jeff I couldn't think straight."

"You were?"

"Yes. I just didn't know how he could leave you alone like this. I'm still not sure I understand."

Lily was shocked but hid it. However, her impassive face still managed to alert Bailey.

"Don't get me wrong, Lily. You're welcome here for as long as you need, but you came to see your brother, and he's not here. We all understand how painful that must be. Gabe's heart was genuine in his offer to Jeff, and we're glad you could come, but talking about it and watching you go through it have turned out to be two different things."

This Lily understood. A part of her mind wanted to panic that she had not pretended to be having a good time, but then she saw how foolish this was. If she was miserable, it was best that they knew this. Even as the thought surfaced, Lily's face heated. How would she ever explain her feelings to these strangers? She glanced up to see Bailey smiling at her—a kind and understanding smile.

But anything Bailey might have been preparing to say had to wait as her husband and brothers came on the scene.

"Can we get some food?" Evan said.

"Sure. What do you want?"

"We'll get it. Do you want anything, Bailey?"

"Yes. I'll have a sandwich, I think."

In what felt like a heartbeat, the atmosphere of the kitchen changed for Lily. She was not afraid of men, but neither was she as comfortable around them as she could be around women and children.

The four family members worked on a snack, sending occasional comments and questions to Lily. But unless she was told to, she did not raise her eyes.

When it was at last time to head to bed, Lily was relieved. Her own efforts had wearied her, not to mention her failures. She wondered until she fell asleep whether she would ever grow comfortable with these people.

~

When dinner ended on Thursday night, Lily immediately went to work on the pots and pans that had been left in the kitchen. Peter trailed behind her, and Ashton went to give a hand, but Gabe stayed back to question Bailey. Having extended the invitation to Jeff, Gabe felt the most responsible for their guest, but the week had flown by. He had even missed two evening meals with the family because he had meetings. It was time to do some make-up work.

Lily's feelings about her brother leaving and her new position in their family had been greatly on his mind, but he had not had time to act on them. He knew now, with the week almost over, that this must change.

"So what does Lily do all day?" Gabe asked his sister as soon as the room was emptied of everyone but himself, Bailey, Evan, and Celia.

"She works, reads, or plays with the children. When Terri arrived Monday and again today to help me clean, the three of us started on the house. Lily has fallen into our schedule, either with the kids or the house, as though she's been living here for years."

"And did she seem comfortable?"

"As long as no men are in the room. The quiet woman you see at the dinner table and in the evenings is not the woman who works and plays all day in this house. The kids have already fallen in love with her."

Gabe nodded but had no comment. He had already talked to his brother before dinner, which left just Lily. In truth they would all be rather busy for another week, but they could still squeeze in time to teach Lily some new pursuits. Gabe had worked it out on paper. Now he had only to explain the first step to Lily.

～

"So what did you do today, Pete?" the little boy's uncle asked.

"I played and watched videos with Lily and CeCe. Lily likes Pooh Bear."

"She has good taste."

"Lily and I like Tigger too."

"Well!" Ashton said, his voice managing to sound matter-of-fact and comical all at the same time. "Who doesn't like Tigger?"

"Rabbit," Peter told him, and Lily heard Ashton hoot with laughter.

"How's it going?" Gabe came on the scene just then, a stack of dishes in his hands.

"We're almost done with these pots," Ashton filled him in. "Who's doing plates?"

"I think Evan. I'm drying. Hey, Lily?"

"Yes?"

"Could you please look at me, Lily?" Gabe requested for the first time. He wanted to shake his head all over again at how busy he had been.

"When I talked to Jeff about your staying here," he said once eye contact had been made, "I told him we would teach you to swim and do all that stuff. Did he tell you about that?"

"Yes, he did."

"Good. Tomorrow after lunch, Ashton is going to teach you to swim."

Lily barely managed to nod.

"Does that work for you?"

"Certainly. Whatever you wish."

It was not the reply Gabe hoped for. How did he explain to Lily that she could go home if she wanted to without sounding like he wanted her to leave? Gabe had no clue. Evan had told him some of the things that Bailey had said to Lily on Sunday, and he feared that adding his own voice would make it sound as though they wanted her gone.

"Do you have a swimsuit?" he asked, sticking to more practical matters.

"Yes, I do."

"Okay then, that's all set."

"Do you know how to get to the pool, Lily?" Ashton asked.

"I don't think I do," Lily answered, realizing not for the first time how little she had been outdoors.

"Okay. I'll just meet you here tomorrow at 12:30. The beach towels are in that linen closet outside the bathroom door."

"Okay."

Lily's eyes had already gone back to the work she was doing, so the brothers were able to exchange a glance.

They were still asking themselves Bailey's question from Sunday afternoon: Should Lily have returned to Kashien?

Lily's whole body trembled as she looked at herself in the mirror. Her brother had told her the suit was very modest and that she looked nice, but it hadn't helped. So much of her showed! She wasn't used to her legs being exposed above the knee, or her upper arms, not to mention the suit fit like a second skin. The clothing she wore in Kashien was long and loose-fitting. Even most of the clothing that Jeff had bought for her tended to be along that line. There were some shorts, but Lily had shied away from them.

But time was creeping up on her. The clock on the dresser said 12:28. Taking a deep breath, she made herself walk to the door and out into the hall. The brightly colored towel from the linen closet was in her hand only a moment before she realized she could wrap it around herself. Her heart still pounded in her chest as she walked down the stairs, but at least most of her was covered.

"Lilyee." Celia said her version of their guest's name as soon as she walked in the door, and Bailey turned to see her.

"Are you all set?"

"I think so," Lily answered, but she was on her way over to Celia, who was finishing her lunch at the table.

"You missed this piece," Lily said to the little girl as she pushed a scrap of bread into view.

Celia stuffed it in her mouth and smiled at Lily. Lily's heart did a little flip-flop.

"Where is Peter?"

"He's eating Daddy today."

Lily knew there was a translation somewhere for that statement, but she didn't try to find it. Indeed, there was no time. Ashton showed up just a moment later, and they were on their way to the pool.

~

The swimming pool at the Kapaia Resort was spectacular. Set among palm trees and lush flower beds, the rectangular pool had wide steps that went into the three-foot end, which soon graduated to five, and then had a brisk drop-off to the nine-foot deep end, where one could dive from the board. The five-foot mark in the pool even sported a slide. And since the whole pool area was empty and clean, for a moment all Lily could do was stare.

"Okay, Lily, get in. I'll be right with you."

Lily had been dreading just that but saw no hope for it. She moved slowly to a chaise lounge where she could place her towel, but then she glanced to see that Ashton's back was to her. Thinking that she had been given the perfect opportunity, Lily swiftly discarded her towel and almost ran for the cover of the water. She nearly gasped at the temperature change but didn't stop, even when it hit the level of her stomach. She wanted as much water over her as she could find. What she hadn't counted on was how swiftly the levels changed. Lily almost had the water where she wanted it when it felt like her foot was slipping off a cliff.

Not able to stifle the small cry of surprise and with nothing to reach for, Lily's head was underwater before she knew it. There was only water below and above her. Where had the bottom of the pool gone? Panic as she had never known consumed her. Her hair was in her face, and try as she might to find the surface, it eluded her. She thought she was going to die when suddenly strong arms lifted her.

Her head broke free of the water, and she gave a huge gasp. Coughing and panting in terror and pain, she felt herself being lifted and carried. Not until she felt the seat beneath her and a towel pressed into her hands did she open her eyes. Ashton was very close. Lily glanced up to see his eyes huge with shock.

"I'm sorry," she gasped, eyes back down, her whole frame shaking. "I'm so sorry."

"It's all right, Lily. Just sit here a minute. It's all right."

In truth, Ashton was trying to convince himself as much as his pupil. When she had cried out and he had turned to see her going under, he had not immediately reacted. Not until he had realized that she was not coming up did he dive in to get her.

"I'm sorry," Lily said again, her whole frame still trembling.

"You have nothing to be sorry about, Lily. It's my fault."

Lily couldn't have disagreed more, but at that moment her father's face swam before her eyes.

You will not shame me, Lily.

With a Herculean effort, Lily willed herself to stop shaking. She glanced at the water but made herself stop thinking about what had just happened.

"Lily," Ashton said from beside her, "you can't swim at all, can you?"

"No."

Ashton put a hand to his face. "I can't tell you how sorry I am. I thought this was going to be some sort of refresher course. If I had known you couldn't swim at all, I would not have let you in the pool alone. I can't tell you how sorry I am."

"Oh no, Ashton. It was all my fault."

Lily would have gone on but stopped when he laid a hand on her arm. She felt his hand shake, and before she could think otherwise, she lifted her eyes to his. The face she saw shocked her with its sobriety.

"I'm so sorry, Lily. When I think of how easily you could have drowned, I—" Ashton looked away from her, and as Lily dropped her eyes again, she saw how wet he was. He still had his T-shirt on.

Lily used the towel then and dried off as best she could. She wished she had pulled her hair back with a tie, but she did her best to smooth it away from her face.

"I'm ready to swim now," she told him quietly, so wanting to make things right. What a horrible thing to have happen the first time the Kapaias tried to teach her something. Lily purposed in her heart to do better.

Ashton looked at her profile.

"Are you sure?"

"Yes."

The swimming instructor glanced down just then and spotted a bottle of sunblock by the leg of the chaise lounge.

"Do you need some of this?"

Having gone back to thinking about what had just happened, Lily answered without even focusing on the plastic container.

"Will it help me swim?"

Ashton laughed at her joke and stood up.

"It sounds like you're as ready as you're going to be, Lily. Come on. I'll go in with you this time."

Discarding his T-shirt, Ashton walked to the edge of the steps, and Lily made herself follow. When they finally stood in the three-foot area, Ashton directed her to the edge of the pool.

"Okay, the first thing I need to tell you is that I'll be between you and the deep end. You're not going to slip off again."

"Okay." Lily knew she sounded breathless but couldn't help herself.

"The next thing I need is for you to look at me every time I speak."

Lily's eyes came up.

"Even if I don't call your name, as soon as you hear my voice, you look at me. Can you do that?"

After Lily nodded, he showed her how he wanted her to lean her forearms against the edge, put her legs back, and kick.

And with that, the lesson commenced. Lily was a swift learner, and her desperate need to have Jeff and her father be proud of her propelled her to keep on, even when she felt afraid. In less than an hour she had learned the survival float and was moving toward the five-foot area.

"I can't believe you never swam before," Ashton kept saying. "You're doing a great job."

"I'm a little worried about the deep part."

"Well, I'll be right with you. In no time at all, you'll be jumping from the board."

Lily couldn't help but laugh, but as the lesson grew more difficult, time faded away. Lily's head was in and out of the water so often, she lost all sense of the day. She was learning to breathe properly, kick her feet, and keep her hands perfectly cupped for her straight-arm strokes.

"How's it going?" Bailey called from the edge of the deep end. It was well after 3:00.

"Great. After trying to drown the woman, I think I might have taught her to swim."

Lily laughed again.

"If you're going to stay out much longer, Lily," Bailey said conversationally, "you'd probably better get some more block on. You're looking a little red."

Before Lily could ask the question that was inside of her, Ashton spotted it too.

"You are red, Lily. We had better finish up for today."

"All right. Thank you, Ashton."

"You're welcome. You did a great job."

Lily swam to the shallow end and climbed from the pool, still self-conscious about being in a swimsuit, but when she toweled off, she did notice that her shoulders and arms were tender. That faded, however, when she felt hunger gnawing at her insides. The bowl of fruit in the kitchen came to mind, and after thanking Ashton again and wrapping up in her towel, Lily headed that way.

After the snack, Lily went up to take a shower. She smelled of chlorine and wanted it out of her hair. She would have enjoyed learning about the workings of the pool, but there had been no opportunity to ask.

Lily had been in the shower just a few minutes when a wave of nausea hit her. She thought she might have eaten too fast and was glad when it passed. However, when she climbed from the shower and looked at herself in the bathroom mirror, this time without her suit, a feeling of dread covered her. She was red. Very red. And a dull headache had started to throb around her forehead.

By the time she got to her room she felt very tired as well. After dressing in her loose, comfortable clothing, Lily decided to lie down. In less than five minutes she was sound asleep.

〜

Dinner was on the table before Bailey realized she hadn't seen Lily since the pool. From the living room, she could see that Lily's door was closed and thought maybe the swimming had worn her out. Nevertheless, dinner was on, and Bailey wanted to give her a chance to eat.

When a soft knock on her door brought no response, Bailey quietly opened the portal to the shadowy room. She could see that Lily was in bed.

"Lily?"

Lily moved a little.

"Come in," she called, although her mouth felt very dry.

"Lily, it's Bailey. Dinner is on."

"Oh, I'm sorry you had to come for me, Bailey. I must have fallen asleep."

"Okay. Do you want to come down?"

Lily tried to lick her lips.

"I'm not at all hungry," Lily finally said, her voice low. "Would it be all right if I didn't?"

"That's fine. Did you burn today?"

"I did, yes."

"Okay. I'm going to run and get you some aloe lotion."

Lily didn't move while her hostess did this, thinking how easily she could go right back to sleep. Even when she heard Bailey returning, she could not find the energy to move.

"Here you go," Bailey said, coming through to put it on her dresser.

"Thank you."

"You're welcome. Come for me if you need something, Lily. And be sure to drink plenty of water."

"All right. Thank you."

Bailey left and shut the door. Lily could tell that she had burned quite badly. Her skin felt awful, but she had no energy to get up and use the lotion. Before she could contemplate the matter much more, she fell asleep again.

When Bailey turned in, a little after 10:00 that night, she checked on Lily one last time. This time the younger woman did not wake up.

Chapter Six

Although Lily had been lying awake since three in the morning, she did not join the family until breakfast. Moving slowly so as not to shift her arms, shoulders, or back, Lily walked in a state of near shock over the way her body felt.

The lotion had done nothing. It felt cool the moment she used it, but the burning sensation was back so fast it startled her. And what was worse, she felt cold. She felt so chilled that she wanted to shake, but she had let herself do that once and knew from the pain it caused she must not let it happen again.

She could hear everyone at the table as she descended the open stairway. They were talking and sharing the paper as they had done other mornings, but Lily didn't try to look up. She wanted to care what her brother thought, but right now nothing mattered. The closer she got to the smell of food, the more she felt she could be sick. But she still forced herself to take her seat.

What Lily didn't notice was how silent the table had become the moment everyone spotted her. The family had looked at her to say good morning but had not uttered the words. Even Bailey's soft "Oh, my," was lost on Lily. Not until Gabe was suddenly next to her chair did Lily realize much of anything.

"Here, Lily," he spoke quietly, "I'm going to pull your chair out."

"I'm not hungry," she said, thinking he wanted her to sit elsewhere to eat.

"Go for the car, Ash," Gabe ordered, and Lily heard him leave swiftly.

"Here we go," he said, his hands coming out to take hers. "Stand up for me."

"I don't feel well, Gabe," Lily told him, even as she stood.

"I know you don't. That's why we're going to the hospital."

"I think I need Jefferson."

Since the admission tore at his heart, Gabe said nothing.

"Mama crying," Celia announced, but it didn't register with anyone but Evan, who went to his wife.

Knowing there was little they could do, the two followed as Gabe took Lily toward the front door. Ashton came in just as he got there, and with only Gabe holding her hands, they took Lily to the car.

"Call the number Jeff left," Gabe told a stunned Evan as he shut Lily's door and Ashton climbed into the back. "Tell him what's happened and that we'll be in touch."

"All right."

"Tell her we're praying," Bailey said, tears still filling her eyes.

"I will," Gabe said, continuing his own prayers as well.

What followed for Lily felt like hours of being trapped in the same nightmare. The seat belt rubbed her skin because she did not want to sit back against the seat. Then she was in a hot, stuffy room with Gabe on one side and Ashton on the other. Her stomach was so upset, she thought she might die from holding everything down. Then a strange woman was telling her to undress. She was asked to climb into a bed with scratchy sheets, one that felt ten feet off the floor. And finally, a needle was pushed into her arm and stayed there. With that, Lily could not hold the tears. They seeped out at her temples and soaked into the pristine white pillowcase under her head.

Sometime later, she opened her eyes to see Gabe sitting at her side. Without even the energy to drop her gaze, she stared at him numbly, just wanting her father or Jeff to come and take her away.

"I'm sorry," she said finally. "So sorry."

"Why are you sorry?" Gabe asked, even as his hand came up to gently touch her hair. He was a tactile person—he wanted to hold her hand at the very least, touch her brow and soothe the hurt, but she was a mass of burned flesh, and with just the slightest touch to the side of her hair, he took his hand away.

"I don't know. I'm just sorry."

"Lily, this is our fault. There's so much we didn't understand. Jeff tried to tell me, but I didn't get it. I thought if you could come to us we would be just fine. But your culture is so different, and now we've let you get hurt."

"I can't fly like this."

Gabe smiled. "You're not going to fly at all. Before I saw you this morning, I would have agreed to send you back to Kashien. You just needed to ask. But not now."

"Why not now?" she asked, suddenly comfortable with him.

"Because now we're going to take care of you. Now I understand, and everything is going to be fine."

Lily still didn't know what he hadn't understood that was so clear now, but she had run out of steam to think.

"Where am I?" she asked, her eyes closing.

"At the hospital."

"I've never been in a hospital."

"Not even when you were born?"

"No. I was born in Lhasa. My father delivered me."

Gabe smiled.

Ashton peeked around the door just then and came to stand by Gabe's side.

"How is she?" he whispered.

"She was just talking, but I think she might be asleep."

"I called and talked to Evan. He said Bailey would be finding a sitter so they can both come."

"Did they get ahold of Jeff?"

"Yes. They called the number, and he called right back. They set up a time for him to call again."

Gabe nodded.

"Are they keeping her, Gabe?"

"I think so. She was getting dehydrated, and they've got her on morphine for the pain."

Almost as if on cue, a doctor came in the door.

"Hello, I'm Dr. Grant," he said. "I understand that you're friends of Lily's."

"Yes. I'm Gabriel Kapaia and this is my brother, Ashton. Lily is staying with us."

"Okay. Was she wearing any block?"

"We don't think so."

The doctor looked up at them but didn't comment. The nurse came in, and a moment later the brothers were asked to leave.

Even as they moved from the room, they heard Lily wake and say her brother's name. Once in the hall, the men leaned against the wall to talk.

"I hate it that Lily has to suffer for my lack of insight."

"How are you to blame for this, Gabe?"

"I knew how unfamiliar she was with the culture. Jeff and I certainly talked about it enough times. But then she had had a few days with him, and from that I made way too many assumptions."

"We all have," Ashton put in.

While they waited quietly, the doctor and nurse came out and explained what the next few days would look like.

"I want to keep her for a few days, mostly for pain management. As you can see, she's in a tremendous amount of pain, and this way we can keep the morphine going and monitor her pain level. She's also going to need another IV bag, maybe two. If she stays here with the catheter, she won't have to be climbing out of bed just yet. But once you get her home, she's still going to be miserable and want to take it very slowly."

"We'll see to that."

"Good. I'll check on her again in a few hours."

The doctor had no more finished with his explanation when Evan and Bailey showed up. Bailey waited only long enough to

hear the doctor's prognosis from her brothers before she went in
to see Lily. It hurt to look at her. Bailey thought she might be
asleep, but as soon as she bumped the chair, Lily's eyes opened.

"Hi," Bailey said, thinking on the fact that hindsight was always
20/20.

"Hi, Bailey."

Bailey sat down. "I'm sorry this happened, Lily. I feel terrible."

"It's all right. I should have thought more about it."

"Do you use sunblock in Kashien?"

"No, we stay covered all the time."

Then I don't know how you could have thought on it were Bailey's
thoughts, but she kept them quiet.

Evan peeked around the corner just then and slipped in when
Bailey waved to him.

"Hi, Lily. How bad is it?"

"Oh, it's bad, I guess," she said quietly, trying not to shiver. "Is
Gabe here?"

"Right here," Gabe answered from the end of the bed, and all
watched as Lily looked up at him without prompting.

"Did the doctor tell you I have to stay?"

"Yes, for a few days."

Lily licked her lips—a labored movement—and Bailey stood
to give her some ice.

"I'm sorry I'm so tired."

"It's all right," Evan told her. "We'll get out of here so you can
sleep."

Lily didn't respond, but the foursome left, at least for a
moment. When they reached the hallway they had a short
meeting before Gabe headed back inside to sit by Lily's bed and
quietly read the newspaper Evan had brought with him.

∼

"Evan talked to Jeff," Gabe told Lily when the nurse woke her
to take her blood pressure.

"How is he?"

"He's concerned about you. He'll be calling again tonight."

"Did you tell him I'm all right?"

"No."

Lily looked at him. "Why not?"

"Because you're in a lot of pain and not all right."

Lily glanced around the room. Her hot skin hurt so badly, but she was cold. It made no sense.

"You don't have to stay, Gabe."

"Okay," he said kindly, and Lily looked to him.

Somehow she knew he would remain. She hadn't wanted to be a bother.

"You're not a bother," he said, and Lily couldn't believe she had said that out loud; she then realized she hadn't.

"How did you know what I was thinking?"

"I put myself in your shoes. I thought about being in Lhasa and getting hurt. You and your father would be sitting with me instead of getting on with your own life. I wouldn't want you to do that."

"But you're willing to do it for me."

Lily watched Gabe smile. His teeth were nice to look at—very white.

"Jeff is like another brother to me, Lily. I'm not sure if he's told you how close we are or not, but my wanting to be here for Jeff's sister is like wanting to be here for Jeff. It would never occur to me to do anything else."

"That was a nice thing to say. Does Ashton feel bad about my being burned?"

"Yes. You're not that fair, Lily. It doesn't seem that you could burn that badly. But that's not the main problem. We offer hospitality for a living. We warn guests about the sun on a weekly basis, and here we let you fry." Gabe shook his head. "We're all kicking ourselves, and I'm sure you can understand why."

Yes, she could, but again she was too weary to say anything.

A knock at the door drew Gabe's eyes upward and dropped Lily's.

"Well, Gabe." A man in a white coat came in.

"Barry!" Gabe said before the two embraced.

"How are you?" Barry asked. "You look great!"

"I feel great, thank you."

Barry glanced toward the bed.

"I'm Dr. Barnes," the man said.

"Hello," Lily greeted him, her eyes still down.

"This is Jeff Walsh's sister, Lily," Gabe filled him in. "She's visiting us from Kashien."

"And you got a major burn," he said with compassion. "Are your legs burned, Lily?"

"Very little, sir. It's mostly my face, back, shoulders, and arms."

"Okay," he said, his eyes on the chart. Lily stole a peek at him and saw that Gabe was watching her anxiously. The moment caused Lily to wonder what she looked like. She knew she felt miserable and assumed she looked the same.

"I need to listen to your lungs, Lily."

"All right," she said faintly; it had hurt so badly before. She knew the moment Gabe slipped out and thought she might cry. He was like her brother right now, and she wanted him near.

You will not shame me, Lily.

Even hearing the words in her mind were enough to break Lily's heart. She was in so much pain and had been thoughtless about the sun; her father might be ashamed of her. She closed her eyes against a rush of tears and heard the doctor's soothing voice.

"It's miserable, isn't it? I'll be as quick as I can."

And he was swift, but just moving her gown away was not only painful, but humiliating. No man had ever seen her naked until these doctors, and Lily was mortified with it all.

"Your lungs sound clear. That's good. We'll keep your bed cranked up, and that will help. Have you been able to sleep some?"

"Yes."

"And what about lunch? Did you eat?"

"A little."

"Do you normally have a large appetite?"

"No."

"Okay. Well, keep sucking on the ice chips and sleep as much as you can. Do you have any questions for me?"

"No, sir."

His heart wrung with compassion for how miserable she had to be.

"I'll get Gabe back in here, shall I?"

"Thank you."

He was on his way out when Lily realized she could have asked him why she was so cold, but on further thought realized she didn't really want to talk any more. Her eyes closed, she heard Gabe enter the room. If she talked to him, maybe it would take her mind from her skin. It had before. Nevertheless, Lily was just too weary to make the effort.

"How is she?" Jeff asked over the phone to Evan after dinner that night.

"Miserable. They're keeping her pumped with morphine, and she's staying for a few days in an effort to keep her as comfortable as possible."

"Good."

"Gabe is with her. He has been all day. Do you want any messages sent to her?"

"No, but if you'll track down the number for me, I'll call her."

"I'll do it. Why don't you call back here in about ten minutes?"

"Thanks, Evan."

"You're welcome, Jeff. Goodbye."

Evan had the phone number and Lily's room number ready in far less than ten minutes. He hadn't thought of himself as anxious until he realized he was drumming his fingers on the table and sitting right next to the phone as though he might miss the call. On top of that, Peter was tapping him on the leg.

"Papa?"

The little boy finally got through.

"Yes, Peter?"

"Is Lily better?"

Evan took him into his lap and tried not to think of Lily's own father. If one of his children was hurting the way Lily was, he imagined his own agony would be great.

"She's not better yet," Evan told him honestly, "but they're taking good care of her. She's going to stay at the hospital for a few days, and when she does come home, she'll need lots of rest."

"CeCe and I can be quiet."

"I'm sure you can. Lily will appreciate that very much."

"Can I make a card for her?"

"You certainly can. She would like that."

"I could put a boat on it. Do you think she likes boats?"

"I don't know. Maybe she could tell you about—"

The phone rang in midsentence, but Evan made himself finish.

"Maybe Lily could tell you about the boats they have in Kashien."

Peter nodded as Evan reached for the phone.

"Hello."

"Evan? It's Jeff."

"Hi, Jeff," the man in Hawaii said with a small sigh; he had been more tense than he realized. "I've got those numbers for you right here."

～

When the phone rang in Lily's room, Gabe quickly reached for it, but Lily still woke. Gabe could see that she had started awake, but he kept his voice soft as he answered.

"Lily Walsh's room."

"Is that you, Gabe?"

"Hi, Jeff."

"Hi. How's Lily?"

"Well, she's been better. Do you want to talk to her?"

"Yes."

Lily had started to cry when Gabe said, "Hi, Jeff."

"Can you take it?" Gabe asked the woman in the bed.

"I don't know if I want it touching my ear."

"Then I'll just hold it for you. Can you hear?"

"Jeff?"

"Hey, Lil."

"Oh, Jeff," was all she could manage as she tried not to shake with her sobs.

It would not have been Gabe's choice to be in on this private conversation, but he heard every word.

"Now listen to me, Lily. Your body is hurting enough; don't work your heart over as well. Just concentrate on getting better so you can enjoy your visit."

"I think I should have gone home."

"Lily, you're right where God wants you. Don't forget that. He's in control, and He can see you through this."

"All right."

"You must tell Gabe everything you need. You've got to, Lily. He'll take care of you. Do you hear me?"

"Yes."

"What hurts the most?"

"My shoulders. They're covered with blisters. The skin just above my upper lip is also blistered. It hurts to touch it."

"What are they doing for you?"

"Bathing my skin in a brown liquid and giving me morphine."

"And Evan said they're keeping track of any signs of infection?"

"Yes."

"Good. We'll ask God to keep you free from any additional pain."

"Jeff," Lily went on after she had thanked her brother, "please tell Gabe he doesn't have to sit here. Tell him not to bother."

Lily heard her brother laugh on the other end of the line, but it wasn't a mirth-filled sound. Not until that moment did she think how this might affect him.

"I can't do that, Lil. I need Gabe to stand in for me. He'll take care of you. I know he will."

"All right."

"Are you tired?"

"Yes. The morphine—it makes me sleepy."

"Don't fight it. Go ahead and sleep and be as comfortable as you can be."

"I will."

"I'll let you go. Evan is keeping me informed. I'll call again tomorrow."

"Okay, Jeff. Thank you."

"Gabe?" Jeff took a chance that he was able to hear.

"Right here."

"Is it just you? Is Lily still listening?"

"No."

"Should I come?"

"I had a feeling you might ask that. Can you check with me again in 24 hours?"

"I'll do that."

"And of course, I'll call you if things change."

"Right. Thanks, Gabe."

"You're welcome, Jeff, but I'm still sorry it had to happen."

Gabe listened a moment longer, said goodbye, and hung up. Lily's eyes were on him. They were sleepy and pain-filled.

"Can you sleep for a while?"

"I'll do that."

"If you wake and I'm gone, it probably means I've gone home for the night. I'll be back first thing in the morning."

"Thank you, Gabe."

"You're welcome."

Lily decided not to fight falling asleep anymore. She had thought he might be staying the night. Now she was only glad he had the good sense to go home and sleep in his own bed.

Chapter Seven

Lily left the hospital to return to the resort at noon on Wednesday. The staff advised her on symptoms that signaled infection and told her what lotions to use. Although they could keep her more comfortable at the hospital, they told her she was over the worst.

Moving gingerly and wishing she could take off her blouse and undershirt, she came in the front door of the Kapaia home.

"Where will you be the most comfortable right now?" Gabe asked, having come in behind her.

Lily looked indecisive, and Ashton spoke up.

"Why don't you take the sofa over here, Lily? Peter can put in a video. It might take your mind off everything."

"Okay. Thank you."

"Hi, Lilyee," Celia greeted her, still using her own pronunciation.

"Hi, Celia. How are you?"

"Are you hurt?"

"A little, yes."

Celia had been warned repeatedly about not hugging Lily, but her uncles still kept a close eye on her to make sure she was not going to get too close.

In the midst of this, Bailey came on the scene, a sheet in her hand. She left it folded over several times, and then laid it where Lily's back would be.

"The fabric on this sofa is rough, Lily. This might help."

After thanking her, Lily carefully sat down, not quite able to cover her wince of pain. She glanced up at the occupants of the room to find all three siblings staring at her. Where she got the courage to do what she did next, Lily didn't know, but with no small amount of effort, she spoke.

"I would like to speak to all three of you, if I could."

"Certainly," Gabe said.

Although Lily kept her eyes down, she could tell that he came and sat down. After Bailey asked the children to color at the dining room table for a few minutes, she and Ashton did the same.

"I can't tell you how thankful I am for all of your care and concern, and I would rather pull my tongue out than sound ungrateful, but you must go on with your lives. If I need something, it's time I learned to ask for it. I don't find that very easy to do, but as of today I will commence to tell you of my needs, so you won't need to unduly concern yourselves.

"I didn't know this kind of pain existed, but sitting around isn't going to help me get better. Anything I can get for myself, such as food and water, I'll see to on my own. If I can't do something, I'll tell you."

Lily took a peek at them and found them all quite sober. In turn, she finished on a somber note.

"It's no one's fault that this happened. I've had to pray constantly since I woke early Saturday morning. It's not often that I have pain great enough to induce me to such thoughtfulness of my Savior. I'm thankful that this happened, if only to remind me of the horrible place hell is. Not that I'm comparing my pain to that, but it does give one a glimpse. Many people still need my prayers and blameless witness so they will turn their lives to Christ.

"It's always tempting to ask God why He chooses hard paths for me. This time, however, I did not ask. I worked hard to see the reason myself, and I found it. I think this happened to make me more aware of the lost world we live in."

Lily glanced up, first at Ashton and then swiftly to Bailey. At last she looked at Gabe and could not look away.

"Was it wrong to say that to you?"

"No. You rescued us, Lily. Thank you," said Gabe.

"Thanks, Lily." Ashton put his word in, and both men went on their way.

Lily's gaze went back to Bailey. The older woman was smiling a little.

"I have something for you."

"Okay."

Bailey held up a scrap of fabric.

"I got sunburned a number of years ago, and the worst part was my shoulders. I wore this in the house and found it offered great relief."

"What is it?"

"A tube top."

"I don't think I've heard of it."

"It's exactly what it sounds like. It's stretchy and surrounds the body without straps or sleeves, just like a tube. In fact, with as slim as you are, you could step right into it and pull it over your breasts, and then you can slip out of your shirt. You're not wearing a bra, are you?"

Lily answered in the negative, even as she was gaining a picture of what Bailey was suggesting.

"I'm not sure I can sit around here and be that bare," she made herself admit.

"It's true that your shoulders will be exposed, Lily, but you're not going to be immodest. Your small figure will be perfectly covered in this tube top, and you'll be remarkably comfortable compared to wearing any type of top or shirt that touches your shoulders."

Lily was tempted, but her face heated at the thought of the men returning and seeing her sitting there without a shirt.

"I don't think I can."

"Okay," Bailey said, knowing she would have to let it go. "I'll leave it with you, though. Maybe you'll just want to wear it to bed with a pair of shorts."

"Thank you."

"Are you up to seeing the children?"

"Yes, that's fine, but I think I should mention one other thing to you. These water blisters are going to start to burst, and my bed is such a nice one. Maybe I should try to sleep elsewhere."

"No, it's fine, Lily. Your bed has a mattress pad, and whenever the sheets need to be changed, we'll just do it."

"Okay. Thank you."

The children came and a video was started, but Lily didn't last very long. She dozed in and out, wondering if she would ever have energy again.

～

"I didn't know she had that many words inside her," Ashton said to Gabe when they both ended up in the kitchen an hour later.

"And so eloquently said too. Had she looked at me too soon, she would have found my mouth hanging open."

"I must admit to you, Gabe, that the different things Jeff has said over the years didn't make sense until Lily spoke to us today."

Gabe was on the verge of agreeing when the phone rang. He was closest and picked it up.

"Hello."

Ashton watched him smile as he listened and knew exactly what was going on.

"By the way," he heard Gabe say matter-of-factly, "I've decided not to marry you."

Gabe listened then and laughed at his own joke.

"Give me the phone," Ashton ordered, and after a few more words, Gabe obeyed.

"Is it really you this time?" the woman on the other end asked. It was Ashton's fiancée, Deanne Talbot.

"Yes. One of these days he's going to keep from laughing, and you'll think I've really broken off with you."

"We'll have to come up with some code word."

"Either that, or you could drop out of school and come home and marry me right now."

"You don't know how tempting that is."

"Why? What's going on?"

"I'm just tired, I think, and even though I studied for hours on my U.S. history exam, I didn't do that well. But mostly, California is not Hawaii."

"It's just a few more months," Ashton said for himself as much as Deanne. Just hearing her voice made him ache with longing.

"It's three months, eleven days, and approximately six hours."

"I love it when you do the math."

Deanne laughed on the other end, and they talked for most of the next hour. By the time they hung up, California was no closer to Hawaii, but both of them felt a little better.

∼

Evan didn't see his wife until he was almost done with his laps. She had pulled a chair close and was sitting at the edge of the pool, watching him. After spotting her, he swam the length of the pool underwater, his blond head breaking the surface at the three-foot end and coming up to smile at her.

"Hi."

"Hi, yourself."

"Wanna come in?"

"Maybe later."

"You sound sad," he commented.

"I'm not—just tired."

"Typical for this time of year."

"I'm always surprised by that. I always think I'm going to have more energy when the guests are gone, and here I need a nap."

"Give it a few more weeks. How are you doing with Lily around?"

"You know," Bailey said, as though she had just thought of it, "it's easy. She's neat and polite and keeps to herself so much of the time. I mean, I feel a certain amount of stress and pain with her being so burned, but she's one of the most undemanding people I've ever known."

"What is she doing now?"

"She's still sitting with the kids in front of the television, but I think most of the time she's sleeping."

"I told the kids we would swim later. Are you going to join us?"

Bailey looked at him a moment.

"Are we going to swim a little later on our own?"

Evan smiled. "I think that could be arranged."

Bailey smiled as she moved to put the chair back.

"I'd better check on the kids."

"All right. I'll be coming in a bit."

Evan watched her walk away, enjoying her figure from the back. He eventually went back to his laps, but exercise was not really what he had on his mind.

～

"This is Nan," Celia said to Lily, nearly shoving a photo in her face.

"Oh."

"Her name is Deanne," Peter filled Lily in. "She's gonna be our aunt."

"How nice," Lily said, still feeling a bit out of it.

She blinked owlishly at the screen and then noticed that Bailey was asleep next to Peter. At almost the same moment Lily realized that she needed to be excused. She tried to focus on the video but soon gave up. There was no help for it. It was going to hurt to move, but move she must.

Walking slowly, Lily headed for the small bathroom situated just off the foyer. It seemed to her that everything took forever, and she wondered at the fact that most body parts were taken for granted, at least until they were injured.

"I think I need food," Lily said quietly to give herself courage as she finished in the bathroom and walked to the kitchen. Something cold and sweet sounded good. Maneuvering gingerly, Lily went straight to the refrigerator.

When Gabe came in a few minutes later, Evan on his heels, they found her trying to cut a slice of watermelon.

"I'm glad to see you," Lily forced herself to say the moment the outside door closed. "Will you please help me get some watermelon?"

"Sure." Gabe was already headed her way. Although he had thanked her for rescuing them, it had been hard to leave her today. He had gone for a run on the beach in an effort not to sit around and stare at her. Evan had finished his laps in the pool, and they had come in together.

"How wide?"

"Maybe half an inch."

It was hard to cut it that thin, so Lily ended up with more than she needed, but in a blissfully brief amount of time, she had a plate in front of her and was taking that first cool bite. It tasted so good that the nausea she had been experiencing immediately began to recede.

"How are you feeling?" Evan asked, taking a seat across from her.

Lily stopped and thought. "My stomach needed food, so that's better, but the burning is unlike anything I've ever known. I almost want to shiver at the thought of what happened to my skin, but then that would be moving, and I don't wish to do that."

Evan blinked at the change in her voice. She still didn't have much eye contact with them, but she sounded the most confident he had ever heard her.

"Did you get some sleep?" Gabe asked, having started on his own slice of melon.

"I did, yes." Lily glanced up as she answered, absently wondering why it was easier to have eye contact with Gabe.

"Good. And what will you do for the rest of the day?"

"I don't know. Do you know if my brother is calling today?"

"I'm not certain. Maybe he will this evening."

Lily nodded, thinking that would make sense because Jeff was working. On the heels of that thought, she tried to remember the time difference on the mainland. While taking another bite of watermelon, Lily wondered, not for the first time, exactly where Jeff was.

Suddenly she wanted cheese. She had eaten only about five bites of the fruit in front of her and might want more, but cheese sounded very good to her at the moment. Going against the feelings inside of her to keep to herself and wanting to make a genuine effort to make this "home," Lily rose and went to the refrigerator again. She knew where the cheese was kept and pulled out a block.

For a moment the pain on her shoulders was so intense that she halted. She shut the door to the fridge but moved no farther.

"Are you all right?" Evan asked to her back.

"I think I will be," she said.

Celia chose that moment to join them. She saw the food and went right to Lily.

"I have cheese?"

"Certainly," Lily said, but her voice was strained.

The men hadn't even waited to hear from her. Gabe was not about to let Lily wait on Celia in her condition. So while Evan saw his daughter to a chair, Gabe took the cheese from Lily.

"I'll cut you some and put it on the table. You can sit back down when you're ready."

"Thank you."

Gabe hesitated. "Can I do something for you first?"

"No, thank you. I just need a moment."

Gabe took her at her word, although it took some effort, and returned to the table. He made himself carry on, but the horrible helplessness and blame was returning. He had told Jeff they would take care of her, and he'd let his friend down.

It did much for his heart to see Lily eventually come back to the table and eat some of the cheese he had cut. It wasn't much, but he figured her stomach might still be upset.

And he was right. Lily would have enjoyed a little more food, but her skin still smelled like the hospital, and that was making her feel a little ill. She would have liked a bath but knew how much she would have to use her arms to get in and out of a bathtub. Without giving it much thought, she asked, "Did the doctor say if I could swim or not?"

Gabe had all he could do to keep his mouth closed.

"You can't go out in the sun, Lily," Evan informed her.

"Oh, that's right."

"Did you want to swim?" Gabe questioned.

"Not really," she answered, wishing she had kept her mouth shut. "I can still smell the stuff they put on me, and I wasn't sure I could stand a shower or bath."

"If we could make the pool work, we would get you out there, Lily," Gabe told her before he realized he had the answer. "I know! We'll cool the water in the hot tub and have you get in that. It's small and easier to manage."

Lily wanted to ask if he was certain, but she kept quiet, partly because he was old enough to tell her the truth, and partly because the pain was crowding in again.

"Hey, Lily." Bailey came to the kitchen to find her. "Someone set a little bag of medicine on the dining room table. Have you been keeping up with this stuff?"

Keeping up with this stuff was a new phrase to Lily, so for a moment she didn't answer.

"Is it mine?" she asked at last.

"Yes," Bailey said and handed it to her.

Lily remembered as soon as she looked inside.

"If those are pain pills, Lily," Bailey went on to say, not wanting to sound like a mother but no longer willing to assume anything where this woman was concerned, "you're probably in need of one. You've been home for almost four hours, and that's about how long they last."

Lily could have sighed with relief. At the hospital they had led her to believe that she would feel a little better every day, and here she was feeling quite miserable again.

"Thank you, Bailey," she said simply and began to read the instructions. She rose to get a glass of water, hoping and praying as she took the pills that relief was on the way.

～

"It's time for the tube top." Bailey surprised Lily when she came to her room after dinner to find her.

"Why is that?"

"Aren't you going in the hot tub?"

"Yes."

"It's like this, Lily. Trying to get the suit over your shoulders and miss your burns will kill you."

The older woman gave her a moment to compute this. It didn't work.

"I'm afraid I still don't understand."

"You have strap marks on your shoulders, right?"

"Yes."

"Well, trying to get the suit in just the right place never works until after you've rubbed your burn more than you want to. And I would have to guess that you don't want your burned shoulders rubbed at all."

"No, I don't."

"You can just wear the tube top and some shorts. I'll go out with you. Don't worry about the guys. They'll leave us to ourselves."

Lily knew it was time to acquiesce.

"Maybe it is for the best."

"Come down whenever you're ready to go."

"All right. Thank you, Bailey."

"No problem," she said with a smile and went on her way.

They're so kind and caring, Lord. I still feel like an interloper, but not because of them. Help me to be a gracious receiver. I had determined to come here and contribute to the household, and now that I can't, my pride has surfaced.

Lily found utter peace as she continued to stand in her room, dressing slowly in her swim outfit and confessing her sins to the

Lord. She saw how much she had been moving on her plan and not His. She had not been thankful, and by constantly second-guessing all of her actions and words, she was making herself ill.

Is God in charge here or not, Lily? When did He call and tell you to take over? Be yourself with these people! Say the things you're thinking and stop fearing their rejection. What kind of friends would Jefferson have if they treated you with scorn because you might say the wrong word or thought?

Confession made, pep talk over, shorts in place, and tube top stepped into, Lily moved to the door. She stopped for a towel in the hallway and then went below, thinking that no amount of physical pain could compare with being at odds with God, her Creator.

"It simply doesn't work," she said quietly.

"What doesn't work?" Bailey asked from the bottom of the stairs.

Lily had not even seen her, but she still admitted, "My being in charge. I'm just not that good at doing God's job."

Bailey laughed and added, "And you know the worst part? I have to relearn that almost every day."

"I know just what you mean."

The children accompanied Lily and Bailey to the hot tub. It was right in the pool area, which was now quite shaded, but Lily had never noticed it. And it was large. It looked as if eight adults could sit in the molded seats very comfortably.

"I'm going to get out and look all around this place one of these days," she said as she followed her hostess. "I didn't even know this was here."

"We'll do a grand tour as soon as you feel up to it."

"Have I thanked you, Bailey?" Lily stopped and asked. "Have I told you how much I appreciate all of this?"

"Yes, Lily, you have. You not only say the words, but we can tell you're thankful."

"Our memory verse on Sunday was about thankfulness," Peter suddenly told them.

"What was it, Pete?" his mother asked as she stepped aside to let Lily go in.

"'Oh give thanks to the Lord.'"

"Where is it found?"

"I forget."

"1 Chronicles 16:8?" Lily asked.

"That's it!" Peter said, his little mouth rounding in surprise. "Do you know that verse?"

"I think I do. Does it go on to say, 'Call upon His name; make known His deeds among the peoples'?"

"I don't know. We just learned 'Oh, give thanks to the Lord.'"

Lily also wanted to thank the little boy. Talking with him had taken her mind off getting into the water, and so she had simply done it. It was not completely comfortable, but getting better all the time. The temperature was at almost the same level as her skin, and so other than her back, shoulders, and arms, she could barely feel it.

"Do you want to be splashed?" Celia suddenly asked. She was standing on one of the built-in benches next to Lily.

"Well," Lily began, a little confused.

"Another time, CeCe," her mother intervened. Then she explained to Lily: "Our rule on that issue is that you only splash people who want to be splashed."

Lily nodded and turned back to the little girl.

"As soon as I can go swimming again, you can splash me. How will that be?"

Celia nodded. "I do splashing good."

Thinking that Celia looked adorable in her little blue swimsuit, Lily smiled and shifted her back so her shoulders could sink below the water a bit more. At the same time, her head went back against the curved seat. She closed her eyes, and for the first time since she woke with the burn, Lily let herself relax.

Chapter Eight

"You know," Lily suddenly said, her head coming up to find Bailey sitting on the side of the tub across from her, "this tub is going to get that antiseptic solution in it, the wash they used on me in the hospital. I know the short shower I took didn't get it all off."

"That's okay. Ash will add some chlorine and it'll be all set."

"May I ask you something, Bailey?"

"Anything."

"What does everyone do around here? How do you make this work?"

While Bailey helped Celia find a toy to play with, she answered, "Gabe is the official manager of the Kapaia Resort. He makes the main decisions and takes the heat if anyone is unhappy. He deals the most with the public, and he has his own office in the rear of the resort office so he can field problems with guests or reservations or whatever.

"Ash manages the grounds and all the groundskeepers, along with all the cottages. He sees to repairs or makes sure they're done, whatever is needed. Evan sees to the restaurant and all equipment."

"What type of equipment?"

"Well, not everyone comes with tennis rackets and balls, but we have four courts, so he rents those out and keeps them up. He manages the beach area, snorkeling equipment, paddle boats— you name it."

"And the restaurant too?"

"Yes. We have a great staff, but he oversees the manager, who does most of the ordering, the hiring, and the firing. Evan also handles any changes to the menu, business hours, or building."

Lily was amazed.

"But right now is your time off?"

"Yes. We don't book any guests in September or October. Some of our competitors say we're crazy, but we found that staying open 12 months a year when we're family owned and operated as we are was just wearing everyone out. We've only done it this way for four years. It definitely takes a toll on the money side of things, but it's well worth it for the rest and family time."

And during your time off, you got stuck with me.

Lily hated the thought and didn't know where it had come from, but she worked to swiftly push it aside. As her brother had reminded her, this was where God wanted her.

"Can we swim?"

"You mean in the pool, Peter?"

He nodded in excitement.

"Not unless your dad comes out with you."

"Can I go ask him?"

Bailey glanced at Lily. Her head was back and her eyes were closed again.

"In a little while."

"I'm going to peel, aren't I?"

Bailey looked over to see that Lily's head had come up and she was staring at her.

"Like a snake." Bailey had no choice but to tell her, laughing just a little.

Lily was still inspecting the skin on her arm when Gabe came toward them. He had a cordless phone in his hand.

"It's for you, Lily. Jeff."

"Oh!"

Lily started to reach for it but stopped.

"I can talk in here?"

"Sure," Gabe said, a smile coming to his lips. "It would probably be best if you didn't drop it in the water as I have in the past."

Lily smiled at him as she took it.

Gabe went back to the house, but now it was Bailey's turn to stare at Lily. For the first time, Lily was talking on the phone to her brother and not tearing up in the least. It looked as though she was finally going to make it.

～

"I think you should stay here."

"Do you?"

"Yes, Lily," Gabe answered, his voice kind but also firm. "A week ago you were in the hospital, and there's no reason to rush this. By the time we drive to church, have early service, stay for Sunday school, and drive home, we're away from the house for hours. You have the rest of your stay to get to know the church family."

Gabe couldn't tell what she was thinking, but he thought she might be reluctant to do as he asked. In an effort to make her feel better, he added, "You'll be much more comfortable here, Lily, and we'll come home and tell you everything."

Lily nodded in obeisance, even though she wanted to argue. She was still sore, that was true, but getting better every day, and she so wanted to go to church. Jeff had talked often about the church family. She realized she wanted to get to know them better.

But the matter was settled.

Lily ate breakfast with the family and even had the newspaper to herself when they all left, but before she was ready to accept Gabe's word on the subject, they were out the door and gone. Lily finished reading the articles of interest to her in the newspaper, but she was distracted.

She cleared her place at the table, washed up the dishes, and then wandered aimlessly around the house. Not until she glanced up to see a surfer offshore did she pull out of her mood. In a moment of recognition, Lily realized that she had not gone out onto the beach since coming to the resort. Her first few days she had been intent on helping and not saying the wrong thing, and then she had been burned.

Able to be outside but still under cover from the sun, Lily stepped out one of the patio doors and onto the covered veranda. She took a seat on a footstool—it still felt better not to lean back against anything—and simply watched.

Unless her eyes were deceiving her, the man's leg was manacled to the surfboard by some type of cord. He wore a black wet suit and had very blond hair. His board was bright yellow. Lily found herself captivated.

The surfer never rode into shore. After riding a wave just so far, he would spin around in a fascinating move and ready himself to catch the next wave. Lily had no idea how long she watched, but the whole show was mesmerizing.

At one point the surfer took a spill, and Lily actually came to her feet with a small gasp. That surfers fell often was not something she would know, so it was with great relief that Lily saw him come up and start again.

I was terribly grouchy in my heart to Gabe, Lily suddenly confessed to the Lord. *Here he was offering to see to my best, and I was angry at him. Why do you suppose that I'm so selfish? You would think I would know better by now. I'm still fighting You over my schedule here. I get it in my head that it's going to be one way, and when it's not, I'm very angry with You.*

Please help me not to fall into this again, Lord. Help me to be strong and want Your will more than my own. Bless the family as they attend church and Sunday school this morning. Help them to study hard. Give Pastor Stringer clarity of thought.

Lily went on to pray for everyone she could think of, at home and in Hawaii, and to thank God for taking such good care of her. The surfer was still at it when she finished, but Lily had lost a certain amount of interest. Seeing that she could still remain out of the sun, Lily moved until she could reach the sand. She spent the next hour writing words, building little roads that resembled a small town, and then simply enjoying the texture of the sand as it ran over and through her fingers.

～

Lily was on Gabe's mind as the sermon began later that morning. He didn't know anyone, woman or man, whose eyes and face did not give him away. Gabe thought back on his early association with Jeff and realized it had been the same. Was two months enough time for Lily to take her guard down? Gabe wasn't sure.

A little hand tapping his leg brought Gabe's thoughts back to the present.

"What is it?" Gabe bent to whisper to Celia.

The sound of her uncle's voice was all the invitation Celia needed. She climbed into his lap and laid her head back against him. It was harder to take notes with her in his lap, but for the moment he wanted to have her close.

In an instant unbidden memories flooded through him. Gabe thought back to harder days—days when the future looked bleak and brief. Days when he had made choices, or rather hadn't made choices, that would affect his remaining time on the earth, be it lengthy or fleeting.

"Look at what the next verse says." Pastor Stringer's voice broke through Gabe's thoughts, and he knew he was missing the sermon.

Asking the Lord to help him, and shifting Celia a little so he could read his Bible, Gabe firmly brought his mind back to the present.

～

Celia was the first one to spot Lily when the family arrived home. Her Sunday school paper clutched in her pudgy hand, she made a beeline for the veranda.

"Lilyee," she called.

"Hi, Celia." Lily welcomed her with a smile and even held her arm out.

"I can't hug," Celia told her, stopping short.

"It's very sweet of you to remember my burn, Celia, but maybe if we hug softly... Can we do that?"

The little head bobbed, dark hair moving, as she crept forward, moving carefully as though she and Lily were already touching. Lily smiled as she watched her earnest expression, afraid to laugh lest she stop. When they finally hugged, Lily realized how much she missed contact. Bailey didn't know her well enough to hug her, and of course with her burn would not have even tried.

"What are you doing, CeCe?" Peter asked as he came to them.

"Having hugs." Her brow lowered in her own defense; she had a tendency to grow cross rather easily. "Lilyee said."

Lily smiled at Peter who returned the grin.

"How were church and Sunday school, Peter?"

"They were fine. I had a itch on my foot."

"Was that during the sermon?"

"No, during Sunday school. I had to take my shoe off."

"Did that help?"

"Yeah. I itched it."

"Scratched it," Lily corrected.

Peter only nodded and asked, "What did you do?"

"After I finished inside, I sat out here and watched a surfer. I had never seen one."

"We have big waves."

"Do you?"

"Bigger than Waikiki. The North Shore always does."

"I didn't know that."

"It's the winds."

Instantly interested, Lily began to question him. Evan wandered onto the scene, and with Celia playing in the sand nearby, the three discussed the reasons for the huge waves.

"All the big competitions are out here," Evan told Lily. "The waves can be downright treacherous, but that's what we look for."

"Do you surf?" Lily asked, leaning close with interest.

"We all do."

"Not CeCe," Peter clarified, and the little girl came over upon hearing the sound of her name.

"I'n hungry," she stated and made her way into the house.

The mention of food caused them all to head that way with Lily bringing up the rear. She looked back at the waves—the surfer was long gone—and tried to picture herself on a surfboard. A small shudder ran over her as a large wave crashed into shore. Not in her wildest dreams could she imagine riding one of those waves.

～

Lily didn't find out until late in the day that there was no church that night. She knew that Gabe would have discouraged her from going, so she found it rather nice to know that she wouldn't be alone again. She had ended up enjoying her solitary time, but company was pleasant too.

"We're going to watch a movie," Peter told Lily, who found Bailey in the kitchen fixing bowls of popcorn.

"How fun. What movie?"

"A Disney one. What is it, Mama?"

"*The Computer Wore Tennis Shoes*. We've heard it's fun."

"We borrowed it from Matthew Daily at church."

"I don't think I've met him."

"He's big. He's bigger than me."

Lily smiled at the way Peter's eyes rounded before she noticed that Bailey was slicing fruit. Fetching another knife, she moved to help her. In no time at all, the men were on hand gathering soft drinks, glasses, ice, and the cookie jar. Clearly it was going to be a feast.

"Okay, Pete," Evan urged when everyone had moved to the TV area of the great room. "Let's start 'er up."

The little boy did not need to be asked twice. He pushed the video into the machine and then scrambled into his father's lap.

It didn't take long for Lily to see what Bailey meant about the film being fun. Dexter Havens, the main character, was a charming scamp who was at college for the social life more than an education. Not known as a brain, Dexter accidentally gets an electrical jolt from a wire that's connected to the school's computers, and his life is transformed. He and his friends join the College Knowledge Bowl for their college and end up in competitions with other schools.

Lily and the Kapaia family were thoroughly engrossed when the debate questions began. Lily didn't hear herself, but just before the answer was given each time, she quietly answered the question.

"The sensation of one's limbs falling asleep is known as?" the quiz master on the movie asked.

"Neuropraxia," Lily said quietly.

"Why was the Taj Mahal built?"

"As a tomb for Shah Jahan's wife."

The quiz master went on to ask for the six largest bodies of water, in order.

"Pacific, Atlantic, Indian, Arctic, Mediterranean, and Carribean."

"Malaysia's currency is the ———?"

"Ringgit," Lily said, having answered at least ten other questions correctly.

"How did you know that?" Ashton finally asked her. He had only known half of the answers.

"Oh." Lily looked surprised and then shrugged a little. "I've probably read it somewhere."

A moment later, Ashton wished he had kept his mouth shut. He realized that Lily had clammed up.

"Go ahead, Lily," Gabe directed, having caught on as well. "Answer the questions."

Lily wasn't sure what he meant. She assumed they all knew the answers since most of them were pretty basic. She wondered that no one had told her to be quiet earlier so they could hear the movie.

On the next question Gabe glanced at Lily, who caught his look from the corner of her eye, but she kept her eyes on the television and said nothing. The scene shifted away from the competition, and Lily was glad to be off the hook. She told herself to watch with her mouth closed.

To help her do this, she reached for one of the paper plates and took some popcorn and fruit. Filling her mouth worked fine until something made her laugh unexpectedly and she felt as though she was going to choke on the popcorn in her throat.

"I'd pound you on the back, Lily, but I'm afraid of hurting your burn," Bailey told her.

Having gained control on her own, Lily thanked her with a strained voice and streaming face.

"Here." Gabe handed her a glass of root beer.

Lily took a few sips, still feeling as though she had something jammed in her throat. Everyone went back to the movie, and Lily realized how blessed she was. The Kapaias treated her like family. They made sure she was all right, but they included her without special treatment and acted as though her presence were an everyday thing.

When the movie ended, the children were put to bed. They rode up the stairs on their uncles' backs, their father bringing up the rear to pray with them, dole out kisses, and tuck them in.

"That was fun, wasn't it?"

"Yes," Lily agreed. "Can you imagine gaining all that knowledge so swiftly?"

"No, I can't. I can't even imagine knowing what you know."

"Oh, Bailey," Lily shook her head, "it's not as much as you might think. You knew most of it, didn't you?"

"Most of it? No. I knew some of it."

"That's understandable, Bailey," Lily kept on, her voice kind. "You have children to raise, a large home to keep, and a husband to take care of. I have none of those things, so I have more time for reading."

"I think you're too modest."

Lily had no idea how to reply to that, so she sat quietly.

"How is your burn doing?" Bailey asked, looking at Lily's still-red face.

"Much better. A week ago I wondered if I was going to live, but now I think I am."

"And how about Jeff? Do you still miss him so much?"

"That's better too," Lily was able to say. "I'm still sorry that our time had to be interrupted, and I find myself hoping he finishes early, but I think I'll be fine."

"Why don't you write and tell your father that you're going to stay a bit longer? That way you and Jeff could maybe have six weeks or so together."

Lily only nodded. How did one explain that you couldn't write Owen Walsh and tell him what you were going to do? At least his daughter couldn't. You could write and ask permission, but not tell.

"I'll have to think on that," Lily said, hoping Bailey would not press her.

"You're easy to have around, did you know that, Lily?" Bailey suddenly said with a smile.

"No, I didn't, but I'm glad to hear you say it. I was wondering how this has been for you. I can see that you're used to having family everywhere, but another woman is different."

"That's true, but I'm doing fine. You're such a big help that this might be the most relaxed time off I've ever had."

"May I ask you a question?"

"Sure."

"Will Ashton and his wife live here too?"

"Not for the first year. They'll take one of the cottages and then move here later."

"And how will that be for you? Will Deanne help out and such?"

"Yes. It helps that Deanne grew up around here. We've all known her for years. And something else you need to understand is that I've grown more laid-back over the years. As long as things get done, the method doesn't concern me anymore. If it's someone else's night for the dishes, he can do them at midnight if he chooses. I'm able to let it go, and then when it's my day, I do it my way."

"When will Deanne be coming to marry Ashton?"

"She finishes with school in December, and the date is set for early March."

Lily smiled. "The children keep talking to me about it. I can tell they're very excited."

"They're both going to be in the wedding, and they also miss Deanne because she's been gone," Bailey said with a chuckle. "Not to mention Ash. He's been just a little bit quiet since she left at the end of August."

"May I ask you another question?" Lily vocalized the now-familiar phrase.

"Sure. You can even ask me a question without asking if you can ask a question."

Lily laughed a little but still said, "What is laid-back?"

"Laid-back means easygoing."

Lily blinked in confusion. That had been no help. Bailey tried again.

"Not easily upset about things. Ready to take life as it comes. Does that help?"

"Yes, thank you," Lily replied, still taking it in. But she had another thought. "So there was a time when you were not easy-going?"

"That's right. It had to be my way or no way."

"What changed for you, Bailey? What happened?"

"God worked in my heart. I had never seen anger as a sin. The boys are more naturally easygoing, but I was determined to have things my way. My parents just thought that was the way I was. But then Evan came into my life, and Pastor Stringer became our pastor, and they challenged me to see my actions through God's eyes.

"I used to get angry at Evan and Peter when they didn't do things my way. Then I understood that all anger is directed at God. If He's in control—and of course He is—then my growing angry at any situation means that I disagree with His rule and authority."

"What a wonderful thing to realize, Bailey," Lily said, even as she thought of her father's tendency toward anger and some of the moods she had been in since Jeff had left.

"I think so. CeCe tends to have my personality, so we're working with her early. We don't want her to see anger as an option."

"You do such a good job, you and Evan both. The children are precious."

"Did someone say I'm precious?" Evan teased as he joined them.

"Yes, dear," Bailey said, her voice deliberately patronizing. "You're the most precious thing in the house."

Evan plopped next to her and planted a kiss on her mouth. The couple then smiled into each other's eyes before Evan picked up his wife's hand.

Had Lily thought about such an action ahead of time, she would have been certain it would have caused her embarrassment, but she was wrong. It seemed natural and right and...Lily couldn't place the other word right now, but she knew this: Seeing Bailey and Evan in love made her heart smile.

Chapter Nine

"Lily, this is Wang Ho."

Almost two weeks after Lily was burned, Evan introduced her to a small, older gentleman who had come unannounced into the kitchen.

"He's our cook at the Little Bay Restaurant. Wang, this is Jeff's sister, Lily. She's staying with us all the way from Kashien."

"It's a pleasure to meet you," Lily said, her eyes down. She had been getting better about eye contact, even with Evan and Ashton, but this man looked like the men from her corner of the world, and long-taught habits die hard.

"Lily Walsh," Wang said softly. "This is not a Kashienese name."

"No, sir."

"And your eyes are not Kashienese, but they are down."

Lily nodded, a smile coming to her mouth—one that matched the smile she heard in his voice.

"You are in America now."

"Yes, sir."

Lily made herself look up, and although eye contact was very brief, it was long enough to see that he was smiling.

"Now listen, Lily," Evan went on. "Wang is family. The only reason you haven't seen him before is because he's been on vacation. He'll be in and out all the time, and if you're smart you'll visit him in the kitchen of the restaurant often. He always has something to offer, all of it mouthwatering."

Lily smiled.

"I'll plan on that."

"Today," Wang said. "Come today."

"All right. I will."

"Are you set, Lily?" Ashton now came through, Celia on his back.

"Yes, I am."

"Wang!" Ashton spotted him, swung his niece around until she was in his arms, and went to give Wang a great, one-armed hug. "How was your trip?"

"Very good. I took pictures."

"I want to see them."

"You shall."

"Good. Right now Lily and I are off to check on the cottages. She hasn't seen them yet."

"Do you have sunscreen on?" Evan asked.

Lily assured him that she was covered. She also had her bamboo hat along, and in just a few moments she was headed out the door with Ashton. Talking all the while, explaining almost more than Lily could take in, Ashton took Lily around to the large garage area and toward a small four-wheeled vehicle.

"Climb in."

Lily did as she was told, and in no time at all they were scooting out onto the beach. Ashton took it easy, as Lily was still somewhat sore, but it didn't take long for Lily's skin to recede to the back of her mind. Since Sunday Lily had made a point to come out and see the ocean every day. She knew she would never grow tired of it. It was too glorious for that. But today was even better. Today she was off the veranda. With the wind blowing in her face and the glorious smell of the salty air filling her senses, Lily couldn't find the words to describe what she was feeling.

"I'll show you the nicest one," Ashton told her as he drove past other cottages to a small house with a number six over the door.

After first going onto a spacious covered porch that sported bamboo chairs and a table, they entered the small structure, and Lily saw just what he meant. The door opened immediately into a nice-sized living room, dining room, and kitchen area. Everything was clean and neat, and Lily saw that a person could live there permanently and in remarkable comfort. Large windows in the living-room area looked out over the sea.

"And back this way are the bedroom and bathroom."

Lily was impressed with all the space and wondered what a night in such a cabin would cost.

"And you say this is the nicest one?"

"Actually, they're all very nice. This just happens to be my favorite."

"Are they all the same layout?"

"No, they're very diverse. Some even have two bedrooms."

"So more than two people can sleep there?"

"Actually, this cottage sleeps five, because the sofa becomes a bed, and there's a roll-away in this closet."

Ashton was opening doors and showing her everything as he talked.

"The two-bedroom units have the same amenities and then some, so they can sleep up to eight."

"And did you and Gabe and the others build these?"

"No, our grandfather did. He started the resort in 1951."

Questions flooded Lily's mind, but she didn't wish to be presumptuous. Instead she centered on the things in the cabin, hoping that Ashton would not grow frustrated with her.

"Ashton, could I possibly see how a sofa becomes a bed?"

"Sure. I'll show you."

After the demonstration, which Lily found quite wonderful, Ash showed her the small back porch where a grill and a compact clothesline for hanging wet items were provided.

Once outside, Ashton patiently stood back, smiling a little over her wonder, and watched as Lily thoroughly examined the clothesline. It was the type that folded down into itself when not in use, and he could see that she found the mechanism utterly captivating.

That inspected, Lily looked around at her surroundings. She didn't say so, but what most impressed her was the privacy. The ocean was visible from almost all the windows of the cottage and of course the porch, but with the way all the small dwellings had been set back amid the foliage, she had the feeling she was alone.

"And how many did you say there were?" Lily asked as they headed back out front.

"Cottages? Thirteen."

"And what do you call this vehicle?" Lily asked as they climbed back in.

"It's a large golf cart. We have four of them."

Lily had read about the carts that golfers took around the course. It made her wonder how many acres the Kapaia Resort was. Ashton drove her past the rest of the cottages, telling her different aspects as he thought of them. More questions occurred to her, and Lily kept Ashton talking until they suddenly stopped at the rear of the Little Bay Restaurant.

She watched her host get out of the cart but did not presume to follow.

"Come on," Ashton urged her. "We've got to check out what Wang is cooking."

Lily finally knew where she was. Not having seen this building from the rear, she had not been able to guess.

The two walked through a rear door that put them almost immediately in the kitchen. Everything was impressively clean, and Lily thought the aromas that filled the busy room were marvelous. Wang greeted both of them with tremendous grace, and before Lily planned on it, she was sitting at a huge steel island amid the hustle of workers, a bowl with some type of pineapple mixture in front of her.

"Eat this, eat this" was the order, and she obeyed.

"How do you like it?" Ashton asked around a mouthful.

"It's wonderful."

Wang had wandered off, but Lily suspected he knew she enjoyed it.

"Your eyes are starting to look green again."

Lily stopped eating and looked at the man next to her.

"Can you explain that to me?"

Ashton smiled.

"For a few days there, the burn was so intense that your eyes didn't look as green. Now the color is coming back."

Lily nodded in a way that was becoming familiar to them all. Her head would nod a little, and her mouth would make an "oh," but no sound would come out.

"I take it you didn't notice?"

Lily's eyes dropped, and she admitted, "I don't care to look in the mirror much right now."

"You don't look bad, Lily—just a little toasty."

His wording and the tone of his voice made her smile before she went back to eating, but he had not understood. It wasn't her looks. It was the reminder of what had happened to her skin. When she caught sight of herself in a mirror, she felt something akin to horror, and even though it might be in her head, the pain would return.

"Tell me, Lily. If I left you here, could you find your way back?"

"I think so," she answered, even as she thought fast about the direction from which they had come.

"Well, I don't really want to do that, but I just remembered a phone call I need to make."

"I can finish quickly," she said, setting her spoon aside.

"No, don't do that. Wang would love to show you the workings of the kitchen. Stay as long as you like."

The offer was too tempting by half. Lily glanced around. The room was full of gadgets and appliances she had never seen before.

"Thank you, Ashton."

"You're welcome. Are you sure you can get back?"

"Why don't you just tell me the way, and then I'll find it."

The youngest Kapaia gave her clear directions, thanked Wang as well as told him that Lily wanted a tour, and went on his way.

It took some time for Lily to feel comfortable alone with Wang and his staff, but in a very short time she was gaining knowledge about the kitchen such as she never had before.

～

"Where's Lily?"

Having tracked some of his family down at the pool a few hours before dinner, Gabe asked the question. He wanted to check with Lily about some ideas he had to further her education.

"Last I knew she was with Ash," Bailey told him.

"They went to see the cottages," Peter added.

"That was right after breakfast this morning," Evan said, just as Ashton made an appearance.

The younger brother had some business to talk over with both Evan and Gabe, but eventually Gabe was able to ask his question.

"I left her with Wang. Isn't she back yet?"

"I don't think so. How was she getting here?"

"I gave her directions, and she was going to walk."

"You should check her room before you go looking, Gabe," his sister suggested. "She might have come in when no one noticed."

Gabe did just that, but not five minutes passed before he was in his own golf cart and headed to the restaurant. He slipped in the back, much as Lily and Ashton had done earlier, but was met with an entirely different scene.

Lily Walsh, flour covering her hands as she rolled out piecrust, was conversing with Wang and the day manager, Rick Wong, in Chinese. Gabe, who had a fairly good command of the language, approached.

"Gabriel," Wang said softly, turning to face him and switching to English, "you have come for Lily."

"Not exactly. We just wanted to make sure she was all right."

Lily was still speaking to Rick. She was asking the man about shipments of produce and vegetables, which were locally grown, and how they worked their delivery schedule, so it took a few seconds for her to notice Gabe. She was so focused on Rick's answers that she didn't realize at first who it was.

"Hello." Gabe smiled when her eyes came up, and Lily beamed at him.

"I'm learning to run a restaurant."

Gabe chuckled.

"Let me know when you go on the payroll. How are you, Rick?" Gabe now said, extending his hand to shake the other man's.

"I'm doing well, Gabe. How are you?"

"Enjoying my time off."

Rick nodded. "It's the same here. We get plenty of outside business in the evenings, but I can tell that the cottages are empty when I can shoot a cannonball through here during breakfast and lunch."

"May I ask a question?" Lily put in, surprising even herself.

"Yes."

"People have kitchens in their cottages, but they still eat breakfast and lunch here?"

Rick explained the preferences of different people, and Lily listened intently. There wasn't a single aspect of this business that was new to Gabe, but he still enjoyed Lily's fascination.

"Gabriel has come for you, Lily," Wang said as soon as Rick was done.

"Oh, I'll wash my hands and come right now."

Gabe was opening his mouth to tell Lily she didn't have to leave but then caught Wang's eye on him. After Rick had gone his way, the older man spoke.

"You did come for Lily, did you not, Gabriel?"

"I just wanted to talk to her about something, not interrupt."

"But she is easy to talk to, do you not find?"

Gabe smiled before saying, "In truth, Wang, I don't know her well enough to answer that."

It was Wang's turn to smile.

"We shall have to see that this situation changes."

Before Gabe could frame a reply, Lily was back. "Thank you for everything," she said to Wang.

He bowed his head to her.

"The pleasure is all mine. We will do it again."

Lily smiled before dropping her eyes, glad that Gabe was waiting and she could exit. Wang was too like the men from home, and finding him here, Lily felt utterly out of her element on the issue of looking men in the eye.

At the door Lily slipped back into her bamboo hat, tying the strings below her chin.

"That hat must be from home," Gabe commented.

"Yes, it is. How did you know?"

"I've never seen one like it here."

"I made it," Lily admitted quietly.

"I'm impressed."

Lily could have told him it was not a great effort, but she was quiet as she climbed into Gabe's cart. The silence didn't last too long.

"May I ask you a question?" Lily asked just after Gabe shifted into gear and set them in motion.

"Certainly."

"Do you know the etymology of the word *payroll*?"

"Offhand I don't, but we can check out the dictionary when we get back."

"Will the history be in there?"

"Not necessarily all the particulars, but the date and origin of the word will be."

Lily's dictionary at home in Kashien could not boast these features, and she wondered if Jeff would be willing to help her to find one like Gabe's before she flew home.

"How's the burn?"

"As long as I stay out of the sun and away from the oven, it's fine."

"You don't look burned anymore." He glanced sideways as he spoke. "You're tan enough to be a native."

Lily laughed because she knew how far that was from the truth. Her skin was tight and already starting to peel in places.

Lily wondered why Gabe needed her. She wanted to ask him but kept quiet, hoping he would volunteer. Gabe, on the other hand, thought she knew. He forgot that he had told Wang he didn't mean to interrupt before Lily returned.

He swung the cart into the wide garage and then asked to talk to Lily on the shady veranda. Lily hoped that nothing was wrong and tried to ignore the tenseness she suddenly felt, but of course nothing showed on her face.

Not at all aware of her thoughts, Gabe started right in.

"Lily, would you say you're up to doing some things, or would you rather wait awhile longer?"

"No, I can do anything you want me to."

Warning bells went off in Gabe's mind even as he nodded. Lily volunteering to do anything he wanted wasn't quite what he had in mind. He continued, but his eyes were watchful.

"The whole plan was to teach you the things Jeff had on his list, but I don't want to rush you."

Lily didn't know if there was an actual list but still said, "We can start on the list anytime you like."

Again Gabe nodded, choosing to take her at her word.

"If you think you can move your arms without pain, we'll head to the tennis courts tomorrow. How does that sound?"

"That's fine."

"You're certain your arms don't hurt?"

"Yes. I should be fine."

"Okay. Do you have any shorts you can wear?"

"Jeff bought some for me."

"Okay. I think you'll be the most comfortable in those, and tennis shoes, of course. Be sure to put sunblock on all exposed skin. We'll head out early and try to beat the heat."

Relieved that nothing was wrong, Lily nodded but wondered if tennis would be the disaster swimming was. Her gaze dropped with the memory.

"Lily, would you mind looking at me?"

Lily complied.

"Are you sure you're up to this?"

She forced herself to keep eye contact and admit, "I was just thinking about how poorly my swimming lesson ended. I don't want to fail in tennis as well."

"But you didn't fail in swimming. In fact, Ash told me you amazed him with how well you did and how fast you caught on."

"He said that?"

"Yes, he did."

"Oh, my," Lily said rather weakly.

"What's the matter?"

"I just wrote and told my father what a mess I had made of things."

Not understanding the seriousness of the situation, Gabe laughed.

"You'll just have to get another letter off to him, telling him you did great."

Lily managed to smile and nod, but a knot of dread had formed in the pit of her stomach. Her father would not understand if she wrote and changed her story. She knew that the burn had not been anyone's fault, but she also knew her father wouldn't see it that way, so she had made a point to take whatever blame there was. She hadn't really mentioned learning to swim.

For a moment Lily thought about her time in the pool. Until her shoulders had started to hurt, Lily had felt very good about what she had accomplished. The thought of getting in the deep end, even after she had gone under and been afraid, was no longer an issue. Nevertheless, it was a little late to mention that to her father.

"Sometimes I wish he had a telephone so I could just call."

"Your father?"

"Yes."

"That would be nice, wouldn't it?" Gabe agreed, coming to his feet and thanking Lily for her time. He had things to do, so as soon as he established a time for their tennis lesson and asked if Lily had any more questions, he left her to her own thoughts.

Lily watched him go on his way, even as she remembered placing the letter where Bailey had directed. It was a common spot in the kitchen that everyone used. The first one to head out mailed whatever letters had gathered.

Moving swiftly, Lily made for the kitchen, hoping the letter might still be there. The basket was empty.

Lily sighed. She so wished she could tell Jeff what had happened. Maybe he could write and explain it somehow, but spending the money on a long-distance call over such a trivial matter seemed wasteful to Lily.

It didn't take long for Lily to realize she was fretting. On her way back through the great room, she walked to the patio door and looked out at the sea.

You're such a huge God that You can create an ocean, but I don't think You can handle my problems. Help me to know what to do, Lord. Help me to know the best path to take. Let Jefferson call or open up some other option that only You would think of to clear this up with my father.

And please, Lord, Lily ended the prayer, *help Father not to be too upset. Help him to trust You too.*

Chapter Ten

"Ready or not, here I come," Lily said in a singsong voice.

It was after dinner—Evan and Bailey had gone for a swim—and the children were hiding from Lily, who was figuring out a way not to find them too swiftly. Celia's giggles and Peter's attempt to shush her were making it a bit hard. The giggles were coming from behind the sofa, and the hushing noise was in the vicinity of the TV cabinet.

"Let me see now," Lily said in an exaggerated tone. "Is Celia under this sofa pillow? No, not there. Maybe Peter is hiding under this picture frame."

It was too much for both of them. They sprang out, giggling uproariously, declaring that they had fooled Lily. Lily plopped down on one of the sofas, and they scrambled to sit with her.

"You didn't find us," Peter exclaimed.

"I thought you were under that picture frame," Lily said, her eyes large with teasing. "And you, Celia, I thought you were under this little pillow."

"I'n too big," she told her, all the while looking very logical. Lily laughed and asked, "Do you know what I want to do?"

"What?"

"I want to go out and sit in the sand. Do you want to?"

Without even answering, Celia began to pull the sandals from her feet. Peter and Lily did the same. Not two minutes later, they were just off the oceanview veranda, working on small sand houses and roadways.

"I think we need a little house right here," Lily proclaimed as she began to wet sand and shape it into a little box. Celia's little fingers came in to help, which meant that Lily had to start over when the toddler became distracted, but Lily didn't mind. Their city was shaping up nicely.

"CeCe!" came a cry of impatience a moment later. "Get off my house!"

"Here, Celia." Lily tried to intervene.

"Wanna sit here," CeCe told her.

"But if you do that," Lily replied, her voice kind, "you'll smash all Peter's work. Come and sit right here next to Peter."

Celia did as she was asked, but her face showed a measure of disapproval. Lily chose to ignore her. She wouldn't have done so with her own child, but Celia was not her own.

"How are you doing, Peter?" she asked of that small boy.

"Okay," he said, working to put the house to rights.

"Why don't I help you?"

"I can help," Celia offered, but Lily did her best to finish the job swiftly and distract the little girl. It worked for a time, but Celia seemed determined to be in the middle of Peter's project. Lily was casting around for something else they might do when she realized they had company. Gabe was sitting on a lounger, a book open in his lap, his eyes on the threesome.

"Hello," he said when Lily's eyes came to his.

"Hello. We didn't see you."

"I didn't want to disturb this construction project, but I suddenly remembered that we never looked up the word 'payroll.' I was afraid I would forget again if I let it go."

Lily smiled and pushed to her feet.

"No, Celia!" The words came out of Peter before Lily could take a step. Lily turned, but the children's uncle stepped in.

"Celia Alani Markham! Come here this minute."

Lip out a mile, the little girl obeyed. The wet sand covering her bottom and hands gave proof of her crime.

"You may sit right here on this seat until you are ready to apologize to Peter."

Celia did so, but it was clear she was none too happy about it.

"Here, Lily," Gabe directed, turning slightly away from his niece. "Pull a chair up and look at this."

Lily bent over the book and started to read where Gabe pointed. "Oh, 1740," she said, her eyes large. "That's earlier than I thought it would be."

"I felt the same way. Here," Gabe shifted the book so she could see better, "read the whole thing. There isn't much, but—" Gabe cut off when his niece moved. Thinking she was headed to her brother, Gabe only watched. The little girl had no eye contact with him as she came around his lounge chair and started to climb into Lily's lap.

Lily was rapt with the book. She had finished reading the definition of "payroll" long ago, but several other words had caught her eye. Without even looking down, she felt Celia, lifted her into place, settled her arms close around her, and continued to study the dictionary. Only Gabe's voice got her attention.

"Celia," he began, his voice telling everyone that he meant business, "you may come and cuddle with Lily just as soon as you apologize to Peter. Until you do that, you will sit on this other seat. Now, what are you going to do?"

Tears threatened at this point, so Gabe reached for the little girl's hand.

"CeCe," he said gently, "if you had built a sand house and Peter sat on it, you would be very sad. You need to love Peter more than wanting your own way."

"I lub Peter" was the tearful reply.

"I know you do. Why don't you go over now and tell him how sorry you are?"

An occasional sniff punctuating her nod, Celia climbed from Lily's lap and went to her brother.

"Peter," Gabe said before Celia got to him, "you need to watch how impatient you get, okay?"

"Okay."

"I'm sorry," Lily said to Gabe.

"For what?"

"I was supposed to be watching the children."

"Actually, I was trying to rescue you. Ash and I try not to get involved for fear that the kids will think they're surrounded by parents, but it's not your job to put out the fires between them. Evan would be none too pleased to learn that Celia gave you a hard time."

Lily's lips formed her silent "oh," her face thoughtful, before she turned to look at the children.

"Celia reminds me of a little girl from home," Lily began to say, her eyes still on Peter and Celia, who were again playing in the sand. "She had to be taught the difference between good attention and bad attention." Lily looked back at Gabe. "She was eager for either kind. Once she understood that negative attention wasn't pleasing to anyone, she changed."

"Good and bad attention. I don't know if Evan and Bales of Hay have ever thought of it that way before."

"Bales of Hay?" Lily questioned as she watched the man in the lounger shout with laughter.

"I don't know how that surfaced from the past," Gabe finally admitted, laughter still filling his voice.

"But that's what you used to call Bailey?"

"As kids, all the time. She used to chase us, but then she got used to the name and ignored us."

Lily smiled. "It sounds like you know all about negative attention."

Gabe's brows rose. "I think you must be right. It's certainly easy to see that CeCe comes by it honestly."

Lily's gaze went back to the dictionary. "Is this type of dictionary readily available here in Hawaii, Gabe?"

"Yes. Just about any bookstore would have it."

"I think I'll ask Jeff to help me find one when he returns."

"Has he called lately?"

"No," she said, her smile a little sad. "I think he must be very busy, or he figures I'll do better if he doesn't call all the time."

"And which is it? Are you doing better?"

"I hope so. I hope I'm not walking around in a self-centered little haze like I was the first week."

"No one thought you were self-centered, Lily. We knew you were scared."

"And how foolish was that?" Lily asked, looking him right in the eye. "Jeff wouldn't leave me somewhere where I would be harmed." Lily shook her head in self-derision.

"So you don't miss him so much?" Gabe tried to guess.

Lily's gaze went to the sea as she admitted softly, "I miss him every day."

Gabe studied her profile for a moment and thought how much he liked Jefferson Walsh's sister. Through his friend he had come to care for this woman, but not until he met her and experienced her openness, honesty, and keen mind did he realize how much he appreciated her as a person.

That he found her quite lovely and very sweet certainly didn't harm the picture, but Gabe's thoughts were not romantic, just tender and caring.

"Why don't you call him?"

"Because it's not an emergency."

"Is that what he told you?"

Lily looked surprised. "I don't know. I just assumed that was the wisest choice."

"Go inside and call him," Gabe suggested. "When the person on the other end answers, just explain that it's not an emergency and would they please ask Jeff Walsh to call when he gets a chance."

"And you don't feel this is wasteful?"

"How would it be wasteful?"

"Because it's long-distance and expensive."

"Much as I appreciate your sensitivity on the issue, Lily, you're not abusing the privilege. Your desire to talk with Jeff is a very easy wish to grant."

An easy wish to grant. Lily liked the sound of that so much she smiled.

"I'll do it. As soon as Evan and Bailey come in, I'll call."

Gabe almost offered to stay with the kids, but something told him that Lily would want to finish the job.

As it was, they took care of the children together. Peter said he was getting hungry, and the four went in for a snack. When Bailey showed up some 20 minutes later, Lily took Gabe's suggestion. Just an hour later, the phone rang. It was Jeff calling for Lily.

～

"Are you dreadfully busy?"

"I am, Lil. More so than I expected to be."

"Well, that's good. The time goes fast then."

"Yes, it does," Jeff agreed, not willing to admit to her that his return might be delayed. He was working night and day to change that fact, but it wasn't going well.

"So tell me," Jeff started again, "now that you've had a few weeks, are you glad you stayed?"

"I am, yes, but I hate how short our time together will be."

"I've been thinking about that."

"What exactly?"

"Just that. Our time *will* be short. Did you know I originally wanted you to come for six months?"

"I think so."

"Well, maybe you should just write Father and tell him you're staying longer."

"You know better than anyone, Jeff, that you don't tell Father anything."

"Lily, I'm not trying to lead you to be disrespectful, but what is he going to do?"

Lily did some fast thinking, but it wasn't in the direction her brother thought it might be.

"You're going to be delayed, aren't you, Jeff?"

"It's looking that way," he admitted, wishing he had told her at the beginning. "I'm working hard, but some of this is out of my control."

In a heartbeat Lily came up with a decision. "I'll give you one extra week, Jeff. I'll trust that you'll do everything within your power to be back when you said you would, but if you're going to be any more than a week late, I'll write Father and tell him I've changed my date."

"Are you sure?"

"Yes. I think he'll understand. I've come all this way, and I know he wanted us to have a good time."

"Thanks, Lily. I'll admit that does take some of the pressure off me."

"Good. I don't want to be a source of worry for you."

She had been just that, Jeff could have told her, but he knew that was no one's fault but his own.

"So how are your lessons coming? What are you learning?"

"You would be so impressed. I can run the bread machine *and* the coffeemaker. I've mastered the washing machine and dryer. I can swim, and in the morning I'll be learning to play tennis."

"Is Gabe teaching you?"

"Yes. How did you know?"

"Because he's very good. What else will you do?"

"I don't know. But when I visited the Little Bay Restaurant today, I learned so much."

"What do you think of Wang Ho?"

"He showed me everything. He was so kind."

"He is kind, but let me warn you: He's a foxy old matchmaker, so watch your step."

Lily had a good laugh over this. In fact, she had a hard time catching her breath.

"Are you all right?"

"Yes, I'm just surprised. He doesn't strike me as the type."

"Well, he is. You can take my word for it."

"So why hasn't it worked with you? I want to be an aunt someday."

On the other end of the line Lily heard Jeff burst into uproarious laughter.

"Where did that come from?" he gasped out.

"I've told you that before."

"You have not."

"I'm sure I have."

He could hear a change in her voice, and it made him smile. He could tell she was relaxing and having fun. And when they finally rang off nearly an hour later, Jeff's heart was light with the knowledge that his sister was doing well.

～

It's getting easier, Lily told the Lord that night. *But the little speaking up I do and having all this eye contact is wearing me out.*

Lily wondered at that moment if any of the Kapaias had a clue. They were such a warm, accepting family, taking people at face value, that she wondered if they had an inkling of how hard it was to be Kashienese-raised and now living in the USA.

Do they know how often I hold my tongue? Should I be speaking up more? Should I share my opinion more and not go along with everything?

The moment these questions materialized, Lily realized she was getting better. She still wanted to please everyone, but she had been rather bold on the phone with her brother.

"Of course," she said to the ceiling, "it's easier when you can't see someone."

Thinking back on the conversation with her brother, Lily knew she would do as she said. If Jeff didn't come back within a week of the scheduled time, she would write her father that she was delaying her return. Tired as she was at the moment, her resolve was firm. She wouldn't be able to see her father, and at times that made him easier to disobey. And for more time with her brother, she would risk the confrontation.

～

Lily studied the lines that Gabe pointed out to her on the tennis court: the service line, singles and doubles sidelines, and baseline. He showed her how to hold the racket and explained the scoring, which she understood right away. But when he actually stood across the net and hit a ball in her direction, only fear of her father's wrath kept her from running.

Gabe saw the anxiety on her face and knew another tactic was needed.

"Why don't you start here, Lily?" he said, signaling her to his side and taking her to a solid wall at the rear of the courts; everything else was fenced. "You stand here and practice hitting the ball against the wall. When you're ready, you can hit one to me."

"Is this playing tennis?"

"It's learning how."

Lily looked at him from under her bamboo hat. "Jeff told me that you're very good."

Gabe smiled a little. "I've been playing a long time, which might make it hard to teach you."

"Because you do it automatically."

Not for the first time Gabe was struck by how swiftly she caught on.

Lily didn't wait for an answer but began to carefully position herself to hit the ball. She held the racket correctly, so Gabe stayed quiet and let her work. In just five minutes he saw that he had made the right choice. Lily's eyes and reflexes were fast, and she was swiftly getting the hang of it.

She and Gabe were back to the net a very short time when Ashton came looking for his brother.

"Gabe," he called as he came, "Mom and Carson are here."

"Thanks, Ash. I'll be right in. I'm sorry, Lily," he said to his student. "We'll have to postpone the rest of the lesson."

"That's fine," Lily replied, while internally working up her courage. "Gabe, may I ask you a question?"

"Sure."

"Would it be all right if I went for a run on the beach?"

Gabe looked surprised. "I had forgotten that Jeff told me how much you like to run. Have you gone at all while you've been here?"

"Not since Jeff left."

"Give me your racket and have at it."

"Well," Lily tried again but thought that perhaps she shouldn't keep him.

"What is it?"

"Would it be all right if I ran more than just today?"

"Lily," Gabe said, a smile on his face, "you may go for a run anytime you like."

Still she looked hesitant, her gaze down.

"What is it?" he tried again.

"If I go early when no one is up, I don't have a key to let myself back in."

"Don't lock the door when you leave, especially if you go out onto the beach. No one comes near the patio doors from the veranda."

Looking up, Lily smiled, her face instantly relaxed. She had been so tense, wanting to run but afraid to ask.

"When you're done," Gabe continued, putting frosting on the cake, "I'll introduce you to my mother and stepfather."

"All right. Thank you for the lesson, Gabe."

"You're welcome. We'll come back to it as soon as we can, but if you get a chance to come out and hit balls on your own, that's good practice as well."

"Okay."

Lily, who was slowly learning the lay of the land, went from the tennis courts to the beach. Gabe made his way inside, always glad for a chance to visit with Carson and his mother.

⁓

Liho Kapaia—Bailey, Gabe, and Ashton's father—had been dead for ten years. Liho had run the resort his father had left to him, with plans that his own children would one day take over. That he would die when they were all so young had not been his plan. But his wife, Gloria, knowing the wish of his heart, kept things going strong until his children were old enough to step in and take the job.

Gloria had never planned to be apart from the resort. She loved the business of hospitality, the nearness of the church family, and the life they had built. But five years after her husband's death, she had met Carson Hana. He lived on the big island of Hawaii. The two were still as smitten with each other as the day they married. They were semiretired and tried to come over to see Gloria's family every month or so.

And the visits always began the same way. Any and all family members who were available would gather in the living room for a time of catching up. The sharing of news was in full swing by the time Gabe arrived, but after hugs were exchanged he settled right in.

"How did Lily do with tennis?" Evan asked when there was a break.

"Very well. She's a fast learner, and I think it helped when I told her she could go out and work on her own."

"Is she homesick?" Gloria asked. "I keep thinking about her with Jeff's being gone."

"I think she must be at times." Bailey fielded that question. "But for the most part, she's very content."

"Grandma?" Peter slipped into the conversation suddenly, and his grandmother looked down to see that he could not get his piece of gum unwrapped. Grandma Gloria always brought gum.

"I'll help you, dear." She bent close to assist him and then noticed Celia. Her little jaw was already working away; she resembled a small cow.

"How did CeCe get hers off?" Gloria asked.

"I don't think she takes the paper off," Peter stated quite logically.

The family had a good laugh over this as Evan signaled his daughter over and asked to see the gum in her mouth. Sure enough, she had been chewing a wad of paper and gum.

"I'm impressed, Mom," Bailey gently teased when the laughter died down.

"With what?"

"I think Gabe has been inside for a full 15 minutes, and you haven't asked how his appointment went."

Gloria smiled. "I was getting to it."

"What did the doctor say, Gabriel?" This came from Carson.

"That everything looks good. He doesn't want to see me for a year."

Gloria and Carson exchanged a smiling look.

"Had you been worrying, Mom?" Gabe asked.

"No, but it's been on my mind for some reason, and I keep bringing it up to Carson."

"Do you want me to call you next time?" Gabe offered.

"It's all right, Gabe. If it's on my mind again, I can call you."

Mother and son exchanged a smile—a smile the family knew well.

Chapter Eleven

Lily came in by way of the kitchen. She had cooled down some on her way back up the beach, but thirst had now hit, and when Peter pushed open the door, he found her drinking a large glass of water.

"My grandma is here!" he told her excitedly.

"How fun for you," Lily said, coming to sit in a chair so their faces would be closer. She noticed he had some pink paper in his hand. "Did she bring you something?"

"Gum." He displayed it proudly as he told her. "Wanna piece?"

"Yes, please," Lily said fervently; she had been hoping to try some.

"You have to peel it back like this," Peter instructed as he gave her the piece and tried to help with the wrapper. It took a little doing, but Lily finally popped the cube of gum into her mouth.

"It's sweet!" she said in surprise, forgetting her manners and speaking with her mouth full.

"I can blow a bubble."

"Show me!" Lily commanded, coming to the edge of her seat to watch, her mouth moving to manage the wad.

Peter produced a small bubble that popped almost immediately, but Lily was still amazed. The little boy went into gales of laughter over the excitement in her face.

"Do it again! Teach me!"

129

This was the scene that Ashton and his mother came on a few minutes later. The bubble-blowing pair did not immediately see them.

"Can I try it, Peter?"

"You might have to wait."

"Okay."

"I mean, is your gum still sweet?"

Lily nodded yes.

"It doesn't work as well."

Having seen the confusion in her eyes, Ashton came forward and said, "It's the sugar." Gloria remained by the door. "Until the gum is more rubbery, it doesn't make for the best bubbles."

"I can feel the grains of sugar in the gum," Lily told him.

"Right. When those dissolve to where you don't notice them, that's the best time to blow bubbles."

Ashton smiled when Lily began to chew her gum in earnest, her brow knit with concentration. He knew his mother wanted to meet her, but he thought Lily might be very embarrassed if the introduction took place just now.

"Is it ready?" Peter asked Lily just as he spotted his grand-mother. "Come here, Grandma. Watch Lily."

Seeing they were not alone and with her gum-covered tongue just beginning to protrude from her mouth, Lily was embarrassed indeed. She tried to get the gum back out of sight, but it caught on her lip. Her right hand came up to snatch it from her mouth. She stood, feeling the wad stick in the palm of her hand.

And amazingly, Gloria and Ashton missed the whole thing.

"Lily, this is my mother, Gloria Hana. Mom, this is Lily Walsh."

"It's good to meet you, Lily," Gloria said warmly, her hand coming out to shake Lily's.

Lily's composure almost slipped, but she caught herself just in time. With a slight bow of her head she spoke, her voice at its most formal.

"Forgive me, Mrs. Hana. It's an honor to meet you, but my hands are not clean just now."

Gloria was surprised by this until she felt Peter pulling on the hem of her shorts.

"She's holding her gum, Grandma. She doesn't want to stick to you."

Lily smiled down at Peter, but her eyes held a hint of strain. Thinking nothing of it, Gloria laughed and filled in the breach.

"Shaking hands doesn't matter, Lily. I'm just so glad to meet you. Are you settling in well?"

"I am, thank you." Lily relaxed very little. "Your family is beyond kind."

Gloria smiled at her. "I rather like them. Will you come and meet my Carson?"

"It would be a second honor. Would you forgive me again if I take a moment to clean my hands?"

"Not at all. Come out when you're ready."

Ashton went with his mother to the door while Lily made a beeline for the sink.

"She was tense with you, Mom, but usually Lily is very—" Ashton began the moment the kitchen door shut behind them, but he stopped when his mother put a hand to his arm.

"Ash, do you think Gabe has noticed Lily?"

The youngest Kapaia stared at his mother.

"Well, has he?"

"Why would Gabe need to notice Lily?" Ashton asked, completely at sea.

"They would be perfect together," Gloria said so simply that she managed to astound her son. He barely managed to keep his voice low.

"I don't believe I've ever heard you talk like that, Mom! What's come over you?"

Gloria didn't answer. Instead, she had another question.

"Is she as relaxed with Gabe as she is with Peter?"

"Not quite as much, but almost."

"Good."

"Mom, what is this all about?"

"I don't know right now," she admitted, "but you know my feelings for Jeff, and this is Jeff's sister. And not just any sister, but a special one."

"How can you tell in so little time?"

Gloria smiled. "I just can."

"And Gabe fits in where?"

"He needs a special woman."

Ashton, who thought his brother more than capable of finding his own wife if he chose to, could only shake his head. He honestly had never heard his mother speak this way.

"Where's Lily?" Bailey called from all the way over by the sofa, where she sat with the other adults.

"In the kitchen."

"Is Pete with her?" Evan wished to know.

"Yes. I think they'll be along shortly."

Ashton had nothing to say. He was still trying to reckon with the idea of his mother as a matchmaker.

The gum wasn't coming off, and Lily was on the verge of panic. Peter had stayed to talk with her, but right now she needed quiet. She needed to think.

"Is it off?" he asked when Lily grew very still at the sink.

"No."

Peter looked up at her profile. She was staring out the window. "What are you looking at?"

Lily glanced down at him.

"Peter, do you know how I could get this gum off my hand?"

His little brow creased.

"Sometimes CeCe gets it in her hair and Mama uses ice."

You're so foolish, Lily. You're using hot water instead of cold.

"Do you want me to get ice?" Peter asked when Lily turned the water back on.

"Maybe one piece would be nice, Peter. I would appreciate that."

Peter was swift to aid her, and after a bit more work, this time with the ice, the gum was gone. The parts of her palm that weren't frozen felt raw where she had dug at the gum with her nails, but at least the sticky substance was off.

"Come and meet Grandpa Carson," Peter invited.

Lily smiled at him, thinking she had made a complete mess of things. Nevertheless, she didn't want Peter to feel any blame.

"It was nice of you to stay and help me, Peter. Thank you."

"Do you want another piece of gum?"

"Maybe another time, all right?"

Peter led the way through the kitchen, and only as they were about to join the others did Lily realize she was still in her exercise clothing and hadn't done a thing with herself since returning from her run. It was not the way she would have chosen to meet people, but hopefully Carson would be as gracious as his wife.

"Here they are," Evan said when they were spotted.

"Lilyee," Celia called as Peter took Lily's hand and brought her along.

Carson *was* as kind as his wife, and in no time at all, Lily was seated with the family and included in the conversation.

"May I ask you a question, Lily?" Carson asked, turning to her a short time later.

"Certainly," Lily answered, finding she had to force herself to have eye contact with this male stranger.

"How many languages do you speak?"

"Three."

"What are they?"

"Kashienese, Chinese, and English."

"What about Japanese?" Gabe asked. "I thought both you and Jeff spoke Japanese."

"Only enough to get by, so I don't claim it. Jeff has a Japanese neighbor, so he gets more practice than I do."

"So you speak Kashienese and Chinese as well as you do English?"

"Yes."

"Have you ever tried Hawaiian?"

"Only a little with Jeff. It does not come easily to me."

"Did the others?"

Lily nodded and explained, "But only because I grew up with all three."

"So your parents spoke all three to you?"

"No. At home they spoke only English, but in school it was only Kashienese, and then I had a Chinese teacher from the time I was very young."

"Have you ever considered getting a job as a translator?"

"I already have one," Lily said.

Everyone gawked at her a little at this point, so she explained.

"I translate the Bible into Kashienese for the church in the village."

"I didn't know that!" most of the family said, everyone speaking at once. Lily didn't know what to think of their reaction. She remained quiet until Celia tapped her leg.

"I have gum," the little person whispered.

"How fun," Lily whispered back. "Did Grandma give it to you?"

Celia nodded, her eyes large.

"You have gum?"

"Not right now. I'll have some later."

"See mine?"

Lily smiled when Celia opened her mouth.

"It's pink," Lily told her, leaning very close to continue whispering into her face. Everyone else was talking, so she felt free to have a private moment with the child.

"Pink?"

"Yes. Does it taste sweet?"

Lily bit her lip to hold laughter when Celia needed to think about this.

"Does it taste good?" Lily tried this time.

Celia nodded, eyes large, even as she realized that Lily's lap was open. She climbed into it without invitation and then looked up at her. Lily had been watching her adorable face the entire time.

"Are you going to learn to blow bubbles?" was Lily's next question, even as she thought about how swiftly she was sliding away from the rules she had always known. Never at home would she have carried on a conversation, albeit a quiet one, when someone else in the group was speaking, even though the words were not directed at her.

It troubled her no small amount, and whenever something did, her face took on a rather inscrutable look. Gabe and Bailey both caught it but knew that now was not the time to question her.

Gabe, for his part, was thinking about the time altogether. How long had Lily been with them? In their hearts she had always been there, but in reality, not long at all. This was a Friday, and Lily had moved in on a Sunday. Could it be coming up on only three weeks? They had been through so many things already that it seemed much longer. And how long did it seem for her? An eternity or a matter of days? Gabe had seen the way she had dropped her eyes when Carson turned to her and realized he had come to take for granted that she was growing comfortable with them and looking them in the eye—at least he hoped she was growing comfortable.

"I think swimming sounds fun," Gloria announced. "Is anyone up for it?"

Celia nearly choked on her gum in her excitement, and in the next few minutes a mad scramble ensued as Gloria and Celia rushed away to change and get towels. Peter was begging Evan to come, and the phone began to ring. With people going in all directions, Lily was left to think for a moment on what she wanted to do. Swimming sounded fun, but it was still hard to go out in the daytime wearing her swimsuit.

Suddenly someone sat down next her. Lily turned to see that it was Ashton, already in his baggy suit, towel in hand.

"Not going to swim?"

"I'm still deciding."

"What are the pros and cons?"

Lily smiled at his teasing tone.

"Being with the family is a pro, but I'm still getting used to wearing a swimsuit, so that would have to be a con."

"So what you're saying is that people in Kashien swim without swimsuits?"

The idea was so shocking to Lily that a small burst of laughter slipped out before she could cover her mouth.

Ashton, looking very innocent, shook his head in mock dismay. "I can see why you would have a problem with us."

"Oh, Ashton," Lily said, even as she turned red from laughing.

Smiling in delight at having caught her out, Ashton stood and made his way to the door. Lily found herself appreciating the fact that he hadn't pressed her for an answer. One by one the family all went out to the pool. When they had finally gone, she realized she was alone in the house for the first time in days.

Settling back, her head going against the soft cushions, Lily decided that at least for the moment she would stay right where she was.

～

"We got a letter from Deanne," Gloria told Ashton as they relaxed on chairs and loungers around the pool. "She said you had just been to see her folks."

"I went last week. We had a good time."

"How is Mic?" Carson asked, referring to Deanne's younger brother, a senior in high school. "Is he in football again?"

"Yes, he's almost as big as I am and starting on offense. I'll be headed to his game next week, so—"

Ashton kept talking, but Gabe found that his mind had wandered. The family's time off was going swiftly. They had planned to have several gatherings with the church family and had not gotten to one of them. It had come up at dinner the night before, but no plans were made.

"Are you going to sleep?" Evan asked from the seat next to his.

"No, but the time is going fast, and sometimes that makes me tired."

"Yeah. We always have so much we want to do, but it takes a good two weeks to get some energy back. This year it's taken longer."

"Yes, it has, and I haven't figured out why."

"It's bound to be several factors. It's never just one."

As though they thought of her at the same time, both men realized that Lily had not come out with them to swim.

"Bailey," her brother called to her, "did Lily say if she was coming out?"

"Not to me, she didn't."

"She was still deciding when I talked with her," Ashton threw in.

"I meant to ask her more about her translating," Carson said. "Do you know what books she's done?"

"We didn't know anything until she told you."

"Well, I hope she has time for two dozen more questions."

The conversation shifted at that point. People were getting drowsy at the same time the children were asking for lunch. Ashton hoisted himself out of the chair to do the honors. Bailey, who wanted only to sleep in the warm sun, thanked him with a wave.

～

"Mom," Ashton called to his mother later that day, catching her when she was alone, "do you plan to ask Gabe what you asked me?"

Gloria put a hand on his arm. "No, Ash, I don't. I'm even sorry I said something to you."

"But you still think it's true?"

Gloria thought for a moment.

"I guess I do, yes."

"So what will you do?"

"Only pray. I'll pray that Lily will notice Gabe if she's supposed to, and that Gabe will notice her. If this is not something the Lord wants, then no harm has been done. If they do get together, I can tell them someday that I prayed, and God wanted it more than I did."

Ashton smiled at his mother before bending to kiss her cheek. They joined the others without further words.

～

Carson and Gloria left on Saturday a few hours after lunch. It was hard to say goodbye, even though they knew that very soon they would all be together on the big island for Gloria's birthday. It had been a good visit. Everyone had enjoyed themselves and knew from past years that the days to Gloria's birthday would go fast.

After they were gone, nearly everyone in the family moved on to their own pursuits. Lily didn't know where the other brothers had gone, but Evan played with the children while Bailey did some laps in the pool. Lily decided to write to Ling-lei, her father, and brother. It took longer than she expected, and when she came downstairs, it was to find Bailey sleeping on one of the center-room sofas, an open storybook next to her. She was so soundly asleep that she wasn't even aware of the way a drowsy Celia was sliding out of her limp lap.

Deciding quickly what to do, Lily came forward.

At almost the same moment, Evan came from the kitchen, having just finished a quick run on the beach. He came to a halt when he saw Lily lifting a drooping Celia and then pressing a finger to her lips as Peter looked up at her. Evan approached as Lily, who hadn't seen him, took the children quietly out the patio doors and onto the veranda. Once by the sofa, Evan found his wife asleep. He followed the threesome outside.

"Hello." Lily greeted him from the rocker, a sleeping Celia in her lap.

"Hi, Lily. Do you want me to take her?"

"She's fine, thank you."

"Look at it, Papa." Peter had brought a seashell for his father to see. "It's perfect."

"Yes, it is. I think you might need to keep this one for your collection."

Peter went into gales of laughter.

"It is from my collection!"

Evan laughed too. "What is it doing out here?"

"I was showing it to Grandpa Carson."

"You rascal," Evan proclaimed before snatching him close and kissing his small neck until he squirmed. Evan let him escape after just a few seconds, and when the little boy moved away, Evan turned back to see Lily's eyes on him.

"May I ask you a question, Evan?"

"Certainly."

"It's none of my business."

"You can still ask."

Lily hesitated only a second.

"Does Bailey know she is expecting?"

Evan blinked in a way that Lily found comical, but she didn't laugh. Their friendship was so new, but Bailey worked hard, and Lily wanted her to know about her condition as soon as possible.

Evan, on his part, was desperately trying to catch up. He was on the verge of asking Lily whether Bailey had said something to her when he realized Lily's question made that impossible.

"Let me get this straight, Lily," Evan tried, his voice low. "You believe that Bailey is pregnant?"

"Yes."

"Why do you think this?"

"It's in her eyes."

Evan studied her, and Lily dropped her eyes before she remembered to look up. Evan took some more time to think about what she was saying. He wondered if he would ever run out of fascination for this guest. At last one question slowed down enough to be caught.

"Did you do this with the women at home?"

Lily nodded, her expression unreadable.

"And were you ever wrong?"

"Just once."

Evan's eyes shifted to the sea. It was a calm day, the waves hitting the shore in a gentle rhythm. It was the kind of day Bailey liked to stroll on the beach, but she was asleep.

Bailey never sleeps in the day! Evan's mind nearly shouted at him.

"Tell me something, Lily," he asked, a small note of urgency in his voice as he turned back to her, "would it be a great inconvenience if I ran a quick errand?"

"Not at all."

"Okay. If Bailey wakes up, just tell her I had to run to the drugstore."

Lily nodded.

"Can I come?" Peter asked, having heard from a distance.

"Yes, Peter, that's fine, and thank you, Lily."

The gentlemen were gone a moment later. Lily was more than happy to sit and rock Celia in her arms, but she did wonder what Evan was up to. Had she but known it, he had taken her seriously. He would make his trip to the drugstore, and then tonight, as soon as he and Bailey were alone, he would tell her what Lily had said.

Chapter Twelve

"She asked you what?" Bailey spoke to her husband in disbelief once they were behind closed doors that night.

"You heard me right. Is there any chance it's true?"

Bailey stared at him, thinking that she had been more tired lately.

"When is your period due?" Evan tried.

"It was due yesterday, but it's not unusual if I'm a few days late." Bailey sat on the edge of the bed, her eyes still on her husband. "Maybe we should get one of those test things like I did with CeCe."

"I already did."

"When did you do that?"

"When you were asleep this afternoon."

Bailey smiled at him. "That was very sweet of you."

"I'm a sweet guy," he teased her. "So do you think it's true?"

"I don't know. My breasts are a bit sore, but that could mean my period is coming."

"Lily did say she was wrong once."

Bailey looked amazed. "Tell me again what she said."

Evan filled her in as best as he could remember and ended with, "She says it's in your eyes."

All Bailey could do was shake her head and laugh a little. Evan left the chair he was sitting on, came forward, and gently pinned his wife to the bed. He didn't say anything until he had first taken a moment to look into his favorite pair of large, dark eyes.

"I hope it's true, Mrs. Markham."

"And if it's not?"

Evan's smile was mischievous. "We'll just have to keep trying."

∼

Lily could tell it was early without looking at the clock, but she was still wide awake hours before it was time to leave for church. Moving as quietly as she could manage, she rose and slipped into running shorts and a T-shirt. She saved her shoes and socks for the veranda, deciding to take Gabe's suggestion and head out toward the beach.

And all went fine, right up to the moment she sat down to put on her shoes. Thinking she was all alone, the door's opening nearly frightened her out of her wits.

"I'm sorry," Gabe spoke quietly after he had seen her start. "Are you all right?"

"Yes, I was just thinking I was on my own."

"Well, feel free to tell me if you would rather run alone."

"Actually," Lily began after seeing that he was in running garb as well, "I was going to say the same thing to you. I might slow you down."

"I doubt it. Do you like to stretch a little?"

"No, I just start slowly."

She was so like her brother at times that Gabe smiled before saying, "Well, let's get going."

They headed away from the veranda and started down the beach. Lily glanced at the empty cottages as they passed them, realizing that running with Gabe meant she could ask some questions.

"Is it noisier when you have guests, Gabe?"

"Somewhat. We rarely have the beach to ourselves when we have guests, but it doesn't bother anyone. It's just a way of life. A lot depends on how many children the guests have. They naturally tend to be more noticeable. If, however, we're booked with couples, we see only snatches of our guests."

Lily, who could easily see how romantic this place could be, found her mind distracted for a few minutes. Romance was not something she dreamed about all the time, but for a moment she let her mind go. She always thought she would marry, but being 24 years old with no prospects made her wonder a bit. Nevertheless, she wasn't giving up hope. She knew that God might have someone for her yet.

A glance to the side told her that Gabe's mind was on something too. Had she been running with Jeff, she would have told him that someday she might honeymoon right in one of these cottages, but it wasn't something she thought Gabe would wish to hear.

"Have you been back to see Wang lately?" Gabe asked.

"He was in the kitchen on Thursday, but I haven't been back to the restaurant. Is he doing well?"

"Yes. I saw him yesterday, and he asked about you."

"He's very kind."

"Yes, he is. Did he do any matchmaking the day you visited?"

Lily laughed. "No, but Jeff mentioned that to me. It's almost impossible to believe."

"Believe it," Gabe told her dryly. "It's done with great reserve and subtlety, but it's still done."

Lily shook her head and sped up a bit when Gabe increased the pace and changed their direction.

"Is that how Ashton got engaged? Does Wang take credit for that?"

"No, but he probably wishes he could. He put Evan and Bailey together."

"I didn't know that!"

"Ask them about it sometime. It's a fun story."

"How often does he work on you?" Lily teased him with the first thing that came to mind.

Gabe shook his head good-naturedly before saying, "A little more all the time. He left things alone when I was battling with cancer, but now he's back in full—" Gabe cut off when Lily came to a complete halt, her breathing coming hard as she stood and stared at him.

"Gabe," she whispered, her eyes telling him she was upset, "it's been so long since Jeff's written of that. I completely forgot. How are you doing?"

"I'm doing fine. I was just given a clean bill of health."

"Do I need to apologize for anything I've just said?"

"No!" Gabe stated emphatically, starting to run and catching Lily's arm long enough to get her restarted. "And if you start changing toward me, watching every word and checking for signs that I'm all right, I'll be forced to dump you in the ocean."

"I won't change," she said quietly. "I'm just disappointed in myself for not remembering."

"Don't worry about it."

"Do you hate to talk about it?"

"Not at all."

With that Lily fell silent, but Gabe was coming to know her quite well.

"All right, Lily, spit it out."

"Spit it out?"

"Yes. I know you have about ten thousand questions racing through your mind. Let's have them."

Lily laughed a little but still asked, "Was it awful for you?"

"At times, yes."

"What was the worst?"

"How sick I got from the treatments and being so tired all the time."

"Was there a particular verse that helped you?"

Without hesitation Gabe quoted, "I love the Lord, because He hears my voice and my supplications. Because He has inclined His ear to me, therefore I shall call upon Him as long as I live."

"The first two verses of Psalm 116," Lily said when he paused.

"That's right. The next two verses go on to talk about the cords of death and asking God to save us, but I just claimed verses one and two. I had no guarantees that God would heal me—it might not have been His will—but I wanted to call on Him for as long a time as I had, knowing He would listen."

"Thank you for telling me, Gabe."

"You're welcome."

Again silence fell between them. Gabe glanced at Lily's face, which gave nothing away this time, but he was coming to sense more than see when she had something on her mind.

"What? No more questions?"

Lily laughed but did feel free to ask one more.

"It was Hodgkin's lymphoma, right?"

"Yes."

"What do they do to give you a clean bill of health?"

"They take a blood test and an X-ray."

"Is it uncomfortable?"

"No, but because of my treatment, I'm allowed only two X-rays a year."

As she usually did, Lily caught on quickly and said, "So you don't want to break a limb."

"Exactly."

"Thank you for explaining it to me."

"You're welcome."

They arrived back at the house before Lily noticed where they were.

"How long have we been out?"

Gabe looked at his watch. "Almost an hour."

"It goes so much faster when you run with someone, doesn't it?"

"Yes, it does," Gabe said as he held the door for Lily to go inside.

All was still quiet, but Lily was hungry. She thanked Gabe for running with her and made her way to the kitchen. Gabe didn't follow. At least, not right away. Something had come to mind that surprised him. He turned back to the patio door, his eyes on the beach, but his mind was on something else altogether.

～

The test Bailey took the next morning was positive. Evan held his wife in his arms while she cried. The children were sure to be looking for them at any moment, but right now they needed this time alone.

"Are you all right?" Evan finally asked.

"I would be better if I wasn't so faithless."

"Why were you faithless?"

"I thought I was too busy and tired right now to conceive. I was sure it would never happen."

Evan smiled down at her.

"Why do we think that it's only our faith that makes things happen?"

"Arrogance."

"I think you're right." Evan gave her another hug and asked, "When shall we tell the kids?"

"Not until we're ready to have everyone know. I'm not sure CeCe can keep this under wraps."

"How about the guys and your folks?"

"Today if we get the chance. That way if I act weird, they'll understand."

"I'll call my dad tonight."

These small details out of the way, the two went back to morning preparations, but Bailey did everything on automatic. Her heart was pondering this small new person in their life and the day they would finally meet.

～

"Okay, the tune we're using this morning," Pastor Stringer said as the morning service began, "is 'Jesus the Very Thought of Thee.' You'll find the words on your worship sheets. Let's stand and sing."

The music piped up as Lily found the song, but she never got past the first few words of the second line. Her eyes looked in horror at the words on her paper, not needing an explanation to understand the pastor's intent.

> Jesus the very thought of Thee,
> Bores me, I must confess;
> Putting You first in all my life
> Int'rests me even less.
>
> I'll give you time on Sunday morn—
> Then I will sing and praise;
> But after that, my time's my own—
> Mondays through Saturdays.
>
> Demand no more of me, O Lord—
> There is so much to do;
> I have a life, I can't afford
> To waste it all on You.

"It's not exactly what you thought it would be, is it?" Pastor Stringer asked softly when the music died down and his congregation stood soberly before him. "But it's often the way we think. In no way do I wish to mock the original song, but I know for my own life that sometimes I need these wake-up calls. Please be seated." Pastor Stringer gave everyone a moment to settle.

"We're going to keep talking about God's expectations for us this morning," he went on, and Lily opened her Bible to the passage where he directed. She had only a vague sense of his preaching in this book before and, with that sense, Lily felt disgusted with herself. *What have you been doing each time you've sat in this church, Lily Cathleen?* That this was only her second time to attend a Sunday morning service did not immediately come to mind. She was determined to be hard on herself, and that was the end of it!

She remembered in time to be hard on herself later and not to miss a word of the sermon again.

～

Sunday dinner was a feast. Lily bit into the ham, which tasted of pineapple, and let her eyes slide closed. For a moment she didn't even want to chew.

"Lilyee's praying!" Celia announced in a voice that would not have helped her had it been true.

Lily's eyes came open as she stopped herself from laughing. Seeing the merriment in her eyes, the other occupants of the table joined her.

"I take it you think the ham is good?" Ashton questioned.

"It's delicious," Lily answered once her mouth was empty.

"Thank you," Bailey said with a smile. "It's my mother's recipe."

"Speaking of our mother," Gabe put in, his own plate giving evidence of how much he liked the meal, "did anyone mention to you, Lily, that we'll be going to visit Mom and Carson in ten days?"

"No, they didn't. Is there something I can do while you're away, or do you just want me to keep things going as usual?"

"You're going with us" at least three people said at the same time.

Lily's eyes got a bit round over this announcement, but no one bothered to elaborate. Evan wanted to talk about the sermon, and the table talk was soon off on that.

When everyone had commented, Evan added, "I especially liked what Pastor did with that song."

"That was an eye-opener, all right."

"He has perspicacity," Lily said quietly, thinking how much she had enjoyed the service too. She kept eating after this, so it didn't come to her attention that everyone at the table was staring at Gabe, and that Gabe was staring at her.

Since some time in high school, Gabe had loved to use that word. And for years, whenever any of his siblings or Evan teased him about getting married, he would say that he would marry the first woman he found who knew what "perspicacity" meant.

"What was the word?" Peter asked, causing everyone to feel rescued.

Lily assumed she was to answer.

"'Perspicacity' means acute mental vision or keen discernment. And what that means, Peter, is that Pastor Stringer is able to see things very clearly. He's able to explain things he has in his mind very well. If he has a thought, he's able to tell someone about it in a way that he will understand. Did that make sense?"

Peter nodded.

Lily then noticed that everyone was looking at her.

"I'm sorry," she said right away, her eyes dropping. "I should have let someone else answer that."

Everyone at the table denied it, but because this event had been somewhat unsettling to all of them, they changed the topic. They ate together for another ten minutes while the children shared what they had learned in Sunday school, and then Evan rose and moved Peter and Celia to the kitchen for their dessert. This rarely happened, so Gabe and Ashton were watchful. Lily felt a little tense but couldn't have explained why.

"We have news," Evan said when he came back, not wasting any time. "Bailey's expecting."

"That's great," Gabe said, immediately pushing away from the table and going to give his sister a warm hug. Ashton was next, his smile huge as he hugged his sister and then Evan.

"Congratulations," Lily said to both of them, but other than that, she remained quiet. She had been sorry she had spoken up on the matter the night before when Evan and Bailey turned in early. Lily didn't know them well enough to broach such a private subject, and she had been bothered by it ever since.

"Have you called Mom?" Ashton asked.

"I was going to, but I think it will be more fun to wrap a baby bonnet for her birthday."

The men loved this idea, and before it was over, the suggestions grew outrageous.

"How about a bassinet? Do you think she would catch on then?"

"I know," Ashton put in, "let's have a diaper service pull up while we're there. She won't be able to miss that."

The children heard the laughter and came to the door, albeit quietly, since they had been told to stay put, but their father motioned them out. That the subject had to be changed immediately did not occur to Evan right away, but thankfully the children were too young to notice how many shared glances were exchanged as the cleanup crew went to work on the dishes.

Lily was having a great time but still wished she had kept her mouth shut. For the rest of the day she prayed for a time when she might ask Bailey to forgive her.

～

On Monday morning Lily sat at the bottom of the front steps and forced her feet into the in-line skates that Evan and Peter had handed her. She already had a helmet on, along with elbow and knee protection. Peter had tried to give her his wrist protectors, but they were too small.

"Okay, Lily." Evan skated over from where he'd been circling the driveway to see how things were going. "How do they feel?"

"All right, I think."

Had Lily waited until she stood up, she would not have answered so agreeably. They hurt! And they didn't hurt just her feet, but the back of her legs as well. She was distracted for a moment when Peter skated up to her with ease, but just watching him told her she was never going to master this. It was on the tip of her tongue to ask if Jefferson had wanted her to learn this, but she realized just in time how rude that would sound.

"This is what I want you to do," Evan instructed. "Hold onto the porch railing and just move along the pavement, real easy-like. Can you do that?"

Lori Wick ~ 151

"I think so," she said on a gasp she wasn't able to control. Her feet felt encased in rocks.

"It hurts a little at first," Evan encouraged, "but you'll get the hang of it in no time."

"Hi, Lilyee," Celia called from the porch.

"Hi, Celia," Lily managed but didn't dare look up at her. She was certain if she took her eyes from her feet, she would go sprawling onto the pavement.

"You're doing good, Lily." Peter came up to skate next to her. He smiled up into her face, but Lily wasn't willing to shift her eyes for him, either.

"How's it coming?" Evan skated up after a few more turns around the drive.

"Okay," Lily said, knowing she was lying through her teeth.

"Does it hurt too much?" Evan asked.

Lily didn't answer. She was trying not to fall, but mostly she didn't want to lie anymore. That she could tell Evan how this felt did not occur to her. They were taking time to help her, and she wasn't going to repay them with complaining.

Not sure if he should tell her to quit or give her time, Evan looked up to see Gabe headed their way, some papers in his hand.

"I'm going to put these on your desk, Evan," Gabe began. "I just came across them on my desk. I thought I had already given them to you."

"What are they?"

"Those contracts from Mains."

Evan nodded. "They knew they wouldn't hear from me before the first of the year anyway, so it's not a problem."

"How's the skating going?"

Evan smiled. "I would say she's pretty miserable."

Gabe laughed a little as both men watched Lily trying to make her way along the porch.

"Are you going to let her off the hook?"

Evan suddenly looked at his brother-in-law and asked quietly, "Why don't you go see how she's doing?"

Gabe's eyes came to his. "And what would be your point in my doing that?"

"I don't know. She's always been the most comfortable with you and Bailey. And I guess I find it hard to believe that you're not just a little interested."

"I've only known her for three weeks."

"You *met* her three weeks ago; you've *known* her for years. But all that aside, I'm not suggesting you propose. Just get closer."

While the men discussed this, Lily finally made it to the end of the porch. All she could think about were her feet. Peter was trying to talk with her, so Lily forced herself to listen.

"When you get really good, Lily, we can go all the way out to the road and back."

Lily wanted to groan at the very thought but did her best to smile at Peter. She turned around slowly, wondering how long she could do this.

"How is it going?" Gabe asked.

He had come up without Lily noticing. When she turned around, it was to find him directly in front of her.

For just a moment Lily's eyes pleaded with his. She then glanced in Peter's direction before saying, "I'm not sure I'll ever be as good as Peter."

"Whose skates are those, Pete?"

"Mama's."

"Do they fit you, Lily?"

Lily looked him in the eye and shook her head over her own stupidity. Her voice held wonder when she admitted, "I thought it was my not being used to them. They are too small."

Gabe smiled. "And you're in agony."

Lily dropped her eyes.

"Can you look at me?"

Lily did, her face now composed and still.

"Was there some reason you felt you couldn't tell Evan and Pete?"

"Do you not find me ungrateful when I complain, Gabe?"

"When have you complained?"

"How's it going?" Evan approached.

"The skates are too small," Gabe informed him.

"Oh, mercy! I'm sorry, Lily." Evan was genuinely contrite. "Let's get those off."

"I'm sorry it didn't work out, Evan," Lily said as she and Peter worked the buckles. "I appreciate your trying to show me."

"It doesn't matter, Lily. You're still working on your tennis, and I think Gabe is going to teach you to golf this week."

That Gabe had no idea this was the plan was communicated with eyes that told his brother-in-law that he knew what he was up to. Since Lily was bent over busily removing the skates, Gabe even had time to roll his eyes at Evan's mischievous grin.

By the time Lily and Peter looked back up, all vestiges of teasing and motives were gone from the men's faces. Lily thanked Evan and Peter again and headed back to the house. Peter ran to put the skates on the porch for Lily, and for a moment the men were alone again—something that was fine with Gabe. Clearly the scene yesterday at the dining room table had put thoughts into everyone's mind. Well, it had put thoughts into his mind too. But before he let them run too far, he had a few questions he wanted answered.

Chapter Thirteen

Her feet still throbbing from the pressure, Lily went indoors and found Bailey alone at the computer.

"How did it go?" she called, turning to face the younger woman.

"Not too well. My feet are longer than yours, and the skates didn't fit."

"Oh, well," Bailey said with a smile. "At least you tried."

"That's true."

This said, Lily set her shoes on one of the bottom steps and then turned back to Bailey, her heart praying about what she needed to say.

"Are you terribly busy right now, Bailey?"

"No. I'm only working on my grocery list, and I've almost got it done."

Lily looked very serious to Bailey, so she grabbed another chair and set it close to hers.

"Here. Sit down, Lily."

"Thank you," Lily said as she came forward, her face and voice subdued. She was ashamed to have eye contact with Bailey over what she had done but forced herself to do the right thing. After a moment she began.

"I feel I must ask your forgiveness, Bailey. I did something very improper. I spoke with your husband and told him I thought you were expecting. On further review, I feel that was very rude and presumptuous of me, and I'm very sorry.

"And on top of that," Lily finished, "you didn't even need me. You already knew."

"We didn't know," Bailey shocked her by saying, placing a soft hand on Lily's hand. "Evan bought one of those home pregnancy tests when I was asleep on the sofa. We did it this morning, and it was positive."

Lily's mouth made one of her silent "ohs" as she stared at her hostess.

"We have you to thank, Lily, or we might not have known so soon. Now I can be careful of what medicines I take and also have plenty of time to schedule my first checkup with the doctor."

"So you don't feel I need to apologize to Evan?"

"Not at all. We've been planning to thank you but wanted to do it privately. We just haven't found the right moment."

"I'm so relieved, Bailey. It's bothered me more than I can say. You're quite certain?"

"Very certain."

Lily smiled. Bailey was so easy to like and be around. Lily hated the thought that anything would ever come between them.

"Do you know what I just realized?" Bailey asked, her brow furrowed.

"No, what?"

"That we've never given you any time to use the computer. Did Jeff show you his?"

"No, there wasn't time," Lily said, eyes already on the screen.

"Well, come in close. I'll show you how I do my menu for the month and the shopping list, and then you can play around some."

Lily looked as if she had been handed a sack of gold. The phone rang, the family came and went, but Lily saw and heard little of it. She was finding out firsthand that computers were amazing.

～

"Tell me something, Evan," Gabe asked when both Peter and Celia were busy on the porch and out of hearing range. "What happens if you all start pushing me toward Lily and she wants nothing to do with me?"

"That's not going to happen."

Gabe gawked at the other man.

"Have you become prescient on us, Evan?"

"No, but I can already see that Lily cares for all of us. If you were to show her any special attention, her heart would melt."

"How can you be so sure?"

"First of all, Gabe, I hope you know that I don't want this if you don't."

"I understand that."

"Okay, just as long as you do."

Gabe's nod encouraged Evan, and he continued. "Even amid thoughts of this new baby, it's been pretty hard to forget what happened at the table yesterday. Lily has been so easy and unde-manding to have around, and then suddenly she wasn't. Suddenly she was wife material for you, and I personally want that very much."

"But she hasn't done any changing," Gabe reminded him qui-etly, his heart clearly in turmoil.

"True, but nothing is the same for me. Now that I've had my eyes opened, I can see how well she suits you. She's godly, sweet, and intelligent, and if anyone can handle all you've gone through, it's Lily Walsh."

Gabe was suddenly swept back to the way he felt after his run with Lily the morning before. When she had left him alone in the living room, he had realized what a good time he had been having and how much he wanted to hear her laugh again.

But what had Evan just said?

"What did you mean just now when you said Lily would melt if I showed her some attention?"

"I can't say that to too many people, Gabe, but I know you're not going to take advantage of Lily's vulnerability in this matter. If I had to describe her, I would say that she's very intelligent and analytical, but I doubt if she's ever had someone hold her hand or send her flowers. Just having watched the gentle way she handles the kids makes me think there's a sweet and romantic heart inside her, but she may not even know it's there."

"And do you think it's fair of me to do anything that might unlock that, Evan?"

"Who better than the man she's going to marry?"

Gabe had all he could do not to throw his hands in the air. Instead, he said, "You've lost your mind; I hope you know that, Evan Markham."

But Evan wasn't convinced. "Do yourself a favor, Gabe. Give Jeff a call. Tell him your feelings have changed and ask him what he thinks. You know he'll tell you the truth."

"Papa," Celia called. She had been calling to him for a few minutes, but he had ignored her.

"Coming," Evan called to his daughter as he clapped Gabe on the shoulder and went on his way.

The younger man stayed where he was, left with more to think about than he had bargained for.

It was luau night at the cove. The children had been talking about it all day, and because Lily had never been to a luau or visited the cove, she was excited too. Guests started arriving at 4:00, and by 4:30 everyone was headed toward a secluded rocky area of beach, each person laden with items for the ensuing feast.

To Lily's surprise, Ashton was already there, tending the pig that was roasting on a spit. She had seen the barbecue pit and picnic area that was closer to the cottages, but this area, she learned, was private, reserved for the family and friends. And the meal was delicious. Lily didn't think she would ever get used to tasting new dishes that she thought could melt in her mouth.

After blankets were spread out, Lily sat with Pastor Harris Stringer, his wife, Barb, and their youngest son, along with

Ashton and the McFarland family, a couple fairly new to the church who had a six-month-old baby.

"Let's have a sharing time," Ashton suggested when most folks were almost finished eating. "And then maybe we can sing a little."

"What'll we share?" Mrs. Stringer asked.

"I think it would be fun to hear how the different couples in the group met and fell in love."

Gabe, who had been working on the last of his fruit salad, looked up at his brother. Nearly everyone was teasing Ashton about having romance on the brain because he was missing Deanne, but he only smiled. Gabe, on the other hand, was not saying a thing. His eyes were trained on his brother, who eventually looked in his direction, his expression too innocent to be real.

From there Gabe looked to Evan. He too looked much too nonchalant, and Gabe knew he had been had. It looked to him as though these two were going to give Wang Ho a run for his money.

"Harris," Evan spoke up in an effort to dodge Gabe's perceptive eyes, "why don't you start?"

"All right. Well, as most of you know, I'm originally from Texas."

Everyone smiled over this since the man still had a slight twang to his voice.

"I did my seminary training down there. That's where Barb and I met. Barb's father was one of my instructors, and I needed his help on a special project he had given me in my senior year. I went to his home, and who should answer the door but this lovely young woman."

"Barb," some in the group guessed.

Harris and Barb Stringer exchanged smiles.

"As a matter of fact," the pastor went on, "it was Barb's sister, Linda. Not until I had walked into the living room and saw a woman who was even prettier than the first did I meet Barb. To put it mildly, I was distracted. I heard almost nothing my instructor said, and when I look back on it now, I know for a fact that he had me figured out."

Everyone was smiling in delight as Harris told his story, Lily included. Gabe was trying to listen, but his eyes kept straying to Lily's face, which was wreathed in soft smiles.

Selfish as it is, Lord, I don't want to suddenly find myself in love alone, Gabe's heart prayed. *I don't know what to do with these feelings I'm starting to have, and I'm filled with so many fears. What if I get close to Lily, but her feelings for me never get strong? Or I get close and she falls for me, but I realize she's not the one? I can't stand the thought of her being hurt.*

"After I made a fool of myself for almost an hour," Harris continued, and Gabe made himself listen, "Barb's father took pity on me and asked her to drive me back to my dorm. I asked if she was free to attend a lecture with me the next week, and she said yes. I can't tell you who spoke or what was said at the meeting, but Barb and I were engaged to be married by the time I graduated."

Everyone clapped in delight as the Stringers leaned close for a moment and kissed. Ashton then called on his brother-in-law.

"I think everyone knows our story," Evan protested.

"Lily doesn't," Gabe put in, working to look as innocent as his family. His and Evan's eyes met for a moment, and the older man had to fight laughter as he began.

"Well, okay," Evan said, even as his eyes swung to his mate. "Be sure and fill in the parts I miss."

"All right."

"I was finishing up college when I decided to get a weekend job in case nothing panned out right after I graduated. Since we lived out in this area and I had heard there was an opening, I applied at the Little Bay. The manager was out, so Wang interviewed me, and to my surprise he never once asked me if I had any expertise in restaurant work. He barely glanced at my application, and we spent the whole time talking about my schooling, where I had grown up, what church I went to, and what my life's goals were.

"Wang was charming, and because he ended up giving me the job, I thought little of it for a long time. Later I realized I had been interviewed for a much different job."

Everyone laughed as Bailey threw a paper cup at her spouse. Not deterred, Evan only caught it and kept on.

"I remember Wang kept asking me if I was a person who would stick with something. I told him I thought I was, but he kept questioning me in different ways. Well, anyway, it wasn't a month after I began that I discovered what he meant. Each weekend this beautiful girl came to help in the kitchen, and every single guy in the restaurant fell apart. We forgot orders, dropped things, and in general, made fools of ourselves. We all knew she lived at the resort, but she was so shy and quiet that we couldn't get ten words out of her—not even her last name."

Evan turned to smile at Bailey, who was shaking her head at him.

"I think maybe I should have told this story," Bailey started. "I don't remember it quite that way."

"Like I was saying," Evan jumped back in, much to everyone's amusement, "this beautiful girl kept coming in. Prior to that I had never known the meaning of the word 'perseverance.' I did everything in my power to get her to talk to me, but nothing worked. Then Wang, foxy old matchmaker that he is, deliberately put us together to clean out the big cooler. I was supposed to be waiting tables—they were even shorthanded—but I was in the cooler with the girl of my dreams for two hours." Evan gave a dramatic sigh that had everyone laughing again. "Somewhere along the line I finally got permission to see her outside of work."

Evan looked at his wife again.

"I didn't find out until much later that she liked me all along."

This story was also greeted by cheers and clapping before the McFarlands were asked to share. Ashton ended the topic with his story about Deanne, and by then everyone realized that a sing-along was not going to work. Darkness was falling, and they still had the fire going, but the children were beginning to droop. As a group they returned to the house, remains of the meal in hand. Spirits were still high for the adults, but sleepy little ones could not be ignored. The family saw everyone to the door, and when they got back inside, Lily had already started on the dishes. Since Evan and Bailey needed to put the kids to bed, the boys helped Lily in the kitchen.

"That was fun," she said, a smile on her face, her arms elbow-deep in suds.

Ashton was on the verge of telling her she might have her own story one day, but something stopped him. In that instant he realized he didn't know Lily all that well. His heart had been saddened over the way she had been so painfully uncomfortable around them when she first arrived, and at the beginning he had done everything in his power not to make it worse for her. Lately he teased her and she always laughed, but this was different. This was a matter of the heart.

"How did your parents meet, Lily?" Ashton, having a brainstorm, asked as he turned to watch her face.

Lily smiled. "In an airplane. My father was already living in Kashien, and on one of his trips back to the States, he and my mother sat next to each other on a flight from California. He had never planned to marry, but by the time they landed, he couldn't stop thinking about her."

"How long before they were married?"

"Only three months."

"And where were your parents originally from?"

"My father was born in Chicago, but he was placed in an orphanage before he was a week old. My mother's family was from the South, New Orleans, but when she came to Christ, her family wanted nothing to do with her. She tried writing and being in touch with them her entire life, but they never responded. They didn't reply even when my father wrote to tell them she had died."

"How did she die?" Ashton wished to know; Gabe could have told him but stayed quiet.

"Breast cancer. My father was ready for us to return to the States, even though we wouldn't have had a home. But by the time they discovered the cancer, it had started to spread all through her. We went back to the village and lived as normally as possible until she could no longer function. Then we made her as comfortable as we could until she died."

"How old were you?"

"I was 12 and Jeff was 16."

The men were silent after this, and Lily glanced at them, wondering if maybe she had said too much.

"And you said they were both believers when they met?" This also came from Ashton.

"Yes. My father had already put together a small church, and the village was coming to respect him. When he told my mother about the work he was doing, she got very excited. That was another reason he was so drawn to her."

The threesome fell quiet then, each with his or her own thoughts. Lily's mind was transported back to a time when she lay in her mother's bed and heard about life before she was born. Ashton's mind was on Gabe, and Gabe was thinking of Lily.

"So tell me," Gabe began, "why didn't you feel you could tell Evan and Peter that the skating wasn't going well?"

Lily looked up to find they were alone. She didn't know when Ashton had exited the room, but Gabe was watching her, one hip leaned against the counter as though he had all the time in the world.

For a few minutes, Lily's eyes went back to the sink. The dishes were all washed, but she took her time washing the suds down the drain.

"I think there were a few reasons," she began, eyes still on her work. "I wanted to try my hardest, and I didn't want to disappoint Peter."

"Anything else?"

"Yes, but I'm not sure how to put it."

"Please try."

Lily glanced at him and then away.

"You've all taken your time and energy to help me. I'm not going to be foolish and tell myself that I owe you for the rest of my life or anything like that, but the least I can do is be appreciative of your efforts."

"Even when you don't like something or you're being hurt?"

Her voice matter-of-fact, Lily said, "Yes, even then."

"If you can, I want you to do something for me tomorrow, Lily."

"All right."

"I want you to come to me and complain."

"Complain?"

"Yes."

"About what?"

"About something you don't like."

She frowned in confusion but still asked, "What if there isn't anything?"

Gabe thought about this before saying, "Will you please try this instead: Complain about something from today."

Lily stared at him. Was he serious? She looked for some sign of teasing and saw none. Her mind cast about for something to say, but she was too surprised.

"Was there any sand on your plate or in your food at dinner tonight?" Gabe prompted. "Did you get tired of sitting with your legs to one side for so long? Did you like the juice Bailey served at breakfast this morning, or did you just make yourself drink it? Did the in-line skates kill your feet because they were too small?"

This all asked, Gabe kept watching her. He wasn't sure he was going about this the right way, but he knew they had to start somewhere.

"May I ask you something?" Lily sounded breathless and confused, but Gabe tried to ignore it.

"Yes."

"Why would you want me to be unthankful and complain about such small matters?"

"Because you need someone you can talk to. You need someone you can be completely truthful with, instead of always being forced to hide your opinion for fear of bothering or hurting someone else."

Lily looked completely shaken. How he had known that no complaining or grumbling whatsoever was allowed in her father's home she did not know, but this was so unsettling that she could barely think. In fact, it was so much so that she almost turned from Gabe and walked across the room.

"Go ahead," Gabe instructed gently. "You can walk away from me if you like."

Lily had all she could do to keep her mouth closed.

"But that would be rude."

"Not to me. If you're upset and need to move around, that's perfectly fine. Or if you want to tell me that you don't wish to discuss this right now, I'll drop it on the spot and ask you about it later."

The tone of his voice, the look in his eyes—had anyone ever shown her such compassion? Lily actually felt as if she could cry. She didn't. Instead she turned back to the sink, her eyes on nothing.

"Is this a bad time?" Bailey suddenly said from the door.

"Actually, it is, Bailey. Thank you," Gabe said as she gave a little wave and slipped out the door. He turned back to see that Lily was staring at him in horror.

"What if she needed something?" Lily asked, thinking this man had lost his mind. "This is her kitchen."

"You're important too."

At first Lily didn't comprehend his words. She heard them, but they were said so plainly and simply that Lily didn't at first catch on. When she did understand his meaning, she couldn't take her eyes from the man across from her.

At last she admitted, "I don't have a single argument in my head."

Gabe's gaze grew very tender.

"But you can argue with me, Lily. I want you to know that."

Lily looked at a complete loss and needed to blink away the moisture that threatened to fill her eyes. She took a moment to compose herself and found that she had a question after all.

"What if Bailey's need had been an emergency?"

"Then she wouldn't have even asked about intruding. She would have come in and stated her need."

This was clear to Lily now, but a moment ago she had still been in the dark.

"Are you going for a run in the morning?" Gabe asked.

"If I wake early, yes."

"When do you not wake early?" Gabe teased a little.

Lily smiled. "Now that you mention it, I can't remember the last time."

"Maybe I'll be up and go with you."

"Okay."

"And then we have a golf lesson."

"Oh, that's right," Lily managed to say, keeping all disappointment out of her eyes.

Gabe thought he might have seen something, but believing Lily had had enough for one evening, he said nothing more.

They parted company just moments later. Lily walked to her room, thinking about Gabe's request that she complain. She knew that was not what he had literally meant. He wanted her to be herself, stating her preferences, and saying what was on her mind.

I can't do that, Gabe, Lily's heart said once she was behind her own closed door. *You want me to be who I am, and I think this is it. I can't tell you what I feel deep inside. It's just not allowed. I can't even tell you that as much as I want to learn to golf, Bailey was going to take me to the grocery store tomorrow, and I've never been to one.*

Chapter Fourteen

Gabe could not sleep. He felt that he had handled things all wrong with Lily. He wanted her to be wide open with him, but in a way he still had control over her. And did she actually understand what he had meant? Did she realize that he wasn't looking for a complaining shrew but a person who could speak her mind? He knew that she would never turn into a harridan, but the thought of never being able to share what you had on your heart was very painful to him.

Even David cried out to God from the depths of his heart, Gabe reasoned. Often in the Psalms David began by asking God if He had forgotten him, or why He had even let him be born. But David always ended his prayer with praise for his Creator and recognition of God's mighty power and love.

Gabe had learned to speak all the thoughts of his heart to the Lord when he was too sick to speak or utter a sound. Maybe Lily was able to be that open with the Lord too. But as soon as Gabe had been better, he had also been surrounded by family and friends who were willing to listen. At this moment, Gabe was asking himself whether Lily was able to talk even to Jeff or her father.

Thoughts of Jeff took Gabe's mind in another direction. Evan had told him to call Jeff, but he didn't know if he could do that. The thought of verbalizing to Jeff his changing feelings toward Lily—even on the phone—was a little too hard to imagine.

Nevertheless…

Gabe got up quietly and left his room. He padded his way through the dark and quiet house until he was at his sister's desk. He knew where she kept her writing supplies. It would have been easier to type it on his computer, but he didn't want to go over to the office at this hour.

The letter began *Dear Jeff,* and continued,

> *I would like you to call me when you get this, but not until you feel the time is right. I wanted to call you, but as close as we are, I feel awkward on this one. The truth is, my feelings toward Lily are changing. Because of our close relationship, I have cared for her as your sister for many years—as I do your father—but not until I had a chance to be a part of Lily's world did I realize how special she is.*
>
> *But here are my numerous dilemmas. First of all, you. How do you feel about what I've just admitted? Second, your father. What would he have to say if he knew? After that it gets worse. What if I find myself in love alone? And now the worst yet. What if I get close to Lily and she falls for me, but I find she's not the one? The thought of hurting her is more than I can bear. Maybe that feeling alone should tell me she's the one, but as you can see, I am a mess!*
>
> *When the time is right, Jeff, please call. If Lily is standing at my elbow, clearly we won't be able to talk of this, but I need to know your heart, and as best you can figure, your father's heart.*
>
> *I just realized that all of this leaves Lily out of the mix. Well, if she learns of my feelings and doesn't share them, at least she'll be back in Kashien and I won't have to face her every day. If I am the only one harmed, I'll deal with it. As you know, I'm not a stranger to pain, but Lily must not be hurt—not by me or the disapproval of her family.*
>
> *Again, I await your call, Jeff. I don't need to say it, but I will anyway: We're brothers of the heart, and we must never let anything change that.*
>
> > *Love,*
> > *Gabe*

By the time Gabe got back into bed, it was quite late and he was finally tired. He opted not to set his alarm—something he would be forced to do all too soon. As late as the hour was, he knew he would never be out of bed to run with Lily.

But maybe that's for the best, he told the Lord, turning on his side to get comfortable. *Maybe she needs her space after the way I handled things in the kitchen tonight.*

～

Lily was up early, but there was no sign of Gabe. She didn't wait for him but made her way to the beach and began a slow run. The morning was beautiful, and in no time at all Scripture passages about God's goodness and His creation were coming to her mind.

Right now Lily was translating the book of Genesis into Kashienese. Because of that, she had more than half the book memorized, so it was at times like this that she liked to start with the first verse and go down through the order of creation, thinking about when everything would have been new: the gathering of the waters, the dry land and mountains appearing, the sea and air teaming with life.

But that wasn't Your greatest accomplishment, was it, Lord? Lily prayed, thinking that the intricacies of the human body were beyond compare.

Lily took some time to thank God for her strong limbs and stamina. She picked up the pace, loving the feeling of heat emanating from her body and the way her heart beat faster. She pushed herself some ways down the beach but then realized she hadn't been this far before. Slowing her pace so she could take in the morning, Lily jogged along easily, her mind going to Proverbs 8, where God's Word stated that wisdom was even older than creation. It was one of Lily's favorite chapters from Proverbs because from the twelfth verse on, it was as though Wisdom herself was speaking. Right then verses 22 and 23 came to Lily's mind.

"The Lord possessed me at the beginning of His way, before His works of old. From everlasting I was established, from the beginning, from the earliest times of the earth."

I need that wisdom, Lord, Lily's heart went on. *There's so much I don't know, so much is still new. I want to be able to tell my father that I worked hard, but the time is drawing to a close, and I still want time to relax with Jeff and not have to be so studious. But that doesn't change the fact that it's all so new and different.*

Lily was barely aware of coming to a stop, but she was no longer running. Her eyes were on the waves that lapped onto the shore. For a time she watched the rhythm and order of the water, and when she prayed this time, she whispered in the wind.

"You're so huge and brilliant. You can make perfect waves come onto the shore. My heart can only imagine what treasures of creation lie within the waters themselves. I wasn't praying to You earlier; I was fretting. Help me, Father. Help me to be strong and do what I'm told to do. And whatever each day presents, help me to be thankful and work my hardest."

It felt good to start running again. It helped clear Lily's mind and show her that she didn't have to be in control. She had a God who could handle it all.

～

It was a small thing, really, but Lily's heart was telling her differently. Her thoughts from the beach that morning were far from her as she sat in Gabe's car. He was driving them to the golf course. He even had two sets of clubs in the back.

Lily wanted to learn to golf—she truly did. Jeff knew how to play and would be proud of her, but doing this today meant forfeiting something else.

"Oh, there goes Bailey," Gabe said conversationally. Unbeknownst to Lily, the other vehicle had been close behind them all along. Not able to hide her interest, Lily's head turned so fast that she nearly hurt herself, but Bailey passed with only a honk and sped on her way. Lily had at least hoped for a glimpse of something more. It had cost Lily much to tell the other woman that she couldn't go with her, but she had done it. Her heart aching over what she must be missing, she suddenly realized all was not lost.

"Gabe, may I ask you a question?"

"Certainly."

"How often does Bailey go to the grocery store?"

"Like she is today, to the big market, only once a month."

"So she'll buy a lot all at one time?"

"Correct."

"And the store will have enough?"

"Yes," Gabe answered slowly, even as bells began to go off in his mind.

"Is it a large store then?" Lily asked next.

Gabe assured her that it was, even as he took a side street just a quarter mile up the road, one that would swing them back the way they had come without being too obvious.

"And will the children be able to stay with her in the store?"

"Yes. She'll get a basket that has wheels under it, and there will be a place for CeCe to ride. Pete will walk and help her with things on the shelves."

"There are shelves?"

"Many of them," Gabe said, now maneuvering through town. He waited for Lily to comment on the location, as it wasn't conducive to a golf course, but it didn't happen. A few minutes later he pulled into a parking space at the grocery store, cut the engine, and turned slightly to watch his passenger. For this reason Gabe saw the exact moment it all hit her.

Lily took in the large store, the smattering of shopping carts in the parking lot, and signs in the windows proclaiming items on sale, and at the same moment she felt Gabe's eyes on her. With a hand to her face, she spoke.

"Please don't make me look at you, Gabe, please."

The plea tore at Gabe's soul, even as he answered.

"That's fine, Lily, but I need to talk with you. I need to tell you how easy it can be."

Lily wanted to shake her head, but she only sat and stared straight ahead, too mortified to move.

"All you needed to say to me was that you wanted to join Bailey when she went grocery shopping. We could have golfed another time."

"I can't do that," she told him, panic clawing at her throat at the very thought.

"Why not?"

"It's not right. You made room in your schedule."

"Why do you think I'm more important than you are?"

Lily didn't know what to say. He had so neatly put his finger on the center of the matter that Lily had no reply.

"You know what," Gabe cut in, "I don't want our discussion to ruin your first visit to a grocery store, so let's go in now and we'll talk about this some other time."

Lily was still sitting stock-still when Gabe opened her door. She made herself get out, finding it very easy not to look at him, but knowing she had no choice except to accompany him inside.

Do you have any idea how angry my father would be right now, Gabe? Do you know how ashamed of me he would be? You have your own life, yet you've set aside the day for me and I've rejected your efforts.

"What you have to understand, Lily," Gabe continued, his voice playful as he put a plastic, handheld shopping basket into her hands, "is that a first-time trip to the grocery store is not to be missed. So take this basket and go to it."

Lily's eyes became huge.

"I didn't bring any money with me."

"I'll cover it."

"Oh, all right," Lily agreed, very uncomfortable with this but trying not to disdain his generosity again. "Should I tell Bailey I'm here?"

"I'll find her and do that, and then I'll come back and track you down. Take all the time you need."

Lily wanted to stop him. She wanted to say this was all wrong, but she didn't. Instead, the reluctant shopper watched until Gabe was out of sight and then glanced around, wondering what she was supposed to do next.

A sign proclaiming crackers to be on sale caught her eye. She moved toward that aisle and a moment later stood in near stupefaction. Never in her life would she have dreamed of so many jars of peanut butter. She was still taking in the brands and varieties when Gabe rejoined her.

"Gabe," she said immediately, "I can't believe how many containers of peanut butter there are."

"There are a lot," he agreed, thinking she would faint when she encountered the cereal aisle.

"Look at this one! It has jelly right in with the peanut butter."

"Oh, yeah," Gabe agreed, plucking it off the shelf. "You'd better put one of these in your basket."

"Oh, do you think so?"

"Certainly. Give it a try."

Gabe suddenly found himself being stared at. He was several inches taller than Lily, so it was impossible to miss the way her head tipped back to look into his eyes.

"I want to apologize to you, Gabe, for the way I've been acting."

"How have you been acting?"

"Not thankful. You try to do things for me, and I show ingratitude."

"I'll tell you something, Lily Walsh," Gabe admitted with a small shake of his head and wonder in his voice, "you take submission to a whole new level."

Lily's head tipped to one side as she asked, "What do you mean?"

"There are Christian men and women all over the world who do not understand the biblical view of submission. When it's done well—when it's done God's way—it doesn't look like threats or domination, nor does it look like a woman not having a say or being a complete doormat."

Lily had to think about this. The word "doormat" perfectly described the way most of the women in the village lived their lives, but she had never seen it that way. She knew that some of the women were loved, especially the ones in the church family. But if "doormat" also meant second class-citizen, then Gabe had certainly hit the mark.

"Okay," Gabe now said, his eyes bright and eager, "what are we going to look at next?"

"Are you staying?"

"I am, yes."

"What do you need to look for?"

"I don't. I'm just having fun watching you."

Lily laughed at that and then blushed a little.

"I did get pretty excited about peanut butter, didn't I?"

"Wait until you see the cereal," he teased her.

Lily was laughing about this when they were spotted. Barb Stringer was pushing a basket toward them, a smile on her face.

"I just saw Bailey and the kids."

"We're kind of together," Gabe explained.

"And, Lily!" Barb went on. "You're shopping too."

"It's my first time," the younger woman admitted.

"So what do you think?"

Lily shook her head. "There's so much. It's overwhelming."

"What do you have at home for grocery needs?"

"There are open-air markets in the large cites, but in Lhasa you just know who sells what product. My father and I grow wheat, flax, and beans, but we have no milk cow or goat, so for cheese we go elsewhere."

"And you go anytime, or just at certain times?"

"Friday mornings are when most people have their wares for sale, but meat and milk products are available more often."

"Do you miss it?" she suddenly asked.

"The people, yes."

Barb smiled at her and not for the first time wondered at the younger woman's composure. She wasn't sure she could do the equivalent of what Lily had accomplished: leave behind everything familiar and go to Kashien for three months.

"Well, have fun," Barb told them.

Gabe and Lily told her goodbye in unison before Gabe turned back to the new shopper.

"Where were we?"

"You said something about cereal."

Gabe's brows rose expressively.

"Come with me."

It didn't take Gabe long to see that he was right. Lily could not speak when she saw the selection of cold cereal alone.

"And over here," Gabe directed, "are hot cereals—the ones for the stovetop or microwave."

"What are all the dates?" Lily finally managed.

"The dates indicate that the product is freshest if eaten by then."

"Those dates seem like a long way off," Lily said as she eyed the boxes.

"True, but most things have some type of preservative in them, and since cereal is not a perishable item, it naturally has more shelf life."

"Shelf life." Lily tested the words and then moved on.

Gabe smiled and wondered what it would be like to have everything so delightful and new.

"There's Peter," Lily suddenly said. "Hi, Peter."

"Oh, hi, Lily. What have you got in your basket?"

"This peanut butter with the jelly right in it."

"Oh, wow! Grape jelly inside."

"Doesn't that look fun?"

"Yeah! Are you going to buy this, Lily?"

"Yes, Gabe is helping me."

Peter looked to his uncle.

"Can Lily get gum?"

"Lily can get anything she wants."

"Come on, Lily," Peter took no time to say, his little face very sincere. "I'll show you."

Lily didn't even glance at Gabe but, realizing this was turning into a whole lot of fun, followed closely in the little boy's path.

～

"I think we need to eat out for lunch," Gabe announced to his sister and Lily as they ended their grocery-store adventure at the checkout counter.

"What about the perishables?" Bailey mentioned.

"Well, we'll run those home and then head out, or even go to the Little Bay."

"Works for me," Bailey agreed, but no word came from Lily. She was too busy checking out the small booklets available near the checkout counter.

Lose 30 Pounds in 30 Days!, Your Horoscope: What You Might Be Missing!, Birthdays of the Stars! Lily read the titles with great interest before her eyes dropped to the large magazines below. "BABY BORN WITH TWO HEADS" leaped out at her, and Lily stared in horror at the composite drawing.

"Are you going to put one of these into your basket?" Bailey teased her.

"Do people actually buy these?"

"All the time."

Lily's eyes went back, this time to the batteries hanging on the rack. She took a package from the shelf and studied it, but long before she was done, it was her turn in line.

A store employee helped Bailey out with her baskets, and Gabe hung back to give Lily a ten-dollar bill and directions if needed. She thanked him and would have said more, but the conveyor belt moved the food to the waiting clerk, and Lily was at once engrossed. The whole process with the bar codes and computer register prompted a new series of questions in the new shopper's mind, but with only five items in her basket, three of them gum, it didn't take long until she was paying, thanking the man, and moving on her way.

"Do the items ever get so heavy that the belt can't move?"

"I've never seen it happen, but it might. Maybe we can come back sometime, and you can ask your questions."

"All right."

When they arrived at the car, they found that Bailey had brought the van up. Gabe went toward the car, but Lily went to Bailey's window.

"Would you and the children like gum?"

"Oh, thank you, Lily."

"Which one?" she asked.

"Here, Peter," his mother called to him. "Come and pick one for us."

It didn't take long for Peter to select the watermelon flavor, and as soon as the pieces were shared, Lily scooted around to the car.

"Don't even think about it," Gabe said flatly the moment she climbed in and began to open her mouth.

Lily looked at him.

Gabe looked back.

"I'm sorry," he said sincerely. "I was certain you were going to apologize for holding me up, but I realize you might have been ready to offer me a piece of gum. I shouldn't have said that."

"I was going to offer you gum," she admitted, "just as soon as I apologized for holding you up."

Gabe smiled at her before asking, "What flavors do you have?"

Lily couldn't contain her excitement. "This is original, then watermelon, and orange."

"And they're all bubble gum?"

"Yes."

"What are you going to have?" Gabe asked as he pulled behind Bailey's van and waved at Peter, who had turned to see them.

"I don't know! I don't know where to start."

All Gabe could do was laugh.

"I know! Why don't we each have a different flavor and then compare notes?"

"Okay," Gabe agreed, but his mind had gone to a dangerous place. Thinking about chewing gum with Lily made her kissable for the first time.

"Do you want orange or watermelon?" Lily made the decision to inspect those two.

"Orange."

Both went to work on their gum. Gabe concentrated on driving while Lily examined the contents of the fifth item she had purchased.

Gabe had to work to keep his eyes on the road as intelligent, well-educated Lily Walsh took neon-colored Band-Aids from a box and sorted them on her lap. She put the spot sizes together, regardless of color, and sorted the larger sizes in the same manner. She inspected the way the adhesive was exposed when the paper was folded back, and even went so far as to put a small strip on the back of her hand, all the while her mouth was going around the gum and even producing an occasional bubble. By the time they reached the house, she was as relaxed as a cat, her head back and eyes closed as she savored the wad in her mouth.

"So, how is your flavor?"

"It's wonderful. How's yours?"

"Very good."

"Do you want to try a watermelon?"

"Not until after lunch."

"Oh, is it lunchtime already?"

"Yes. We're eating out."

"At the cove?"

"No, at a restaurant."

Lily had all she could do not to swallow her gum. First a grocery store and then a restaurant! It was too good to be true.

"Are you all right?" Gabe asked.

"Yes," she told him, but he could see that she was flustered as she stuffed items into her shopping bag, dropping both gum and neon strips.

"I'm going to go help Bailey with the bags."

"I'll come too." Lily was only too glad for an excuse to do something. If she didn't calm down, she was going to ruin her outing in the restaurant as she had almost done in the store.

On his end Gabe was praying for patience. He could see that something was on Lily's mind, and he wanted her to tell him.

Well, Lord, I won't have to second-guess on this after all. If Lily ever decides to start talking to me, I'll know we've got something here.

Chapter Fifteen

"I was hoping you would see us come in." Bailey greeted her husband with a kiss and handed him a bag of groceries.

"Of course you were. You just love me for my muscles."

"Among other things," she teased him.

"Lily bought gum," Peter said to his father as he started to walk toward the kitchen door. "And we're going out to eat for lunch."

"We are?"

"Yeah. It was Gabe's idea."

"Is Gabe paying?" Evan asked with a wiggle of his brows, but Peter only laughed as the two trooped toward the house, groceries in tow.

"All right, Miss Celia," Bailey instructed as she took her from her car seat and gave her a job, "you find Ash and tell him we're going out to lunch. Can you do that?"

"To lunch."

"That's right. Check in his room, and if he's not there, look all over the house, but don't come back outside without him. All right?"

"Right," Celia agreed but continued to stand where she was.

"Get going," Bailey instructed.

"I has to carry," she told her mother, her little brow furrowed with worry.

"Oh, right. Here," Bailey handed her a roll of paper towels. "You can take this to the kitchen and then find Ash."

Bailey was still laughing at Celia when Gabe and Lily showed up. Lily's face was red, and for a moment Bailey was distracted.

Lily had taken some bags and started toward the house, but Gabe had climbed into the back of the van to pull things forward. Bailey suddenly realized they had a moment alone.

"Lily looked a little flushed, Gabe. What have you been doing to the girl?" she teased.

"Making a complete mess of things, I'm sure."

Gabe's voice was so serious that Bailey dropped all teasing. "What happened?"

"I don't know," he answered her, sounding frustrated. "She must think I'm waiting to pounce on everything she says, but I want her to see that she doesn't have to live like that with us."

"Like what?"

"Oh, you know, never saying what she wants, always going along with every idea. Did you know that she didn't feel she could tell me she wanted to go to the grocery store instead of golfing? She felt she was being disdainful of my taking the time to golf with her."

At the same moment the couple heard the house door open, so the subject was dropped, but Bailey had heard enough. In just a matter of seconds she realized she could be doing her part too.

〜

Lying back on his bed, a smile on his face, Ashton read Deanne's latest letter. They talked on the phone every week, but it wasn't enough. Deanne wrote to him at least twice a week, and Ashton usually wrote just as often.

This letter told about a Christian concert Deanne had attended and how it had taken her mind from wanting to be home. But then she recalled the verse about not grumbling and realized she hadn't been all that thankful about this opportunity to finish her college education.

I've taken it all for granted, Ash, she continued.

How often did I dream of being able to do this, and then when the Lord gives me the chance, I'm not thankful. Since falling in love with you my future looks different than I originally planned, and at times I wonder why I'm even going for my degree. But whether or not I'll ever use it as I thought I would, I'll have accomplished my goal, and only because God afforded me this opportunity. I think that alone needs to be at the front of my mind. Does that make sense? Maybe we can talk about it next time you call.

Did my mom call you? Mic had two touchdowns in his last game. Isn't that great?

The letter went on about general things but then ended with comforting news:

Not long now, Ash—2 months, 24 days, and 13 hours until I'll be home.

All my love,
Deanne

Ashton set the letter aside and just lay thinking about what she had said. He hadn't been as thankful these days, either. He naturally missed his fiancée, but that didn't excuse the way he had been moping around since she left.

"Well, no more," he whispered to the Lord. "I'm going to be thankful for every day, and not because of Deanne, but because You saved me."

The words were no more out of his mouth than someone banged on the door.

"Ash," a little voice accompanied this pounding, and he knew he was getting a visit from Celia.

"Hey, you," Ashton said when he opened the door and she rushed at his legs.

Arms up to communicate her desire, Celia looked up and waited for her uncle to reach for her. Once in his arms, she put her little hands on his cheeks and spoke directly into his face.

"We're going lunch."

"We're going to lunch?"

She nodded.

"Where are we going to lunch?"

"Out."

Ashton kissed her cheek and held her close for a moment.

"Am I invited?"

This was met with another nod.

"All right. Tell your mom I'll be down in a minute. Okay?"

"'Kay."

Ashton watched her run down the hall, fall without mishap, pick herself back up, and then take the stairs on her stomach, feet first, at a speed that was frightening. He turned back into his room to ready himself to leave, thinking that Celia had been a good reminder of what he had just told the Lord.

Even that little girl needs my example so she'll find You, Lord. I can't show her the joy I have in You if all I do is wander around and wait for Deanne to come home.

〜

Gabe was starting to know "the look." It was another hour before he realized what he had witnessed in the car with Lily, but now he had her figured out.

Whenever Lily grew very still and watched everything very carefully—her face a picture of composure, he knew she was in a new situation. Sometimes she would be so taken by surprise that she would forget herself, but from the moment they walked into the restaurant, Gabe knew that any peace he read in her expression was forced.

"What are you having, Peter?" his mother asked.

"Do they have hot dogs?"

"Let's see."

Lily watched Bailey lean toward her son and study his paper place mat. Lily looked at her own place mat, but it was not the same. She watched Evan reach for a booklet of some type and look in it, but still she hesitated.

"What are you having, Lily?" Ashton asked.

"I don't know. Can you recommend something?"

Gabe hid a smile. She was covering very nicely.

"I heard you went shopping today," Evan said before Ashton could answer.

"We bought gum!" Peter chimed in. Lily smiled.

"It was very interesting. I learned quite a few new things."

As Lily said this, Gabe laid down his "booklet," and she was able to see that various food items were listed inside. She reached for one, and as though the knowledge emerged from a hidden corner of her mind, she knew what she was supposed to do.

"I'm having the taco salad," Ashton proclaimed as he set his menu aside. He then noticed Lily again. "Lily, did you cut your hand?"

Lily looked confused for a moment, and then her face swept with color.

"Oh, no, I just, um, that is, I wanted to see what it was like."

Ashton tried to follow but failed miserably. He didn't say anything but watched as Lily swiftly peeled off the pink strip and rolled it in her fingers.

"There's nothing to be embarrassed about, Lily," Gabe said quietly from beside her. "Ash would understand that Band-Aids are new to you."

"Is that it?" Ashton asked with a smile. "Did you buy those this morning at the store?"

Lily nodded, smiling at his understanding eyes.

"I thought you were going golfing," Ashton said, having just remembered.

Gabe smiled. "There was a change in plans."

"So when will you golf?"

"I was going to ask Lily about that later."

"We can anytime you wish," she told Gabe.

"Okay," he said simply, still planning to ask her about it and not just tell her.

"Okay, folks." A woman came on the scene in a clean uniform and apron. "Can I start anyone with something to drink?"

Lily was unprepared for this. They had already been given water, and it was her turn to answer the woman much too soon.

"I'll have the same," she said, thinking she had had a moment of genius, but the person before her had been Bailey who wanted only water, and Lily hadn't caught that.

The waitress, however, took it in stride and moved on. Evan, on the other hand, finally saw what Gabe had been witnessing.

"Lily," he asked kindly, "is this the first time you've eaten in a restaurant?"

She nodded, feeling quite tense and hoping she hadn't done anything wrong.

"Honestly, Lily," he went on, "you're so good for me."

Lily only stared at him, wondering what that could mean.

"I live so much of my life without giving a moment's thought to the everyday aspects. Will you please do me a huge favor and explain something that I wouldn't understand or naturally know how to do if I came to Kashien?"

Lily looked surprised, but pleased too.

"Gabe and I saw Mrs. Stringer in the grocery store, and she was asking me how we did our marketing at home. I think that might be a little bit different for you."

"So what would I have to learn?"

"In our village you would need to understand that Cam sells cheese and butter, but he won't accept any trades. He only wants coins. Jenai sells fabric, but we can always pay her with wheat or flax. Yau Ta is one of the few men who will give us coin for our wares, but that's because he goes into the city and can peddle them for much more than he paid to us. And most things are negotiated, but not all, so one has to be careful not to give offense."

"And what happens if someone gets offended?"

"It can cause quite a stir. Feelings get hurt, and then the person assumes he's lost respect with you or the whole village. The repair work is so difficult that one learns at an early age not to offend."

"So how do you ever tell anyone that he needs to be saved from his sins?" Bailey asked.

"We don't attempt to open any doors. We wait for a door to open for us. The church has over 50 men, women, and children now, and when someone sees a difference in us and inquires about it, we see that as an open door. When Jeff went off to college in California, he wrote back and told me about the practice of greeting strangers and handing them a booklet or a piece of paper that explains the gospel and then walking away.

"It's not that easy in Kashien. Your life has to be different enough to open the door, or you must keep your mouth closed."

"And what differences would the people of the village see in you and your father?"

"We are honest in our trade. We don't use drugs or alcohol. My father does not beat me. We do not grow angry and shun the neighbor with whom we are upset. We give away some of our time and wares without expectations of reciprocation. I am an honorable daughter in that I am not seen out at night with men, nor am I known to speak back or be disrespectful, especially before the men of the community."

"And is the color of your skin ever a barrier?" Gabe asked this question.

"When my father first came he was not trusted, but all he did was buy a plot of land, build a home, and begin to work the land. It took almost two years for someone to ask him why he was so honest. Six months later he led that man to Christ, and the church began.

"Then he met and married my mother, and more walls came down when the village realized they could trust a white woman. By the time Jeff and I came along, we were very accepted in the village. Visitors sometimes have a hard time, but we deal with it as best we can, and the walls come down if they stay among us long enough."

"What do you miss the most?"

Bailey had no more voiced this when the drinks arrived and the waitress stayed to take their orders. When it was her turn, Lily was ready.

"I'll have a hamburger, please."

"How would you like it done?"

Lily blinked.

"Try medium, Lily," Gabe helped her out.

"Medium, please."

"And would you like cheese on that?"

After only a moment's hesitation this time, she managed, "Yes, please." When the woman moved from their table, Lily admitted in a low voice, "I didn't know I could have it with cheese."

"Have you not had a hamburger?" Bailey asked, trying to think if they had grilled out since Lily arrived.

"I don't think so. Will I like it?"

"I think you will. What did you get to drink?"

"I have water," Lily said when she saw that nothing else had been delivered to her.

"We need to get the waitress back, Lily. You need to have a milk shake with your hamburger."

"Bailey?" Lily made herself say.

"Yes?"

"I need to look at my money and make sure I can afford a milk shake."

The only people at the table not to protest the idea of Lily paying for her meal were under the age of six. Lily listened to the chorus of arguments without comment. She sat very still until Gabe put a hand on her arm.

"Is there some reason you wanted to pay for your meal?"

"I think Jeff would not wish me to always be a burden to you."

"What if you're not a burden to me? I did invite everyone out to lunch," Gabe reminded her.

Lily had no comment for that.

"Here are the flavors," Ashton said, reaching for the menu again and pointing to the right spot.

Just reading the selection made Lily's mouth water. When Evan called the waitress back, the novice diner ordered without further comment.

~

Lily rode home with Evan and Bailey. Peter was in the back with her and they had been talking, but now it was quiet and Evan's voice came from the front. Lily tried not to listen, but it was almost impossible.

"Zulu called when you were out," he said, referring to one of the elders at church. Evan was preparing to become an elder and had been involved in a rather delicate matter with a certain family at the church.

"Can you tell me about it?"

"Things have come to a head with Ginny."

Bailey sighed in irritation. "Honestly, Evan, the woman wants to homeschool her kids! I don't think it's that great of an idea in her situation, but if she wants to, what's the big deal? You and I have even talked about it for Pete and CeCe."

"Well, you put your finger on it."

"On what?"

"The crux of the matter: We've talked about it."

Bailey could only stare at her husband.

"Ginny is the problem, Bailey," Evan said gently, "not the homeschooling issue. At this point it's not about her wisdom on whether or not she should do this. It's about how tightly she's holding onto the entire issue. She won't even dialogue over it. She's made up her mind and feels that's the end of it."

From the back, Lily heard no more. It was as if Evan had been describing her father. How many things did Owen Walsh hold onto too tightly? Lily knew she would never be able to count them all. And as far as dialoguing on an issue, well, that just didn't happen. Lily had been raised to accept that his word was law, and his decisions were not open for discussion, especially where his daughter was concerned.

Lily's thoughts raced wildly in the time it took to get home. She desperately wished she could talk to Jeff. She felt as if she had just gained a new understanding of her father. Jeff had offered to speak to her father on her behalf, and Lily now saw that this is what she would want him to say: *Can we please just talk about things, Father? Can we just do that much?*

Lily was so eager to get home and write to Jeff that the rest of the trip was made in a blur.

~

When Evan came to the bedroom that night, he found a surprise on his pillow. Bailey was still in the bathroom, so for a moment he sat and simply held the newborn-size disposable diaper she had set on his pillow, his head shaking in wonder.

Even though Celia was still young, he realized he had forgotten just how tiny a new baby could be. He unfolded the diaper and smiled.

"You found it," Bailey said as she joined him on the bed. She sat close and put her chin on his shoulder.

"Can you believe this size?"

"Isn't it cute? I knew it was a bit premature, but I'm so excited."

"How are you feeling?"

"Pretty good. I'm tired after today's activities, but all in all, I'm in good shape."

"Wang said he was coming to cook dinner tomorrow night."

"Yes, he did! I had forgotten about that."

"Did you also forget that next week we go to your mom's? She'll keep the kids, which means you can come home and lie around."

"Well now, I can't miss with that plan."

Evan looked into her eyes. "You're going to be more tired this time—you already are. So you have to take your rest when you can get it."

"I'm not more tired!" she protested.

"You're a bit on the short-tempered side."

Bailey sat up, suddenly very alert.

"Am I really?"

"Yes. It's slight and mostly with the kids."

Even though she looked upset, Bailey said, "Thank you for telling me. I'll have to talk to them about it and apologize." She then sat thinking and finally added, "But I don't feel tired."

Evan's brows rose before he looked at his watch. "I followed you up here ten minutes ago when you said you were going to bed, and you're already in your nightgown. It's not even 10:00."

Bailey looked at the bedroom clock. It read 9:54.

"Oh."

Evan smiled.

"But if you're not tired…" he said, letting the sentence hang.

Bailey smiled in return and hugged his arm with both of her arms.

Still sitting on the side of the bed, Evan lay back, taking his wife gently with him.

～

"I've made a poor assumption where you're concerned, Lily," Gabe confessed as they sat on the sofas by the television in the living room. Lily had stayed up to watch the 10:00 news with Ashton and Gabe, but now Ashton had gone to bed.

"How did you do that?"

"When Evan asked you about your home today, I learned two things. I thought because I was so close to Jeff that I knew most everything, and I don't. And then I thought that discussing Kashien would only make you feel worse, but I could see how pleased you were to talk about it. So for that, I'm sorry."

"Thank you, Gabe, but I haven't been feeling left out at all."

"That's good to hear. Now before I turn in, I do need to check with you on golfing, and I would request that you not answer too fast."

"Okay."

"Would you like me to show you how to golf tomorrow, or is there something else you would rather do?"

Lily kept her mouth shut but realized that she still wasn't doing what he had instructed. She had the answer already settled in her mind, but he had told her to think. Lily tried to do that swiftly: Bailey had not said anything about her plans. Wang was coming to cook that evening, but they would certainly be done golfing by then. Or would they?

Knowing she had done as Gabe had asked, Lily actually smiled a little before answering.

"Wang is coming to make dinner tomorrow night, and I rather hoped to watch him. Would we be done before he arrives?"

"Yes. We would go in the morning before it gets too warm."

"Then I would like to golf very much tomorrow."

Gabe couldn't help but smile at her. "Okay," he said quietly, his heart filling with more new emotions. "It's a plan. They open at 7:00, so I'll call first thing and get a tee time."

Lily was instantly at sea. She nodded but couldn't think why they would need to drink tea before they golfed. It must be some strange sort of tradition, but it sounded like something you would do in England, not Hawaii.

The two went back to watching the news. Lily was intent on an international story when a tiny scrap of knowledge emerged from the back of her mind, and she suddenly understood Gabe.

"You start a golf game by teeing off, don't you?"

"That's right. And since you need to golf in groups of two or four, you have to schedule a time so everyone is not at the same spot at the same time."

Again Lily smiled, feeling quite pleased that she had figured it out.

Gabe stood, thinking that if he stayed near her any longer he would never fall asleep.

"I'll see you in the morning."

"Okay. Thanks for everything, Gabe."

"You're welcome. Good night."

"Good night."

Lily did watch a little more of the news, but she was distracted. She thought that Gabe Kapaia might be the kindest man she had ever known.

Chapter Sixteen

"It's not a very large ball, is it?" Lily asked as she stood with Gabe in the practice area at the golf course, studying the golf ball in her hand. They had gone ahead of their 8:15 tee time in order to practice.

"No, it's not."

"And the whole point is to get it into the hole with as few hits as possible."

"Correct."

"How many other games have a low scoring system versus a high scoring system?"

"Let me see." Gabe thought a moment before continuing, "In cross-country your score is your placement at the finish line, so you want to finish as soon as possible because all of the scores are added up."

"What do you mean?"

"There are seven men or women to the team and the top five runners' places are added up for the team score. So if your team finishes third, seventh, tenth, fourteenth, and nineteenth, all those numbers get added together for a team score of 53. The team with the lowest number wins."

This was met by one of Lily's silent "ohs," something Gabe never tired of seeing. He was also finding it very distracting of late.

"Okay." Gabe knew he'd better stick to business. "Let's work on your grip."

Not many minutes later Gabe was asking himself how many romantic movies he had seen over the years where the man takes advantage of teaching a woman to golf or swing a bat in order to put his arms around her. Fun as he thought it might be to hug Lily, he wasn't going to start playing games with her heart.

Standing next to her so he could show her with his own club, Gabe demonstrated the proper grip and stance. This did not come as easily to Lily as tennis had, and the stillness of her carriage told him she was tense.

"How did you sleep?" Gabe asked.

Lily blinked at the change in subject but still said she had slept fine.

"Good. Is the bed here very different from the one at home?"

This made Lily laugh.

"Very different. At home we sleep on thick mats, and the frames are very close to the floor."

"Is the bed here too soft? I mean, does it hurt your back?"

"Oh. I'll have to think about that."

"Your hands are perfect," he said quietly, and Lily's head whipped over to look at him.

"This is it?" she asked, clearly excited. "This is how I'm to hold it?"

"That's it," Gabe said with a laugh. "Now I'll put the ball on a tee, and you try swinging at it."

By the time Gabe got her set up, Lily had shifted her hands, so it didn't go well. The ball rolled off with a strange little plop, and Lily frowned at it.

"Let's try it again."

That was to be the first of many suggestions to try again. One time Lily would bump the ball and it would roll away, another she would swing and miss it completely.

"It's harder than it looks," Lily said when she looked over some 50 yards to see a man tee off and send his ball straight up the fairway.

"You'll get it."

Lily was starting to wonder, but she kept going, telling herself that the key was concentration. Her shoulder and arms were aching, but she ignored them.

Lily looked down at the ball one more time. She kept her legs still. She didn't shift her hips. She kept her hands and arms just the way Gabe had told her. She didn't hear him call her name. She swung.

The sound of a dull thud came to her ears just a heartbeat later. Lily looked with something akin to horror as a man rushed to his golf cart to inspect the dent she had just delivered to a spot above the front tire.

"Oh, no," she said softly.

"Stay here." Gabe swiftly decided to rescue her and headed over to speak to the man. What followed was an hour of work: finding the course manager, discussing the damage of the cart and ascertaining primary responsibility. Gabe kept Lily almost completely out of it, but near the end she stood with Gabe while he spoke to a maintenance man he knew from church, her eyes down. Lily's eyes stayed down all the way to the car when it was at last time to leave. Her body ached from the way she'd been holding herself, but she didn't relax even when Gabe pulled from the parking lot to take them home.

"Are you all right?" Gabe asked Lily when they hit the main road; she had been much too quiet during the whole ordeal.

"I feel awful about what happened."

"You must remember what the manager said, Lily. That man had no business parking his golf cart there. Even the man admitted to ignoring the sign."

But all Lily could say to herself was *I failed you, Father. I didn't learn to golf and even harmed another person's property.*

Gabe let it go until he pulled into the driveway and parked in the garage. With a hand to Lily's arm, he kept her in the car and worked to keep his voice gentle.

"We're just going to keep at this golfing thing until we get it right."

Lily didn't look at him.

"I'll call again for another tee time, and this time we'll just head right out onto the links. We won't be near anyone's cart or car."

"You have better things to do with your time."

"That's a matter of opinion" was all Gabe said to that. "Will you please look at me, Lily?"

She complied.

"We'll go at the same time tomorrow. Please don't let this ruin your day."

"Thank you for taking me and being willing to try again."

"Is that what you really wanted to say, or did you want to tell me to leave you alone?"

Lily looked as shocked as she felt. "No, Gabe, not at all!"

Giving her arm a little squeeze and dipping his head some to make sure they held eye contact, he said, "But if you ever feel that way, you can tell me."

"Why would I ever be so rude as to tell you to leave me alone?"

"I don't mean in a rude, uncaring way, Lily, but it's all right for you to tell me you need some time off. This whole experience is a learning one for you, and that can be exhausting. Do you see what I'm saying? I'm not telling you to ignore Scripture and be unloving to others. I'm just telling you that your feelings and opinions count for something."

Gabe was warming to his subject now. Letting go of her arm, he shifted his whole body to better see Lily.

"Lily, I can't believe what help you've been in teaching me to do things I don't want to do! You're so good at bucking up and taking care of business, and I've been lax about that at times. But at the same time, isn't it all right for you to say you enjoy tennis but golf isn't your thing? Of course it is!"

Lily could only stare at him. She didn't know what "bucking up" might be, but he had just said that she had been a help to him. The day before Evan had said she was good for him. It was almost more than she could take in.

"Okay, Lily, I'll drop this right now. I've been overwhelming you for days. We'll golf in the morning. I'll let you know the time." Gabe stopped and just looked at her, his heart aching to explain what was going on inside, but right now it ached for something more.

"And one of these days," he added, "I'll stop giving you orders right and left."

"I don't think you give orders right and left," Lily told him in quiet sincerity, even managing to keep her eyes on his.

Gabe only looked back into Lily's gaze and didn't try to stop her when she moved to climb from the vehicle. He watched as she went toward the beach. And still, his heart prayerful, he let her go.

～

"How was golfing?" Bailey asked the moment Gabe walked into the kitchen.

"Lily hit a golf cart that was parked in the wrong place."

"Is she upset?"

"Yes."

"Did it break?" Peter wanted to know.

"There's a little dent," his uncle said.

"Hey, buddy," Bailey said, "I think it might be best if you didn't ask Lily about it, all right?"

"Okay. Did she cry?"

Bailey looked to Gabe.

"No, and I don't know how thrilled she is to try playing again tomorrow, but that's what we're going to do."

"If I've gotten to know Lily at all, she'll go golfing with you tomorrow without so much as a whimper," Bailey offered.

It was on the tip of Gabe's tongue to say, "That's what I'm afraid of," but Peter was still standing with them. The way his sister was watching him, however, gave him the impression that she knew what was on his mind.

"Where's Miss Celia?" Gabe hunkered down and asked his nephew.

"She's out to eat with Papa."

"How fun. Where did they go?"

"We don't know, but it's my turn later."

"That'll be great. Do you by any chance have time to go swimming with me?"

"Yeah!"

"Get your suit."

Both adults watched the boy dash from the room. Bailey was still smiling when she said, "That was nice of you."

"The nice person is Peter," Gabe stated plainly. "He never clamors for my attention, but he's always receptive to it. Standing here I suddenly realized we haven't done anything in ages, and I simply miss him."

Bailey looked touched, but Gabe didn't stop.

"I hope you know how much I love him, Bailey."

"I do, Gabe. And while we're on the subject of feelings, Evan tells me I've been short, especially with the kids. If I've done or said anything to hurt you, Gabe, I'm sorry."

"Thank you, but I can't think of anything."

"Are you the person who folded that load of laundry and put it on my bed?"

"Yes."

"Thank you for that."

"You're welcome, but unless I find socks and T-shirts in the next load, I won't be doing it again."

Bailey looked confused until Gabe said, "You had a number of rather feminine garments in there, Bales."

Bailey smiled a little. "You've never given it any thought before."

"Trust me," he stated, his voice dry as he headed for the door to find his own swimming suit, "I do now."

Bailey just barely held her laughter, even as she asked God to work a miracle in Lily Walsh's heart. She didn't know exactly what it should look like, but in the end she wanted Lily watching her brother the way he watched her, and staying with them in Hawaii until they were all gray with age.

~

Lily took her shoes off the moment her feet hit the sand, never tiring of the feeling. The sand was hot and coarse, and her feet weren't that tough yet, but somehow it always felt very soothing.

So intent was Lily on her feet that it took a moment to see that Ashton was on the veranda. He was waxing a surfboard.

"Hi, Lily," he greeted her.

"Hi, Ash. Are you going surfing?"

"I am. Want to come?"

Lily smiled. "Can I watch instead?"

"Sure, but if you change your mind…"

Lily only laughed and joined the youngest Kapaia, taking a chair to watch him work.

"How was golfing?"

Lily's eyes went to sea.

"Not too good," she said quietly.

"Did you get hurt?"

"No."

"Did Gabe get hurt?"

"No," Lily answered, now turning to look at him.

"Did *anyone* get hurt?"

"No, it wasn't like that."

"Well, that's certainly a relief."

Lily wasn't sure if she agreed with him or not, but he had given her something to think about.

"So what did happen?"

"I hit a ball into a golf cart and dented it."

"How did Gabe react?"

"Quite calmly."

"And how did you react?"

"I just stood there."

"And how about now? Are you still upset?"

"I am, yes."

"Is Gabe?"

Lily thought about their conversation in the car and had to admit, "I don't believe he is."

Ashton's brows rose before saying, "Being the youngest, I learned something a long time ago, Lily: Take your cue from the person in charge."

Lily wasn't exactly sure what this meant, but she was figuring it out fast. Why did she insist on being so upset when Gabe was ready to forget the whole episode and try again tomorrow? The answer wasn't long in coming: her father. Somehow she didn't think he would take the harming of someone's property this lightly.

"Penny for them," Ashton's voice broke into her contemplations.

"Excuse me?"

"Penny for your thoughts."

"They're not worth that much."

"Tell me something, Lily. Does anyone in Kashien make you feel as though you matter?"

Lily had all she could do to keep her mouth closed, even as her heart asked the question, *Is my self-image truly so low?* The answer was not a simple one. Off the top of her head she would say yes, it was low. But upon further reflection, she realized that women from her village in Kashien gave little thought to how they were treated. It was simply a way of life. A woman learned at an early age from whom to gain emotional support. It usually didn't come from male family members, but other females. Women friends were another element in the picture, but here it was so different. Bailey had been a great encouragement to Lily, but so had her brothers. Lily's own brother was a source of reassurance, but Jeff was different. He had lived 18 years in the Kashienese culture but was now very much "an American."

Lily sat thinking on all of this until she realized that Ashton was watching her. Lily immediately knew why.

"I didn't answer your question, did I?"

"No, and you don't have to. I'm just trying to figure out if I need to apologize."

"You don't."

"I wish it were that simple."

"Why isn't it?"

"Because I can't take your word for it. You don't expect anything from anyone, so you might not have the right view of how I just treated you."

Lily was growing upset; she even came to her feet.

"That's just plain insulting," she said, her voice low with anger.

"Why is it insulting?"

"You're saying I don't even know my own mind."

"I didn't mean to say that. I'm sorry it came out that way. I meant to say that your bias might not let you be as honest with me as you need to be."

Lily had to think on this, but her thoughts were in a muddle. In the midst of them, Ashton stood.

"For the record," he went on, "it's good to see you get angry. I was sure you were capable of great passion. It's nice to know I was right. It gives me great hope."

"Hope for what?"

Ashton smiled hugely, his board going under his arm.

"I'll tell you about it someday." This said, he shoved a stick of gum in his mouth and handed one to Lily.

"Ashton," she began in her normal voice, not even looking down at the gum, "I feel I need—"

"Don't even go there," he said, his voice not at all teasing.

Lily blinked.

"Were you about to apologize to me?"

Lily gave a small nod.

"I'll make a deal with you, Lily," Ashton began, his voice completely back to normal as well. "You can get angry at me, and when I think you were unjust or that you sinned against me, I'll tell you so you can make it right. Prior to my telling you that I think you were wrong, I want you to speak your mind to me, even if you feel angry. Deal?"

"Deal," Lily said, not thinking she had a choice.

"I'm off," Ashton stated. He turned toward the sea but then paused and looked back. "Unless we still need to discuss this."

"No, that's fine" was all Lily could muster just before Ashton gave a wave and jogged across the sand. Realizing her legs would no longer support her, Lily let her body sink back down to the chair, wondering if there had ever been another time when she was quite this emotionally exhausted.

~

"Okay," Peter called. "Watch this one."

Peter did a silly jump from the diving board to his uncle, who waited for him in the deep end.

"That was a good one. A nine at the very least."

"Let's dive for rings!"

"Okay. Where are they?"

"I'll get 'em."

Gabe lay on his back, his eyes on the sky as Peter made quick strokes to the edge of the pool and then scrambled over to the hot tub for the rings. He was back before Gabe was ready to move, but he forced himself to dive with his nephew when all his body wanted to do was sleep.

"Gabe?" Peter said when he had tired of that game; they had played at least a dozen since getting in the pool.

"Yeah?"

"Do you think we can eat lunch out here?"

"I'm sure we can. What sounds good?"

"Can you barbecue hamburgers?"

Gabe laughed, finally understanding why Peter's voice had been so hesitant and hopeful.

"I doubt if we have any meat thawed, buddy, but we can check."

"Do we have hot dogs thawed?"

"Even if we don't, hot dogs will work if they're frozen."

Peter's answer to this was to throw his arms around his uncle's neck; only Gabe's strong legs kept their heads above water.

"So drowning me is my reward for agreeing to barbecue?" Gabe gently teased Peter, holding him close in the water.

"I love you, Gabe," Peter said, leaning back to look into his uncle's eyes.

"I love you, Pete. You're my favorite nephew."

The little boy smiled. "I'm your only nephew."

That we know of were Gabe's private thoughts as he remembered his sister's condition and gave the little boy a kiss.

"Shall we go see if we have some hot dogs?"

"Yeah! Chips, too, and Pepsi."

"Works for me."

The twosome made their way from the pool to dry off. Peter climbed onto Gabe's back for a ride to the kitchen, both with the makings of a feast in mind.

Chapter Seventeen

"Here you are," Gabe said as he stepped onto the veranda and found Lily just coming back from the beach.

Still feeling very weary, Lily only looked at him, not certain how she was supposed to respond and wishing that the walk she'd just taken along the shore had done something for her turbulent emotions.

"We're having lunch by the pool if you want to join us."

"Thank you."

Gabe looked at her. The words were said in a wooden voice, and Gabe had never seen Lily looking so tired.

"Are you all right, Lily?"

"I don't know."

"Can you tell me what's wrong?"

"I think I can. I mean, Ash wouldn't mind, I'm sure, and I would really like your advice about what to do."

"Okay."

"I got angry with Ash, and he was pleased."

Gabe's face lit up with delight. "You got angry at Ash?"

Lily had all she could do not to burst into tears. Her hand came to her mouth, and all she could think was *Please help me, Jeff. I'm so lost and confused right now. Someone please help me.*

"I'm sorry, Lily," Gabe was swift to say. "Here, sit down and tell me what happened."

Lily took a moment to collect herself and then told the story. She ended with, "Gabe, I'm so confused. Why would Ash wish me to be angry with him?"

"He doesn't want you to be angry with him as much as he wants you to feel free to have your say. It's about how much we value you."

"It's like you tried to explain to me in the kitchen the other night, isn't it?"

"Exactly. You have very few rights where you come from, Lily. In my opinion, Americans have too many rights, but a balance is needed here. You don't have to lower your eyes to show that you have respect for us—I think you've learned that—and in the same vein, you can also say that you don't wish to do something or that a comment hurt your feelings. We're not going to make you feel like you don't matter."

Lily nodded slowly and heard her stomach rumble. She then realized that Gabe had offered her lunch. Had she kept him from his? Lily was ready to ask when she realized this was just the kind of thing he was talking about.

"I'm afraid to be a bit of bother to anyone. Did you know that?"

Gabe nodded, his gaze growing a bit tender over his pleasure that she was seeing this for herself.

"I don't know why exactly. I mean, I know my father cares for me, but you've used the word *value*, and that has given me much to think about."

"The time is going by swiftly," Gabe forced himself to face that fact and admit. "You have only about a month left with us. We want this time to be great fun. We want you to be able to return to Kashien so full of good memories and our good care of you that you'll never forget. But mostly we want our relationship with you to be all it can be. You've seen the way we treat each other. We want you to be part of the family too."

"Thank you, Gabe." Lily made herself answer and not chatter on about how much they had already done for her. If she lived to be a hundred she would never forget that they *had* made her feel like family, if only she could relax and enjoy it.

Gabe nodded, not sure he could say anything more.

"Did you say something about lunch?" Lily ventured forth to ask.

"Yes, I did. We're out by the pool."

Lily stood.

"I think I'll go have a little something to eat."

"Sounds good."

Lily led the way, and Gabe was thankful. His emotions were tumbling a bit, and it was good to have a few moments with no one looking him directly in the face, especially Lily.

By the time they arrived at the pool, Gabe had things under control.

∼

Lily woke slowly and stretched like a cat. Still out by the pool, she had fallen asleep in a lounger, thankfully in the shade. A turn of her head told her that Bailey was still asleep in the lounger next to her.

For a moment Lily remembered the conversation they had shared before dozing off. Lunch was over, only the women were by the pool, and Bailey had seated herself next to Lily's lounger, surprising her with a question.

"If you could do anything you want this afternoon, Lily, what would it be?"

"Oh, let me see…" Lily thought a moment, thinking that a nap sounded good, but so did something else. *"I would walk through that grocery store again."*

Bailey laughed.

"You really liked it, didn't you?"

"I did, Bailey," she admitted with a shy smile. *"All those shelves full of new things! I found it fascinating."*

"Well, the resort store is not as large certainly, or as full of groceries, but you'll have to walk over there and have a look around."

"There's a store within walking distance?"

"Sure, right at the office."

Lily's mouth opened in her characteristic "oh."

"Have you not been to the office store?"

"I haven't even been to the office."

"You'll have to go. You might even find a little something to take back to your father."

"What does the store carry?"

But Lily remembered the way Bailey smiled and got a teasing glint in her eye, telling Lily that she would have to go and see. Lily was thinking about doing just that when she suddenly wondered what time it was. Depending on what Wang planned to make for dinner that night, he might already be in the kitchen.

Moving as quietly as she could, Lily left her chair and then the pool area. She took a moment to freshen up before heading to the kitchen, and when she arrived, she saw that her hunch had been correct. Not only was Wang already working, he welcomed her help. Lily settled in for a delightful afternoon of cooking and learning.

〜

It was the type of meal that would have been nice to linger over. Much to everyone's delight, Wang and Lily had prepared a rice dish to go with lean roast beef, and it was delicious. However, everyone had to be out the door for Bible study by 6:45. The meal wasn't rushed, but neither was it a dining experience. Lily felt a little uncomfortable about this and said something to Wang when they had a moment alone.

"You worked so hard, and we're all rushing off."

"You worked hard too."

Lily shook her head. "I just did as I was told. The hardest work is brain work."

Wang smiled.

"Go, Lily. Have a good time at Bible study."

Lily still looked uncertain.

"I'll be at one of the other Bible studies, Lily; don't forget that. Don't deliver pity where there is no mailbox."

And with that she was rescued. By the time they all got to the van, things had become a bit rushed, so Lily took the driving time as an opportunity to pray and calm down. And she was glad she did.

This was the night that Pastor Stringer devoted to communion and prayer; they spent no time in study. After they broke bread, people all around the room shared their prayer needs. Some were heartbreaking, and Lily was glad that she was not distracted. Then they broke into small groups, and Lily ended up praying with two women she didn't know. Lisa had just miscarried her baby. The other, an older woman—Lily hadn't caught her name—had a mother who was dying of cancer.

Lily was tense when it was her turn to pray, but then she realized how foolish that was and simply opened her heart to the Lord.

"Father in heaven, I thank You that You know all of our needs before we even speak them. You know my heart tonight, Lord, and how unfamiliar I am with so many of the people here, but I still ask for Your grace to be upon each one. Help us to remember that You are in control at all times and we can trust You. Forgive the sins in our hearts, Lord, so You can bless us. Open our eyes to new truths, that we might become more like You. Amen."

"Thank you, Lily," Lisa said when they were through.

"Yes, thank you, Lily," the older woman agreed. "It's hard when you don't know folks, but you covered us all very well."

Lily smiled in genuine warmth, wanting to say thank you right back for the way they had included her.

~

Lily heard the phone ring just ten minutes after they had arrived home, but she was not in the habit of picking it up. And, too, Wang said he would be back for the book she'd told him about, and she wanted to make sure it was in the kitchen before she went to bed.

The aromas of the marvelous dinner they had enjoyed still lingered in the kitchen air, and Lily was thinking of getting out some leftovers when Bailey stuck her head in the door.

"The phone's for you, Lily."

"Oh! Thank you, Bailey."

Lily went to the phone, a smile on her face. It was so fun when Jeff called.

"Hello?"

"Lily?" her father's voice said, sounding as far away as he was.

"Father," Lily said, automatically switching to Kashienese, her eyes dropping unconsciously. "Where are you calling from?"

"Hankuo," he said, his voice sounding pleased. Lily's last moments with him had been rather tense. It was wonderful to hear his light voice.

"How are you?" she asked, genuinely wishing to know and so pleased that he sounded the same.

"I am well. How are you?"

"I'm very well. I've learned so much."

"Tell me about it."

Lily did, her voice excited with the wonder of it all. She rattled on for some time until she remembered that morning.

"I think things were going well until we went golfing this morning."

"What happened?"

"I didn't do well," she admitted. "We're going to try again tomorrow, but I hit a ball into a man's cart and felt terrible about it."

"What did it do to the cart?"

"Dented it," Lily answered with dread. Already her father's voice had started to change.

"Lily," Owen now said, all playfulness gone, "you have shamed me."

"I am sorry, Father."

"You will make a promise to me, Lily."

"Yes, Father."

The door from outside opened behind Lily, but she took no notice.

"You will not eat until you have learned to golf."

"Yes, Father."

"Say it back to me, Lily, so I know I am understood."

Like a child, Lily repeated the words back to him, her voice low and repentant. Her father did not stay on the line much longer, but his voice was no less displeased before he hung up.

Lily stood for some time staring at the wall when the discussion ended. It was not a terribly harsh sentence; after all, they were going to golf again in the morning. But with the turn in the conversation, Lily had not had time to inquire after Ling-lei or anyone else in the village.

Finally taking herself off to bed, Lily realized this made her as sad as having her father angry at her from across the ocean.

〜

"Was that Jeff?" Gabe asked when Bailey came back to the television.

"No, I think it was her father."

"No kidding!" Evan sounded pleased. "That's great that he could call."

"Where do you suppose he calls from?" Ashton asked.

"Maybe Capital City," Gabe guessed.

Celia called from the top of the stairs just then, her voice very wobbly, and Bailey rose.

"What are you doing out of bed?"

Bailey's question was met with full-blown tears, so she moved to the stairs.

The sports highlights came on just a short time later, and all at once the men were absorbed. Had Bailey been in the room when their guest came through, it might have been different. As it was, Lily went from the kitchen to her bedroom for the night without having to speak with anyone.

～

"Something has come up, Lily," were Gabe's first words to her the next morning.

Lily, who was reading on the veranda, looked up from her book. She had been planning to start the day with her customary run but then realized how hungry that would make her. Concern that something would keep her from eating—as was about to happen—had stopped that idea. Lily opted to read instead.

"Can we do our golf lesson tomorrow?"

"Certainly," Lily told him, managing to smile.

"Thanks, Lily. I appreciate your flexibility."

Lily smiled again.

"Well, I've got to run. I'll probably see you this afternoon."

"Okay."

Lily shut the book as soon as Gabe went back inside. She stared at the ocean before shaking her head a little. Her father had required this of her, and it had never occurred to her to question him. And then she had foolishly promised—something both she and her father knew better than to commit to. Lily went back to her book, knowing she was going to have to ignore her stomach all day.

～

The resort store was delightful. Water toys, sand buckets, T-shirts, magazines, gum, mints, candy, and much more, all waited for Lily to feast her eyes on. By lunchtime she had become quite hungry and knew that the book she was reading was not going to distract her any longer. It was then she had remembered Bailey's words about the store. In less than ten minutes Lily was at the door, her small coin purse in hand.

The woman in the office said that no one was actually manning the store today, but Lily could let her know if she found something she wanted.

"Will it be a problem if I take a long time looking?" Lily had asked.

"Not at all," Mollee had assured her with a smile. "We don't close until 5:00."

With that, Lily's mind was taken completely off her stomach. The postcard rack alone kept Lily busy for a long time. The cards were three for a dollar, and Lily chose several to send home and even a few to keep for her own memories.

From postcards she moved to the seashells. Many shells could be found on the beach, but the ones inside the glass case were very special. Perfect in shape, with no broken or chipped pieces, some were so intricate and lovely that Lily knelt down to gain a better view.

Lily read every single T-shirt messag and inspected all of the tourist books and maps, but not until she discovered the water domes did she know what she would take to both her father and Ling. The glass globe with the sunset and palm trees, where tiny pieces of glitter floated in the water, would be for Ling. Her father's was of the beach with minuscule particles of white sand floating all about.

Lily set the two she wanted to one side and continued her perusal of the store. Dozens of bottles of every type of suntan lotion filled one shelf. Other shelves held film, disposable cameras, deodorant, toothpaste, toothbrushes, and so much more. Her hunger receding from her mind, at least for a time, Lily read and explored every item she could lay her hands on. It wasn't the way she had planned to spend the day, but it was going to work out fine.

～

Much later that day, Gabe did a double take when he climbed from his car and found Wang Ho waiting for him. Normally a picture of tranquillity, the older man was the most agitated Gabe had ever seen him.

"You're waiting for me," Gabe said respectfully. "Is something wrong?"

"I am not the one who waits. It is Lily who waits."

Gabe's heart sank with dread, sure that something had gone wrong while he was at Waikiki.

"Has something happened to Lily?"

"She has not eaten all day. When her father learned that she did not golf, he made her promise…and then you left…"

Wang was so upset that he wasn't even finishing his sentences, but Gabe still caught his meaning. His hand was already unbuttoning his dress shirt.

"Where is Lily now?"

"At the cove."

"Make me some sandwiches, will you, Wang? And throw in a little fruit and something to drink. I'll change and meet you on the veranda."

Wang left without further comment.

Gabe rushed around the side of the house and went in through the veranda. He hit the stairs at a run, reminding himself to hang his slacks in case the bankers wanted to see him again in the next few weeks. The temptation to throw his clothes on the bed and jump into shorts was strong, but he made himself slow down.

A glance at the clock told him it was almost 3:30. Lily never ate very much at one sitting, which meant she'd gone for hours on only the dinner she had had last night. Not enough time to starve, but plenty of time to grow tired, have a headache, or feel very dizzy. And all for what? Not learning to golf. If Gabe let his mind go too far, he would be furious with her father by the time he spoke with Lily.

Ten minutes later, shorts, T-shirt, and sandals in place, golf balls in his pocket and an eight iron in his hand, he met Wang on the veranda and took the hefty sack lunch from his grasp.

"Thank you, Wang."

"You are welcome, Gabriel. Take good care of her."

Their eyes met for a moment, and then Gabe turned and went down the beach. He could have taken one of the carts but thought the walk might help to calm the wild racing of his heart.

Did he let on that he knew about the phone conversation with her father, or wait to see if she figured it out? He knew they would speak of it at some point, but he wasn't sure when the time would be right. He also knew that he needed to put a call in to Jeff. This one was a bit out of his league. He could tell Lily not to ever do this again, but he didn't want to be her father all over again. He was more than happy to let Jeff be the heavy if that was needed.

All thoughts of how to handle the situation flew from Gabe's head the moment he spotted Lily. She was not actually down at the cove but above it on a sandy platform, her eyes out to sea. She had a blanket under her and an open book in her lap, but she didn't seem to be aware of anything around her.

"Hello," Gabe called as he started up the knoll, hoping not to startle her. It didn't work. She started and then turned to him, smiling when she saw his face.

"Hi, Gabe. How was your day?"

"It was all right. I don't think I told you," he said as he crested the top and joined her on the blanket, "but I had to meet with our bankers today. We're looking into making some improvements next fall, and the whole thing turned into a rather long, drawn-out affair."

"Did it seem like they will be favorable?"

"Yes, it did. Evan was with me for part of the time, and he's very good at explaining the plan. Hey, did you see what I brought with me?" Gabe asked, reaching for the golf club. "We still can get a little golfing in today."

"You don't want to go all the way to the golf course, do you, Gabe?"

"We don't need to," he said as he pushed to his feet. "Come right down here, and we'll have our lesson."

Lily was so surprised that she didn't say anything, but she did follow Gabe to where he was teeing up a ball. He handed her the club.

"Okay now. You know what to do. Just whack that ball up the beach."

"This way?" Lily asked as she addressed the ball.

"That's it. A little better position with your feet. That's good. Keep your arms nice and straight. Okay. Go."

A sudden case of the shakes overcame the hungry woman, but she made herself concentrate, eyes on the ball, working to remember everything Gabe had said the day before. Not sure if she could ask much more of herself, she swung. It wasn't the prettiest or the straightest, but it went up the beach about 65 yards. Lily watched it land and then looked to Gabe, who was smiling at her.

"You golfed, Lily," he said simply.

"I golfed?" she asked, visibly brightening.

"You golfed. That's all there is to it."

Gabe laughed when she sighed, looking very content.

"Can I join you?"

"Sure. I was just reading."

Gabe gathered the club and tee and followed Lily back to her seat. She could go to the house and eat now, but the knowledge that she had golfed was something to be savored a little longer.

"I missed lunch," Gabe began almost as soon as he sat down. "I hope you don't mind if I eat."

"That's fine," Lily said quietly. For obvious reasons she had not gone near the kitchen or dining room earlier in the day. She might need to head to the house sooner than she thought.

"Do you want a sandwich or anything?" he asked around a mouthful of food.

"I don't want to take your lunch, Gabe."

"I have plenty," he said, passing a wrapped sandwich and a small cup of fruit to her. "Here's a spoon."

The first bite was so good that Lily felt tears fill her eyes.

If you cry in front of this man about the flavor of this food, Lily Cathleen, she scolded herself, *you deserve to go hungry.*

She took a moment to compose herself and then took another small bite. It tasted so good. She couldn't remember the last time anything tasted so wonderful. Finally in control, Lily glanced at Gabe. She found him studying her. Just a moment of meeting his gaze and she knew. They watched each other for a moment, but Gabe didn't speak until Lily's gaze went back to sea.

"What am I going to do with you, Lily Walsh?"

"Did I really golf, Gabe, or were you being kind?"

"You golfed. I would have stayed down there with you the rest of the day if that's what it took."

"How did you know?"

"Wang."

Lily looked at him with a frown and then said, "I had a sense that someone was in the kitchen last night, but I never looked around."

Gabe did not reply.

"My father is not an easy person to honor, but I have been raised to try."

"And you do a wonderful job, Lily, but I must admit to you that I feel I need to call Jeff."

Lily nodded. "I understand."

"Do you ever get tired of being treated like a naughty five-year-old?"

Lily smiled and even laughed a little.

"It is like that, isn't it? I would be inclined to ask you if you're tired of dealing with a naughty five-year-old."

"That would be all well and good if I felt that way, but I don't."

"Then why are you calling Jeff?"

"Because as much as I want to, I don't have the right to tell you to defy your father."

Lily found that she had nothing else to say to this. Her thoughts had been on that very subject for most of the day, but with no conclusions.

Lily quietly ate the fruit and sandwich and even drank the little box of juice she was offered, but she had so much to think about she couldn't say a word.

Chapter Eighteen

"Thanks for calling me back" was the way Gabe started his conversation with Jeff after dinner that night. He spent a few moments explaining the golfing situation, and Jeff thanked him for being in touch before he asked to speak to Lily.

Gabe's look was apologetic as he handed Lily the phone, but she rescued him by smiling at him.

"What in the world went on with Father on the phone?" Jeff wasted no time in asking in a mockingly chagrined tone that made Lily laugh.

"Oh, you know how it is, Jefferson. I was telling him everything—being completely honest—and the next thing you know, I'm in trouble."

"By all normal standards the whole thing was ridiculous, Lil. But even knowing it was from Father, I can't imagine what he was thinking. He's not there to gauge if that was even wise. For all he knew, you had been ill and already down on your food. I mean, it wasn't even safe."

"No, I guess it wasn't. I think with me so far away he feels helpless and needed some method to gain control."

Jeff snorted. "That's not hard to believe, but now listen to me, Lily. At this time in your life, Gabe is the authority. If anything questionable comes along again, you must speak to him about it."

"All right."

Jeff sighed on the other end. "Gabe told me he hates it that you're treated like a child, Lily. Is that the way you feel?"

"I don't know, Jeff. He said the same thing to me, but he also said that he doesn't see me that way. I was a little confused."

"What you don't seem to understand, Lily, is that our father is in a class all his own. Gabe wanted to tell you to ignore Father's orders in the future, but he's not sure it's his place. I assured him that where Father is concerned nothing is normal, and that for now, Gabe can advise you to do anything he thinks is best."

"So he does think I'm a child?"

"Not at all, but he sees that you're out of your element in Hawaii. You're trying to live out your Kashienese upbringing in the United States and finding out firsthand just how difficult that is."

Lily realized it was very nice to have someone understand.

"I'm glad you called," Lily told him. "It's been a long, hard day."

"Well, Gabe tells me you're doing great. Maybe you can get some extra sleep tonight and rest tomorrow."

"I feel I need it, but I'm also tired of always being in so much trouble."

"You're not, Lily, but it's just like we've always said—the human element makes it hard. If we could get rid of people, everything would be fine."

Lily laughed, and for a time they spoke of everyday events. Jeff said things were looking up about his coming home on time, and then he dropped a bombshell.

"I was going to call you this week," he said, his voice growing quiet.

"About anything in particular?"

"Yes. I've met someone."

Lily hesitated. Clearly this was significant, but she couldn't think why.

"Are you still there, Lil?"

"Yes, Jeff. I'm just trying to figure out why you would say that to me. Did you meet a man or a woman?"

Jeff's laughter boomed over the line, and Lily sat in bemused silence.

"I'm sorry, Lily, I keep forgetting my phraseology. I meant that I've met a woman, someone special."

"Oh, Jeff, that's wonderful. Where did you meet?"

"Well, the first time we were introduced we were at work, but then I saw her at church and we got to talking. Her name is Annika Farrell."

"What a pretty name! Does she live where you are right now?"

"No, she's here on the project too."

"What was it about her, Jeff? What makes her special?"

"A lot of things. She's not that happy in her job right now, but she still works hard each day. And we agree on so many things!" In his excitement, Jeff changed topics very swiftly. "She's been reading this book I just started—it's about families and home—and we both think the author is very scripturally based."

He cut off suddenly, and Lily thought he might be embarrassed. Lily was not. She wanted to know more.

"So what happens now? You leave there in a month to come back here. Where will Annika go?"

"She lives in California and will complete her work here in about two weeks. We're going to write to each other and visit if we feel it's time for that."

"What if you do fall in love? Will she join you here?"

"Well, we haven't talked about marriage, but she's told me she would have no problem leaving California and her job. Her mother worked outside of the home all the years she was growing up, and she's never wanted that for her husband and children."

"I'm so happy for you, Jeff. Have you written to Father?"

"No. I think I'll wait just a bit longer with Father, but I wanted you to be aware."

"I'm glad you told me. I can be praying for both of you."

"I need that, Lily. I've only known her for the month I've been here, and I'm definitely ready to know more, but it's all new right now."

Lily assured him once more of her prayers and then realized they had been on the phone for a long time.

"I'd better let you go."

"Okay. Take care and have fun."

"I will."

"Hey, do me a favor and put Gabe back on, would you, Lily?"

"Certainly. 'Bye, Jeff."

Jeff said his goodbyes and waited until after Lily put the phone down. He had wanted to talk to his sister, but that had been hard since very recently he found he had plenty to say to his closest friend.

"Jeff?"

"Yeah, I'm here. Is Lily standing right there?" Jeff needed to know.

"No."

"I got your letter."

"Did you?" Gabe asked, feeling unbelievably tense.

Jeff began to laugh.

"What could you possibly be laughing at?" Gabe asked, thinking his hearing was going.

"Gabe, Gabe, Gabe." Jeff finally found his breath long enough to speak. "You can't believe the way I wrestled with God over having to come here. I desperately wanted a good reason for my being sent away, and the only thing I could come up with was that you might fall for my sister."

Gabe had to sit down.

"Are you there?"

"I'm here. I just needed a chair."

Jeff laughed again.

"Jeff, you're not putting me on, are you?"

"Not at all, Gabe. I couldn't be more excited."

"But what about all the questions I asked you?"

"They were good ones, by the way. I can see you're thinking, and this is all I can tell you: Lily is going to fall for you."

"How can you possibly know that?" Gabe asked, even as he began to relax. Jeff sounded so much like himself, and it felt good just to talk about this.

"Because I know the two of you. There are no two people more suited. If she hasn't fallen already, it's because you're not doing something right. I think if you show the slightest bit of interest in her, she'll tumble."

"That's what Evan said."

"Then I agree with him."

"What about your father, Jeff? What would he say?"

"I can't honestly tell you, Gabe, but I find it hard to believe that he would stand in the way of Lily's happiness, even if it meant her moving away."

"Okay. Thanks, Jeff."

"Thank *you*. I've since come to terms with God about why I'm here; in other words, He doesn't owe me an explanation and I had better be thankful. But if you and Lily found each other, I would be very happy."

The men rang off shortly after this, and for a moment Gabe sat alone in the kitchen. He was rather drained but realized how special it was to have Jeff's blessing.

But what if Lily doesn't do what Jeff and Evan think she will? he asked of God. Naturally there was no answer, and Gabe knew that the only way he would know anything was to keep spending time with the lady in question.

Gabe came from the kitchen to find the Markhams playing a board game at the dining room table. Ashton had gone to see Deanne's parents, and Lily was nowhere in sight. When Gabe asked Bailey about Lily's whereabouts, he was told that she'd gone toward the pool.

Even though he was quite certain of the answer, he still asked, "With or without her swimsuit?"

"Without."

Gabe headed that way and found Lily. She had slipped into some shorts—unless she was exercising, she could usually be found in the lightweight slacks that she wore in Kashien—and was sitting on the edge of the pool, her feet and calves in the water at the three-foot end.

"Are you upset with me?" Gabe asked. He sat directly across from Lily.

"No. Did you think I was?"

"Not exactly, but I guess I wouldn't blame you if you were."

Lily shook her head. "I understood why you called, and Jeff and I had a good talk."

"He seems to be doing well."

"Yes. Did he tell you he met a woman he's interested in?"

"No, but that's great."

"I think so too."

Gabe watched as she said this and could see that her feelings were genuine, but he wasn't sure she was ready to continue that line of conversation.

"So tell me," Gabe began again, "what did you do all day, Lily?"

"I read quite a bit. I visited the resort store. And I wrote a paper."

"On what?"

"Luke 1:18,19. In fact, I was going to ask you if you would be willing to critique it for me."

"Certainly."

"Do you want me to go and get it right now?"

"Sure."

Gabe watched as she dried her slim calves and feet and then waited by the pool for her to return. His heart was headed to a place of no return, and until Lily came back he begged God to lead him in the days ahead.

"Here it is," Lily said, presenting it to him just a short time later.

Gabe was so captivated that he immediately began to read.

"Zacharias said to the angel, 'How shall I know this for certain? For I am an old man, and my wife is advanced in years.' And the angel answered and said to him, 'I am Gabriel, who stands in the presence of God; and I have been sent to speak to you, to bring you this good news.'"

What Gabriel Understood

How often do I question You as Zacharias did, Lord? I think too often. How often do I do as I'm told or instructed from the first moment? Not often enough. I am just as swift as the old priest was to offer excuses for why I can't believe, obey, or trust You.

Is Gabriel at an advantage since he is a heavenly being? I'm so struck by his sentence about standing in Your presence, Lord. I try to picture it, but I'm not sure I can take in the full measure. Do You sit on a throne as Your subjects come before You? Or do You stand when You give orders of the utmost importance? But then, wouldn't all Your orders be of the utmost import?

And what of the subject who has come before You—Gabriel for instance? Can he even walk upright into the room if You are present, or must he crawl or come with face bowed low as he realizes into whose presence he has stepped?

But still it comes back to me. Have I ever once said I am Lily Walsh, and I stand in the presence of God? Nothing in me desires to compare myself to the special agent You have in Gabriel, but do I not stand in Your presence every time I open Your Word? Should not my heart, and possibly even my stance, show immeasurable reverence and awe as I realize that I have a way to You? Do I fully comprehend the magnitude of being in Your presence? Does my human heart stand a chance?

I think what Gabriel understood was who You are. At times I have asked myself if humans can survive a love as huge as Yours, but that is before I remember that You are willing to save us. And that You save us from Yourself, for Yourself.

Gabriel understood what I am still working to grasp: You are holy, just, mighty, all-powerful, and do not suffer fools lightly. But Gabriel also understood the love You have for the frail humans You've created, a love so great that You allow us to come to Your Word, and thus, stand in the presence of God.

Gabe lowered the paper and looked across to where Lily had sat back on the edge of the pool, her feet in the water again.

"This is excellent."

"Thank you."

"What made you think of studying this passage today?"

"I'm not sure that it was anything in particular. I was thinking quite a bit about my father, but with no answers or conclusions. The book I'm reading is interesting, but it was hard to concentrate because I was so hungry. So I eventually turned to Luke—it's my favorite Gospel—and tried reading very slowly and carefully. I was struck by Gabriel's response for the first time."

"If you could do today over, Lily, what would you do differently?"

"I would have told you this morning about the conversation with my father. I know you were in a hurry and needed to go, but I would have asked for your advice."

"What if there hadn't been anyone to ask? What if we'd all been called away and Wang hadn't heard the conversation?"

Lily thought for a moment.

"Maybe I would have tried to golf on my own, or maybe I would have eaten a little just to get through until you could teach me."

Gabe was upset with Lily's father all over again. He didn't want to show his anger, but he wished for answers to the questions rolling inside him. He suddenly wondered if Lily could help.

"It's hard for me to imagine a person like your father," Gabe admitted, working to be tactful. "I want to understand, but that type of treatment is a bit out of my realm. How do you deal with it?"

"When I'm at home or here?"

"Both."

"Well, at home I just know my place, and I keep it. And here, well," Lily had to stop. Gabe watched her shrug a little before she said, "Please do not picture me miserable and ill-treated at home, Gabe. My father does take some things too far, but I have been raised to submit to God and to authority, and I think that is a very good thing." Lily paused a moment before going on. "My father is not a young man. I know that does not excuse wrongdoing on his part, but he's been this way for a long time, and I wish to honor him, even from afar. It was foolish of him to ask me to promise, and just as foolish for me to agree, but even at that, I wanted to do everything I could to keep my word."

"I think your father must be so proud of you, Lily. I don't know how he could be otherwise."

"I think he is, at least most of the time. And it's very kind of you to say so, Gabe."

"It might be kind, Lily, but it's also true. I'm not trying to make you feel better, I'm giving you a genuine compliment. I too have worked hard to honor my mother, but I haven't come as close as you have."

Silence fell between them. Lily felt slightly uncomfortable and found her eyes lowering with embarrassment. She then realized she hadn't done that for a long time and saw very clearly how much she was changing.

The word "change" reminded Lily that one of the men at Bible study the night before had talked about change during his prayer request. This led to one more thought.

"May I ask you a question, Gabe?" Lily asked, all reserve falling away in her ongoing search for knowledge.

"Certainly."

"Why have we not been to Bible study on other Wednesday nights?"

"Oh, let me see. I think it was canceled the first week you were here because Harris was sick. The second week and third you were still quite burned, so Evan and Bailey stayed home. And now last night we finally all made it."

"What day did I come to the resort?"

"The fifth."

"And what's today?"

"September 30. Tomorrow is October 1."

Lily didn't know how so much life could have been lived in such a short time. Life was slower in her village in Kashien; everything moved at a greatly decelerated pace. Amid these thoughts, Lily realized that people could have been anywhere during the time when she was burned, and she would not have noticed or even cared. For a moment, a chill swept over her skin. It had been so awful, and right now she was tremendously relieved to be past it. At times her shoulders were still a little tender, but nothing compared to what they had been.

"What does that look on your face mean?"

Lily glanced up, not aware that she had been under Gabe's scrutiny.

"I was thinking about my sunburn."

Gabe only nodded. Knowing what a trauma that had been, he didn't need to hear more.

"Do I have a lesson of some type tomorrow?"

"I don't think so. What would you like to do?"

"Oh! I don't know."

"Must you do something?"

"What do you mean?"

"Only that a few days of lazing around might be nice. You've either been burned and in pain or going nonstop since you arrived. And don't forget, we leave for my mom's next week. There'll be plenty to learn there."

"Like what?"

"Well, they live in a neighborhood, so they have houses close by. You might find that interesting. There's a shopping mall within walking distance, and they have several boats."

Gabe smiled when he was the recipient of Lily's silent "oh." His heart did a flip-flop as he watched her eyes light up with anticipation. At the same time he prayed for wisdom and patience, because all he had wanted to do lately was take this woman in his arms and tell her he loved her.

〜

Kahaluu

"When Deanne called last night she mentioned that you have someone visiting right now, Ash. Is it a guest? I thought you still had time off."

"We are still off," Ashton answered his future mother-in-law, Anita Talbot. "Lily Walsh is staying with us. I think you've heard me talk about Jeff Walsh. Well, it's his sister. She's not in a cottage. She's actually staying with us in the house."

"Where does she live?" Hadden Talbot, Deanne's father, asked.

"Kashien. She's here visiting for three months."

"Is she enjoying it?"

"I think so. She tends to be quiet and hard to read, so I'm not exactly sure."

"Can you tell if she's falling for Gabe the way Deanne hopes?" This came from Anita, and Ashton smiled, thinking his fiancée had done quite a bit of sharing.

"I can't tell. I wish I could. Maybe Gabe can tell, but I'm in the dark on this one."

"You were in the dark on Deanne too," Anita now teased him, "so that doesn't surprise me a bit."

Ashton laughed but had to agree. He had been so afraid of saying the wrong thing and chasing Deanne away that he'd nearly scared her off with his silence.

"You know—" Ashton had a sudden thought— "I should probably remind Gabe of that. If he's like I was, he's afraid of making a mistake. But if Lily's the woman for him, then even if he blows it for a time, it will work out."

"What'll work out?" Mic asked as he joined them midsentence.

"Mic." His father said his name quietly before Ashton could explain. Mic had a tendency to enter a room talking, and Hadden was trying to make him aware of that fact.

"Oh, that's right," he remembered when he saw his father's face. He quietly joined the group and then looked up to find Ashton's eyes on him.

"How are you?" the older man asked.

"I'm all right. Is something wrong with Deanne?"

"Not that I know of. Do you know something?"

"No, but I know I missed what was said and wondered if it was about Deanne."

"It wasn't," Ashton stated simply, not willing to admit that he and his entire family were engaged in matchmaking. Anita had no such qualms.

"There's a young woman staying with Ash and the family. They all hope she and Gabe will get together."

"Is she cute?" Mic asked, looking very much like the high school boy that he was.

Ashton only laughed.

"What does she look like?" Anita now put in, just curious. "Is she Kashienese?"

"No, she's American, and she's very attractive, but I would not call her cute. She's too classy for that."

Not to risk giving his fiancée's parents the wrong impression, he didn't add that Lily was one of the sweetest women he had ever known.

"And in all of this," Hadden's dry voice now asked, "is Gabe interested in her, or is Deanne just doing a lot of wishful thinking?"

Ashton answered very quietly. "It occurs to me that my brother would be very embarrassed if he knew we were discussing this, so I would beg your discretion, but yes, Gabe is interested."

"We'll just pray for them, Ash," Anita said with understanding. "And we won't say anything when we visit in a few weeks."

"Thank you," Ashton said gratefully, and hoped that would be the end of the conversation. It was all too taxing. The woman he loved was far away, and that was proving to be very hard. His heart never banked on how difficult it would be to watch his brother fall for someone so close by and not have a clue where he stood with her.

Chapter Nineteen

Lily couldn't believe she was back on an airplane before it was time to go home. And this time she wasn't alone. The large, comforting presence of Gabe Kapaia was on one side of her; Ashton on the other. Lily glanced up at the female flight attendant until a man came down the aisle behind the woman, causing Lily to drop her eyes. The moment Lily's gaze was in her lap, she realized that the uniformed woman's eyes had lingered admiringly on the men who sat on either side of her. For the first time, Lily thought about what good-looking men they were.

From the time she was a child, Lily had longed for the dark complexion of the people of Kashien and knew now why the Kapaia family was so attractive to her: They looked as she had always dreamed of looking. Her hair was dark, but it wasn't the glossy black locks that both brothers could claim. And her eyes were green! In Lily's opinion she couldn't look less like an islander if she were blond-haired and blue-eyed.

"What goes on in that head of yours, Lily?" Gabe's voice came from her right.

The slim brunette looked up at him.

"I don't know what you mean."

"You're sitting very still with your eyes down. What are you thinking?"

"I was thinking about blond hair and blue eyes."

Gabe leaned forward in his seat to get a better angle on her face. His brows had shot up, and Lily could see that she had surprised him.

"You're not actually unhappy with your looks, are you, Lily?"

"Not exactly," Lily said rather slowly.

Gabe held her eyes for a moment, but she didn't elaborate. "Do you think you'll ever tell me what that meant?"

Lily suddenly found it impossible to explain. Feeling her face heat slightly as her tongue tied, Lily was glad when Gabe sat back with just a light touch to her arm.

Never had anyone read her as well as Gabe. Lily thought it uncanny. It was almost as if he knew what she was thinking. She had lost count of the times he asked her about her thoughts at the worst possible time.

A voice came over the intercom at that point, and Lily was glad for the distraction. She did everything the head flight attendant instructed: tray table up, seatbelt in place, bag stowed under the seat in front of her, exits located. A short time later, they were in the air.

～

Hilo, on the Big Island of Hawaii

Lily immediately saw what Gabe had been talking about. Carson and Gloria's home was on a palm-lined street with houses that sat on large parcels. With the rise of the lot, the ocean seemed a long way away, but Lily had been told that it could be seen from the back of the house, and the beach was an easy walk along a paved path.

The house she walked into with the rest of the family was spacious and smelled of flowers. The front door opened up into the living room, with a galley kitchen to the left. A hallway exited out of the living room, and somehow Lily knew that it must lead to bedrooms. A small family room was adjacent to the kitchen, and on the back of the house was a large covered porch.

While Lily was taking this in, she noticed Peter and Celia heading for a box of toys in the family room. She smiled at how well they knew their way around.

"Look!" Peter could be heard calling as he found new toys that his grandmother had added.

"Here, Lily," Carson, who was suddenly beside her, offered. "Come this way, and I'll show you your room."

"Oh, thank you," Lily replied, taking a moment to remember to look up. She was now quite at ease with Gabe, Evan, and Ashton, but having eye contact with other men still took a conscious effort.

Carson took Lily through the living room, both Gloria and Gabe bringing up the rear, to the large enclosed deck on the back of the house and into a small room where the walls were almost all windows. A daybed was made up, but the room was clearly for sitting and enjoying the view.

"Are the children in here with me?"

"No, we had planned that but decided to put you out here on your own. Will this be all right?" Gloria asked.

"Yes, thank you."

"This is Carson's runaway room," Gloria explained as she plumped a pillow on one of the chairs. "When he can't sleep, he comes out here and opens all the windows. Sometimes the sound of the ocean and wind can put him to sleep."

Lily opened her mouth but closed it again as she listened to Gloria telling her where she could store her things for the duration of her visit. After they had been thanked one last time, Carson and Gloria made their way back inside the house. Gabe stood at the door to speak to Lily.

"You didn't ask them if you would be in the way when Carson needs this room."

"I was thinking of doing that," Lily admitted.

"No!" Gabe exclaimed, eyes large with mock amazement.

Lily's hand came up to cover her smile, but her eyes gave her away. For the first time since she arrived, she tried to give as good as she had gotten.

"I've decided something."

"What's that?"

"I'm going to be so much trouble on this trip that you'll be changing your mind about bringing me."

"What will you do?"

Lily opened her mouth but nothing came out.

Gabe laughed at the bemused look on her face.

"I'll think of something!" she told him, hands coming to her waist.

"You do that," Gabe said very softly, his gaze warm.

A moment later Lily stood alone, Gabe's eyes still in her mind as she wondered at the strange fluttering she felt in her chest and stomach.

∼

"Have we been bad?" Peter asked after his father directed him inside and shut the door of their bedroom; Bailey and Celia were there too.

"No, Pete. Your mom and I just need to tell you and Celia about something. Okay?"

"Okay."

The four lay on the bed, heads close. Evan took a moment to look into the faces of his children, so like his beautiful wife with their soft, dark eyes and black hair. It occurred to him that it wouldn't hurt his feelings in the least to have another little person who looked just like them.

"Something special is going to happen in a few months, and we want you to know about it."

"What is it?" Peter asked.

"What's it?" Celia echoed.

"We're going to have a new baby at our house. Mama's going to have a baby."

Taking a moment to react, Peter asked, "A boy or a girl?"

"We don't know yet. We won't know until the baby comes."

"Do Grandma and Carson know?"

"No. We want to tell them, but first we wanted you to know."

"Can I tell?" Peter asked.

Evan and Bailey exchanged a look before Evan decided.

"I think that would be all right."

"I brought a special gift for Grandma's birthday, Pete," Bailey said. "It will help give the surprise away. So if you give her that, she'll figure it out."

"Where is it?"

"I want to." Celia had suddenly realized she was being left out, and her brow came down. Bailey and Peter moved off the bed to get the present from the luggage, but Evan kept his daughter on the bed to talk about her attitude.

A short time later the four were ready to go out. Evan asked Peter to let Celia share in the gift, and Bailey had a fit of giggles over the way they attempted to hold it between them.

"Okay," their father urged, "let's find Grandma."

"What's this?" Carson asked in a loud voice as soon as they'd come into the living room. "Looks like an early birthday present for someone!"

Gloria nearly shot in from the kitchen. It was a family joke how much she enjoyed gifts and her own birthday in particular, and Carson's loud tone had worked.

"An early gift?" she asked the adorable children who were holding it for her.

"Here, Grandma! Open it."

"Okay. Can you help me?" Gloria invited when she'd sat with the present in her lap.

"Mama's a baby," Celia chose to announce just then.

"What's that?" Gloria asked, not looking at her but trying to help Peter with the ribbon. A moment later she withdrew a bib, rattle, teething ring, and soft cloth baby book.

The family that was gathered watched as Bailey's mother looked down at Celia—just realizing what she'd said—back to the baby gifts in the box, and then up to her daughter.

"Oh, Bailey," Gloria said on a laugh as she came forward to hug her daughter. "When are you due?"

"It looks like June."

"And how are you feeling?"

"Other than being tired, I'm fine." Bailey lowered her voice and added, "I'm looking forward to having the kids stay with you."

"Well, then we agree on that. You can ask Carson if it's all I've talked about for weeks."

Mother and daughter hugged again, and Bailey thought, not for the first time, how wonderful a grandmother her mother had turned out to be.

~

Lily had stowed her things quite a while before, but she still lingered in the room assigned to her. In some ways, the resort's view of the ocean was better, but this was different, and thus fascinating. Lily watched a mother with two small children and then a couple who held hands and walked with heads close. She could see several runners, some running shoeless in the surf. Lily had brought her running shoes and shorts, but she didn't know if it would be appropriate to head out or not.

Now that's just what Gabe is talking about, Lily, she thought to herself. *You are so afraid of doing the wrong thing that you do nothing. You're the only one who knows what you're interested in, so the least you can do is ask someone's opinion on the subject.*

But even after this pep talk she sat still, not wanting to tell anyone what she was thinking. She was still sitting quietly when someone knocked on the door.

"Come in," she called from her seat by the window.

"Hello," Bailey said as she stuck her head around the corner. "Can CeCe and I visit?"

"Please do."

The door was opened and Celia ran for Lily, climbing into her lap as fast as she could maneuver.

"Mama's having babies!"

"Mama's having a baby?"

Celia nodded so fast that it looked as though she made herself dizzy.

"So you're going to be a big sister?"

Celia nodded this time, but it was far slower, her brow drawn in puzzlement. She finally turned to her mother.

"Lilyee says I'm big."

Bailey only laughed and then tried to explain. She was still speaking to her daughter when she looked up to see Lily looking back out the window, her eyes huge. Bailey followed her gaze and found herself thankful that it had first happened with just her and not when the men were present.

A woman was on the beach, and she had just slipped out of her cover-up to reveal a swimsuit of minuscule proportions. A two-piece outfit, it was little more than strings in the back with tiny scraps of fabric in the front. It wasn't unusual to see these types of suits on the beach at the resort, but of course the resort had been empty for Lily's visit.

Bailey's gaze now shifted to Lily, who had turned red in embarrassment.

"Haven't you ever seen a swimsuit like that, Lily?"

"No," she whispered. "Is she not ashamed?"

"Evidently not."

"I'm embarrassed for her."

"I think you might have seen something similar to that at the resort before now if we had guests."

Lily turned to Bailey with surprised eyes.

"Your guests dress like that?"

"Yes and no. We make it very clear that ours is a family atmosphere, so rarely does anyone come to the pool like that, but some couples want to swim only on the beach, and at times the women, and even the men, can be very immodest."

"So you're used to it?"

"No, I've never grown accustomed to it, and we talk to the kids about modesty issues whenever the time seems right. But these events go with the job, I'm afraid."

Lily nodded and glanced once more to the beach. The woman was lying down now, so her nudity wasn't as visible. Lily prayed for her, and then for her own attitude, finding it would be very easy to forget that this woman was loved by God.

"CeCe and I actually came with a mission, Lily," Bailey said. "We're having a snack in the kitchen and wondered if you were hungry."

"I am, thank you. Are you eating right now?"

"Yes. Come join us."

The ladies made their way inside and found Gloria serving up food to Ashton and Peter.

"Here they are," she said as the threesome approached. "Just in time for cheese and crackers. Have a seat, Lily, and tell me what you would like to drink."

"Oh, anything is fine, Mrs. Hana."

"Please call me Gloria. How about some juice?"

"Thank you."

"I've been making plans," Ashton told Lily when she sat across from him.

"Okay."

"You're on a whole new island and you need to learn some new things."

"Oh, all right. Do you have books for me to read and study?"

Ashton's grin was downright cheeky as he admitted, "No, my idea is for Gabe to take you around."

Lily laughed a little. "Don't you think Gabe might have better things to do?"

"No," Ashton blew her comment off, his hand waving to make his point. "As long as he doesn't have to take anyone to the zoo, he would love to show you around the area."

Lily looked a bit skeptical, but Ashton only smiled again. And because Gloria was giving her something to eat and Peter was asking her a question, she let the matter go. However, not an hour after Evan, Gabe, and Carson arrived back, Gabe sought out Lily on the porch that led to her bedroom and invited her to go sight-seeing in the morning.

"Do you really have time for that, Gabe?"

"Sure. We'll use Mom's car and see everything there is to see. I think you'll love it."

"But will you?" Lily boldly asked for the first time.

Gabe nearly did a second glance but managed to keep his pleasure inside.

"Trust me, Lily, I would not have offered if I didn't want to. And I know all the great places to visit."

"Have you lived here on the Big Island, Gabe?"

"No, but when I was in the midst of the cancer, I spent some of my recovery time here with Mom and Carson."

"Will it bring back bad memories for you now?"

Gabe smiled. "It's nice of you to ask, but it feels so good to feel good, Lily, that the memories fade a little more all the time."

"May I ask you something?"

"Sure."

"Do you ever fear it will come back? I mean, I'm dreading just the long plane ride back to Kashien. I can't imagine wondering what it would be like to dread the return of cancer."

"I do have moments when I think that way, but I've learned that God doesn't do things without reason. The cancer won't come back unless that's what's best for me."

"It's a huge trust issue, isn't it?"

"Yes, and I must be honest and tell you that it's harder to trust in some areas than others, but the possibility of the cancer returning is usually a settled issue for me."

"What isn't so settled for you?" Lily asked, but immediately shook her head. "I'm sorry. That was intrusive of me. Please don't feel you must answer."

"No, I don't mind at all. It's probably good for me to talk about it."

Lily nodded and waited for Gabe to define what he meant by it.

"I was only 22 when the cancer was diagnosed. We were all in shock—mostly me—and so when the doctors told me I needed to prepare ahead of time if I ever wanted to have children of my own, I didn't do anything. I guess I had accepted the fact that I probably wouldn't live through the ordeal, so I missed my chance."

"And that's what plagues you at times?"

"Yes."

"So you don't believe in adoption?" Lily asked, hardly believing she had voiced that thought.

"I think adoption is wonderful, but I'm not certain with my medical history that I would ever qualify."

Lily nodded. "I've read about how hard adoption can be in America."

"It's not hard in Kashien?"

"To adopt a baby? No. In fact, if I don't marry, I hope to adopt at least two children. I think it's best if children have a father and a mother, but I would still like to try."

"Is it easier for folks who live in Kashien?"

Lily looked at him and saw that he was listening very closely.

"Not necessarily. As you can guess, boys are more treasured, so more questions might be asked, but many babies leave the country every year."

Gabe had many other things he wanted to know, but Evan and Peter joined them on the porch before he could continue.

"Am I interrupting?" Peter asked, and Lily could see that Evan had schooled him before they came out.

"We were talking, Peter, but that's fine," Gabe said. "What did you need?"

"I want to know if Lily can go to the beach with me for a little while before supper."

"Yes, I can," Lily said right away. "Shall we go now?"

He nodded and looked so sweet that Lily didn't think she could deny him anything.

"I was going to ask you, Peter," Lily said as she stood, "when is your grandma's birthday party?"

"Friday night. Niko will be here."

"Who is Niko?"

"His real name is Nikolo, but we call him Niko."

"How do you know him?" Lily tried again.

Still on the porch, Evan and Gabe missed the rest of Peter's answer as he and Lily walked toward the path that led to the beach.

"Did we come out at the worst possible time?" Evan asked, eyes on his brother-in-law.

"No, it's all right. We're headed off tomorrow, so if I want to pick the conversation up again, I'll have a chance then."

"How are things going?"

Gabe sighed. "Well, all lights are green. I just don't know how to put my foot on the gas."

"Meaning?"

"Meaning Jeff couldn't be more happy, and all of you are ecstatic, but Lily doesn't have a clue."

"What will you do?"

"I won't be sneaky; I can tell you that. If Lily and I can't dialogue over the way I'm feeling, then there's no hope."

"I can see how you would want that, Gabe, but you might need to give her time once you bring the subject up."

"That's true," Gabe agreed, his eyes still on Lily and Peter's progress. "I know she's comfortable with me, and that's at least a start."

"That's how things began with Bales and me."

"Where is Bailey? I haven't seen her for hours."

"Sleeping. She was in a bit of panic about not wanting to forget any of the kids' things and wore herself out before we left."

"Her condition doesn't help, either. I remember at the end with Celia she slept all the time."

"Yeah. It's pretty typical to be worn out at the beginning and end."

Talk about naps made both men drowsy. Evan slouched down in his seat, and Gabe watched Lily in the distance until he couldn't keep his lids open. Not surprisingly, he dozed off with her on his mind.

Chapter Twenty

"The Big Island is famous for its orchids," the tour guide at Orchids of Hawaii said. Lily hung on every word, Gabe at her side. The colors and varieties they were shown were spectacular. Following the brief tour, they were taken inside and shown how to make leis.

Again Lily paid close attention, but this was a challenge. She concentrated through each step, but her lei did *not* look like Gabe's.

"How did you do that?" she asked when she looked over to see a perfect flower necklace hanging from his hand.

"I've had a little more practice than you have," he told her.

"I broke a few of my flowers," she told him, brow lowered in Celia fashion. "You didn't break any!"

Gabe had all he could do not to shout with laughter.

"Tell me what I did wrong."

"It's your first time, that's all."

Lily scowled down at her flowers and realized it wasn't such a bad job after all, but compared to Gabe's and the ones in the gift shop, it lacked a bit.

"I was going to give this to you," Lily told him, "but I don't think it's nice enough."

"It's fine," Gabe said as he placed his own necklace around her, placing his hands on her shoulders so he could bend and kiss her on both cheeks.

"Thank you," she said softly, a little color coming to her face, not out of embarrassment, but pleasure. "You don't have to wear mine if you don't want to."

"I would be proud to wear yours."

Gabe wanted to tease her about not getting kissed when she put it around his neck, but another couple was close by, so he kept the thought to himself.

With that the time was over and they made their way out to the car. They buckled up once the air-conditioning was blasting into their faces, and Gabe pulled onto the street.

"Do you think you would like lunch now, or maybe you would like to see the zoo?"

Lily turned to look at him.

"Ashton said you don't like to take anyone to the zoo."

"Well, you're not just anyone. You're special."

Lily continued to look at him.

"Because I'm Jeff's sister," she stated.

"Well, that was the reason at the beginning," Gabe said, finding it easy to answer and use the excuse of driving to spare him from looking in her direction.

"But it's not the reason now?"

"Not the main reason, no."

Lily felt something she'd never known before. Just the odd sensation alone should have been enough to make her back down and stay quiet, but words came out of her before she could stop them.

"What's the main reason now?"

As though he'd timed it, the light turned red and Gabe had to stop. He turned to the woman who sat staring at him, met her eyes, and answered.

"The reason now is that I know who Lily is. She's more than just Jeff's sister. She's smart, and godly, and beautiful. But most of all, she's the sweetest woman I've ever known."

The two stared at each other until the light changed. When Gabe turned back to drive, Lily also looked out through the wind-shield and worked at breathing.

"What are you thinking, Lily?" Gabe had to ask as he negoti-ated the car through traffic.

Sounding slightly breathless, Lily answered, "That it would be nice to talk to Jeff right now."

"What would you say to him?"

"I would ask him what he thinks of the two of us having feel-ings for each other."

"He's all for it."

Lily's head turned swiftly back to Gabe.

"You've talked to him?"

"I wrote him about my feelings, and then when I called him last week, he and I talked after you got off the phone."

"Can you tell me what he said?"

"He said that the only good reason he could find for his going away was if the two of us fell for each other."

"He said that?" Lily asked, her eyes huge and mouth opened. "Jefferson Walsh said that?"

Gabe had to smile. "That's what he said."

For a full minute the car was utterly silent. Gabe had no idea where he was going; he just drove. Lily was the first to speak.

"Gabe, I don't want to go to the zoo. I just want to sit some-where and talk, even if it's just in the car. Can we do that?"

"We certainly can," Gabe answered, even as his heart tried to beat out of his chest.

Just as soon as he was able, he headed the car into a shady, palm-covered area. Using the automatic controls on his side, Gabe put all the windows down before turning the engine off. Removing his seat belt, he shifted to see Lily. His heart sank when he saw tears in her eyes.

"Can you tell me why you're ready to cry?"

Lily looked out over the hood.

"I think I can, if it's all right not to look at you."

"That's fine."

"I feel almost disloyal," Lily admitted after a few moments. Hot air was coming at her from all sides, but she took little notice. "I love my father and my brother, but no one has ever made me feel as special as you have."

Lily glanced at him and then away. "At first I understood that it was who you are—a warm, caring person—but then I found myself hoping it could be more. I felt so selfish at times, but I wanted the way you treated me to be more than just the kind way you treat everyone."

"Do you now understand that it is?"

"I think so, but part of my heart is afraid to believe it. I know how I'm feeling, but I never really imagined that you might be feeling something too."

Gabe gave a soft laugh. "Well, it's good to know that I didn't overwhelm you. I thought the whole world could tell that I was falling for you."

Lily turned to look at him, and since Gabe had never taken his eyes off her, he was waiting to meet her eyes.

"Can it be possible that I've known you only a month?" Lily asked.

Gabe smiled. "It feels like much longer, doesn't it? But it's probably a good idea if we both remember that it has been a short time."

Lily nodded. "Feelings run fast. That's what my friend Ling-lei would say."

"Ling-lei sounds like a wise woman."

Lily nodded. "She's a special friend and, yes, she is wise. She's taught me much and doesn't even know it."

"Why doesn't she know it?"

"Because it's not 'book learning,' as she would call it. She's taught me by example."

"In what way?"

"Like so many women in the village, Ling is uneducated, so I'm teaching her to read. Because of that, she thinks I'm smart enough to have all the answers, but she's taught me so much about respect and how to love and take care of others, especially children.

"She was the person who was with me the most after my mother died. She's too young to be my mother, but she could easily be my sister."

"It sounds like she is," Gabe said. "A sister of your heart."

Lily looked at him. "That's what I mean. You're always so understanding and caring." Lily made herself keep eye contact, even as she felt her cheeks heat. "I didn't know anyone like you existed."

"Nor I you," Gabe said and reached for her hand.

Lily melted a little when their fingers met.

"I'm going to look so forward to getting to know you, Lily Walsh."

Lily found herself smiling. Gabe smiled too but noticed a small bead of sweat near Lily's temple.

"How about we find a nice, air-conditioned place to eat lunch?"

"That sounds very nice."

Gabe gave her fingers a little squeeze before letting go, and when the car's air-conditioning blew in her face, Lily closed her eyes.

I'm going to lose my heart to this man, Father, if I haven't already. I've never felt this way before, and I think that's why I know what my heart is going to do. Help me. I don't even know what I need help with, but please help me today.

～

"That's a faraway look," Evan said to his wife as he joined both Bailey and her mother on the porch.

"I was thinking about Ashton," she said with a drowsy sigh. "I think he misses Deanne so much that he doesn't quite know what to do with himself."

"He's trying, though," Evan said.

"Has he spoken to you, Evan?" Gloria asked.

"Briefly. He wants to be thankful, and he's working to be, but he is very distracted, more so than he thought he would be in Deanne's absence."

The object of their conversation was coming toward them on the path, Celia on his back and Peter hanging on his front.

"He'll make it," Evan said confidently.

The women didn't reply, but watching Ashton laughing with his niece and nephew, they were inclined to agree.

～

"How is that sandwich?"

"Very good. Do you want to try some?"

"No, I'm in good shape. How about you? Do you want some of this fruit?"

"Maybe just a piece."

Gabe pushed his dish toward Lily, but she hesitated.

"May I change my mind and take two?"

His sigh was huge. "If you have to."

Lily heard his long-suffering tone and smiled as she speared a chunk of papaya and a slice of kiwi.

"And you're sure you don't want any of mine?"

"Yes. If you order dessert I might steal some, but I'm not all that crazy about corned beef."

"Is that what I'm eating?"

Gabe set his fork down.

"Did you not know what you ordered?"

"Yes and no. I knew it was a sandwich, but not what kind."

"So why did you order that?"

"Because the woman taking our order seemed to be in a hurry, so I just asked for the special."

"And you've never had a Reuben before?"

Lily shook her head.

"My dad used to love them. You're eating corned beef, sauerkraut, Thousand Island dressing, and Swiss cheese on grilled rye bread."

Lily looked down at her sandwich in surprise.

"All that on one sandwich?"

"Yes, it's an unusual combination, but there are folks who love them."

"It is good."

Gabe looked thoughtful. "I was a kid the last time I tried one; maybe I should try again."

"Here." Lily lifted the sandwich toward him. "Have some bites."

For Gabe there was an intimacy in her offering him the sandwich she had been eating, but as he took a bite he knew Lily was oblivious to it. She was just being her usual sweet self.

"How is it?" Lily asked, leaning forward expectantly.

"It's good!" he said with surprise.

"Keep it. I'll eat the other half."

"Thank you."

Lily smiled as she went back to her plate, picking up a potato chip to put into her mouth.

"What's become your favorite food since arriving in Hawaii?" Gabe asked.

The chip was still in Lily's mouth, so it wasn't hard to decide. "Whatever I'm eating at the time," she said but then paused. "Unless gum is a food."

"You and your gum," Gabe teased. "I think we're talking about a serious addiction here."

"You might be right. I don't know what I'll do when I go back to Kashien."

Those words silenced the couple. They ate for a time, just the sounds of the restaurant and other diners around them.

"Is there any chance you could stay?"

"You mean longer or permanently?"

"Permanently."

"No. I told my father I would return to him. I will extend my trip if Jeff does not come home on time, but I told my father I would be back."

"I do admire the respect you show your father, Lily, but your leaving is not going to be fun for me."

"Will you write to me?"

"Yes, but I hope you won't be away too long."

Lily's face filled with regret. "It's expensive to come back, Gabe. I can't think it would be very soon."

"If money is the only problem, Lily, then it's not a problem at all."

"My father would never agree."

"Tell me about him."

Lily's head tipped. "He's a man who loves people the way he thinks they need to be loved. He would never see himself as harsh, only just. But that's not the most difficult part. The hardest part only occurred to me after I arrived here."

"What is it?"

"You can't discuss things with him. I think you say 'dialogue.'"

Gabe nodded. "It's funny you should mention that. All I've prayed for the last week is that we would be able to dialogue about our feelings for each other. When you asked if we could skip the zoo and just talk, I knew that God had gone before us. I don't know what the future looks like, but being able to dialogue with you has meant everything to me.

"But now you tell me about your father, and I can't help but ask myself how you can be so open and ready to talk when your father isn't. Why aren't you more like him?"

"Because I've had people to talk with all along, Ling being one of them. Women in my country learn to be responders. If someone is kind to us, we respond with kindness. If someone is harsh, we know to retreat and hold our place and not trust that person so swiftly the next time. I have many kind women friends in Kashien, but to most Kashienese males women are invisible. Outside of Jeff, you are the first man who has treated me with deference. If my father would do the same, we could dialogue too."

"Your father doesn't know what he's missing."

Lily felt shy at the compliment and dropped her eyes, but not before thanking Gabe. They both went back to their food, but not two minutes passed before they were talking again.

～

"Hey, Mom," Gabe sought her out in the family room as soon as they were back at the house, "I'm going to let Lily use the phone in your room. Is that all right?"

"Certainly. Did you two have a good time?"

"Yes. Very."

Gabe found Lily still by the front door and took her through the living room and down the hall.

"Are you sure about this?" Lily asked for the fourth time.

"Yes. Just give him a call and tell him we're at this number. I know you want to talk to him."

"But the cost. We'll be back at your house on Saturday."

Gabe looked at her. He didn't want to treat her like a child, even though the temptation to protect her was very strong within him. He made himself listen and not roll over the top of her objections.

"So it's really okay that you wait? You're not eager to discuss any of this with Jeff right now?"

"No, I'm fine. I would like to talk to him, but I can wait until we get back."

"Okay," Gabe agreed, "but just tell me if you change your mind. Don't worry about the cost; Mom and Carson won't give it any thought. If you want to talk to Jeff sooner than Saturday, say the word."

"I will. Thank you."

Standing in the hallway outside the bedroom door, Gabe looked down at her. Lily looked back. With a gentle hand, Gabe pushed the hair from her forehead and then placed his hand on her slim shoulder.

"Of all the things we need to talk about in the weeks to come, the one that's most on my mind is the conversation that we started on the porch yesterday."

Lily nodded. "Were you serious about your feelings on adoption? Could you raise another person's child?"

"I think I could, but there are other issues just as important as that. How would you feel if you could never be pregnant? What if you could never have a biological child?"

Lily looked thoughtful. "I see what you mean. My first response is to say I'd be fine, but it would be wise if I think about it for a time."

"Good. Tell me when you're ready to talk some more."

"Okay."

The twosome went in search of the family and found them here and there. They settled in the family room to talk to Gloria, who was keeping an eye on Celia so Bailey could sleep. And it didn't take long for Gloria to see that something had changed.

"Where did you eat?"

"At Mo's."

"That's one of my favorites. Did you have a Reuben?" Gloria asked to tease her son.

"How did you know?" Lily asked.

Gloria laughed. "Did you really have a Reuben?"

The three had a good laugh as Gabe explained what had happened.

"So after all these years, you find you like Reubens." Gloria was clearly pleased. "Your father would be delighted."

Gabe was telling her how he'd thought of his father in the restaurant when Carson joined the group, Peter and Evan in his wake.

"You're just the lady I'm looking for," Carson said to Lily as he took a seat next to his wife. "I have a question for you."

"Okay," Lily answered, reminding herself to look up.

"What books of the Bible have you translated into Kashienese?"

"Oh, let me see. All of James, 1 Peter, and John. Then select passages from Psalms and Proverbs. Right now I'm working my way through Genesis."

"Is that all?" Gabe teased from beside her, and Lily turned to smile at him.

Carson, however, was not finished with the subject.

"So by the time you're done," he asked, "do you basically have the books memorized?"

"Pretty much."

"Give us James," he commanded good-naturedly.

Everyone laughed when Lily said, "In English or Kashienese?"

"English, please," Carson got out between chuckles, but then stopped Lily before she could start. "Can I test you in James?"

"Certainly."

Carson went for the Bible he and Gloria kept on the kitchen table, excitement showing in his eyes.

"Okay," he began once he'd found the text, "give us James 2:5."

"Listen, my beloved brethren: did not God choose the poor of this world to be rich in faith and heirs of the kingdom which He promised to those who love Him?"

"Word perfect! How about 1:8? What kind of man is unstable in all his ways?"

"A double-minded man."

"That's two for two," Carson said, now warmer to his subject than ever. "How about 4:10?"

"Quote it?"

"Yes, please."

"Humble yourselves in the presence of the Lord, and He will exalt you."

Carson beamed at her. "That was great."

"You don't have a television at home, do you, Lily?" Evan asked with a smile.

Lily smiled back at him, the fondness showing in her eyes. "No, not even a radio."

"Is it terribly time-consuming for you?" Gloria asked.

"It would be if I didn't control it. Every other week I devote three days to it, and on the off week just one day. My father still wants me involved in the village and not spending all of my time bent over the translating."

"So you know Greek and Hebrew?" Carson asked.

"Yes, my father was taught those languages in seminary and he has taught me."

"And how long does it take to do just one verse?"

"It depends on where I am in the text. I try to stay within the context of the passage. So if I'm just starting, it's very long and drawn out, but once I know where I am, it moves smoother until the story line changes. Genesis has been the most challenging that way."

"And you've been doing this for how long?"

"Since I was 15, so about nine years."

"Is there anything about translation you don't like?" Gabe asked from beside her, and Lily thought him most perceptive.

"When the church isn't doing well, I sometimes ask myself why I bother. If I'm not careful, I can have a poor attitude."

"So what do you do to combat that?"

"I remind myself that I'm not doing this for this life but for eternity, and that it's a privilege to be in God's Word for any reason."

Gabe smiled into her eyes, and Lily smiled back. For a few moments the couple just looked at each other, something that only the children in the room did not notice.

Chapter Twenty-One

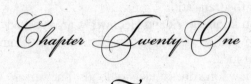

"Lily, this is Melika," Gloria said on Friday afternoon, "Carson's daughter, and her husband, Koma."

"It's a pleasure to meet you," Lily told the couple who had come for Gloria's birthday party.

"That little streak of lightning that ran to find Peter is Niko," the birthday girl continued, "and the butterball in Carson's arms is Kimi."

"How old is your daughter?" Lily asked Melika, finding it easier to meet her eyes.

"Ten months, and the apple of her grandfather's eye."

"She's beautiful."

"Well, we tend to think so," Melika admitted, "but then we admit to being biased as well."

"Can you wave at Lily?" Carson took Kimi's arm and moved it. "Wave at Lily."

"I can do waves," Celia came close to Grandpa Carson's knee to say.

"Of course you can," he said as he gently put her on his other knee, needing no time at all to see the jealousy. "You're such a big girl," he praised her as she cuddled close.

Celia heard him, but at the moment she noticed Kimi watching her. The two little girls grinned at each other and, a moment later, Carson put them both on the rug. Kimi took only a moment to crawl over and try to sit on Celia. That three-year-old laughed in delight, which made everyone in the room laugh with her.

Lily saw her opportunity and rose quietly. She had volunteered
to help Gloria in the kitchen and still had a few jobs to do. This
was where Gabe found her.

"Oh, what's this?" he asked when he saw the little hors d'oeuvres
she was putting together.

"I don't know what they're called, but your mother showed
me how to make them."

"Can I try one?"

"Yes, but take it from this side. The others have mustard."

"So my secret's out," he stated as he leaned against the counter
and took a bite of what looked like a tiny hot dog wrapped in a
crust.

"What secret?"

"That I don't like mustard."

"Now that you mention it," Lily teased, "you have been rather
difficult. You don't like corned beef, and you don't like mustard.
I'm starting to wonder about you, Gabriel Kapaia."

"Is that so?"

"Yes, it is," she told him, not able to hide her smile as he did
so often with her.

"Okay, I'll make a deal with you. I'll keep trying corned beef if
you'll go swimming with me after we get back."

"Why wouldn't I go swimming with you?"

"Because you don't like to be out in your swimsuit."

"Oh, that's right." Lily paused as she thought about it, remembering back to the day she and Jeff purchased it. "Why do you
want to go swimming with me?"

Gabe hesitated. They were alone in the kitchen, but that could
change at any moment.

"Ask me later."

"Okay," Lily said, still watching him. "Is it something bad?"

"No, but the answer isn't a short one, and I don't want us to be
interrupted."

"Okay," Carson's voice came to them even before he showed up, "we're headed into the kitchen now, and yes! We have found some people."

Gabe began to laugh as Carson approached with a video camera held so he could view the tiny screen.

"You'll have to get used to this, Lily. Carson has taped all of Mom's birthdays since the day they were married."

"How does it work?" Lily asked, fascinated with the small camera.

"Come over here, and I'll show you," Carson offered. "You stay there and pose, Gabe."

Gabe tried for a sophisticated and debonair look and then stuck his stomach out and slouched.

"Which one did you like?" he asked innocently.

Lily was trying not to laugh because Carson was taking the time to explain his camera to her, but it wasn't easy.

"Okay now, Lily," Carson instructed, "you get in front of the camera and wish Gloria a happy birthday."

Lily felt suddenly shy about this but gave it her best shot.

"Happy birthday, Gloria. You do me an honor when you include me in your special celebration. Thank you for your wonderful hospitality in this beautiful home. I pray God's blessings on you today and in the year to come."

Carson hit the pause button and lowered the camera.

"Was that all right?"

"That was great, Lily. No one has ever mentioned honor before. What was that phrase you used?"

"I think I said that I'm honored because Gloria included me."

"And honor is important in your village?"

"Honor is important all over Kashien. In fact, it's so important that I can't find the English words to describe it."

"Say it in Kashienese."

Glad that he was not recording her, Lily quietly vocalized the foreign words that spoke of the high value of honor—not just her own honor, but also that of others.

"And what word or words in all of that don't translate?" Gabe asked.

Lily told him and helped him pronounce it when he asked her. Carson put the tape back on for this and then thanked them when he was ready to move on.

"I'm falling in love with you," Gabe whispered the moment they were alone. "You know that, don't you, Lily?"

"How is it possible, Gabe, that we care so much about each other after such a short time?"

"I think it's because of our connection—" Gabe had no choice but to cut off when Bailey and Celia came looking for a drink, but somehow Lily knew that Gabe was going to mention her brother. She went back to work on the hors d'oeuvres, her hands moving without a lot of thought as her mind was centered on her brother and how well she knew Gabe because of him.

The party was an unqualified success. Carson's son and his family had come just before the meal, and with 18 in the house, it had been a loud and joyous celebration. The children were drooping a bit—Celia had already been put to bed, and the two babies were sound asleep in laps—when Gabe asked Lily to go for a walk with him. After they left, the adult conversation in the living room turned to the absent couple.

"Am I out of line," Carson's son, Kale, asked, "to ask if Gabe and Lily are seeing each other?"

"We think so, Kale," Evan took the liberty to answer, "but it's rather new."

"As in today," Ashton put in. "Or have I had my head in the sand?"

"No, I think you're right. Something must have happened when they were out today."

"And Lily is here for how much longer?"

"Till the end of November, but I think she's talking about delaying her departure if Jeff doesn't come back on time."

"Did you hear about that, Kale?" Melika said to her brother. "She had no more arrived than Jeff was called away. She was only coming for three months, and he was sent away for two of those."

"How did she handle it?"

"Like she handles everything," Bailey answered. "With quiet grace and dignity."

"And does that come from her upbringing?"

"I would say so, yes," Bailey answered before Evan spoke again.

"And the funny part is how sorry we all felt for her. She didn't know what a bread machine was. She had never used a computer or learned to swim, and we thought in some ways she was just a little bit pathetic. But she's never been distracted by the media, so she's had all sorts of time to read and learn.

"One night we watched a movie that had scenes from a quiz show. Some of the questions were impossible, but she knew every answer."

"Not to mention having books of the Bible memorized," Carson added.

"Entire books?" Koma asked.

Carson smiled hugely as he nodded. "I quizzed her on the book of James. You can give the reference of any verse and she'll recite it for you."

"And you think Gabe has fallen for her?" Lydia, Kale's wife, asked.

"I hope so," both Gloria and Bailey said at the exact same time, putting the room into enough laughter to wake the babies.

～

"Was it rude of us to leave the party, Gabe?" Lily asked as they walked side by side down the beach path.

"No, I don't think so. We've had good visits with everyone, and things are winding down. When the two families get together, you never know—they might still be talking when we get back."

Lily didn't reply to this. It was nice just to walk in the warm sand and feel the breeze on her face. The sky looked extra wide tonight and full of stars. Lily could have easily lain down and counted them until she fell asleep.

"I want to answer your question now, Lily."

"Oh, all right, Gabe. I'm glad you remembered."

Gabe took a moment to start, his voice sincere.

"The water and swimming have been major parts of my life since the day I was born. I've used water for exercise, for fun, for sports, and at times for therapy. I've watched other people use it for romance. I've watched my sister and her husband and Ash and Deanne cavort and chase each other in the water, and they made me wish for someone special of my own. I'm not suggesting anything improper, but I want to go swimming with you, Lily. It's something I want to share with you. I want to lie back on the surface of the pool and float and talk while we look at the clouds. I want to sit in the hot tub and hold your hand."

The man in him wanted to do more than that, but he knew he couldn't let his mind go there. The last thing he wanted to do was give Lily the impression that he couldn't control himself.

"Thank you for telling me."

"Did I say too much? Are you afraid to swim with me now?"

"No, but it is hard to be outside my room with so little on. I'm not used to that."

"First of all, I want to say that I think your swimsuit is very modest, Lily, but beyond that, do you feel that way even if it's just me swimming with you?"

"I think I do feel more comfortable with you, Gabe, but how would I know that it would be just you?"

"The family has a schedule."

Lily looked at him. "A schedule?"

"In a loose sort of way, yes. Right now only Bales and Evan use it, but once Ash and Deanne are married, I'm sure they'll want some time alone in the pool too."

"How does it work?"

"The pool and hot tub close to the public at 9:00. If Evan and Bailey want to be alone at the pool, they tack a ribbon on the bulletin board in the kitchen."

Had there been any more light, Gabe would have witnessed one of Lily's silent "ohs."

"Please don't misunderstand me, Lily. I'm not suggesting that we head alone to the pool at night, but I do want to swim with you, both in the pool and in the ocean."

"I've never swum in the ocean."

"It's very safe in the bay."

"Is that the almost-round-looking area over by the restaurant?"

"That's the one. It's a great place to swim."

Lily nodded, not thinking about the fact that Gabe couldn't see her. He had taken them in a wide circle, and they were now headed back toward the house. It was well lit from within, and the sight made Lily feel warm.

"I'll swim with you, Gabe." Lily suddenly realized she needed to give this man an answer. "I can't say that I'm completely comfortable with it, but I would like to try."

"Oh, Lily," Gabe said on a sigh, "you do wonders for my heart."

"How is that?"

"You don't really know, do you?"

"No, I don't think I do."

She sounded so uncertain that Gabe almost reached for her hand.

"Let's just say," he said kindly, "that you're one of the bravest people I've ever known."

Lily had all she could do not to look around.

"Were you talking about me?" she finally asked.

Gabe's laughter sounded in the night, but he didn't answer. Fatigue, both emotional and physical, was starting to find him. On top of that, they were almost back to the house.

"I shouldn't have said that unless I was willing to explain myself right now, Lil, but I must admit to you that my brain is getting fuzzy."

Lily wasn't tired at all, but she still understood. "Can we talk about it another time?"

"Absolutely. Thanks for understanding."

They finished the walk back to the house in silence, Lily thinking on the events of the day and all they had talked about.

Getting to know someone is nothing like I imagined, she ended up telling the Lord, a smile in her heart. *But I'm still having fun.*

～

"Will you miss the children?" Lily asked Bailey once they were in the van and leaving the airport for home.

"Yes, but this will still be good for me. The week will alternately drag and race by, and before I know it, they'll be back, and I'll be more than ready to have them. However, Evan has already told me to rest and not work on projects like I usually do when they're gone."

Lily smiled. She could well imagine how easy it would be to dash around and get things done when you finally had the time, but Evan was wise. Even though the projects would be waiting, Bailey should rest while she had the chance.

And at the moment it seemed everyone in the van felt that way. The remainder of the ride was finished rather quietly. Lily's thoughts roamed to many places until the resort house came into view. Then she smiled. It had just been a few days, but now it was familiar and dear. The sight of it also brought about questions. Had Gabe lived there all his life? Lily thought he had but suddenly wasn't certain.

"I need a nap," Ashton proclaimed as he climbed from the back of the van.

"And you don't even have CeCe here to use as an excuse," Evan teased him.

"True enough. I guess I'll just have to lie on the sofa and watch television."

"Behind your eyelids," Gabe remarked dryly.

The five of them trooped into the house, luggage in hand, and disappeared in various directions. Lily was going to take her bag to her room, but Gabe stopped her at the bottom of the stairs.

"If you want to call Jeff, the number's on Bailey's desk."

"Okay. Thank you."

Lily then looked at him, and because no one was close by, decided to ask what was on her mind.

"Do you want me to call him, Gabe? Is there some reason you're concerned?"

"I'm only thinking about your needs. There might be things on your mind that you need to bounce off someone. I don't want you to hesitate to call Jeff and do that."

Lily nodded and looked thoughtful. Gabe found her so appealing that he smiled.

"*Are* there things on your mind?" he dipped his head a little to ask, liking it when he could look directly into her face.

Lily smiled. "Just a few."

"Want to share?"

"What I would tell Jeff, you mean?"

Gabe shook his head. "I was just teasing you. If I drag everything out of you, I will have spoiled your time to share private thoughts with your brother."

"But I do want to ask your opinion on something," Lily continued.

"Okay."

"Can love develop out of liking someone?"

"I certainly think so. What do you think?"

"I don't honestly know."

"Where did that question come from?" Gabe asked, just as Evan came down the stairs. He sailed right past them, but Gabe still took Lily's arm and led her to the sitting area of the living room. When they had sat side by side on one of the love seats, Gabe repeated his question.

"Do I have to look at you when I answer?" Lily needed to know.

"No."

Lily's eyes dropped to her lap. "I realized this morning, when I was talking to the Lord about all of this, that I like you more than anyone I've ever known." Lily glanced at him but looked down again. "I think that's where the question must have come from."

"I like you too," Gabe said softly, not really afraid of being overheard but wanting to go slow and easy with these new feelings. "I've liked you for a long time, even before we met."

"Did Jeff talk about me that much?"

"Not constantly, but enough that I knew you were special."

"Gabe," Lily said, having just remembered his earlier comments, "I need to tell you that I have also been thinking about the adoption issue. I've realized how special it is that Bailey is expecting right now."

Gabe waited, not sure where she was headed.

"However, I'm not jealous, Gabe, not in the least. My mind has also been on my friend Ling. She was seven months along in her pregnancy when I left. I'm not jealous of her either, but if I had the chance and was needed, I would take her children and raise them as my own. Bailey's too. In a heartbeat I would gladly become a mother to Peter and Celia, or to my friend Ling's children, Faith, Hope, and Charity, and love them with all my heart. I think it's wise that this subject stays open between us, but this is the way I feel right now."

"Thank you for telling me. I've had more time to accept the situation, but at times I've struggled terribly. Never having considered foreign adoption, I now have a whole new direction in which to think. I thought I would have to content myself with being an uncle, but you've helped me to see that there might be challenges in whole new ways."

"I don't think I know what you mean."

"I'm not borrowing trouble, Lily, but I am trying to be practical. The first obstacle in the path is that I can't father children myself. The second frustration is that I would probably never qualify for a U.S. adoption. I would be foolish to think that all will be smooth sailing now that you've suggested foreign adoption. Some complication could easily come up on that road as well.

"All that to say I've got to keep trusting and not holding on too tightly to what I think would be the ideal. I've got to let God, in His time, introduce me to all of the options. Have you heard of foster child care?"

"Yes, I've read about that."

"It would be my goal for us to adopt so the children would be our own, but I need to hold that loosely because it might not be God's plan. Foster parenting might be the way God could use us best."

"I hadn't thought of that. How does it work exactly?"

Gabe told Lily what he knew, and as he was coming to expect from her, she had probing and insightful questions. He wasn't able to answer them all, but when she was through, he then questioned her about the adoption methods in Kashien.

The family roamed in and out, and while the two were aware of them, they were not interrupted. They talked for a solid two hours before Lily realized she had needed to use the bathroom when she came in and never had. Excusing herself, she finally went on her way, her heart thinking once again that getting to know someone was nothing like she'd ever imagined.

Chapter Twenty-Two

Gabe was in the process of slowly changing his clothes—his mind was too full of Lily to be rushed—when someone knocked on his door. Even before Gabe could open his mouth, Ashton's head popped around the door.

"You decent?"

"Rarely."

It was their standard joke, and Ashton came into the room as though he'd been invited. He flopped onto his brother's bed and lay on his side, head pillowed in his hand, staring at Gabe.

"Come on in, Ash." Gabe said dryly.

"Thanks. So tell me."

"Tell you what?"

"When you asked her."

"When I asked who and what?"

"When you asked Lily to marry you."

"I haven't."

The youngest Kapaia looked comically skeptical.

"What are you up to, Ash?" Gabe questioned him, going back to folding his shirt and finding an old T-shirt to wear with his swimsuit.

"What am *I* up to? *I'm* the guy on the sofa, dozing in and out, blissfully minding my own business when I wake to hear Lily say, 'We would get our baby from Capital City and be free to leave with her that day.'"

Gabe smiled but didn't say anything, and Ashton became very serious.

"I take it you've talked about your cancer?"

"Right."

"And Lily thinks you can adopt from Kashien?"

"She's sure of it."

"How do you feel about that?"

Gabe smiled. "Excited. I mean, Lily and I have a long way to go, but foreign adoption never occurred to me."

"Am I wrong in thinking that Kashienese adoption would be even easier with Lily having dual citizenship?"

"I think you must be right, but that didn't come up."

"But you haven't asked Lily to marry you?"

"No."

"Why not?"

Gabe laughed. "It's a little soon for that."

"It's not too soon to talk about adoption, but it's too soon to talk about marriage?"

Gabe threw a balled-up piece of paper at him.

"I'm not sure what you think you heard, but Lily was not being specific to the two of us. She was only explaining the process to me."

"But you love her," Ashton stated.

"I care for her very much."

Ashton fell on his back, put his hands behind his head, and spoke to the ceiling.

"That means you'll love her eventually, which is great." With a huge sigh of satisfaction he added, "She doesn't ever have to leave."

"She'll still go back to Kashien."

Ashton rolled back to his side.

"Why?"

"She told her father that she would."

"But just for a visit, right? I mean, she won't go away forever."

"It's hard to say what it will all look like. So much depends on her father."

"Will she write him and tell him she's falling for you?"

"I don't know. She was going to put a call in to Jeff. He's probably the best one to counsel her right now."

The men fell silent for a moment. Gabe picked up a pair of socks, added it to his laundry basket, and then lifted the basket in his hands.

"I'm going to start my wash and go surfing. Want to come?"

Since surfing was a huge passion for the younger man, he didn't need to be asked twice. With a plan to meet on the veranda in ten minutes, the men went on their way.

⌒

"Thank you for calling me back," Lily said into the phone. "Did I interrupt anything?"

"No, but I'm headed out in a little while, so that's why I called back right away."

"Will you be seeing Annika?"

"As a matter of fact, I will. She leaves the middle of this next week, so we're trying to do the weekend up big."

"Sounds fun."

"Speaking of fun, how are you doing?"

"I'm doing fine," she smiled, not aware that her voice had grown very soft.

"Is there something you want to tell me?"

"Oh, Jeff, I don't know where to begin."

"Do you love him?" Jeff guessed correctly.

Lily sighed. "I didn't know you could feel this way about anyone, Jeff. What will Father say?"

"I don't know, Lil." Jeff's voice was full of compassion and understanding. "Will you write him or just tell him when you get home?"

It didn't escape Lily's notice that Jeff knew she would go home. She didn't say anything, but that meant a lot to her.

"I don't think I'll write. I'm not sure what I would say. We're going to keep exploring this until I have to leave, so I won't really know where things stand until then."

"And will you keep your original go-home date?"

"How are things looking on your end?"

"Like I'll be a week late."

"Okay," Lily said, and Jeff could tell she was thinking. "I'll probably wait until you let me know for certain, but then I'll ask Gabe to help me change my flight. After that, I'll write Father."

"We'll have a good time, Lily."

"Jeff," Lily said suddenly, almost cutting him off, "where did this new boldness come from? At one time I would never have dreamed to tell Father anything. Why am I able to do it now?"

"It's probably tied into how safe and secure you feel in Hawaii with the Kapaias. Are you looking at the men?"

"Yes."

"Is it easy?"

"It is with Gabe, Evan, and Ash. It's a little harder with others."

"But you're doing it?"

"Yes."

"That's probably part of it too. You're feeling more confident all the way around. But don't be fooled, Lily. Father is the type of man who commands subservience from his children. One minute of being in his presence, especially in Kashien, and you'll be cowed under again."

"Just hearing his voice on the phone did that."

"And how did that make you feel?"

"Tired. I understand that I need to show him respect when we're in the village, Jeff, but why can't I look at him when we're alone in our home?"

"I don't know, Lil. It wasn't like this when Mom was alive. I still think you and I should sit down when I get back and decide what I should say to him in a letter. I think my representing you will help."

"Okay, Jeff, we'll plan on that."

With a little more talk about relationships—Jeff and Annika's, Lily and Gabe's, and both Walsh children to their father—the two rang off. Something niggled in the back of Lily's mind, something she didn't like, but for right now she couldn't put her finger on it.

〜

At midmorning on Monday both Lily and Bailey were to be found at the bay, bamboo mats spread out as they lay under an umbrella and visited on the warm beach. Bailey was in a one-piece suit. Lily also had her suit on but had only gone so far as to remove her T-shirt, not her shorts. Atop her head was her bamboo hat, but her feet were bare so she could push her toes into the sand.

"I love sand," Lily suddenly proclaimed.

"That's a good thing to love when you live in Hawaii."

"True."

They were quiet for a moment, but Bailey had too much on her mind to let it last.

"Did that one little word mean that you plan to live here?" Bailey asked, her head turned so that she was looking at Lily when she smiled.

"I don't know," Lily said softly, her eyes on the bay.

"I hope you realize that we've all been plotting against you for ages."

Lily turned in confusion. "You have?"

"Um-hm."

"What kind of plotting?"

"Oh, mostly praying, but also asking questions and trying to think of ways for the two of you to spend time together."

"In hopes of what?"

"That you would notice Gabe."

"Why, Bailey?"

Bailey laughed as she said, "Because you're perfect for each other. And since Gabe had already found you, we just needed you to notice him."

Lily looked at her, her face a picture of pleasure and bemusement.

"I had no idea."

"Well, we tried to be subtle, and in truth, Evan was the busiest one."

"Evan?"

Bailey laughed at the now surprised look on Lily's face, but before either one of them could comment further, they looked up to see Gabe headed their way.

"Is this just girl talk?" he asked as he came to Lily's side.

"No, you can join us," Bailey said, "especially if you're sharing some of what's in that cooler."

"We'll just have to see about that," he teased, and Lily smiled at how laden down he was. He had his own mat, the cooler, a basket, and several towels. Lily thought she could see a book and some magazines as well. Clearly he had come for the day.

"How are you?" Gabe asked when his mat was next to Lily's and he'd passed bottles of juice to everyone.

"I'm fine. How are you?"

"Just dandy," he said, throwing in a wink for good measure.

Lily smiled in pleasure and looked away in embarrassment. Bailey had been watching them but now picked up the book she'd brought along and began to read.

Lily looked out over the water for a time, but she didn't want to read with Gabe next to her. She just wanted to look at him and talk. She glanced his way to find him watching her.

"Will you go to dinner with me on Thursday night?" he asked quietly.

"Oh, certainly. To the Little Bay?"

"No, we're going to go someplace a little fancier."

Lily hesitated. "Will I have something to wear?"

"Yes, that teal and blue dress you have will be fine."

Lily nodded, feeling very pleased. Their eyes locked for a moment, until both shifted their eyes away.

"I learned to swim in this bay," Gabe said, his eyes on the water, his voice thoughtful.

"How old were you?"

"Just a baby, I think. I don't remember it, but my mom talks about it now and again."

"And when did you learn to surf?"

"I think I started that when I was maybe four or five."

"Were you at all timid or frightened?"

"Not at that age. I was too young to realize how seriously I should take it. My dad knew the dangers and kept a tight rein on me, but I was raring to go at all times."

"Were you ever hurt?"

"Not seriously. I tumbled off my board enough times early on to learn respect for those waves, and that's all it took. I was still dying to go surfing every waking moment, but I knew my limits."

Lily was silent with awe—learning to surf at such a young age.

"It's all a matter of where you live," Gabe continued to voice his thoughts. "Kids who grow up in the mountains of Colorado learn to snow ski as babies. On a horse ranch, you're in the saddle before you can walk. On the beaches of Oahu, you learn to surf."

"I think I'll learn to surf someday," Lily suddenly proclaimed.

Gabe shifted to get a better view of her face.

"Are you serious?" he asked.

Lily's smile was nothing short of cheeky. "No."

As Gabe laughed, Bailey commented that Evan was headed their way. Lily frantically reached for her T-shirt. Stopping her actions, Gabe put a hand on her arm and spoke quietly.

"Your suit is very modest, Lily. You don't need to cover up."

Lily looked into his eyes. "You're sure?"

"Very sure. Jeff helped you buy this, remember?"

Lily nodded.

"He would not mislead you, and you can trust me that I would tell you if something was inappropriate."

Lily nodded and set the shirt aside, but she kept her hand on it. Evan greeted everyone, put a mat next to his wife, and reached for Bailey's hand. Lily had no sense that he was looking at her, but still she felt bare. Her figure compared to Bailey's was very small, but having her arms and neck so exposed and the suit fitting snug against her body was a whole new experience.

Lily found, however, that it didn't last. In time they were all eating, visiting, and reading, and Evan's presence soon became a complete non-issue.

～

The Tuesday night luau at the cove was for adults only this time. Deanne's parents, Hadden and Anita Talbot, were invited. Ashton was in attendance, as were Evan and Bailey, Harris and Barb Stringer, Wang, Zulu, who was one of the elders from church, and his wife, Aleka, Davis and Pam Merrill, plus Gabe and Lily. The group of 14 were in high sprits from the moment they arrived and enjoyed much laughter as they ate.

The last time they had eaten together the conversation had turned to romance and how the couples met. Tonight's discussion focused on when folks came to Christ. The mood of the party grew a little more serious then, but no less enjoyable. Time was taken for everyone to tell how he or she had come to a saving knowledge of Christ, the stories so diverse they could have been in a book. The evening passed all too swiftly, and before anyone was ready, folks needed to head home.

"We had a wonderful time, Evan," Harris Stringer said warmly shaking his hand as he and his wife were leaving. "It won't be long until you're back to work."

"Just a few weeks now."

"Do you think you'll be rested?"

"I think we're getting there. We haven't told many people yet, but Bailey is expecting, so I've been asking her to take it easy. I find that she does that better when I do."

"God knew what He was talking about with male leadership, didn't He?"

"Indeed." Evan laughed. "Have a safe trip home, Harris."

"We'll do our best. We'll see you at Bible study tomorrow night."

～

Harris Stringer waited only until Bible study ended the next night to nab Evan and ask for a word with him in private.

"Evan, am I stepping over my bounds to ask if Gabe and Lily are getting to know each other?"

"No, I don't think so." Barely managing not to smile, he asked, "What are you seeing?"

"Well, last night at the luau they seemed to be getting close, and now tonight they sat together."

Evan could no longer hold his smile. Harris, a bit of a romantic, smiled in self-congratulations.

"I'm right, aren't I?"

"Yes, but I don't know how much they're sharing right now."

"But I can pray," the excited pastor said, nearly rubbing his hands together.

Evan could only laugh.

～

On Thursday evening, Lily checked her appearance for the last time before moving from her bedroom to the hallway and down the stairs. Gabe had said they were dressing up a bit, and for some reason this made her a little excited and nervous.

As she was descending the stairs, she heard a soft whistle and looked to see Ashton watching her from the sofa. Lily laughed.

"Were you hoping a taxi would come by?" Lily teased him as she reached the bottom.

"No!" The man was playfully outraged, coming off the sofa to be heard. "I was telling you that you look pretty!"

"With a whistle?" Lily was still teasing. Gabe had done this to her just the day before, and she had needed a full explanation.

"Well," Ashton said trying not to smile, "it is a bit crude, but I meant well."

"Thank you, Ash."

The two smiled at each other in genuine friendship.

"Where are you two headed?"

"I think Gabe said something about Turtle's Bay."

"He's probably taking you to the Cove restaurant at the Turtle Bay Hilton."

"That's the place," Gabe confirmed as he came down the stairs, looking very nice in dress slacks and an Aloha shirt. "Are you ready?" he asked when he reached Lily's side.

"I have to put my sandals on," Ashton answered with as straight a face as he could manage. "And comb my hair."

"I hate to tell you, Ash, old buddy, but you're not invited."

"Why not? I'm a lot of fun."

"That's true," Gabe agreed. "You rate right up there with a toothache."

The couple exited on Ashton and Lily's laughter, but they weren't in the car five minutes when Lily asked, "How does Ash feel about our getting to know each other?"

"I think he's fine with it. Why do you ask?"

"I just wanted to be certain."

"Well," Gabe returned wryly, "as of last weekend he wanted to know why I hadn't asked you to marry me yet. So if that's any indication, he must be all for it."

Not only his words, but also his tone gave Lily the giggles— something Gabe had never heard from her. He enjoyed thinking about it for the next few miles, a little sorry that they didn't have farther to go.

Once inside the elegant restaurant, however, Lily's giggles were nowhere to be heard. Lily and Gabe were soon seated, and hovering at their side was a perfectly groomed waiter in a white coat. He took Lily's napkin from the table and placed it in her lap. All expression had left her face, and Gabe immediately saw the signs. Gabe waited only for the man to step away from the table to speak.

"Are you all right?"

"Yes."

"Can you tell me what you're thinking?"

"I'm thinking that I don't want to do anything to embarrass you."

Gabe slid his hand along the tablecloth so he could touch Lily's fingers. She relaxed a little.

"You're not going to embarrass me. If anything, I'm in great danger of having to confess the pride I feel over being with you. I wanted to come here because the setting is special. You can relax and enjoy this."

"Maybe you should just order for me."

"I can do that, or you can ask all the questions you want."

Lily nodded and tried to do as he told her.

"It is fancy, though, isn't it, Gabe?"

"Yes, but they pride themselves on making your dining experience a memorable one, so just ask for whatever you need and you'll enjoy yourself."

"All right."

Gabe took his hand back, and Lily smiled at him.

"Still like me?" Gabe teased a little.

"Yes, but I should be the one to ask you that question."

"Go ahead."

"Do you still like me?"

His dark eyes studied her for a moment before saying, "Oh, yes," very slowly.

At that moment the waiter returned with tall glasses of iced tea and began to explain the evening's specials. Gabe could tell that some of it was new to Lily, so when the man asked if they wanted more time, he said yes.

"Do they actually serve dolphin here?"

"Dolphin fish."

The silent "oh" was punctuated by the relief he saw on her face.

"So what sounds good?"

For the next five minutes they discussed their options. Lily began to worry about the time and then realized that this was their night; there was no need to rush. With this in mind, she finally sat back.

"Have you decided?"

"Yes. I'll have whatever you're having, or whatever you want to order for me, as long as I can just sit here, look at you, and talk to you."

"Do you have any idea how much you've changed?"

"Good changes or bad ones?"

"Good. You've gone from a girl who couldn't look anyone but Bailey in the eye to a woman who knows what she wants."

Lily smiled but still said, "Let's just hope I can keep it up, even when I come face-to-face with Owen Walsh."

"I'll be pulling for you."

Lily needed an explanation for that expression. Gabe took care of that before ordering their food and doing what Lily wanted: talking and looking at each other for the remainder of the evening.

Chapter Twenty-Three

For a while it had seemed the weeks were going to last forever, but to Lily's amazement, time had moved on. Having gained definite confirmation from her brother, she had already written to her father about staying two extra weeks. Her return date was now December 15.

But that was not what was on Lily's mind today. Today her thoughts were wholly centered on her brother. He was flying in that afternoon. Lily could hardly stand the wait. She was working on her packing but kept growing distracted as she worked.

"I need to talk to you, Lily Walsh." Bailey's disgruntled voice could be heard in the hall just before the woman herself appeared in Lily's doorway.

"Okay," Lily said with a laugh, knowing that her friend wasn't actually angry. Lily turned to Bailey but continued folding the blouse she was working on.

"Now you listen to me, Lily Walsh! You can move back to Jeff's, but before he goes to work in the mornings, he needs to bring you here."

"He's not going to work for about three weeks."

Bailey's hands came to her expanding waist.

"Then he can just move out here and stay with us!"

"I've become very bold, Bailey, but I'm not sure I can order my brother to move out here."

Bailey perked up with a new idea.

"Evan can order him."

Lily laughed and asked, "But who's going to convince Evan?"

Bailey's look was a tad smug and a little bit provocative.

"Leave that to me."

Leaving the younger woman shaking her head with amusement, Bailey went in search of her mate. Time had moved on for Bailey and the family as well. Their two months off were gone, and they had guests in all the cottages. Nevertheless, this was a Saturday, and Bailey knew her husband might still be in the vicinity. She was pleased to come down the stairs and find him making a phone call at her desk. She waited until he had hung up and then put her arms around his neck from the back.

"I'm here," she said into his ear, "to work my female wiles on you."

Evan held his laughter before saying, "I can hardly wait. What is it that you want?"

Bailey sat in his lap.

"Evan, Jeff comes home today."

"Right."

"We can't let him take Lily away from us."

"What do you want me to do?"

"Order him to move out here until he goes back to work."

Bailey tried not to smile when Evan hooted with laughter, but it didn't work. Unfortunately for Bailey's plan, the children heard their father's mirth, and a moment later Bailey and Evan weren't alone.

"Will you at least talk to him?" Bailey asked before both children tried to climb into her lap.

"Because you want Lily around even though Jeff is home?"

"Don't you?"

"Yes, but she's waited two months to be with him. I think we'd better let them handle it."

Bailey sighed.

"And don't forget, Bales, there's someone else's heart involved here too. I have a feeling we'll be seeing plenty of Lily."

"So what you're saying is that I need to convince Gabe?"

Evan's brows rose. "That's a thought. He probably won't need much persuading at all."

Looking like a woman on a mission, Bailey asked the children if they wanted to take a walk and visit their Uncle Gabe.

～

"My sister accosted me in my office this morning," Gabe said to Lily on the way to the airport.

"What did she do?"

"Well, she started out in a friendly enough fashion but ended up threatening to make my life miserable if I let Jeff take you away."

"What did you tell her?"

"That I would see what I could do, but even she had to agree that Jeff might wish to have some time with you."

"So we're taking our cue from Jeff?" Lily asked.

Gabe glanced at her as he realized what she'd just said.

"Lily, would you rather stay at the resort than move back to Jeff's?"

"Certainly. Did you think otherwise?"

"I don't know what I thought. Will you tell Jeff?"

"No."

Gabe looked at her again. "Because you don't want to hurt him."

"Correct. Not even wanting to be with you would make me risk hurting Jeff."

Gabe took her hand.

"We'll take our cue from Jeff," Gabe agreed, not sounding upset or resigned, just matter-of-fact.

Lily agreed with a nod, but she wasn't entirely certain how she felt at the moment.

～

Lily put a hand to her chest as the first passengers came through the door. He was almost here. Jeff was almost back! Lily knew she was going to cry and didn't even care. Gabe was behind her, able to see over her head. So many people came through the door that Lily wondered if her brother had missed his plane. She was turning to ask Gabe about it when Jeff appeared.

Spotting them almost immediately, Jeff came their way with a huge smile on his face. He wrapped his arms around his sister, who was already getting teary.

"Oh, Lily," he said when he stepped back to look into her face, his mouth open in surprise. This was not the sister he had left. She was tanned, with a healthy bloom about her that had not been present when he'd left two months earlier. And her eyes! They were sparkling.

Jeff couldn't find any words, so he hugged Gabe and then stood looking at the two of them.

"How was your trip?" Gabe asked, giving Lily a moment to compose herself.

"Good. Everything was on time."

"And do you have to go back anytime soon?"

"Not for three months, and only then if I'm needed."

The threesome started walking toward the baggage claim area, but Jeff kept turning to look at Gabe and his sister. And his sister looked back!

"Well, it's a good thing you didn't try to keep your feelings a secret." Jeff finally said, finding the words he'd been looking for. "I would have known in an instant."

"Known what?" Lily teased, and Jeff had all he could do not to shake his head. The change in her was remarkable. And he learned a moment later that it wasn't just her appearance. As he watched she took a piece of gum from her pocket, unwrapped it, and popped it into her mouth.

"My sister is chewing a piece of gum," Jeff commented to Gabe.

"It gets worse," Gabe informed him. "She's completely addicted."

They had arrived at the baggage area, so Jeff was able to stop and face his sister. She blew a quick bubble.

"You're addicted to gum?"

"I think I am," she said brightly. "Want some?"

All Jeff could do was laugh.

A loud buzzer sounded, and Lily stood back while the men went forward to gather Jeff's gear. Lily's heart filled with dozens of emotions as she watched the two men she loved. She couldn't stop smiling as they trooped out to Gabe's car. Gabe opened the trunk and shifted Lily's bag out of the way.

"Lily, why is your bag in here?" her brother asked, loading his gear.

Lily frowned in confusion. "I thought I was coming back to the apartment with you."

"Well, I plan to sleep in my own bed tonight, but I figured we would live at the resort until I went back to work."

"Are you certain?"

Jeff's brows rose. "Lily, if I had a choice between having Annika with me or five miles away from me, she would be with me."

"Bailey will be so pleased" was all Lily said before she climbed into the rear seat of the car so her brother could have the front, suddenly very glad they had taken their cue from Jeff.

"Now, as a lot of you know," Pastor Stringer said Sunday night as the evening service began, "Jeff Walsh was called away just as his sister arrived from Kashien. But now Jeff's back, and we've gotten to know Lily in his absence. For the next five weeks they've agreed to tell us a little about growing up in Kashien. We're going to start tonight and have just a ten-minute segment with them each week.

"Okay, Jeff and Lily, come on up and get us started."

Jeff came out of the pew, Lily behind him. She had deliberately dressed in Kashienese garb, bamboo hat and all, and she walked ten paces behind Jeff, head down. Jeff went directly to the podium, but Lily stayed behind and to the side of him.

"What you just watched," Jeff began, "is the way a Kashienese woman lives her life. To show obeisance and respect to the male head of her household, be it her father, husband, or brother, she walks behind him with her head down. And her eyes must be lowered. She must not look a man in the eye unless she is commanded to do so."

With that, Lily removed the hat and came to the microphone with her brother.

"You may have noticed that even now Lily sometimes drops her eyes in the presence of the men here at church. It was something she was taught from early childhood. What Pastor has asked us to do now is have a short conversation in Kashienese. Lily is going to be better at this than I am since I've been away so long, and she's always had a better ear for languages.

"What we're going to act out for you is the buying of her hat. Watch the way Lily compliments me with just her stance and attitude, even as she tries to diplomatically dicker me down on the price."

Pastor Stringer came forward with a separate microphone. Jeff had given him the gist of the conversation, and in between Lily and Jeff's conversation, he "translated."

Lily came forward, head bowed. She spoke and indicated the hat. Jeff handed it to her and stated a price. Lily said very little, but by her hand movements and the way she handled the hat, she told Jeff she thought it was very nice. She spoke about the top of her head not being covered and said how the sun beat down on her. She drew out a tiny coin purse, opened it, and looked inside.

Everyone laughed when Jeff looked affronted and waved at her to put the coin purse away. Lily's manner of apology was fascinating. She bowed and groveled, and in a few moments Jeff forgave her and sold her the hat. Everyone clapped when Jeff turned back to the congregation.

"Had we been in Kashien, it would have taken a lot more groveling on Lily's part to get me to notice her again. As Pastor pointed out, her offering price was insulting for what was obviously a fine work, and I was angry. I would have gone without a sale before I would have given in too soon."

"Can we take some questions, Jeff?" Pastor Stringer cut in.

"Certainly. Aleka," Jeff called on the woman whose hand came up first.

"Is there no compassion, Jeff? Would there be some caring that she didn't have a hat and had to work in the hot sun?"

"Not for a woman. As the seller, I might feel some compassion if I hoped to marry her someday, but even if that were the case, I would have to be careful not to show too much of that in public and lose face."

"Is the hat actually from Kashien?" was the next question from a girl in the back pew.

Jeff looked to Lily.

"Yes, I brought it with me," Lily explained.

"She did more than that," Jeff interjected. "She made it herself. The weave is so tight you could carry water in it."

As people throughout the room murmured with appreciation and more questions were asked, Ashton leaned toward his brother.

"If that smile gets any bigger, Gabe, it's going to split your face."

Gabe didn't even try to hide it. His chest was out a mile as he watched Lily up front. Her smile was on the shy side even as she worked not to drop her eyes before all the men of the church. Her gaze swung over in his direction repeatedly, and Gabe asked God to help her relax and do a good job.

A few minutes later she was back in the pew next to him.

"You did great," he told her softly.

Lily gave him a look, said a single word in Kashienese, and shook her head a little. Gabe waited only until the service ended to ask her about it.

"Didn't you think you did well? And what was that word?"

"That word was 'terrified.' Couldn't you see me shaking?"

"No, you did great."

"I'm glad to hear you couldn't tell, but it's a bit daunting to know that I have to go up there four more weeks."

"You're going to do fine. You already know most of these folks, so you're getting more relaxed," he reasoned. "You love the work you do with the translating, so when it's time to talk about that, you just share with us like you did that day with Carson."

Lily glanced toward the podium.

"It's scarier up there than it would first seem."

"Yes, but could you tell that everyone enjoyed it?"

"I could, Gabe. Thank you."

It was on Gabe's mind to say something more, but people were headed their way. They greeted Jeff if they had missed him that morning, and then had more questions for Jeff and Lily. The family was late getting home, but since Jeff was staying with them, it felt like a continuation of their time off. They talked and laughed until much too late, but all agreed that it was worth it.

∼

"So, do the two of you have a plan?" Jeff asked Gabe when he'd been home about ten days.

The two were alone in Gabe's office. Jeff had gone over to ask him an entirely different question and then saw a snapshot of Gabe and Lily on Gabe's desk.

"It's interesting that you should ask that, Jeff. You know how I love maps and charts and such, so just last night I was looking at the calendar and putting some of this down on paper. I met Lily when you brought her to us on September 5. On October 7—just a month later when we were in Hilo—we talked about our feelings. You came home November 6, which meant we'd had a month to get to know each other under closer circumstances. And now, Lily leaves for Kashien four weeks from yesterday.

"I love her, Jeff," Gabe said simply. "Has it happened very fast? Yes, but that's not my problem. My problem is having no idea how to approach your father."

Gabe stopped talking for a moment, but he added something before Jeff could speak.

"I also want you to know that I've done nothing more than hold Lily's hand."

"I appreciate your telling me, Gabe. I recently found out how hard it can be. But tell me something. What does Lily want you to do about our father?"

"She thinks it would be best if she talked to him first and asks him to write to me. She's hoping he'll be willing to dialogue through the mail."

Jeff looked thoughtful, trying to gauge if Lily was on the right track. It was so hard to know.

"Maybe I'll talk with her," Jeff said, his mind still working on it.

"Or the three of us could talk."

"Yes," Jeff said immediately; that was the idea he was looking for. "Let's do that tonight."

"Okay. We'll let Lily know as soon as she gets back from the store."

"I'd better go and let you get to work."

"Before you leave—" Gabe stopped him—"tell me how things are going with Annika."

Jeff smiled. "I got a letter yesterday."

"And she's doing well?"

"Yeah. We miss each other. For the first time I think I know how Ash feels."

"And how I'm going to feel in a few weeks."

"Well, there's one consolation," Jeff said, this time on his way out. "We'll all know how to pray for one another."

∼

"Look at this one," Lily said to the children, Celia in her arms and Peter standing beside her. Bailey was on her own with the shopping cart. Lily and the children were shopping with the little handheld basket.

"It's red, and this one is yellow," Peter told her.

"And you say they have tiny M & M's inside, Pete?"

"Yeah! They're real good."

"I think we'd better add some to our basket."

Peter and even Celia lit up over this.

"Eat an now," Celia said.

"No," Lily said with a shake of her head; she had become quite good at translating. "We'll eat them later, maybe after lunch. Would you like to walk for a while?"

Celia's little head bobbed. Lily gladly put her down; her arms and shoulders had started to ache.

The threesome shopped on. The whole point was for Lily to entertain the children so Bailey could make better use of her time, but in truth Lily was the one being entertained.

The bathroom was in the produce section, and when Peter needed that, Lily stayed close by but looked her fill of luscious fruits and vegetables. Not until Celia said she missed her mother did they go and report back.

"How is it going?" Bailey asked.

"Someone needed to see her mother."

Bailey took Celia in her arms. "Did you want to shop with me for a while?"

Celia nodded, her face a bit sleepy, and Lily made room in the seat area of the cart for the little girl to ride. Bailey had just moved on her way when Peter quietly spoke Lily's name.

"Yes, Peter?"

"Lily, can we look at the baby things?"

"We certainly can. Do you know where they are?"

"No."

"Well, we'll find them."

Not many minutes later Peter stood in front of the stacks of diapers, his little face serious.

"Were you hoping to get something here, Pete?"

"No, I'm just looking for blue diapers."

"Why is that?"

"Well, if Mama has a boy, I think he should have blue diapers."

Lily had no idea that he'd thought that much about this. Her heart was very touched by his admission.

"And why is it important that a boy wear blue diapers?"

"So people won't think he's a girl."

"Will you be all right if your mom has a girl?"

"Um-hm," he said, his face completely open. "I think they have lots of pink diapers."

Lily looked at him, her heart filling with love.

"Have I told you, Peter, that you're one of my favorite people to shop with?"

"I am?"

"Yes, you are."

Obviously pleased, the little boy only smiled at her, his eyes shy. Lily was ready to stand and study this aisle for as long as he wanted, but evidently he'd seen what he came to see. A moment later he suggested they look at the candy section again. Lily was only too happy to comply.

∼

"I finally have things figured out, Jeff. The last time we spoke of this—you were still away—I didn't know what to tell you when you offered to represent me to Father."

"But you do now?"

"I think so. At least, I have a plan. I'm going to tell him how I feel. I know it won't be easy, but somehow I think my having been away will have softened him. I might want you to write him someday, but not now.

"My goal is to go home and find a way to dialogue with my father. I don't know how he'll react, but I'm hoping he'll respond to me openly, and through mutual respect we can move to a different level in our relationship, at least within the walls of our own home. And then in the same way I want to introduce the subject of Gabe and me."

"Good," Jeff congratulated her. He was more than willing to write to his father for Lily, but if she could implement changes on her own, that would be best.

"What will you do if he doesn't respond the way you hope, Lily?" Gabe wanted to know.

"I guess I honestly believe he will, Gabe."

Gabe smiled at her. From all he'd heard of this man, his heart was doubtful. But Lily certainly knew her father better than he did, and on top of that, she looked peaceful with her decision. And Gabe hoped she was right. His future with her rested on Owen Walsh's response. God might choose to work in the man's heart, and Gabe needed to make up his mind to believe and trust God, no matter what the outcome.

"Will you approach this as soon as you get home, Lily?" Jeff asked. "Or ease into it?"

"Right away. As soon as we're home and alone."

"We'll be praying."

"Thank you, but out of curiosity, what will you ask God to do?"

"I'll ask Him to help Father to listen. You put your finger on it, Lily. If he gets upset or angry, you can't talk to him. I'll ask God to work in his heart, even before you arrive."

This plan worked for Lily. She did not want to tell God what to do or beg Him in desperation to make her father listen. She did believe that she had some good things to say to her father. She never once wanted to show him disrespect, but she ached for change between them. Even if she could never come back and marry Gabe, the man she was now in love with, she wanted her relationship with her father to be different in the future.

"What if he never lets you come back?" Gabe voiced the question that had been in the back of his mind for weeks.

Jeff and Lily both looked at him, but Jeff answered the question.

"He is a hard man, Gabe, but not completely unreasonable. If Lily writes and tells me that it has all fallen apart, I'll write to my father and introduce you so that you can write to him personally. He knows about you. I can't think how he could possibly object to such a man marrying his daughter. But if he does object, we'll do everything we can on this end to make it work."

"Would it make it worse if I came to Kashien?"

"You mean right now, Gabe, or if he won't listen?" This came from Lily.

"I would love to go with you right now, Lily, but I was thinking more along the lines of if and when it didn't work."

"I'll have to think on that one, Gabe. I mean, it would be wonderful to have you, but if my father is that upset, I can't think of how your presence would help."

"I guess I thought it might help him to see that I'm serious and committed to us."

The two looked at each other for a long moment. Jeff watched them.

It was one of the most wonderful things he'd ever experienced to have his sister and closest friend in love. And for just a moment, Jeff let himself forget that there might be a man in Kashien who could smash all their dreams to pieces.

Chapter Twenty-Four

"What did he have to say?" Evan asked from inside the garage the moment Bailey climbed from the car. She'd had her first doctor's appointment, and Evan had not been able to accompany her.

"He says everything looks great and that I'm due on June 1."

"June 1? Okay. Any limitations or restrictions?" Evan asked with an arm around her as they walked toward the house.

"No surfing."

"And what about your swollen ankles?"

"Prop my feet when I can and take brisk walks."

"Okay."

"How are the kids?"

"Having a blast with Lily."

"What are they doing?"

"They took a picnic to the bay. I ran into Gabe, and he said he can't get a thing done for watching them out his window."

Rather than go inside, the couple walked toward the surf until they could look down the beach toward the bay. Lily wasn't hard to spot.

"It looks like Ash joined them."

As the couple looked on, Lily put her arms in the air and waved as though she was pretending to be a tree. Had Evan and Bailey known it, that was exactly what she was doing.

On the beach, both Peter and Celia were rapt with attention. Lily was telling a story. Ashton had come along in the middle of it and quietly joined them to listen.

"And when the little girl," Lily continued, "saw how glad her mother was to have her home, she realized she'd been wrong to leave. Her mother put ointment on all her scratches, gave her a big bowl of rice, warm milk, and sugar, and tucked her into her own little bed. The little girl fell asleep knowing how deeply she was loved."

"That was a good story," Peter said. "I liked it."

"I'm glad, Peter. Thank you."

"Me too. Good store."

"Thank you, CeCe." Lily smiled at her before cupping her small face in her hands to kiss her. Watching Lily's actions, Ashton realized something for the first time.

"There are children in Kashien that you love, aren't there, Lily?"

Tears filled Lily's eyes so swiftly that she was surprised. She didn't break down, but emotions filled her very fast.

"Three little girls," she said quietly.

"What are their names?"

"Faith, Hope, and Charity."

"How old are they?"

"Faith and Hope are six and five. Charity is little more than a baby."

"We're having a baby," Peter put in.

"Yes, you are," his uncle agreed. "Do you think it will be a boy or a girl?"

"I don't know. I think a boy would be fun, but a girl would be okay too."

"I'n a girl," Celia informed the group.

"You could have another Celia," Ashton said to his nephew.

"Yeah," Peter agreed, looking a bit uncertain.

"I must tell you, Peter," Lily said, "that I think you are a wonderful big brother."

Peter smiled shyly, but Lily could see he was pleased.

"Are you leaving soon, Lily?" Peter asked next.

"In three weeks, yes. I'll miss you."

"I'll miss you too."

Lily glanced at Celia, thinking this was the usual time for her to chime in with a comment, but she had found the grapes.

"How many of those have you had?" Lily asked.

Celia's answer was to put another one into her mouth.

"I think that means it's time to eat."

Although the little group invited Ashton to join them for lunch, he said he had to get back to work. He took the cookies they offered him and went on his way, but he walked slowly so he could listen to the sound of Lily's gentle voice as she talked to the children. Hearing it reminded him to pray for Gabe. Deanne would be back very soon now; Ashton could count the days on the calendar. But when Lily left, Gabe had no idea when he would see her again.

"Where are we going?" Lily asked Gabe the next afternoon as she went with him toward the garage.

"Cottage nine has a problem that no one else can get to right now, so I'm going to check it out. And you know what?" Gabe asked just as they reached the garage.

"What?"

"You're going to drive."

Lily stopped and Gabe laughed.

"I don't think this is a good idea."

"I think this is a great idea," he disagreed.

"Gabe," Lily said seriously, "I'll smash into something or maybe kill someone."

"You won't. I'll be right beside you."

Lily glanced at the golf cart.

"You'll like it," Gabe said enticingly.

Lily looked at him and tried not to smile.

"Come on. Just sit in the driver's seat and see how it feels."

Lily did as she was told, and to her surprise it did look rather fun.

"Okay." Gabe wasted no time, having her where he wanted her. "Here's the key. Put it in right there and start it up."

"Will it move?"

"Not until you step on the gas."

After much laughter, some panic, and a few jerks and starts, Lily found herself driving down the beach in the golf cart. She had liked riding in them all along but now discovered this was a whole new sensation. If she let off the gas, it slowed. If she braked, it stopped. She was in control!

"Oh, my," was all she could say for the first minute. "I had no idea."

"Maybe I'll just let you do all the driving from now on. If I have to move from my office, I'll call you to pick me up."

"I can do that," Lily said brightly.

"I love it when you smile."

"Do you?" she teased him a little.

"Um-hm."

"I can't look at you, Gabe," Lily said, knowing he wanted her to. "I have to concentrate on my driving."

"That's okay. I can look on my own."

Lily smiled again.

"Here we go," Gabe said, and suddenly it was time to show Lily where to stop. Telling her to leave the keys in the cart, he led her onto the porch and knocked on the door.

"Is someone staying here right now, Gabe?"

"Yes, but they said they would be out all day."

"How will you get in?"

"The master key."

"Why did you knock if they're not here and you have a key?"

"Because you never want to walk in on someone. You always take for granted that they are in until you find out otherwise."

Amid this conversation Gabe had knocked again, received no response, and used his key. Lily came in behind him and stood still while he read the note he'd brought.

"Okay, it looks like there's a problem with the showerhead. The bathroom in this unit is a bit small, so you might want to wait here."

"Okay."

Gabe headed in the direction of the needed repair job, and Lily looked around. This cottage was different from the one Ashton had showed her, and of course the guests' belongings were scattered here and there, but certain aspects were familiar.

"Gabe?"

"Yeah?"

"Do you have a favorite cottage the way Ash does?"

"Yes, it's the same one, number six."

"Why that one, do you think?"

"Oh, the layout is nice, and the size."

Lily didn't answer. The toaster, an unusual model, had caught her attention, and she had moved in for a closer look. She didn't see the magazine until it was much too late.

In the bathroom, Gabe wrapped up the repair job quickly. The fitting was loose, and after a little tightening, Gabe ran the water and saw that it was fine. Not until he'd done all of that did he realize that Lily had become very quiet. He gathered his things and went looking for her. He found her standing stock-still, eyes glued on something. When he was close enough, he could see that a magazine had been left open on the kitchen counter. It showed a very intimate scene between a man and woman. Shocked as she was, Lily seemed incapable of taking her eyes from the picture.

"Lily?" Gabe called to her, and she seemed to snap out of her trance.

Face flaming with mortification, she turned away and moved to the door. Gabe double-checked to make sure he'd left all in order, exited, locked the door, and found Lily sitting in the passenger seat of the cart.

"Are you all right?" Gabe asked when he climbed behind the wheel.

"I don't know right now," Lily answered honestly, her eyes on nothing.

Gabe knew they needed to talk. Thankful that he was not expected back for a while, he drove slowly toward the garage but parked outside of it in a shady, secluded area.

"Lily, can you look at me?"

Lily, who had been staring with unseeing eyes the whole time, turned to focus on Gabe.

"I think we need to talk about this."

"The magazine?"

"Not unless you want to. What I'm wondering right now is if anyone has ever talked to you about the ways between men and women."

Lily stared at him.

"Can we talk about this subject or are you too upset?"

Just hearing his calm voice, Lily relaxed. "We can talk, Gabe."

"You're sure?"

"I'm sure."

"Lily," he asked gently. "Has anyone ever explained the act of physical intimacy to you?"

Lily's eyes grew worried, and Gabe could see she was on the verge of panic. For this reason, he reached over and took both of her hands in his.

"Lily, honey, listen to me."

Lily looked at him, her mind racing to take all of this in.

"I want to marry you. I want to make you my wife. You understand that, don't you?"

"I'm sorry I looked at the picture," she blurted and didn't even answer him. "I'm sorry, Gabe!"

Gabe took her in his arms. "It's all right. You were just shocked, and you never have to be sorry about telling me how you feel, even if you're afraid of our coming together. We'll always talk things out."

Gabe moved back so he could look at the face that was so dear to him.

"Tell me something. Are you afraid when I hold your hand?"

"No, never."

"And just now when I hugged you, did it frighten you?"

"No," Lily said softly, already understanding what he going to say.

"It's just me, Lily. I would never hurt you or ask you to do something that was wrong." Gabe smoothed the hair from her face. "When the time comes for us to do more than holds hands, we'll both be ready."

"How will I be, Gabe, when I know so little?"

"Well, we can keep talking about it some, but also my sister has a book, written by a believer, that explains things very well."

"I should read it."

"Or you can talk to Bailey. If we already had your father's permission to be engaged we could talk of it more openly, but it's probably best if at this point you get your details from the book or my sister."

Lily looked into his eyes.

"I love you, Gabe."

Gabe leaned close and kissed her for the first time.

"I love you, Lily. And I don't mind telling you that it's going to kill me to put you on the plane."

"We kissed," Lily said with wonder, having missed what Gabe just said.

Gabe smiled. "Yeah."

"My parents used to kiss. I was just a little girl then."

Gabe touched her soft cheek.

"I'm so glad you're not a little girl anymore."

Lily smiled, and they kissed one more time.

"I'll get the book for you," Gabe said knowing it was time for him to get back to work.

"All right. And if I have questions, I'll ask Bailey."

"Okay."

Gabe made himself start the cart, drop Lily at the front door of the house, and get back to the office, realizing as he went that he could easily forget he even had a job when he was with the woman he loved.

∽

"Just get her out of the house for a few hours," Bailey told the men the day after Thanksgiving.

"Doing what?" Jeff asked. "We've seen just about everything this island has to offer."

"It doesn't matter what you do. But two weeks from tonight she needs to be gone from 2:00 until dinner."

"All right," Gabe assured her. "We'll figure something out."

"Thank you," Bailey said, smiling in delight that her plan was underway.

∽

"Can you believe we're already to our final week of sharing with Jeff and Lily?" Pastor Stringer opened the evening service as he had done for a month now. "It's gone so fast, but I think you'll find tonight extra special. I persuaded Lily to come up and share on her own. If you've never heard what one of her main jobs is in the village, you'll be amazed. Please come up, Lily."

Hoping her heart would stay in her chest, Lily stepped to the podium. She couldn't tell whether her voice was halting and unsure, but she did her best, reading from the paper she'd prepared for the evening.

"The job that Pastor Stringer spoke of just now is translating. For the past nine years I've been working on various books and passages of Scripture, translating them from English into Kashienese. It is long, intense work, but it has provided some of the most gratifying hours I've ever spent.

"I don't know if anything quite compares to watching one of my friends from the village read the Word of God for herself and understand it. And not only that, but having those books in her own language means she can read them to her children and show them the way of salvation.

"If you'll allow me, I would like to share a story with you, one that makes me ignore the ache in my neck and back and keep translating, even on days when my heart's not very willing.

"One of my closest friends is Ling-lei Chen. She's a little older than I am and has been married for several years. When I left, she was expecting her fourth child. I've been teaching Ling to read. We started in easy books, but her husband, who can read, also has copies of the Scripture that have been translated. When Ling was newly married, her brother came through the village and stopped to visit her. Ling's husband, Lee Chen, was not home. Ling is not a bold woman. As with all Kashienese women, she knows and keeps her place, but her brother made a criticism of my father and the church, and Ling spoke out.

"I had just been teaching her John 3:16. She could not read yet, but she quoted it to her brother. He paid her no attention and said she was just rambling, but Ling was not put off. She brought out the copy of the Scriptures and waited while her brother found the reference. He read John 3:16 for himself. He was so taken that this was actually written down in his own language that he waited for Lee Chen to return. He ended up staying the rest of the day with them, and before he left the next morning, he'd given himself to Jesus Christ.

"Please do not see me as anyone special. I am simply the tool God uses to get the translating job done. My father is in the process of teaching others to do what he's taught me. If others will come forward and help, then the Word will get out even faster. If others will see what the Lord has taught me through the intense time I've spent in the Word, then a great work can be done in my village in Kashien. Many souls are still lost, but God is working, and when He brings us to mind, we would covet your prayers on our behalf, not just for those of us who work to put the Word out, but for hearts to be open and receptive upon hearing."

As on previous evenings, the congregation had many questions. Lily explained how the pages were printed on a small printer in the next village, then sent off to the larger city of Qufu to be bound before being sent back to the village. She also answered a variety of other inquiries. Had Pastor Stringer not brought things to a close, it would have taken the whole evening. Lily returned to her seat, a little shaky, but knowing that Gabe had been right. She knew these people now, and they knew her. It had simply been a time of sharing with friends.

～

"Do you realize you've created a monster?" Ashton asked Gabe while standing at Gabe's office window. Gabe joined his brother, and they both watched Lily in one of the golf carts.

"I don't think she's walked anywhere since she learned to drive it. Is that Jeff with her?"

"Yes, she's giving him a tour."

Gabe had a huge laugh over this, but he wouldn't have been so lighthearted if he could have heard the conversation going on in the golf cart.

"I got a letter from Father, Lily," Jeff said to his sister, happy to let her drive and enjoy her company and the view.

"You did?" she asked, her voice dropping to match his.

"He's not very happy that you stayed longer. He assumed that I influenced you, so he's upset with me. He said he's disappointed that my word doesn't mean what it used to."

"What did he mean by that?"

"Well, he said you could have three months, and you've stayed longer."

"Oh, Jeff, that's so discouraging. I somehow thought he would have changed as much as I have in these weeks."

"I think we'd better stop counting on that."

Lily pulled up to the Little Bay Restaurant, where she and Jeff planned to eat lunch. They walked in together and were seated before they began talking again.

"I have felt so optimistic about it all, Jeff, but I realize now that that's been based on my feelings, not facts."

Jeff nodded. "I think Father is much the same as he's always been."

Lily stayed quiet.

"What will you do?"

"About what?"

"Will you still talk to him about changes in your relationship?"

"At this time I'm planning on it, but if he seems upset when I arrive, I won't. I don't want to go in with an agenda so firm in my mind that I forget about Father's needs and wants. I mean, the whole subject will probably be somewhat upsetting, but if my timing is wise, then he might be more receptive."

"That's a good plan. You know I'll be praying." Jeff took a drink of the root beer the waitress had brought him. "Before I forget to ask you, how are you doing with leaving next week?"

"Oh, Jeff, I'm so torn. I miss Father and Ling and the girls, but I would never choose to leave you and Gabe. Or the church family here. They mean so much to me now. I even met a woman at the resort store this week. She's from the area—her name is Ana—and she was just shopping. We had such a good talk, and if I was going to be here I would keep getting to know her, but I feel so limited the way things are."

"But you're doing the right thing," Jeff encouraged her. "Father would never recover if you just wrote and said you were staying. The relationship you have now would be completely destroyed."

"Why is that, Jeff? Father has the same Holy Spirit living inside him that you and I do. Why can't he change as we have?"

"You answered that for me right after you came to Hawaii: He has no accountability. He's a maverick, and since he sees God working, he assumes all is fine. What Father has never understood is that we can sometimes experience God's blessings in spite of the fact we're headed the wrong way."

It was a good time for their food to arrive. Lily liked the way her brother had worded that and wanted to think on it. She found herself wishing that her father could hear the same words.

Chapter Twenty-Five

"*Likewise urge the young men to be sensible; in all things show your-self to be an example of good deeds, with purity in doctrine, dignified, sound in speech which is beyond reproach, so that the opponent will be put to shame, having nothing bad to say about us.*"

Gabe looked at the passage from the second chapter of Titus and worked to accept what he knew God was saying to him. The little word "all" usually caught his attention when he was studying his Bible. It didn't say he needed to be an example of good deeds in the things that were easy, but in *all* things. And if that wasn't enough, Gabe knew there was to be no place for negative comments about his own character.

I've been angry, Gabe confessed to the Lord. *I haven't wanted anything to stand in my way. I haven't told Lily how I feel, but my anger toward her father is there, and it's wrong. Help me, Lord. I can't have this my way. It's got to be Your way, even if it feels painful to me. Please help me to let go of this, and even Lily. Help me to see that if You want us together, You'll make it happen.*

Gabe knew a peace after this confession and continued to search his heart for more hidden motives. It was time to let this go. It was time to come clean before God. Lily thought he was doing great. He knew better. Gabe looked at the clock. It was early, but this was the time Lily usually went out for her run. Gabe swiftly dressed, hoping to find her on the beach.

～

"You've been angry at my father?" Lily questioned him for the second time. They were walking along the shore, holding hands and talking.

"Yes, for a long time. I'm sorry I didn't tell you, Lily. That was wrong of me, but there's more I have to say."

Lily glanced at him and knew nothing but dread.

"Lily, I don't want you to go home and do anything out of desperation to get back here to me. I don't want you to do anything your father would disapprove of." Gabe took a huge breath. This was costing him greatly, but he had to be sure she understood. "I've wanted to write to him. I was sure it was the right thing to do. Then you said you would set it up so I could, but even that might not work, Lily. Hard as it is for me, we've got to take our cue from your father. Even if he never allows you to return, we must wait on him."

"But you still want to marry me?"

Gabe stopped and took her in his arms. Lily felt the way he trembled. In her ear, he whispered, "I would marry you this afternoon and never let you leave me."

Lily hugged him back, her arms tight around him.

"As long as I know you still love me and want to marry me, I can do this."

Gabe shifted so he could see her face.

"You're so special, Lily. I don't deserve you. And for the record, I'll want to be married to you until the day I die."

It was all Lily needed to hear. What Gabe was asking was huge, but she knew he was right. A little more headstrong about talking to her father than even she was willing to admit, Lily had needed to hear the words as much as her father.

～

"Hank, this is my sister, Lily."

"It's a pleasure to meet you, Lily. Jeff has told me about your visit. Have you had a good time?"

"Yes, it's been wonderful."

"And you go home when?"

"In five days. I fly out Wednesday morning."

"Well, I hope you have a good trip home."

"Thank you."

Hank moved on his way, and Lily waited only a moment to speak to her brother.

"Is he your boss?"

"No, he's a coworker."

"Will I meet your boss?"

"Randolf isn't in today. I'm sorry, Lily, that I didn't think to show you the office before."

"That's all right. I'm seeing it now. Actually, it's much the way you described it in your letter."

"Did I write to you about it?"

"Yes, when you were first hired."

"That was six years ago."

"Right."

That his sister would remember what he said amazed him a little, but then it shouldn't have. When Lily cared about someone, she did it with all her heart.

"We'd probably better get going, or Gabe will wonder what's happened to us."

"Oh, all right," Lily agreed, but Jeff thought this might be a little harder than it seemed.

If they had needed to get Lily out of the house for lunch or dinner, that would have been easy, but from 2:00 to 6:00 was going to take some work. Gabe had come up with the idea of giving Lily a tour of Jeff's office at 2:00 while he ran an errand. The rest of the time was Gabe's to kill, and Jeff hoped he had something up his sleeve.

"Where are we meeting Gabe?"

"Just up the street."

"And are you coming with us?"

"No, I've got some things to finish here, so I'll see you for dinner tonight."

"Wang is cooking," Lily told him. "It would have been fun to stay and help, but I'm glad I saw your office."

"Me too. Now you can tell Father all about it."

"Maybe Gabe will be finished with his errands and I can still get back to help Wang cook."

"Maybe," Jeff said noncommittally, hoping Gabe had plenty of ideas.

Ten minutes later Jeff and Gabe had made the exchange, and Gabe took an unsuspecting Lily to a small shop not far from Waikiki. He parked the car at the curb and held the door for her to get out.

"Are you shopping?"

"I am, yes."

"What are you getting?"

"I'm looking at jewelry."

"Oh, how nice. I've never worn any jewelry."

"I've noticed you don't wear any. Is there a reason?" Gabe asked, his hand to the small of her back as he led her into the store.

"No, no special reason. I've never had any, so that might be some of it."

"We might have to change that," Gabe said when the door shut behind them.

"Change what?"

"Your not having any jewelry."

"Gabe," Lily put a hand on his arm, "I wasn't dropping any hints."

Gabe kissed her nose.

"I know you weren't."

This said, Gabe led Lily to the counter where Lee Kamioto, a man she had met at church, was standing.

"Hello, Lily."

"Mr. Kamioto! How are you?"

"Doing well."

"Do you work here?"

"Not only do I work here, I own the store."

"Oh, how wonderful. Have you been in business long?"

The worried look Gabe caught on Jeff's face would have disappeared if he could have seen Lily just then. She had dozens of questions for Lee, who had been warned of her coming, and that was all before she spotted a picture of his grandchildren, who also attended their church with his daughter and son-in-law.

"What can I show you, Gabe?" Lee asked when he and Lily had exhausted every subject.

"I think this tray of engagement rings with the matching wedding bands right here."

Lily looked up at the man next to her, her eyes large. Gabe smiled down at her in hopes of comforting her, but Lily's expression didn't change.

"I'll tell you what," the observant shop owner said. "I'll just leave this tray with you two. If you need anything, I'll be right over there."

"Thank you," Gabe said, but Lily was still staring at him.

"Gabe," she whispered as soon as they were alone, "I just realized I'm not bringing anything to this marriage. I mean, I have a small chest of things, but they're not of any value here."

"I don't know what you're talking about."

"Well, I have a blanket and some cooking items, and then last year—"

"Lily, honey, stop."

Lily did as she was told.

"What was the part about bringing something to the marriage?"

"Oh, the rings just reminded me that at home a woman brings family jewelry or something of value—a dowry of sorts. It helps the couple get off to a good start, but I forgot that it's probably different here. I'm sorry."

Gabe put his arm around her.

"I will want you to bring anything you have that's important to you, but that's not what we're about today. Today, I want you to tell me if any of these rings appeal to you."

Lily looked down at the tray and then sighed very softly.

"Aren't diamonds pretty?"

"Yes, they are. Does anything stand out to you?"

"Oh, my" was all Lily could manage before she stood in painful indecision. Finally she looked back to Gabe. "Can you pick something?"

"Don't you like any of them?"

"I like all of them."

"Then go ahead and try one on."

Still she hesitated. Gabe spotted some tall stools and brought two of them over. He ordered Lily to sit and then slid the tray a little closer to her. Gabe sat close on another stool and watched her. After a good deal more study, Lily picked out a ring with a minuscule diamond.

"Is that the one you like?"

"Yes, and it looks like it won't be too costly."

"I can afford everything in this tray, so you need to select the one you like the best and not worry about the cost. I would tell you if I couldn't afford it."

"There is one I like better."

"Which one?"

Gabe saw what she picked and smiled. It was the very one he'd spotted earlier that day.

"Try it on."

Lily started to do that, but the wedding band moved to the side and the two rings separated.

"I broke it!" she gasped.

"No, you didn't. These two rings will be soldered together, but not until after the wedding. Here, try just the diamond."

It was rather exciting for both of them when the ring fit perfectly over Lily's slim finger.

"It's so pretty," Lily kept saying.

Gabe kissed her temple before going to tell Lee they had a winner.

"I want you to know," Gabe said once they were in the car, one hand holding the small jeweler's box and the other hand holding Lily's, "that I understand you can't wear this home, but will you please take it with you?"

"Oh, Gabe, my heart would break if something happened to it, and without it being on my finger, I would be worried all the time."

Gabe nodded in understanding.

"Will you wear it until you leave?"

"I want to, Gabe—I can't tell you how much—but can we please wait? That way I won't have to take it off again."

Gabe set the box aside so he could reach up and stroke the smooth skin of her cheek. The wait was going to be one of the hardest things he had ever gone through, but Gabe reminded himself that Lily was at the end.

～

"It looks like Bailey has been doing some decorating," Lily commented as she and Gabe parked in front of the house and saw the wreath on the door.

"Oh, yeah," Gabe said, hoping he had given everyone enough time. He didn't see Jeff's car, but maybe he'd put it in the garage to help with the surprise.

Gabe stayed on Lily's heels as she entered through the front door, so he saw at the same moment she did the Christmas lights come on all over the tree they'd put up.

"Merry Christmas!" everyone yelled as the family came toward her.

"Oh, my" was all Lily could manage for several minutes. Gifts were pressed into her arms, and she stared in wonder at her brother, Ashton, Evan, Bailey, and the children.

"Come on in," Evan directed. "It's Christmas right now and time to open gifts."

Lily suddenly found herself the center of attention, gifts surrounding her. She couldn't speak for a time, and when she did, it was in panic.

"I don't have anything for you. I didn't shop! I never even thought of it."

"You have gifts for them," Jeff stated calmly, and Lily blinked at him.

"Jeff," she said quietly, "could I possibly see you in the next room?"

"It's all right," Jeff said, his voice filled with laughter. "You go ahead and pick out a gift to open. Just tell me who it's from, and I'll take it from there."

Lily looked at him for a moment but did as she was told. The gift closest to her was from Peter and Celia. Lily opened it to find a dictionary, the very type she'd been hoping to own.

"Oh, thank you, Peter. Thank you, CeCe. I'll use it all the time."

"Okay!" Jeff said in excitement, reaching into a bag near his chair. "It looks like Lily has a gift for Peter and one for Celia. Who's going first?"

This little routine became hysterical as Lily leaned in close each time to see what "she" had purchased for each person. It didn't take long to see that her brother had shopped while he was away, and she knew he was giving up his own Christmas gifts for her.

"Lily" gave Celia a doll; Peter got a set of tiny cars. From Bailey and Evan, Lily received a thick book on Hawaii's history. She gave them a wooden cheese cutter. Ashton gave Lily a T-shirt from Deanne's university in California—one that Deanne had sent when she learned of the early Christmas party. In return, Ashton got a book on classical cars, a passion of his. Jeff gave his sister a thin gold bracelet, and he was more than happy with the hug she had for him.

When it was finally time for Gabe's gift to Lily, a gift bag was set in her lap. It was heavy.

"I wanted to wrap the gift we just bought together, but you'd already seen it. I had to settle for this."

More curious than ever, Lily moved the tissue paper and laughed in delight when she saw the contents. It was gum, every conceivable type and flavor.

"Are you sure you want to feed the addiction?" Jeff teased Gabe as he took the last gift from his bag.

"I've decided not to fight it," Gabe said dramatically, starting to open his gift from Lily.

"What is it?" Peter asked when Gabe only stared at the frame in his hand. At last he turned it and everyone looked at the five-by-seven close-up photo of Lily's face. It was in a silver etched frame, and the original picture had been taken at Carson and Gloria's. Lily was on the porch, and the photographer had captured her sweetness as she'd been looking down at the children.

For a long moment Lily and Gabe stared at each other, reminded once again that very soon, memories and pictures would be all they had.

～

The days and hours between Lily's surprise Christmas with the family and the time to say goodbye and go to the airport disappeared at a horrific pace. Lily was utterly silent in the backseat of Jeff's car, having just said goodbye to Evan, Bailey, the children, and Ashton. And she had not yet been required to say goodbye to Gabe or her brother. She was glad they were in the front seat. Not having to look at them just now was a mercy.

They had not given themselves tons of excess time, so the wait was not long. The three talked about general things, and when the first seating announcement was made, they began their goodbyes.

Jeff held his sister for a long time.

"Have I told you lately how proud I am of you?"

"I don't think so."

"My mistake," he said. "I should say it more often."

Lily gave him a watery smile. "So I should tell Father that I didn't shame him?"

Jeff only laughed, hugged her again, told her he loved her, and did not attempt to hide the moisture in his eyes.

Lily then turned to Gabe.

"You need to understand that when you come back, I won't let you go again."

Lily could only nod.

"I think it might be easier to get cancer again than to have to say goodbye to you."

Lily put her hands on his face. "Please don't get cancer again, Gabe. Please be here waiting for me."

"I shouldn't have said that. I'm sorry. I'll be here. I'll wait for you, Lily, no matter how long it takes."

"Please hold me one more time."

His arms brought out all the tears that had waited for this moment. She sobbed as he embraced her, feeling that she couldn't do what she had to do. As it was, most of the plane was boarded before she picked up her bag and left them, still crying.

Gabe watched her go, unable to believe she was leaving them.

"Bring her back, Jeff," he said quietly.

"For both of your sakes, I wish I could."

Both men hoped and prayed that Lily would be all right and even enjoy her flight. They would have laughed to know that once in her seat she berated herself for the baby she was, but her scolding did no good. Feeling as though she would never recover, Lily cried all the way through takeoff and for many minutes in the air. By the time she was able to control herself and doze off, she had a huge headache. There was only one consolation: The waiting was over. She was on her way home.

～

Capital City, Kashien

"Lily."

She heard her father's voice as she came from the jet way, eyes down. Without having to look up, she saw that he was off to the side and went to him. She was so tired she could hardly think straight and was thankful she still remembered all the right things to do. It seemed to her that she had not been here for years.

"Are you well?" Owen asked.

"Only tired."

"Then we will go home."

Lily followed behind him, hoping she could keep ahold of her case. It was heavier this time than when she left, and to her weary arm it felt like lead. She wished her father would notice her and take it, but Lily followed him and remained quiet.

The journey home was made more difficult by her fatigue, but Lily was thankful that her father was not full of questions. They traveled by bus and then cart to their village. Lily did not even ask if she could be excused, but once home went directly to her room and lay down, thinking she would be sick if she did not get some sleep.

Had she but known it, her father had been more sensitive to her needs than he let on. He would not have stopped her from sleeping for anything, but he did go to her room and stand looking down on her sleeping form. His heart was overjoyed with praise to God that she had come safely home to him.

"Lily!" Ling-lei gasped at the sight of her friend and nearly pulled her inside her small home.

"How are you?" Lily asked, so glad to see her. "And how is that baby boy?"

"My baby is perfect," Ling said with a smile, "but we will speak of him later. How are you, my friend?" Ling asked. "You look more beautiful than I have ever seen you. How are *you*?"

Lily smiled. "You will make me be selfish by talking about myself first?"

"Yes. Now, what is his name?"

Lily's mouth opened.

"How did you know?" Lily asked softly.

"I am a woman who still longs for my husband's touch, Lily Walsh. Of course I know. What is his name?"

"Gabriel."

"Like the angel."

Lily laughed. "He's wonderful."

"He must be. You have a glow about you."

"Ling." Lily's face was suddenly worried. "My father does not know, and I must pick a time."

Ling put her hand up.

"I will say nothing."

"Thank you. Do you think me deceitful?"

"No. If he asks and you do not tell, that is wrong. But sometimes waiting is best."

The women began to catch up. The girls were with their grandmother, and Daniel was sound asleep. Lily was sorry to miss the girls, but time alone with Ling was rare, and they had so much to share. Ling had loved all of Lily's letters but had written none of her own.

"I have something for you," Lily said when the women had talked for nearly an hour. She brought out the water dome, smiling at her friend's reaction.

Ling had never seen anything like it, and Lily had a glimpse of herself as Ling asked more questions than Lily could answer. They ended up laughing at how many times Lily said, "I don't know."

It didn't take much longer before Ling just threw her arms around her friend, telling her in no uncertain terms that it was wonderful to have her home.

～

Lily settled back into the village with amazing ease. Her heart was never far from thoughts of Gabe and her wonderful time in Hawaii, but she fit back into her old routine as though she'd never left.

The person who surprised her was her father. He was different, but not in the way she had anticipated. She'd been home two weeks, Christmas had come and gone, and he had yet to question her over what she had learned on her trip. Indeed, Lily thought him quiet in all respects. She prayed for opportunities to talk on a personal level with him, but when he did not invite conversation, even when they were alone in the evenings, Lily kept all thoughts to herself.

Letters arrived from Bailey, Jeff, and Gabe. Lily saved Gabe's until last, savoring the words and thinking about his dark head bent over the paper as he wrote. She thought he would type them on his computer and wouldn't have minded, but it was special getting a letter in his neat, bold writing style.

When she wrote back to Gabe, she told him how odd she found her father's behavior. She wrote Jeff about the same thing, but she had no more than mailed the letters when his behavior seemed more normal again. He was talkative about what was going on in the village and excited when Lily showed him her progress with the translating.

The bombshell didn't drop until one night on Lily's third week back. Lily and Owen were alone in their home and the two of them sat reading in the quietness.

"I was so afraid you would have changed," Owen suddenly said.

Lily took a moment to respond, eyes down, before looking up without being told and saying, "I *have* changed, Father, and I've been hoping to talk to you about that."

Hearing the difference in her voice, Owen looked up to see Lily's eyes on him. He frowned, but Lily did not drop her eyes.

"What are you doing?" Owen demanded, his own eyes growing angry.

"Just looking at you," Lily said softly.

"Is this what you have learned from your trip away—to disrespect your father?"

"No, Father, but I was hoping we could discuss it."

Lily would have said more, but Owen stood.

"My hopes were wrong." His voice was flat and cold. "You are changed. I waited to see, but I did not wait long enough."

Owen stalked from the room, leaving Lily feeling crushed and broken. His silence had all been a test. For one horrible moment Lily wished she'd never gone to Hawaii.

"I wanted to go, Lord," she whispered in prayer, feeling breathless with pain. "I thought it would be wonderful, and it was. But now will I forever long for that life while I live in this one?"

Lily couldn't even let her mind think of how far away Gabe was just then. She didn't think her heart could take the memory.

Chapter Twenty-Six

"Hope," Ling-lei called to her daughter during one of Lily's visits. Lily had been home about a month. "Do you wish to tell Lily what happened?"

The five-year-old came over, her little face alight.

"Come sit in my lap," Lily invited. Having received an offer she would not pass up, the little girl climbed into Lily's lap and let herself be held close.

"You grew very big while I was gone."

"I'm five."

"Yes, you are."

"I'm a Christian."

"Oh, Hope…" Lily held her tightly, her heart pounding. "Can you tell me about this?"

"Mama and I looked in the Bible. We looked at the words from God."

"What did they say, Hope?"

"That I'm a sinner, but Jesus wants to save me."

"So what did you do?"

"I prayed," she told her with a peaceful smile. "I told God I was ugly with sin but that I wanted Him to live in me. And now He does."

"Will He ever leave you, Hope?"

"Never."

"What about when you sin?"

"Not then even."

Lily kissed her brow and rocked her a little.

"You have learned, little one, what many take too long to grasp. How wonderful to know that you and I have the same God living inside us."

"He's with me when I'm scared."

"Yes, He is."

Lily's eyes met those of her friend. Ling was crying.

"Thank you for telling me."

Hope climbed from Lily's lap, and the women sat in quiet wonder for a time. Lily prayed for Hope, asking God to bless her with a heart that would be strong and asking that she would walk with Him for all of her life.

"How are you?" In her quiet way, Ling cut into Lily's prayer.

For the first time since that night with her father, Lily let her shoulders droop and her true feelings show. She looked tired and discouraged. She didn't cry, but she did share openly.

"He still won't speak to me, Ling. It's been the most miserable time of my life—even worse than when my mother died. I don't know what to do. I feel he sees my going away as some type of betrayal. Jeff told me to write and he would intervene, but if Jeff gets involved, I think that will just put up a greater wall."

"So you're not writing to Jeff, or not mentioning the situation when you do write?"

"All I'm saying in my letters to Jeff and Gabe is that the time isn't right and to please keep praying."

Ling nodded and then asked, "Have you tried speaking to your father?"

"Well, I call to him, but when he won't answer I just stay quiet. Is that what you would do?"

Ling thought for a moment.

"I think I would say more," she concluded at last. "You are so good on paper, Lily. Maybe he would read a letter from you. But you never yell, so I know if you speak to him it would be with respect."

"So you think I should try?"

"Maybe a little at a time."

Lily thought about this all the way home, and to her surprise, her father was in the house. He did not look up or acknowledge her, and at the moment Lily figured she had nothing to lose. She took her chair across from him in their small living room and did as Ling had advised her.

"I wish to say something to you, Father. I hope you'll listen." Lily hesitated, but even though he did nothing, she went on. "I have not changed completely, but I was hoping that when we were alone, I could look at you without your permission. I know it would be a great change for us, but I don't wish it out of disrespect." Lily finished with what was foremost on her mind. "I wish we could at least discuss it."

When he gave no indication that he'd even heard her, Lily ended with just a few more words.

"I learned so many things while I was away, and you haven't asked about one of them. It feels as though all you want is to keep control of me, and I wish I understood why."

Lily stood then and walked back out of the house. Tears blinded her, but she still began to run. It was too hot in the day for such activity, but she ran until she was overly warm and winded and then sat beneath a tree for shade.

I know You love me, and in his own way my father loves me, but I don't know what to do, Lord. Do I go back to the way it was, forget Gabe, and live out my life in this village?

But even as Lily prayed this, she didn't feel it was right. There was nothing wrong with her loving a godly man like Gabe and wanting a life with him. That her father would expect her to never find love and have a marriage of her own was not only unreasonable, it was selfish. At the same time, Lily knew that no amount of disrespect or anger toward her father was right. Lily asked God to help her curb her emotions and be as blameless as Elizabeth, who had been described in the first chapter of Luke. Only then did she let her thoughts turn to Gabe.

"I'm sitting under a tree in Lhasa, Gabe, and I'm thinking of you," Lily whispered into the warm afternoon air. "Are you thinking of me?"

～

Oahu, Hawaii

One of Gloria and Carson's Christmas gifts to Gabe was a copy of the tape from Gloria's birthday. He had watched the video right after he got it, but not again until tonight.

It was late, and he should have been in bed like the rest of the household. But Lily was so heavy on his mind that he was up—close to midnight—watching her on the tape. It didn't take long to see that it would be sweet torture. He came to the part where Carson had filmed just the two of them in the kitchen, and when the television screen was full of Lily's smiling face, Gabe paused it. He smiled just at the sight of her and knew an ache so deep that he didn't know if he could stand it.

"Are you all right?" Ashton had come down the stairs to ask. "Did I wake you?"

"No, but I saw the light when I used the bathroom."

Ashton sat with Gabe, and this time the older Kapaia didn't pause the tape. They watched the whole party, laughing at their mother's fun response to her gifts and smiling in delight as Carson caught the children on film. The familiar images suddenly disappeared, static followed, and then the blue screen indicating the video was over appeared. Both men were brought abruptly back to the present. Gabe hit the button to shut things down.

"And this year Deanne will be in the film too," Gabe said to his brother.

"So will Lily."

"Do you think so?"

"Don't you?"

Gabe was quiet for a moment before saying, "Let's just say I'm hoping, Ash, but we'll have to wait and see."

Knowing he was finally ready to sleep, Gabe told his brother good night and took himself off to bed.

〜

Lily's face was nothing short of dreamy as she sat at the table in her house and read her letter from Gabe. He made her laugh on several occasions, and one time Lily's mouth actually opened in surprise.

> *I was really down yesterday when I realized you've been gone for seven weeks. Do you know what I did? I gathered what I needed, took myself off, and applied for a passport. I know by the time it comes I'll have calmed down, but as of yesterday I was getting ready to fly to you with little more than my toothbrush in my pocket. I had my hand on the phone to get prices from the airline when I realized I needed a passport. It was an impetuous act, I'll admit that to you, but I think that when it comes, just having it in hand might make you feel a little closer.*

Lily set the letter down and smiled. He was so fun. She desperately wished she could tell him to come, or write and say she was coming, but it wasn't time. And Lily still wanted to do as Gabe had asked—honor her father's wishes.

"Lily, are you home?" Rika called from outside the door. "Can you come help me?"

Lily rose to aid the older woman, a smile on her face.

"What have you got?" Lily asked when she stepped outside to see that her neighbor was dragging what appeared to be an old, broken metal barrel. She had lassoed it with a rope and tied the rope around her waist.

"I don't know, but I wanted it."

Lily laughed hugely over this, even as she spotted her father coming their way. He stopped and greeted Rika and asked if he could help.

"Lily and I can get it," she replied, waving him off. Lily shook her head in amusement.

"So where do you want this?" the younger woman asked.

"In my garden."

"All right, let me have some of the rope."

The two tugged it along the path, both out of breath in a few minutes, and Lily wondered how the old woman had gotten it as far as she had. Once they had it in place, Lily was invited inside for some tea, and they visited for the next hour. It was a good time, but Lily suddenly realized she hadn't started working on dinner.

Not until she walked back into her own house did she remember she'd left the letter from Gabe on the table. Seeing it just as she left it gave her great relief as she knew her father had come in. As Lily gathered the letter and took it to her room, she wondered what her father would have done if she had gotten off the plane and told him she'd met a man. Having Gabe come up even at this stage of the game made Lily tremble with dread.

Lily suddenly stopped. *I've become consumed with worry, Lord. I don't trust You to take care of this. Please repair things between my father and me. Help me to know what to say and when.*

Lily heard her father in his room just then and was reminded about dinner. It wouldn't help anything if she didn't get her work done. She had done her best to keep all her jobs going, even her translating, in an effort to show her father how much she cared. And it wasn't an act. She did care; she cared deeply.

And I must keep working to accept the fact that I may never get to go back and marry Gabe, Lily reminded herself. She didn't know how many years it would take to get over that hurt, but if that was God's will for her, she did not want to let it cripple her. *Not to mention, whether I leave here tomorrow or never again, there's no point in stealing a moment of precious time from my work in the village.*

～

Oahu

"Hey, Gabe," Jeff had caught him on a rainy Sunday morning in late February.

"Hi, Jeff. How are you?"

"I'm okay. Did you get a letter from Lily recently?"

"Thursday."

"Any changes?"

"None."

Jeff stood still for a time.

"What are you thinking?" Gabe asked.

"Something isn't right here. I feel like Lily's not telling us something."

Gabe's heart sank with dread.

"Your father wouldn't hurt her, would he, Jeff?"

"Not physically, but he's tremendously controlling."

This news for Gabe was extremely painful. Lily was so far away, and they couldn't even speak on the phone.

"I'm going to confront her with this when I write next," Jeff concluded.

"Do you want me to say anything?"

Jeff looked at his friend. He knew that what he had just shared would cause Gabe pain and tempt him to worry. Lily would not thank her brother for that.

"Why don't you keep your letters in a lighter vein, Gabe? I think Lily needs that right now. If she's having a hard time and not sharing it with us, there's a reason. I'm not trying to come between the two of you, but until you've been introduced to my father, I'd probably better stay involved."

"All right. I hope you know this is hard."

"Yeah, it is. I wish I had better news."

"Why would Lily not talk to us?"

"I have a sneaking suspicion that she hasn't even been able to mention that she's met you. If my father knew about you and forbade Lily to marry you, she would have written about that and not left you hanging. This is Lily being protective, feeling that it's best if she handles something on her own."

"That's not like her."

"Not when she's here, it isn't, but we're both so far away."

Gabe's eyes closed as he said, "Don't remind me."

Jeff only touched him on the shoulder before they moved to sit down for the service.

～

Lhasa

Lily frowned down at the bread she had just burned and knew she was going to have to do better than this. Her heart was so heavy all the time that she was having trouble doing anything well. When she was out with the folks from the village or church it was easier, but at home, a dark cloud rested over her and it was starting to show. Even Ling told her she looked thin and pale. Since then Lily had been working hard to be thankful, but it was proving to be more difficult than she expected.

"Do you wish to discuss something with me, Lily?" Owen asked so suddenly from behind his daughter that she nearly dropped the loaf she was holding. Moving slowly, Lily managed to turn and look at her father.

"I did not tell you to look at me!" Owen snapped.

Lily dropped her eyes. She didn't want to, but she hoped if she obeyed he would listen.

"May I tell you my thoughts now, Father?" Lily asked softly, eyes down the entire time.

"Proceed."

"It seems to me that your rules mean more to you than our relationship. On Sunday you preached about the Pharisees who were angry with Jesus because he healed a man on the Sabbath." Lily nearly quoted her father when she said, "'Their tight hold on man-made rules left them utterly coldhearted to a man in need.' Now your own daughter just wishes to look at you and talk with you, but unless I obey your rules, not God's rules, you shun me."

Lily trembled in the horrible silence that followed, her body aching with the tense way she held herself.

"You are getting letters from a man, are you not?"

This question surprised Lily, because it was so far from their present topic of conversation, but she still answered truthfully.

"Why have you not told me?"

Lily answered slowly, still keeping her voice level and eyes down.

"Gabe is special, Father. I find it very hard to discuss him with someone who is constantly enraged at me."

"I will not tolerate your disrespect!"

Lily couldn't take it anymore. She slowly raised her eyes, and although her father hid it, he was shaken by the depth of pain he saw in her face.

"What of your disrespect for me, Father?" Lily whispered slowly and in very real agony. "I'm a person with feelings, and I've honored you all my life, only now to be treated like a criminal. I love the people of our village—you know I do—but I'm not Kashienese, I'm white, and while we're alone in our home I want to be free to talk to the father I love and look him in the eye. I used to be able to do that, but when Mama left us, you changed. I want to go back to the way it was. I'm not asking for anything immoral or sinful. I'm just asking to be noticed and loved in a way that makes me feel loved."

Owen's look and tone were colder than he intended.

"You've changed."

"You're right; I have," Lily agreed, "but I'm not sinning against you, Father. I think if you search your heart, you will see this."

When Owen said nothing for several long seconds, Lily didn't wait to be excused but turned and went to her room.

Owen stood looking at the spot where his daughter had just been, his heart in a mix of emotions. Having her gone from him had been nowhere near as hard as he'd anticipated, but that had lasted only until she returned. Once she came back, he realized he never wanted her to leave him again. But that wasn't the point right now. Lily Walsh was a wise young woman, and she had said something Owen could not ignore.

Walking to her door, he called her name.

"Lily?"

"Come in."

Owen moved the heavy drape that served as a door. Lily was sitting on her bed and kept her eyes down.

"What are these man-made rules you speak of?"

"It is not a rule of God that I lower my eyes before you in this house, nor is it one of God's rules that we pray together at a certain time each evening. I see in my Bible that anger is a sin, yet you grow angry with me often. I am confused that you do not see sin in your anger and yet see so much sin in some of the actions of a daughter who wishes only to honor and please you."

"You see obeying your father as man's rule?" Owen asked.

Lily mentally wrestled to explain, fearful that she would make a mess of things. "Do you think that Le Pa's sleeping with a woman who is not his wife is a serious sin, Father?"

"Of course."

"Do you realize that you exhibit the same anger toward me when I do not keep my eyes lowered as you did toward Le Pa?" Lily wanted to look up but was afraid to risk it. "And this was not the way I was raised, nor did you expect this from my mother. At what point did you read in your Bible that to be an obedient daughter I must become Kashienese?"

"But we live in Kashien, Lily. Surely you can see."

"Yes, I can see when we are among the people of the village, but not when we are home alone. You keep me at arm's length, as the Lhasa men do with the women of their families. I wish for a closeness again, an openness between us."

"And you do not feel we have this?"

"You are angry with me often. You are so easily upset with me that I do not feel I can make a move. This is the first time in more years than I can recall that you have allowed me to ask you something and have not become angry when you do not like my answer."

"And you have realized all of this in making this trip to Hawaii?"

"No," Lily was forced to admit. "I have felt this way for years but have not been able to tell you."

"But something did happen in Hawaii that has made you come home and say these things to me."

"That is true. I was able to look my brother in the eye and not feel ashamed. I was able to say what I feel and not be ashamed."

"If it was so ideal, I wonder that you came home at all."

Lily did not see this coming. His voice had been so calm. She couldn't believe how harsh those few words could be. Her whole body was racked with physical waves of pain as her father delivered these barbs, turned, and walked from the room.

Lily had no choice but to cry out to God for help; He was all she had. Finally invited to talk to her father, Lily thought it had done no good.

For many minutes she prayed and asked God for comfort and wisdom. It was while she was praying that she realized the very thing she'd been talking to her father about had just happened. Ironic as it seemed, he had turned into his own example.

With a peace and calm that Lily had not felt in many weeks, she decided to confront him with this truth. Lily walked slowly out to see whether her father was still home. Sitting in his chair and reading a book, he did not look in her direction, but Lily felt firm in her resolve.

"There is one more thing I need to say to you," Lily began.

Owen ignored her, and for the first time Lily began to grow angry.

"I would beg an audience with you, Father. Will you please hear me out?"

Owen did not so much as stir, and Lily's anger boiled over.

"*Look at me!*" Lily ordered her father for the first time in her life.

Owen was so shocked by her words and tone that he did turn to her.

"The very thing I told you that happens between us has just occurred, but you are blind to your own sins. I said things you do not like, and you left my room in anger." Lily's eyes were blazing now, but she was not done. "I left the man that I love with all my heart in the state of Hawaii in order to come home to you because I told you I would return. Do not *ever* accuse me of being a daughter who does not work to honor her father, for in such a statement you lie to yourself about Lily Walsh."

Lily walked out of the house this time, leaving her father shaken. Never had she spoken to him in this way. It came rushing to him that the woman who had come home to him was happy and productive before he stopped speaking to her. She had not said one word about wanting to go back or about meeting a man, but she had been happy and joyful in his presence.

Owen sighed with relief when he saw that it wasn't too late. He would talk to her again. He would find that happy woman again, and everything would go back to the way it was.

Chapter Twenty-Seven

Oahu

It was with a tough mix of emotions that Gabe Kapaia stood as best man for his brother on March 4 and watched him pledge his life to Deanne Talbot. Nevertheless, there was no denying the happiness in the bride's face and the utter joy in his brother's.

The families of the bride and groom, church family, and friends were out in force. Everyone was up for a great time. Gabe was too, but all through the service and celebration he found his heart in two places: rejoicing with Ashton and Deanne in Hawaii, and in a small village in Kashien that he could only imagine.

~

Lhasa

Lily was in a quandary. Her brother had figured her out. She had read his letter while sitting quietly under her favorite shade tree, and now she just sat and thought.

Something is wrong, Lily, had been some of his words. *I can tell by your silence after all we discussed when you were here. I can only guess that Father has become impossible. By the time you receive this, you will have been gone for almost three months, and not being able to talk to you and know how you are truly doing is more difficult than I can say.*

He didn't need to say. Lily knew how hard it was. The last weeks had felt more like years. Her father had been slightly more civil since Lily had made her feelings clear, and Lily had been doing better with her emotions, but this time had been unlike anything she'd ever known.

Lily read the letter again, thinking that "impossible" was a great way to describe her father.

"He's never once told me he was sorry," Lily suddenly realized, speaking quietly even though she was alone. "I think such words from him would be wondrous to hear."

～

Owen gave Lily a week, thinking she might need a little time on her own, but his plan to talk to her and bring her happiness again was sincere. The only problem was how busy she had become. From the morning she'd told him of her feelings, she had been extremely occupied in the village. It niggled in his mind that this might be a tactic to ward off some type of gloom or sadness, but Owen wouldn't let himself go too far with such thoughts.

He kept working on dinner, something he hadn't helped with in years, hoping that because it was early, Lily would have a little time to spare when she came in. Owen had just finished brewing the tea when he heard her steps at the door.

"I made dinner," Owen proudly announced when Lily walked in.

"Oh, my," Lily said with pleasure. "It smells good."

"I got fairly proficient while you were gone. I think I had started taking you for granted."

Lily was slightly amazed by this statement but hid it behind a smile as she looked at the meal he'd prepared.

"Here, sit down while it's hot."

"Thank you."

They ate for a short time in silence, and then Owen did something that shocked Lily.

"I feel I need to apologize to you, Lily. You've been back for weeks, and I haven't asked you about the things you learned."

Lily did not look up, but her mind filled with one thought. *So this is the way it's to be. You're going to ignore the fact that I've met someone and just go back to life the way it was.*

"Was swimming the first sport you learned?"

"Yes, it was," Lily managed to keep her voice normal and even be thankful that they were having a normal conversation.

"You said in your letter that it didn't go well. Did you get better?"

"I did, yes. I can't remember if I wrote to you about my sunburn, but that was all that really went wrong. I did learn to swim."

"You got sunburned?"

"Yes," Lily said, shivering at the memory.

"Was it a bad burn?"

"Very."

"What did you do?"

"They put me in the hospital."

Owen had all he could do not to react. His first thought was outrage that he had not been informed, but for the first time he saw that he was growing angry. He stopped in light of this knowledge, and also as he thought about Lily being ill.

"So Jeff was with you?"

"No." Lily shook her head, wishing she could look up. "The Kapaias took me."

Had Lily been looking, she would have watched Owen's eyes close. The thought of his daughter being so burned that she needed hospital care, and surrounded by strangers, was almost more than he could bear. He looked over at her and just stared. She was not a short woman, but she was slight of build and fine-boned. The horrible image of her burned and blistered caused him to tremble. He changed the subject, but the image stayed with him.

"What else did you learn?"

"Bailey Markham had this wonderful appliance that makes a perfect loaf of bread. I thought it amazing. You put all the ingredients in and it mixes the dough, kneads it, lets it rise, takes it back down, lets it rise again, and then bakes it."

"How long does it take?"

"About three hours, maybe a little more."

"Does Jefferson have one of those?"

"No, but he has a coffee machine that gives you hot coffee in about a minute."

"That fast?"

"Yes."

And the conversation they should have had her first day back ensued. It was not exactly what Lily had been looking for, but she was very thankful. Now she could write to her brother and tell him that it had been bad but things were greatly improving. For the moment she didn't want to think about what she would have to tell Gabe.

∽

Oahu

> *It's time for me to face facts, Gabe. My father is not going to accept my having fallen in love. I told him more than a week ago that I love a man in Hawaii, and he has made no comment of any kind. I can see that he wishes for me to keep on here and for life to be as it was.*
>
> *I can't quite believe I'm writing this to you, but it's not fair that you stay there and keep your life on hold. I hope that Mr. Kamioto will return your money, since we did not need to have the ring sized.*

Gabe could not read any more. Sitting at the kitchen table where he'd found the letter, he remained utterly still and in shock. For a moment his mind ran with wild thoughts, wondering exactly how old Owen Walsh was and whether Lily could come to him after her father passed on.

Gabe realized he was being foolish. Even if the man died this year, it would be the longest year of his life. Looking at the letter again, he finished reading. There was no silly face at the bottom telling him it was all a joke. He had determined to honor Lily's father, and they had done that. Now Lily would never be his.

You've gotten me through things that I never thought I would survive, Lord. I fear I need You to do so again.

～

Lhasa

"Oh, Father, I'm glad you're here. I just finished that chapter in Genesis and wondered if you would have time to look it over."

"Certainly. The mail just came," he said, passing to her the letter that had her name on the front even as he took the Genesis chapter from her hand. He would have gone right to work on that, but one of his letters caught his eye. The postmarks were numerous, and it looked as if the first stamp was from all the way back in September. Setting all else aside, Owen opened that letter to find it was from Jeff and had evidently been lost in the mail.

Dear Father, he began…

> *My request to have Lily come for a visit has gone from bad to worse. I left Lily in the care of the Kapaia family, knowing she would be as safe with them as she would be in my care. What we all failed to realize was how little she knew of American customs.*
>
> *Lily has been badly sunburned. She is in the hospital even now. Gabe Kapaia—I have written of him often—is there with her at all times. He is taking full responsibility, even for her hospital bills—something Lily does not know.*
>
> *I am confident that in time all will be well. Lily is strong, stronger than she thinks, and as hard as it is to have her ill when I'm away, Gabe has assured me that he and the family will see to her every need so that she makes a full recovery. Gabe is a man of great faith and honor. He will see to it that Lily is fine.*
>
> *Lily and I won't have much time together when I return, but she'll have learned much in the period I am away, and*

> *I know it will be fruitful for both of us. I thank you again*
> *for letting her come.*

Owen put the letter down. He looked up to tell Lily, who had sat in her own chair, about the missing letter, but he never spoke a word.

Lily was reading her own letter, a smile on her face so like her mother's that Owen was stunned. As he watched, she smiled a little more and even laughed softly. For a moment she let her eyes go to the window, her face thoughtful, until she went back to her reading, which put the smile back on her face.

Owen had the unsettled feeling that he was witnessing a very private moment. The thought gave him little comfort. Gathering his papers, he stood. Lily never noticed as he exited to his bedroom and stood looking down on his bed. He had been alone in that bed for many years, but it was to this house and this bed that he had brought his wife home. Both of his children had been conceived and born in that very bed.

Do you really want to deny Lily that joy? Owen asked himself for the first time. He didn't need much time to know the answer. His heart wondering how he would ever survive, Owen began a letter to his son.

～

"Why, Lily," Ling whispered because Charity and Daniel were still napping, "I didn't think I would see you today."

"Is this a bad time?"

"No, come in."

Lily entered the Chen home, trying not to cry. She desperately needed to talk to her friend but knew she would break down.

"You are sad. Can you tell me about it?"

"I think so."

"Is it your father?"

"No, he's very normal again—kind even. He hasn't been this kind in a very long time."

"I'm glad, Lily, but something is hurting you."

"I got a letter from Gabe."

Ling stayed quiet to let her friend share.

"I can tell by the way he writes that he has not yet received my letter." Tears came to Lily's eyes; they would not be stopped. "It was such a fun letter, so like Gabe. I can hardly stand the thought of his reading my letter and hurting the way I hurt when I wrote it."

Ling let her friend cry. She ached for her, but there was little she could do but speak the truth to her. After a moment she began.

"I need to tell you something, Lily Cathleen," Ling-lei said gently, having handed her a small handkerchief. "It may not be a comfort today, but in time you will see. You have honored your father, Lily, and God will bless such obedience. Right now it seems that your heart will break without Gabriel, but God can be all to you, since you have kept Him first in your heart."

"Thank you," Lily managed, sniffing a little. Ling was right—Lily did feel as though she would never survive, but her friend had done her a great favor by reminding her that God was to be her all. No person on the earth could substitute for God and His all-encompassing love.

～

Oahu

Jeff didn't knock or stop for any formalities. He walked into Gabe's office, shut the door, and said, "My father wants to hear from you."

Gabe came out of his chair.

"He wrote to you?"

"Yes. He says Lily doesn't know and he would appreciate your discretion."

"Why, Jeff?" Gabe tried to understand. "I told you about her letter. She's in as much pain as I am. Why would he not talk to her?"

"He probably sees it as a mercy," Jeff guessed. "Why get Lily's hopes up if he isn't going to accept your suit?"

Gabe tried to understand, but it was hard. He prayed that he would do things differently if he ever became a father.

"What does he want me to do?"

Jeff consulted the letter and read from it.

> It is my hope, Jefferson, that if you have any doubts about this man being suitable for your sister, you would never mention this missive to him. If after reading this you still feel it is the best, please ask Mr. Kapaia to write and tell me about when he came to Christ, his commitment to your church family, his occupation and ability to care for Lily, and whether he plans to lead Lily and any children they may have to fear and serve the Lord.
>
> Please explain to him that it's all well and good if he feels he loves my daughter, but because I am not there to see how he lives his life, I need to hear his beliefs and goals, mainly spiritual. As you must know, Lily is special. What I'm asking is if Gabe is the special man for her.

Jeff looked up to see determination in his friend's eyes.

"I can't ask for more than that, can I, Jeff?" he stated after a moment. "At least he's giving me a chance."

"I'll be writing him too, Gabe," Jeff assured him. "I've talked about you over the years, but I'll just remind my father of how close we've been and that I have been here to watch you in action."

"Thank you."

Jeff had to get back to the office, but not before the men embraced. Gabe sat at his desk for a long time after his friend left and looked out on the bay where he and Lily had talked so many times and even swum. He asked God to give him the words for this letter he would write, but more than that, to go before him on this entire matter.

～

Lhasa

Owen was not surprised to receive a letter from his son the very next week. As he half expected, he spoke very highly of Gabriel Kapaia and reminded him of their ongoing friendship over the years. Owen was grateful for the words because he had forgotten some of the things Jeff had written about Gabe in the past.

By the time Gabe's letter arrived, Owen was ready for it. It began much as he expected but then took a turn he did not anticipate.

> *Thank you for contacting Jeff, Mr. Walsh, and asking to hear from me. As you might have guessed, I love your daughter, but if I had my way, she would have more than I can give her. I think Jeff must have mentioned that I am a cancer survivor. I am glad to be alive, but I will never father biological children. I didn't know if I would ever meet someone who would understand my situation, but then Lily came into my life. She is not opposed to adoption; indeed, she is all for it, and I feel even this is a blessing from God, since at this point in time, it is my only option.*
>
> *You may wonder why I began this letter on such an intimate point, but in truth, Mr. Walsh, I can't think of anything else you would object to. I came to a saving belief in Jesus Christ as a child when I realized I was lost in my sin. After that I thought I was serving God and was sold out for Him, but when I learned I had cancer at the age of 22, my faith was put to the test in a way I'd never known.*
>
> *During that time I realized that Christ had to be my all. I praise Him for the growth I experienced and would be willing to go through it again if ever I needed it to draw me closer to Him. My church family was amazingly supportive at that time, as was my mother, stepfather (my own father is dead), sister, brother-in-law, and brother.*

My work at the resort our family owns and operates
was put on hold while I was ill, but things are in good shape
now, and we are looking into doing some remodeling and
expanding later this year. God has greatly blessed us.

Reading at bedtime in the solitude of his room, Owen couldn't help but be impressed. He read the entire letter over twice, thinking that everything indicated that Gabe Kapaia was the special man for Lily.

Owen was still coming to grips with losing Lily, but he knew he could not fight this any longer. Feeling the time might be right, Owen went to Lily's room. It was dark, her lantern already out, but still he knocked softly on the wall just outside her doorway.

"Come in," she called, having heard his footsteps.

"Lily, I need to speak with you."

Owen heard the rustle of her covers and told her she could stay in bed.

"I think we need to make a trip to Hawaii," Owen began, finding that speaking his mind was easier in the dark when faces could not be seen.

"Hawaii?" Lily questioned.

"Yes, I desire to see your brother and his life there, and I think I should meet Gabriel Kapaia."

Lily could not muffle her sobs. Her longing to be with Gabe, even as she tried not to think of him, had been so great.

"Come to me, Lily." Her father's hoarse voice sounded in the dark, and Lily ran to be hugged. Owen's own tears joined his daughter's as she thanked him through breathless sobs.

Lily desperately wanted to know where this change of heart had come from, but that was not something she could ask. Jeff or Gabe might be able to tell her, but she would never have the relationship with her father that she had with them.

"As soon as we can manage the details, we'll go," Owen told her.

"Thank you. Thank you, Father."

"And you must pack everything, Lily, and say your final good-byes."

"Everything," she managed, the tears coming again.

"I would make just one request of you, Lily."

"Yes, Papa."

"Will you please continue to dedicate some time to the translating, Lily, and send the pages back to me?"

His voice had been the most humble Lily had ever heard it. She thought her heart would break, but she told him she would gladly translate for him for as long as she was able.

When at last they parted to find their rest, Lily felt exhausted and drained. She would have said that there were no tears left, but it wasn't true. They started again when her heart spoke to Gabe across the miles.

Don't give up on me yet, Gabe. I'm coming as soon as I can.

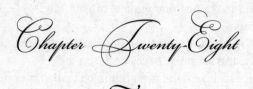

Chapter Twenty-Eight

Six months to the day from the time Lily flew back to Kashien, Owen and Lily's plane landed in Oahu. They were both spent—Owen more so than his daughter—and more than glad to see Jeff waiting outside the customs area.

With as little fuss as possible, Jeff got them to his apartment and into bed. Lily would take the sofa during their stay, but for now she was sound asleep in Jeff's bed.

At the risk of waking his father, Jeff checked on him in the spare room. It had been almost four years since they'd seen each other, and for the first time, Owen Walsh looked old. Something squeezed around Jeff's heart as he looked down at the man who had fathered him, and he asked God to do a work between them so that when Owen left Hawaii, he and Jeff could claim a closer-than-ever-before relationship.

Thankful he hadn't disturbed him, Jeff let himself back out of the room, only to find that Lily had come to the kitchen.

"Are you awake?" Jeff whispered, thinking she looked like a sleepy child with her hair all over her face.

"I think so."

"Do you want some coffee or tea?"

"I think just water, Jeff."

He waited until she'd finished half the glass and then spoke. "Are you up to talking?"

"Certainly."

Smiling, Jeff reached for the phone, dialed, and handed it to his sister.

"Say hello to the man that answers."

Lily smiled just as Gabe picked up.

"Hello?"

"Hello," Lily said softly and heard Gabe's breathless laugh.

"I love you," he wasted no time in saying.

"Oh, I love you, Gabe. It's wonderful to hear your voice."

"How was the flight?"

"It was long but survivable."

"How did your father do?"

"He got very tired. He's sleeping right now."

"Did Jeff tell you you're invited for dinner?"

"No, but I can't wait to see everyone. How's that new baby?"

"She's a doll. You're going to fall in love all over again."

"Have the kids grown?"

"Yes. Pete will be in school in just a few months."

"Oh, my. I've missed so much."

"How were folks in the village?"

"Doing well," Lily told him, amazed just to hear the sound of his voice. It felt as though she hadn't left. He was still Gabe. He talked to her the same way and included her in his life and was interested in hers.

They visited for a little while longer before Gabe said he had a call to make. Lily told him she looked forward to that night.

"How is Mr. Kapaia?" Jeff asked with a smile. He'd been at the table the whole time they talked, not listening, but still hearing things off and on.

"He's wonderful," Lily said, her face wreathed in smiles. "He said we're invited to dinner."

"Let's hope our father is up to it."

"Jeff," Lily started, suddenly putting her hand on his arm, "I'm sorry I haven't asked about Annika lately. Are you still seeing each other?"

Jeff smiled. "We e-mail each other every day."

"But you haven't seen each other?"

"We did briefly in Arizona at the end of February, but the way things had been going for you and Gabe, I didn't want to write about us."

"Is Arizona where you were?"

"Yes. Now that things are up and operational, I can talk about it."

"Well, I want to hear everything, but first I want to know when you'll see Annika again."

"The end of August. She has vacation time, and she'll be coming here."

"I'm glad, Jeff. Again, I'm sorry I haven't checked with you."

"It's all right. I'm looking forward to telling Father about her."

"When will you?"

"When he's rested and we have some time."

"Have you taken some days off?"

"Tomorrow and then a few others in the weeks to come."

Owen joined Lily and Jeff while they were still talking. He looked somewhat rested but still a little worn around the edges. Jeff was careful to keep the pressure light about the evening's plans, explaining that it was entirely up to him. When presented with the idea of meeting and eating with Gabe and his family that night, Owen surprised his children by saying he would enjoy it very much.

Owen was delighted with the Kapaia Resort. He proclaimed the grounds to be beautiful and smiled widely when he saw the house and large covered porch.

"And this is where you stayed, Lily?"

"Yes."

"Did you have your own room?"

"Yes, upstairs."

Jeff and Lily shared a look at his pleasure, thinking he was looking more relaxed by the moment.

Nearly all of the family came to the door, and just moments after Lily and Deanne hugged for the first time, Lily had eight-day-old Sarah Lilia—which was Hawaiian for Lily's name—in her arms.

"Are you sure you're up to having us?" Lily asked Bailey, who looked wonderful.

"I'm fine. Wang is babying me, and Deanne got the house ready."

Lily heard her father's laugh just then and looked over to see him talking to Gabe. They had only shared a swift hug before Lily was swallowed up by the rest of the family. Evan wasn't long in ushering everyone to the table, however, and before Lily knew it, she was sitting right next to Gabe, his hand holding hers under the table.

"Okay—" Evan stood at his place and acted as host—"I'll keep this short because the food is hot, but of course we want to extend a warm and special welcome to Jeff and Lily's father. Welcome, Mr. Walsh."

"Thank you."

"And to Lily," Evan continued, "welcome, and I have a question."

Lily looked at him and smiled.

"Where are you staying?"

"At Jeff's."

"Where will you sleep?"

"On the sofa."

"That won't do at all," Evan said, gaining a laugh from nearly everyone. "We want you to move back into your own room tonight. And now," he continued, moving on so fast that the family laughed again, "let us be thankful for this family and feast."

All jesting gone, Evan offered a prayer that told of his heart's great joy over their gathering. Celia sneezed in the middle of the prayer, which made Evan pause and then continue with a smile in his voice, but it wasn't long before everyone was eating and talking.

And it was not lost on Lily that one of her favorite meals had been prepared: the special ham with pineapples baked all over the top, mashed potatoes, fruit salad, and chocolate pie for dessert. She hadn't feasted like this in six months, and every bite tasted like ambrosia.

"Does coffee in the living room sound good?" Bailey asked when things at the table got a little quiet and the diners were done.

"I'll help," Lily volunteered but was told that tonight she was a guest. Just moments later she found herself on the love seat next to Gabe, her father in the chair to her left, and all but Ashton and Deanne, who had volunteered to do the coffee, gathered around them.

"What was the weather like when you left Kashien, Father?" Jeff asked Owen.

"Mild at home, but on the warm side in the city."

Gabe listened to this conversation, but because he was on Lily's right side, he had to look past her to see Owen. It was a wonderful view in his opinion, but he realized he had not considered one aspect of her return: She had become Kashienese once again. Her eyes were down the way they had been when they first met. The only difference, with the exception of her father, was that Lily would raise her eyes when someone spoke to her. The moment she was done, however, her lids lowered again. Not once did she look at Owen, even when he spoke to her, and Gabe assumed it was because she did not feel free to do that without permission.

Wishing there was something he could do to tell her it would be all right, Gabe remembered what was in his pocket. Owen was sharing about the church family in Lhasa when Gabe discreetly passed a stick of gum between them until it lay next to Lily's leg. She saw it immediately. With her right hand Lily enfolded the gum in her palm. With her left hand she covered her mouth to hide a smile.

"You can chew it." Gabe's voice came for her ears alone, but Lily didn't look at him or try to reply.

The next hour was spent in the same fashion, but when Jeff saw that his father was looking a little worn, he suggested they head out. Owen seemed to have no problem with that, but he did not expect Evan to follow through on his suggestion from dinner.

"You can just gather your things tomorrow, Lily," Evan said. "Bailey will have everything you need for tonight."

Owen waited for Lily to turn and check with him, but all she did was thank Evan before saying, "I'll walk you out."

Clearly, Jeff thought nothing of this. He put a gentle arm around his sister's shoulders, planning to tell her something before he left. As soon as the three were alone on the porch, he spoke.

"Hey, Lil, you're in Hawaii now. You have to look at the men."

"You're right, Jeff. I'll work on that."

"Good job. We'll see you tomorrow."

"Okay. Have a good night, Father."

Owen bid her good night as well, but as soon as both he and Jeff were in the car, he asked, "Why would you advise Lily to have eye contact with men without consulting me?"

"I was thinking of your testimony, Father," Jeff answered as he started the car and got them under way. "People will wonder what kind of monster you are that you won't allow your daughter to look at you."

"Surely there is tolerance for other cultures here in Hawaii, Jefferson." Owen sounded testy.

"Father," Jeff began, his voice a bit commanding, "why have you brought Lily all this way? You do plan to let her stay and marry Gabe, do you not?"

"If Gabe asks me for Lily's hand, I will give them my blessing."

"Then why would you push the point over Lily's eye contact?"

Owen had no answer for this. He was quiet enough that Jeff was certain he was angry or offended, but Jeff opted not to ask.

As it was, they said little else as they finished the ride home. Owen gave no indication with his voice or demeanor that he was angry, but he said he was ready to turn in almost as soon as they stepped through Jeff's apartment door.

∼

Evan answered the phone, but because it was for Gabe he had no choice but to disturb the talking couple. Gabe came to the phone, surprised to hear Jeff's voice.

"Hey, what's up?"

"I thought I'd better let you know about something that came up in the car."

"All right."

"My father expects you to ask for Lily's hand. If you're thinking his blessing is a given, it's not. You need to ask him."

"I planned on that. In fact, I asked him to join me for breakfast on Saturday. We're going to the Little Bay."

"Great."

"Thanks, Jeff."

"You're welcome. I'll see you tomorrow."

When Jeff got off the phone, he sat and thought about the conversation in the car with his father. That man was sleeping now, but why would he make a comment about Gabe needing to ask for Lily's hand?

Why do you think Gabe asked you to breakfast? Jeff mentally asked. *Surely not to talk about the weather.*

Jeff knew he needed to pray. If he felt this frustrated this early in his father's visit and didn't keep his thoughts in check, his frustration would only go from bad to worse.

∼

"I'm back," Gabe said with a smile when he joined Lily in the sitting area of the living room. Ashton and Deanne had gone home to their cottage, Peter and Celia were in bed, and Evan and Bailey were watching television while Bailey gave Sarah a last feeding.

"Is everything all right?" Lily asked.

"Yes. That was Jeff giving me a word of advice."

"About Father?"

"Yes."

"What did you think of him?"

Gabe took her hand. "It's hard to watch his treatment of you."

"I'm fine, Gabe. Please believe me."

"I do believe you, but it doesn't make it right."

"You get used to it."

"I don't know if I ever would."

"Sometime it's harder to imagine something than to actually do it."

Gabe looked at her. "I missed you so much."

For a moment Lily only looked at him. When she spoke, her voice was filled with wonder, as though the thoughts were new, even to her.

"I love Kashien. It's been my home forever, but I left my heart in Hawaii, in your hands." She looked at him for a long moment. "I found it was very hard to breathe without it."

Gabe took her in his arms.

"Oh, my sweet Lily," he said close to her ear. They didn't kiss or even share a deep embrace, but Gabe simply held her, her head on his shoulder.

"I don't want to say this, Gabe, but I'm fading."

"I'll bet you are. Why don't we tell Bailey you're ready to head to bed, and she can find you some things for the night."

Gabe gave her a quick kiss before they went over to the TV area. They sat with the Markhams and talked for a few minutes, but fatigue was covering Lily's very movements. It was a sweet mercy when Bailey finished with Sarah, handed her off to her father, and took Lily off to bed.

"I assume you received my letter, sir?" Gabe asked Owen after the two had taken time to speak of general things.

"I did, Gabriel. Thank you."

"Was everything clear to you?"

"It was. I had forgotten about your bout with cancer. You did not say in your letter how your health is today."

"I'm cancer-free. I have a checkup each year, so my oncologist keeps close track of me."

"I'm glad to hear it. I would not withhold my permission on the worry that you might become ill again, but I would hate for you and Lily to have to go through that."

"I appreciate your words, sir. Cancer is a funny thing. It can creep up on you without warning and change your life forever. I try hard not to second-guess the situation. I won't ignore any obvious signs, but at the same time I can't panic each time I feel a pain."

"You have obviously learned great trust in God."

"I'm getting there. Some days are better than others."

Owen looked at him for a moment.

"Lily is special," he said at last.

Gabe nodded. "You, sir, would know that better than anyone, but I am learning fast."

"I know she loves you, and I can tell that you love her."

Gabe only nodded this time.

"My wife and I shared that type of love, and Jeff told me yesterday that he is seeing someone. God has been good to us."

Again Gabe only waited, seeing what Jeff had seen on the day his father arrived: Owen Walsh was not a young man. There was so much Gabe could say to him, so many things he wanted to lay at his door, but he remembered his long-ago resolve to treat him with honor and respect. If Lily's father were going to stay and remain a part of their daily lives, Gabe might be more vocal, but he did not believe that the right time was now.

"Is there something you wish to ask me, Gabe?" Owen inquired in a moment of compassion, genuinely desiring his daughter's happiness.

Gabe smiled. "Indeed, there is, sir. May I have Lily's hand in marriage?"

"I believe that would do very well," the older man said. "I would make but one request of you."

"Please name it, sir."

"My plane leaves to go back to Kashien on July 14. Will you please marry my daughter before then, Gabriel, so I can be here when it happens?"

If he had offered Gabe the moon, he couldn't have made him happier.

"I'll find Lily as soon as we're done here, sir. And thank you."

Owen nodded. "Lily said something about the workings of this kitchen. I believe I'll go and inspect those and let you go on your way."

Gabe had all he could do not to run. He thanked his future father-in-law again, remembered to sign for the bill, and by the time he saw Lily was very calm, but the moments in between had been a mad scramble for Gabriel Kapaia.

⌇

"Where are we going?" Lily asked Gabe, who held her hand as they walked.

"To the office."

A couple with two little children, all in swimsuits and headed in the direction of the pool, came across their path.

"How are you folks enjoying your stay?" Gabe greeted them kindly.

"It's great, thank you."

"Have fun at the pool."

"Thanks. We will."

Lily waited until they were past before asking, "Do you have some business to see to?"

"I do, yes."

"Oh, maybe I can help."

"I'm sure you can," Gabe said as he led Lily through the resort office, greeted Mollee, and then took her into his office where he shut the door.

"Here," he directed her, "take a seat. I have to boot up this computer."

Lily was glancing around, remembering the last time she'd been there, so she didn't immediately notice that Gabe had come back around the desk. When Lily finally snapped from her reverie, he was already pulling the chair next to her very close and had shifted them both so they could face each other.

"I would have liked a more romantic place than this, but I hope when you hear me out, you'll understand."

Lily only looked at him until he picked up her left hand.

"Oh, Gabe," she said when she saw the ring.

"Will you marry me?"

"My father said yes?"

"Yes."

Lily could only watch in awe as he pushed the beautiful diamond onto her finger.

"You kept the ring."

"I had to. It's your ring. I was just holding it for you."

Lily threw her arms around his neck. Gabe kissed her, and she kissed him right back.

"I'll take that as a yes."

Lily only laughed, but Gabe was already pulling her to her feet. "Okay," he said in his excitement. "Now this is where it gets interesting. Come over here and sit on my desk chair."

Lily laughed at the delight in his face but did as he asked.

"Okay, use the mouse and click on Wedding. That's it. Now click again on Announcement."

What appeared on the screen floored Lily. She read it and read it again.

To be put in the bulletin under special announcements:

> **Sunday, July 9:** *Please join us for the wedding of Gabriel Kapaia and Lily Walsh. The ceremony will be at 12:30 P.M. immediately following the second service. All are invited to the wedding and luau to follow. Lily's father*

is visiting and wishes to see his daughter wed before he returns to Kashien, so things are being arranged very quickly. If anyone would care to help with food, flowers, or music on this special day, please see Lani Pilipo, our wedding coordinator.

Lily turned to look at the man bending over her.

"This was your father's only request, that we be married soon so he could be here for it."

"That's just four weeks away, isn't it?"

"Yes. Do you think we can do it?"

Lily nodded, her eyes filled with excitement, but she had one question.

"Do you think the church will mind?"

Gabe laughed. "Before I came and found you, I put a call in to Lani. I told her she had to stay quiet about it until I got back to her, but she was coming apart at the seams with excitement, and I could hardly get a word in."

"What do we do now?"

"We print this out, go tell the family, and then get this to the church so it can be included in tomorrow's bulletin."

He had done so much planning that Lily was amazed. Just minutes later they were getting ready to leave the office to tell the family, but Lily stopped at the door.

"Oh, no!"

"What's the matter?"

Lily looked at him and admitted quietly, "I've thought for some time now that it would be wonderful to honeymoon in Hawaii."

"Why can't we?"

"You live here, Gabe. It won't be special."

That man's smile was very slow. "Just let me take care of the details."

"You're sure you don't mind?"

"Are you going to be there with me?"

Lily knew she didn't need to answer. She smiled and went up on her toes to kiss him. It was time to tell the family.

Chapter Twenty-Nine

Bailey watched Lily hesitate as she studied the price tag of the first wedding dress and knew they were going to have a little conference.

"Can we have just a moment alone?" Bailey asked the saleswoman kindly.

"Of course. I'll check on you in a little while."

"Lily?"

The younger woman turned to her.

"Does anything appeal to you?"

"They're expensive, Bailey," Lily wasted no time in saying. "There must be something more economical."

"Why don't you just see if something appeals to you?"

To Bailey's utter astonishment, a stubborn look crossed Lily's face as she shook her head no.

"When Gabe and I shopped for rings, he presented me with a tray. Thinking to save money, I looked for a small diamond, but Gabe told me he could afford everything on that tray and not to worry. I want the woman to first bring dresses that are reasonable; then I will choose from those."

"I'll take care of everything," Bailey said, finding she did not have to argue. Evan was paying for Lily's dress, and he had told Bailey what they could spend. Bailey simply informed the woman what the limit was, and dresses began to appear. Nevertheless, Lily did not look thrilled with any of them.

"Nothing?" Bailey asked when the woman disappeared for a few minutes.

"They are all sleeveless."

"It's very hot this time of year, Lily."

A look of sudden misery covered the bride's face. It was brief, but Bailey caught it. When the woman came back, Bailey once again asked if they could have some time on their own.

"There are other stores we can check, Lily."

"I'm sorry to be so difficult, Bailey. Maybe my father should choose this dress for me."

"You're not marrying your father."

"Be that as it may, it would not please him to see me looking immodest."

"And that's how he would feel about a sleeveless dress?"

Lily nodded, wishing Gabe was here, even as she admitted, "It's not just my father's wishes. I am not comfortable in sleeveless clothing."

Someone knocked at the door, and Bailey went to answer it.

"Would you ladies like something cool to drink? Tea or a soda?"

"Water for me, thank you," Bailey said.

"Water, please," Lily added.

"Okay, Lily—" Bailey was not giving up just yet and only waited until they were alone again—"let's try this. When the woman comes back, we'll explain everything to her. If she can't help us, then we'll head on our way."

"She's already done so much."

"It's her job."

Lily had to repeat that fact to herself several times over the next 90 minutes, but when they were done, Lily had a dress—a lovely gown with short sleeves and a modestly rounded neckline. It had no train but fell to the floor with insets of lace and satin. It was so perfect for her that Bailey had all she could do not to cry when Lily had come out with it on.

"Will Gabe like it?" Lily asked when they drove away, both tired but content.

"Gabe will love it. How will your father feel about it?"

"I think he will approve. Will Evan be upset over the cost?"

"No, Lily. It's under what he said we could plan on."

"Thank you, Bailey."

"You're welcome."

Lily put her head back and closed her eyes. By the time they pulled up in front of the house, she was sound asleep. Gabe had seen them and come out, but only Bailey emerged from the van.

"How did it go?"

"She found a beautiful dress."

"Good. Did it need altering?"

"No, we brought it home with us. If you'll help me get it out, I'll take it inside."

"It looks pretty," Gabe said, having caught a glimpse of lace as he pulled it out and laid it across his sister's arms. She got herself in the door and ran into Evan.

"How did it go?" he asked as he took the dress from her arms.

"It took a little doing, but she found a beautiful dress."

"No altering?"

"No. She's a perfect size four."

"A four?"

"Yes, I haven't been that small since I was in the fifth grade!"

"Well, you won't hear me complaining," Evan said, giving her a look that made her smile. "Where do you want this hung?"

"Lily's closet."

"Where is Lily?"

"She fell asleep in the car. Gabe is getting her."

Easier said then done, as that man was finding out. Once Bailey went on her way, Gabe opened Lily's door, but she was out cold. He knew that some of her tiredness was from jet lag and some of it was from the emotions of this time.

"Lily?" he tried softly.

Nothing.

"Lily, honey." This time he touched her shoulder. "Can you wake up?"

Lily shifted and sat up very straight, feeling completely disoriented. She looked at the inside of the garage as though she'd boarded an alien vessel. She turned to Gabe and blinked slowly.

"I found a dress."

"Bailey told me. Do you like it?"

"Oh, Gabe, it's so pretty, but I worry about the cost."

"Evan told Bailey what he expected. She would not have ignored his wishes. Let Evan and Bailey do this for you—they want to—and don't forget how pleased your father was when they offered."

Lily nodded, still feeling half asleep. She looked at him with lazy eyes and admitted, "I just want to be married to you."

"The feeling is quite mutual," Gabe said with a hand to the side of her hair. It was always so soft, and since it was very straight—a texture completely opposite his own coarse waves— he was fascinated with the feel.

"It's hot out here. Are you ready to go inside?"

Lily came out the door and around to the back.

"Bailey took it in for you."

"Did you see it? Did you like it?"

"What little I saw I liked very much."

"I don't want you to be disappointed."

Gabe laughed. "Haven't you figured out that I would marry you if you wore a paper sack?"

"Well, that would have cost less money."

They began to walk toward the house.

"Where is my father right now?"

"He was around for a little while after lunch, but then he said he wanted to walk on the beach."

"Have you seen him since?"

"No, but Evan spotted a lone figure by the cove and was pretty certain it was him."

As soon as Gabe said this he looked at his watch.

"I've got to go. I'm suppose to meet Ash, and I'm already late."

"Okay. Thanks for waking me up."

Gabe took her face in his hands. "I hated to do it, but it's awfully warm out here."

"If the children want to swim, maybe I'll take them."

"Um, I hate to miss that."

"Go on," Lily told him gently, and after giving her a soft kiss, he did.

Lily watched him walk away, her heart amazed that this man would soon be her husband. It was like a dream come true and more wonderful than any fairy tale she had ever read.

"How was your walk?" Lily asked her father when he came in through the doors from the veranda.

"Invigorating. Did you know that the bay is 106 meters around?

"How did you figure that out?"

"With this gadget Jeff gave me," Owen said and pulled out a GPS.

"Is that one of those Global Positioning Systems?"

"Yes. Right now we are 128 meters from the cove and," he pushed another button, "172 from the bay."

Lily smiled, thinking it was wonderful to see him relaxed and having such a good time. She forgot herself and looked up into his eyes. He frowned fiercely, and Lily's head dropped.

"Come here, Lily," Owen said suddenly and led her to the sitting area. "I want to ask you something."

Lily sat, eyes down.

"Look at me."

She obeyed, glad that for the moment they were alone.

"Did I see some clothing in the closet at Jeff's? Women's things?"

"Yes, I believe you might have."

"Are they yours?"

"Yes, he bought them for me on my visit."

"But you didn't bring them home."

"No. I knew I wouldn't have an opportunity to wear them."

"Well, you're in America now, Lily. It's time you wear them. In fact, I've been meaning to tell you that I have a little money set aside so you can get a few more things. I wouldn't want you looking out of place and not having the vibrant witness you've always had."

"Thank you, Father. Did you wish to shop with me?"

"No, no," he waved the thought away. "I know you'll buy appropriate things."

For a long moment Lily looked at him.

"You don't really know what to do with me anymore, do you, Father?"

Owen's attention had been headed back to the device in his hand, but he stopped and stared at his daughter.

"One moment you're upset that I looked you in the eye without permission, and the next moment you're giving me a gift so that I will feel at home here." Lily paused but said again, "You really don't know what to do with me anymore."

Owen's face looked stern but his voice was not.

"I think you must be right, Lily. I hadn't thought of it, but it's quite true."

"I would just ask one thing, Father," Lily now said. "When you fly away after the wedding, please don't leave angry at me. I think my heart would break if you did."

Tears had filled her eyes over just the thought, and Owen's heart was touched.

"I'll gladly do as you ask, Lily. Indeed, I shall try not to get angry for any reason. I never told you, but you spoke wisdom to me that day. I do anger easily, and I have worked to be more mindful of my thoughts and actions."

Lily smiled at him and decided to go for broke.

"Father, why did you change your mind and decide that I could come back to Hawaii?"

"Didn't I tell you?"

Lily shook her head no.

"I thought about the life I'd enjoyed with your mother. I didn't want any less for you."

The very thought Lily had entertained but kept to herself! Lily was incapable of speech over the fact that her father had come to it on his own. She had remained quiet and respectful and let God do His job.

"Thank you," she finally managed, not able to say more.

A moment later Owen went back to his GPS, happy as a child, and Lily was left alone in her thoughts, trying to find the words to thank God for allowing her to talk to her father.

〜

"Lily," Lani Pilipo began almost as soon as she'd come in the front door; the wedding was in less than three weeks. "This is Kenika Uilama. He's going to be your photographer."

"It's a pleasure to meet you, Mr. Uilama," Lily said to the man who appeared to be old enough to be her grandfather.

"It's a pleasure to meet you. Lani has dragged me out of retirement for this one. I hope I haven't lost my touch."

Lani laughed and shook her head.

"Lily, have you seen all those photos on the bulletin board in the hall at church?"

"Yes."

"Mr. Uilama takes them all. Your wedding photos will be beautiful."

"I would make one request," the older gentleman said. "I would like to do the wedding pictures in lieu of a gift."

"Oh, Mr. Uilama, please let us pay you," Lily said, wishing Gabe had been on time for this meeting.

"No, no. I knew Gloria before she even became a Kapaia. Besides, it's a selfish gift on my part, since it saves me from having to pick out teaspoons or towels—something my late wife would have loved. As they say these days, I'm clueless."

"Are you sure, Mr. Uilama?"

"Quite sure. Now, why don't you tell me what you have in mind."

Deanne chose that moment to come in from the kitchen, and everyone greeted her.

"Gabe is stuck on the phone," she told Lily. "He asked me to tell you."

"Thank you, Deanne. Mr. Uilama was just asking me what I want for photos," Lily said before turning to that man. "I would be happy with whatever you want to take. I'll leave it up to you."

"Why don't we put together a simple list," Lani suggested, and in a matter of moments they had a list started on paper: the newlyweds alone, the bride with her father, the groom with his parents, the newlyweds with Owen, with Gloria and Carson, and so on. Lily had never considered all the possibilities, but Lani and the newly married Deanne were pros.

By the time Gabe arrived, it was nearly settled. He greeted Mr. Uilama like the old friend that he was, and other than asking for a few pictures outside with the ocean as a backdrop, he seemed well content with the list.

The group visited for a while, but when Mr. Uilama took his leave and Lily finally had a few minutes alone with Gabe, she remembered she had something to tell him.

"On Thursday before the wedding I'm going to move back to Jeff's."

"Is there a reason for that?"

"Yes. Carson and your mother will already be here, and Carson's family will be coming in that day. It will make it easier for everyone if my room is free."

Gabe did not look happy about this idea at all. He didn't say anything, but some of the warmth had left his eyes.

"Is something wrong, Gabe?"

He didn't answer right away, which told Lily she was right. Lily stayed quiet and waited for him to speak.

"Did Bailey hint that you should do this?"

"No, I thought it was only logical."

"You have remembered that Ash's room is open these days, haven't you?"

"Yes, Gabe, but three families are coming in with only two open rooms. My room is needed."

"Are you sure they're coming that day?"

"Melika and her family are coming that day, and Kale and his family are coming Friday."

"So wait until Friday."

"No, I think it will be easier if I'm moved out before they come."

Gabe frowned at her.

"Why are you frowning at me?" Lily asked quietly.

"I worry about the things your father says to you."

"Like what?"

"That's just it; you never know."

Lily felt wounded. She glanced away from Gabe, not sure what to say.

"Have I upset you?" he asked her profile.

"A little. It's hard knowing that you think my father an ogre."

A tender hand to Lily's face brought her eyes back to Gabe's.

"Sweetheart," he said gently, his hand softly caressing her cheek, "I love your father, and I've enjoyed getting to know him, but in many ways he's a law unto himself. Jeff may not be there all the time, and your father has a hold on you that's hard to deal with."

"What are you afraid he'll say?"

"I don't know, but I don't want him treating you in such a way or telling you things that will leave you an emotional wreck by Sunday."

Lily tried to understand, but it was hard. "My father's been around all the time I've been here," Lily suddenly realized. "What do you think will be different?"

Gabe didn't have an answer, and that was very frustrating. He finally ended with, "I just thought you should know how I felt so

you could be on the alert. I'm not suggesting that your father will
be malicious, but the way he treats you is not always the best. I
wanted your last few days before the wedding to be relaxed. I
thought you might have that here. I'm not sure if you will at Jeff's.
That's all."

Lily took a moment to think about this.

"Thank you for telling me."

Gabe looked at her. "Did we just have an argument?"

"Were you angry, Gabe?"

"A little."

"So was I."

"Is it settled?"

"Yes. If I find that I can't rest like you want me to, I'll call you
and we'll figure something out."

"Good. I'll stop worrying."

"You have to stop worrying anyway."

Gabe nodded as he slipped an arm around her, knowing she
was right. He had just snuggled her close to his side when his
cell phone beeped. Lily started and was reminded that it would
be at his waist almost constantly for ten months of each year,
something she was going to have to get used to.

Having known Lily was coming to the office, Gabe nevertheless found himself very thankful that he'd just been put on hold
when Lily entered, a stack of papers in her hand.

"Oh, I'm sorry," she whispered as soon as she saw the phone
in his hand. She began to back away.

"I'm on hold," Gabe said as he waved her back, his eyes not
quite reaching her face.

This was a Lily he'd never seen. He didn't know where she
had found the slim white slacks and dark-blue print top she'd
tucked into them, but the tiny bit of lace along the square neckline and the way both pieces fit her was causing him to forget
who he was holding for.

"Why don't I just look around the gift shop until you're off?"

"Okay," Gabe agreed, his mind distracted again as he watched her walk away from him.

Lily was completely unsuspecting. She talked for a few minutes with Mollee, who was manning the resort desk, but then made her way to the shop. She was studying an item new to the shop, a small scooter, when Gabe found her.

"Someone has been shopping," he said softly, having to work to keep his hands to himself.

Lily turned with a smile. "Do you like this outfit? Deanne took me."

"I like it," he said. His admission was a gross understatement, but this wasn't the time to tell her what she was doing to him.

"Do you want these papers now?"

"Yes. Why don't you come back into the office?"

The moment they were around the corner in Gabe's office, the door not even shut, Gabe took Lily in his arms and kissed her.

"What was that for?" Lily asked in surprise.

Gabe looked down into her beautiful face, so sweet and full of trust. He asked God to let him be worthy of this special woman.

"Let's just say I needed it," Gabe told her quietly.

Lily only smiled up at him and raised her fingers to stroke his cheek. They didn't kiss again, but both were content to look at each other for a little while, remembering that in nine more days they would be husband and wife.

Chapter Thirty

With just four days left until the wedding, Gabe and Ash went out to breakfast, much the way they had before Ashton and Deanne were wed.

"I'm not at the house all the time," Ashton began, "but it seems as though things are wrapping up very nicely."

"They are, thanks to Lani and the rest of the church family."

"When do the Kale and Koma gangs arrive?"

"Melika and Koma come tomorrow, Kale and Lydia on Friday."

"And that's why Lily is moving back to Jeff's?"

"Yes. I wish she could stay, but it is going to be something of a madhouse."

The men ordered their food and enjoyed their coffee for a time, but Gabe had been heavy on Ashton's heart for several days, and he wasn't going to miss this opportunity to find out how he was doing. Everything was moving so fast, especially because Gabe had not planned on getting married on such short notice. Because of that, the family had not been able to leave a cottage open for a year like they had for him and Deanne.

"Are you and Lily going to be all right living up at the house so soon?"

"We'll be fine. Things will quiet down when everyone goes home, and Evan has already warned Peter and Celia about banging on our door."

"Are you as tired as you look?"

"I am, yes. I'm busier than I would wish to be. I can tell that both Lily and I are going to be worn out before all of this is over."

"Then I'd better warn you about something."

"Okay."

"Take it easy for those few days you're gone."

"I think that's the plan. We'll probably just lie around the pool."

"That's not what I meant."

Gabe looked at his younger sibling. Right now he was the experienced husband. Gabe was very aware that he was not.

"Sometimes I can be rather thick, so be specific with me, Ash," Gabe commanded. "Very specific."

"Deanne and I were so tired by the time we left for our honeymoon that I thought we would be on the same page about things that night, but that was before we were alone. Suddenly I had all sorts of energy, and all my bride could do was cry. She wasn't upset, just exhausted."

Gabe was surprised but kept quiet, knowing there was more.

"If I had said something stupid like 'I've waited a long time' or showed Deanne that I was disappointed, I would still be trying to repair the damages. Are you getting my meaning, Gabe?"

"Yes," Gabe said very slowly and gratefully. "Thank you."

"You're welcome."

Ash watched his brother take a drink of coffee. For a moment he just stared at him. This was the older brother he adored. This was the man who had battled Satan when he had done everything in his power to discourage Gabe during the cancer ordeal and all it had entailed. It hadn't worked. This was the brother who had taught him that their God was huge. There was so much Ash wanted to say; he just hoped he could find the words. And then Lily came to mind.

"I hope you know how special Lily is, Gabe, and how much I'm praying for your marriage."

"She is special," Gabe agreed quietly. "And I'll take any and all prayers you want to offer on our behalf. Thank you."

"It's a lot of work to love someone in the way that makes them feel loved, Gabe, but it's worth it."

Gabe smiled at him. Right now Ashton didn't seem two years younger. Gabe felt like a kid as he realized this might have been the conversation he would have had with his father had Liho Kapaia been alive. In fact, Ashton looked more like their father than either he or Bailey.

"Where are you two headed on Sunday night?" the younger man asked.

"Kevin gave us a rate at the Ihilani."

"Oh, very nice. How long will you be gone?"

"Just until Tuesday morning. Owen flies out Thursday, so that will give Lily one more day with him."

"How do you think she'll do with his leaving?"

"I think all right. Hopefully we'll both have gotten some rest."

It would have been nice to have started on that rest right then, but both men had jobs waiting for them. They talked a bit more as they finished their breakfasts, but it wasn't long before both were headed out the door and back to work.

"How are you doing?" Jeff asked his sister on Saturday night. That afternoon they had had the wedding rehearsal and a light dinner, but now they were trying to make an early night of it back at Jeff's apartment.

"I'm all right, I think. A little tired, but all right."

"Take my bed tonight," Jeff told her.

"Jeff, you need your rest just as much as I do."

Jeff smiled just as their father joined them from his room.

"I don't think I do," he teased her quietly, and Lily blushed.

"Do you think I have the right shoes?" Owen asked as he brought out the patent leather ones they had given him with his tux. "They pinch."

"Just wear your tennis shoes," Lily told him, surprising both her brother and father into laughter. "I'm going to," Lily added and found both men laughing again.

"You are not!" Jeff said, clearly not believing her.

"I'll show you tomorrow," she said complacently.

"Are you wearing tennis shoes?" her father now asked, having taken a seat to try his shoes on again.

"Yes. Bailey did, and she says it's the only way your feet can survive such a day. It's too bad you don't have a dress to cover your feet, Papa."

"But what about when you sit down," Jeff argued. "Your feet will show then."

"Yes, they might, but the shoes are brand new and very nice, and I don't care if they're seen."

Right now Jeff could believe that. Lily was slouched in a corner of the sofa, looking as if she didn't care about anything. It was too bad that the bride had to get so weary before the big day. Jeff knew that some of it stemmed from the rush of everything, but even brides who took months to plan were usually worn out by the time the ceremony came around. With this thought, his mind naturally went to Annika.

"Is there anything fun on television tonight?" Lily asked, wanting to just lie back, relax, and not think about what did or did not get done.

"I'll check."

There wasn't, so they ended up watching a Hallmark movie that Jeff had on video. It was both funny and poignant, and Lily cried at the end.

"Go to bed, Lily," her father told her, albeit kindly.

"You're sitting on my bed," she told him through her sniffles, as he was on the other end of the sofa.

Jeff reminded her that she was taking his bed that night. And because even Lily could see that she was on the verge of falling apart, she took the offer without another word of argument.

～

To Lily's amazement, she was able to concentrate on the sermon by making herself ignore the flowers and bows they had already placed in the sanctuary the day before. They had come to early service, as did the rest of the wedding party, and other than Celia yawning a few times, everyone looked alert and ready for the big day.

After Sunday school, Bailey, who was Lily's matron of honor, saw Lily into a special room so she could dress. She left Celia with her—the little girl was Lily's bridesmaid—and for a time the two sat and talked.

"What did you learn in Sunday school today?"

"We had candy."

"Why did they give you candy?"

"For a verse."

"You said a verse?"

Celia's head bobbed.

"What verse was it?"

The four-year-old frowned in concentration, and Lily had to bite her lip to keep from laughing at her earnest face. The little girl finally started the verse and had just finished it when Bailey returned, Deanne behind her.

"Time to get to work," Bailey proclaimed.

"What did you do with Sarah?"

"My mom has her. Do you want to hit the bathroom one more time before you climb into that dress?"

"Oh, maybe I'd better."

To the strains of the organ that signaled the start of second service, the women went to work. They had plenty of time, which was a good thing as it was hot and no one wanted to rush.

"How are the guys doing?" Bailey wondered out loud at one point.

"Shall I go check?" Deanne asked. She did not have to change her dress, so she seemed the most logical person to go.

"How are you doing?" Bailey asked Lily when only Celia was with them. The little girl had found a flower to play with and wasn't attending to their discussion.

"I'm fine," Lily said cheerfully. "Not even tired."

"Good. Have I told you how honored I am to stand up with you?"

Lily smiled at her. "I wouldn't have anyone else."

The women embraced before Lily stepped into her gown. Bailey blinked like mad to keep from bawling, and Deanne came back just in time.

"Oh, Deanne, help Lily before I sob all over the place!"

"Oh, Lily," Deanne said softly. "You look beautiful."

"Will Gabe like it?"

"Gabe will love it!"

To Lily's relief the time moved swiftly. Running only seven minutes late, she stood at the back of the church and watched Celia walk down the aisle, holding her Uncle Ashton's hand. Bailey went next, her hand tucked into the crook of Jeff's elbow.

Lily glanced up to see her father looking down on her, his eyes intent.

"Are you all right, Papa?"

"Just memorizing your face."

It was almost more than she could take. With a huge effort she didn't cry. A moment later the music sounded, and they started forward.

Had Lily been aware of anything save the man waiting for her at the front of the church, she would have heard sniffles and gasps all the way down the aisle. The church family had fallen in love with this sweet woman, and most of the them thought she looked like an angel in that white dress.

Owen stood proudly as he escorted Lily along, but he was very aware of the way she'd begun to tremble.

"Are you all right?" he asked softly.

"I think so."

"You'll do just fine."

Lily wasn't so sure about that, but Gabe was suddenly there, taking her hand and smiling down at her. She heard a baby cry, and then Pastor Stringer began. It was not a long service, but one that told of Gabe and Lily's commitment to Christ before they committed themselves to each other. Lily's voice was wobbly and just above a whisper as she repeated her vows, but she meant them with all her heart. Gabe felt her tremble, and when Pastor Stringer prayed, asked if she was all right. Lily nodded, and Gabe prayed that they would both make it.

And make it they did! When they turned to the congregation to be presented as Mr. and Mrs. Gabriel Kapaia, everyone cheered. Gabe and Lily laughed in delight as they moved down the center aisle.

The wedding party had been gone only a short time when the bride and groom returned to personally dismiss the rows and thank each person for coming. It took some time to accomplish this, and then it was time for pictures. What seemed like a long time later they were headed to the parking lot of the church for a luau, a feast provided by almost all who attended. For the next four hours they visited and laughed in celebration before Gabe bent and told his bride that it was time to go.

Alone for the first time all day, Lily changed her clothes very slowly. The family would be coming to take everything home, so she packed what she could and was still moving at a thoughtful pace when Gabe came for her.

Their car had been hidden away from "decorators," so it was very hot after sitting in the sun, but neither one noticed the heat much. Gabe held Lily's hand as they pulled away from the church, a CD playing softly in the background.

"Where are we headed?" Lily asked.

"To the other side of the island."

"To a nice place?"

"Very."

"For both nights?"

"Yes. In fact, we'll probably wish we could stay longer."

"Oh, I can't wait. What is it called?"

"The Ihilani Resort and Spa."

"Sounds romantic," Lily said softly, and Gabe smiled at her.

They finished the drive with quiet talk, just glad to be alone, Gabe holding Lily's hand all the time he drove. During times when only the CD could be heard, Lily let her heart be amazed. Just three months ago she hadn't thought she would ever see this man again. As Gabe had a tendency to say, *God had gone before them.*

～

"This doesn't sound good," Evan said as he walked into the bedroom to find his very weary wife working to feed their equally weary daughter. Bailey had delayed nursing her so she could take care of it in the privacy of their home, but now one-month-old Sarah was past the point of consolation.

"Hey," Evan said as he took her and bounced her a little, "Mama's trying to feed you."

His deep voice seem to calm her just long enough to get her back into Bailey's arms. It was with blissful relief for both mother and daughter when Sarah finally settled in and began to eat.

Evan sat next to his wife, taking in the front of the top she'd changed into. The side he could see was soaked with milk. Bailey herself was drooping a bit, but as always, Evan found her lovely.

"You were wonderful today."

"Thank you, and thanks for all your help."

Evan smiled. "I couldn't decide who I liked looking at more: our frowning Celia who kept adjusting her sash, or her lovely mother."

Bailey laughed. "Wasn't she funny? I wondered about that when we picked out that dress, but she liked it so much."

"Well, it's a done deal. How do you think they're doing?"

"I don't know. Lily was awfully tired."

"We'll just have to pray," Evan said, and as though on cue the room became quiet, allowing both of them to do just that.

〜

The room they would have at the resort for two nights was all Lily could have dreamed of. Done in soft pastels, the suite was clean and spacious and sported a huge bed flanked by nightstands and lamps, and a small living room area. But the best parts were a window and balcony that gave a fabulous view of the ocean. Lily didn't even need to go outside; she was happy to stand at the glass and look.

Gabe stood with her, but once their bags had been delivered, he said he was going to get ice.

"Should I stay by the door?" Lily asked.

"No, I'll have my key, so don't worry about it."

The ocean view kept Lily completely captivated while her husband was away. It was different from the view at the resort, and Lily was still taking it in when Gabe returned, coming up to put his arms around her from the back.

Lily gladly turned in his embrace, and it wasn't long before Gabe was shutting the drapes.

"Are we going to turn out the lights too?" Lily asked in between kisses.

"Do you want the lights out?" Gabe asked her.

"I thought they were supposed to be."

"What made you think that?"

Lily bit her lip, looked uncertain, and shrugged a little.

"Come here a minute," Gabe invited, "and sit on the bed with me."

Gabe took her hand and together they climbed into the middle of the king-size bed. They faced each other, legs crossed and knees touching.

"Do you remember that day you came to my office and brought me the papers that Evan sent over?"

"Yes."

"Do you remember the way I couldn't take my eyes off you?"

Lily thought a moment. "I do remember that."

"Other than a few times in your swimsuit, that was the first time I could see your figure."

Lily's eyes widened a little. "That outfit is immodest?"

"Not at all, but there's no comparison to it and the rather baggy clothing you used to wear from Kashien. Your new clothing lets me see your shape."

Lily nodded a little and asked slowly, "And that's why we should have the light on?"

Gabe leaned forward to kiss her before he went on.

"There is no way to describe to a woman how fascinated men are with women, including their bodies. I've saved myself for marriage, Lily, but not just physically. I've tried not to look at women who don't have enough on. I've worked to keep my thoughts pure and not be distracted by nudity—not easy to do when you own a resort. Now I have a wife, and I can finally look—at her.

"I'll understand if we need a little time to get used to the idea, but you're my only option, Lily, just as I'm your only option. Don't hold yourself back from me. I want to look and touch. I want you to look and touch me. And since the Bible says our bodies are not our own, we need to be very nurturing with each other in this area."

Lily nodded, even as she said, "The book didn't cover that."

"What exactly?"

"How interesting women are to men. Why is that?"

Gabe smiled. "You're soft and not built the same way. Let me tell you, that's a pretty heady combination."

Lily nodded, but she was quiet, trying to take it all in. Finally she asked, "Did you say something about taking some time?"

"Yes, I think that's pretty normal."

"So does that mean we can work on having the light on, but it doesn't have to be right now?"

Gabe smiled again. "I think that would be just fine, a good goal for us."

"Do you know how sweet and patient you are, Gabe?"

"I've waited years for you and for this night. I wouldn't want to do anything to spoil it for either one of us."

Lily knew a contentment she didn't think was possible. And when her husband did turn the lights out and she went into his arms, the contentment only grew deeper.

Chapter Thirty-One

At the airport, Owen hugged Lily tightly before turning to his new son-in-law.

"Take care of her, Gabriel."

"I will, sir. And thank you for everything."

Owen turned to Jeff and put out his hand. The men shook.

"Take care, Jefferson. Write me soon."

"I will, Father. Have a good trip."

"Thank you for everything."

"Greet the church family for us, Father," Lily put in, "and please ask Ling to write me."

"I'll do that."

The three stood together as the elder Walsh picked up his bag and went on his way. Lily didn't let herself think about how long it would be before she might see him again.

"Do we have time to see his plane leave?" Lily asked.

"Sure," Gabe answered, and they moved to the window. When the plane backed away and moved out of their sight, the three walked to Gabe's waiting car.

"Are you going to get your driver's license, Lil?" her brother wished to know.

"I think someday, but not right away."

"Why is that?"

"I want to practice a little more in the golf carts."

Gabe found this highly amusing and teased his wife about forgetting how to use her feet.

"But it's so fun," she concluded, looking at Gabe as though he should have already figured that out.

"How long until you're back here to pick up a certain someone, Jefferson?" Gabe asked as he drove them from the airport.

"Six weeks from tomorrow."

"And how long can she stay, Jeff?"

"Ten days."

And with that, the occupants of the car grew quiet. Gabe was thinking about getting married while he was still in the busy season and hoping he and Lily would be able to make enough time for each other until the resort closed in September. Lily was wondering if Jeff was going to marry Annika and what she would be like when they met. Jeff found himself envying his sister and friend and the new life they had started together and the peace he could see written all over their contented faces.

～

"Okay," Bailey told the newlyweds about five weeks later as she put Sarah into Lily's arms, "there's a bottle in the kitchen. She should take that before you put her down."

"All right. Have fun."

"Thank you. Peter, CeCe, come and kiss us goodbye."

The children ran to their parents, who were headed out to dinner, and a few minutes later Gabe was giving horsey rides in the living room.

When both children fell in a giggling mass to the carpet, Gabe asked, "Aren't you going to tell me not to get the kids all stirred up before bed?"

Looking delightfully innocent, Lily said, "But, Gabe, I'll be busy with the baby. You'll have to get them calmed down for bed."

His eyes telling her he was on to her, Gabe said, "We'll just see about that, Mrs. Kapaia."

Lily barely managed not to smile before the children crawled back onto Gabe. The horse play went on until Celia was red in the face and Gabe called it quits. It wasn't long before the children were to go to bed, so Gabe saw them into pajamas, supervised the brushing of teeth, and gathered them to either side of him for a story. Sarah was still in Lily's arms, and she sat on Peter's other side, listening to the story as well.

"Do you want to have prayer time down here with Lily and Sarah or up in your beds?" the children's uncle asked.

"Down here," they both voted, and what followed was a sweet time of listening to the children pray and then hearing Gabe praying for them. His petition included a plea that they would understand how much God loves them, that they would desire to serve Him always, and that they would have a wonderful night's sleep.

After prayer time, Gabe gave them piggyback rides to bed and then gladly joined his wife on the sofa. Lily had found Sarah's bottle and was talking to the baby while she ate.

"You're such a sweet girl," she said softly. "You need to drink the whole bottle, sweet Sarah, and sleep all night."

Gabe put an arm around his wife and looked down at his niece.

"Isn't she beautiful?" Lily asked.

"Yes, she is. She looks like a miniature CeCe."

"Who looks like a miniature Bailey," Lily added.

The couple spent some time talking to each other and Sarah. Annika's upcoming visit to Jeff was mentioned before Gabe volunteered to take Sarah on his shoulder and rock her to sleep.

"By the time we get one of our own," Gabe said as he cuddled Sarah close, kissing her downy, soft head, "we'll be old pros."

"I think you're right."

"I never did ask you what your father said when you told him we hoped to adopt from Kashien."

Lily turned to look at Gabe but didn't really see him.

"Lily?"

She finally focused on her husband's face.

"I don't think I ever said anything, Gabe. I'm sure he knows we want to adopt, but Kashien never came up."

"Oh." Gabe was surprised. He had assumed they'd spoken of it. "Will you mention it to him, or is there some reason you would rather not?"

"No, none at all. I just didn't think of it. We received a letter from him yesterday, and I just have two more verses to go on that chapter I'm working on, so I'll ask him about it when I write back."

"Be sure and let me know what he says."

Sarah had fallen asleep in that brief time, and Gabe took her to the bassinet in her parents' room. He left Evan and Bailey's bedroom door open so they could hear if she woke before going back to Lily on the sofa. They turned the television on and started to watch a movie, but it wasn't often that they had the downstairs to themselves. It didn't take long before they were more interested in each other than the television.

～

Bailey's voice probably sounded normal to her children, but Lily could tell she was having a hard time. Her tone was a little too bubbly, and she kept looking at Peter and then swiftly away.

Breakfast was a merry feast of Peter's favorite foods, but at last it was time. Celia stayed with Lily, as both Evan and Bailey walked Peter out to the road so he could catch the bus for school this first day. Lily was working on the dishes when Bailey came back in, not bothering to hide her tears. Lily turned and watched as she sat at the kitchen table and cried.

"He's so little," the torn mother whispered. "I can't stand it, Lily. He was so excited, but to me he just looked little and vulnerable."

"Did Evan follow in the car like he planned?"

"Yes. He said he would come right back and tell me, but I still feel awful."

The advice from the school was not to bring your child on the first day unless that was going to be their primary mode of transportation. The Markhams understood this, knowing that part of the school experience was the bus, but Bailey desperately wanted to know how Peter arrived. Evan had the idea of following in the car and simply watching from a distance.

"I know what I have to do," Bailey proclaimed and stood.

"What's that?"

"Get to work. Get busy, play with Celia, something!" she said with a sniff. "Sitting around is pointless."

Bailey began to walk from the room, but Lily's voice stopped her. She looked back.

"Don't forget to add prayer to that list, Bailey, especially for Peter."

Bailey bit her lip to keep from crying again, but she did thank Lily before going on her way.

~

To Lily and Gabe's amazement, Annika looked like Lily. She was slim with dark hair, and her eyes were a shade of brown-green. Lily had been rather nervous about meeting her, but when they arrived at Jeff's apartment and Lily saw that Annika was nervous too, all walls came down.

"How was your flight?" Lily asked warmly. The men were making dinner.

"It was fine. I've never been on a plane that long, but then I thought of your coming from Kashien and knew I had it easy."

"You learn to sleep in a seat or bring a lot of books."

"I read," Annika confirmed.

The men came in just then with glasses of soda.

"It's nice to be waited on," Lily told her husband, and he bent to kiss her. Lily then glanced at Jeff. He'd given Annika her glass and still hadn't taken his eyes from her. Annika was staying in a small hotel so she could be close by, and Lily knew that Jeff planned to show Annika every square inch of the island before she left, as well as introduce her to Gabe's family and all the church family. It was going to be a busy time.

Lily found herself praying for her brother and the woman he loved. She didn't know Annika well enough to read her face, but looking into Jeff's love-filled eyes, she knew that if he had his way, Annika would never go back to California.

～

"Are you busy?" Lily asked as she came to the doorway of Gabe's office just two weeks after Annika returned to California. The resort families had already started their time off, but Gabe had occasional business calls to make.

"For you? Never."

Lily smiled as she went in and sat in the chair across from his desk.

"My lap would be more comfortable," he teased her invitingly.

"I'm sure it would, but I've come on business."

"Let me guess," Gabe teased again. "You want a golf cart of your own."

Lily laughed and Gabe just watched her, still marveling that she was his.

"What's up?" he finally asked.

"Were you sincere about adopting a baby from Kashien?"

"No," Gabe teased again. "I was kidding."

Lily smiled but still waved a letter at him. "The day before my father got our letter, a baby girl had been left on the neighbor's front porch. They already have five of their own and don't want her. My father wants to know if we do."

Gabe could not believe what he'd just heard. For a moment he wasn't sure he could find enough air for his lungs. A baby girl was waiting for them in Kashien. Could it be true?

Watching him, Lily realized for the first time what this meant to her husband. Lily had always had a plan: Even if she had never married, she would have adopted at least one child from the village. Until Gabe had met her, he'd had no such options. He thought he would never be a father.

Right now Lily watched as he slowly stood and came around to her. Lily stood to face him and watched as he searched her eyes.

"You wouldn't kid me about this, would you, Lil?"

"No, Gabe," she told him gently, seeing the vulnerability in his eyes and wishing she'd understood before. "Let me read to you what my father said.

> Lily, were you serious about a Kashienese baby? I know you have just married, but the day before your missive arrived, a baby girl was left by Lanling Sanyi's door. She hasn't the ability to care for an additional child. I had just read your letter when I heard the news, and I asked her to keep the baby for the time being. If you are interested, you should get right back to me.

Lily lowered the paper and looked at her husband. It was a huge step.

"What do you think?" Gabe asked when she was done.

Lily laughed. "I think I want her today, but I haven't looked into the savings account to see if we can even afford airline tickets, much less the cost of the adoption. Sarah is still using her bassinet, but we could probably borrow one. It's probably only fair that we discuss this with Evan and Bailey because it would certainly affect them as well." With that Lily ran out of practical thoughts. "What do you think?"

"I'm stunned. I'm excited, but I'm also stunned. She would be ours, right, Lily? No one would come and take her back?"

"No, that rarely happens as it is. But when the mother deserts the child, the authorities see it as a done deal."

"Let's go find Evan and Bailey and see what they say."

∼

Initially they didn't say anything. Gabe was still too stunned to talk about it coherently, so Lily had explained the situation. For a time Evan and Bailey just stared at them.

"This baby was just left to starve?" Evan finally confirmed, his voice filled with pain.

"Not exactly." Lily was still doing the talking. "She was left with a family. The mother knew that at least for the moment the baby would be cared for."

"But this means you could have her?" Bailey asked in wonder, looking to her brother. "You would have your own baby, Gabe? Yours to keep?"

"It looks that way."

"Call the airlines," Bailey said, telling herself not to cry. "There's no one more perfect to take this baby than the two of you. Call right now and go get her."

"You do understand, Bailey, what it will mean in this household?" Gabe had to check.

"Don't worry about that," Evan said firmly. "Sarah could have been twins. Having two babies in the house is not a worry. Understanding whether this little girl has health problems or special needs or restrictions about leaving Kashien—those are things to question, not whether we should have another baby in the house."

With that, the Markhams began to question Lily about Kashienese adoptions. Even Gabe had some questions he had not thought of before. They talked for a solid hour before Evan grew practical again.

"Okay, it's settled. Now what do you do?"

"Write my father," Lily said, "and tell him we want to come."

"What will he do?"

"He'll inform the authorities."

"And they'll listen to him?"

"They always have in the past."

"How often have babies been left in the village?"

"In the village, dozens of times, but my father is not always involved. Over the years he has been personally involved in probably 11 or 12 adoptions."

"And what will his letter back to you say?"

"One of two things. He'll either say to come as soon as we can or that the baby's been taken by another family."

"Let's write to him now," Gabe said, not wanting to run ahead of God on this issue, but also ready to move forward as they were able.

"Before you do that," Evan said, "let's pray."

For Lily it was one of the sweetest moments of her married life. Celia wandered in and had to be hushed, but Evan prayed that God would direct and lead them. He asked God to help Gabe and Lily to hold this baby loosely so their hearts would not be broken, but also to expedite matters if this was the child for them.

Gabe had tears in his eyes when they all looked up. Lily watched him, telling God what a wonderful father he would be, but still knowing that she needed to let God do His job. While she was still watching him, Gabe turned and smiled at her.

"Let's write a letter."

～

"So when will you know?" Harris Stringer asked after Gabe shared with the Bible study on Wednesday night.

"When we hear back from Lily's father."

"Does the mail take awhile?"

"Well, we sent our letter two-day air, but that only gets it to Kashien swiftly, not necessarily to the village."

"And what happens if he writes and tells you to come?" Barb asked this time.

Gabe turned to his wife.

"We book flights and make sure we have everything we need for the baby, but we keep that carefully packed away until we have her."

"Why is that?"

"Because the Kashienese government will accept only cash," Lily answered. "If you're seen coming into the airport with a diaper bag and no baby, the wrong sort of person might figure out that you're there to adopt. Everyone knows that takes cash, and you might find yourself at knifepoint sometime after you leave the airport."

Gabe had been aware of this, but he was certain that the shocked faces he was seeing around the room must have mirrored his own when Lily first told him.

"And is it very expensive?"

"Very."

"We'll be praying," Harris assured them, something Gabe and Lily appreciated very much.

As the next few days passed, Gabe learned some things about himself. Before Lily came with the letter from Owen, Gabe had been completely at rest, newly married and enjoying his time off. Now when he walked around the house, he found himself looking at it through the eyes of a father.

And he wasn't the only one distracted by the possibilities. Each and every person he knew asked him the status of the baby the moment he saw them. It was as if nothing else in life mattered. That wasn't true, but it took a few days for Gabe to see this.

The moment of realization came about a week after they had sent the letter to Owen. Gabe found Lily getting dressed in lightweight cotton pants and a yellow T-shirt.

"Oh, you look nice," he said, coming to give her a kiss.

"Thank you. We're only going to that little diner up the road, so I didn't want to be too dressed up."

"We're eating out before we shop?" Gabe asked.

Lily stopped and looked at him.

"We're going shopping?" she asked.

Gabe frowned. This was getting confusing.

"Why don't you tell me what you're talking about."

"Ana and I are having lunch today."

"I thought you and I were going shopping for some baby things."

"Not today, Gabe. I told you yesterday morning about my lunch with Ana."

"No, you didn't."

"Yes, I did."

Gabe shook his head, and Lily just stood there.

"When did you tell me?" Gabe tried again.

"At breakfast yesterday morning," Lily answered. "Do I need to cancel my lunch plans, Gabe? Is that what you wish me to do?"

Her sweetness made him feel awful, which made him sound even more upset.

"No, just go ahead."

Still, Lily hesitated before asking, "Do you want to discuss it when I return?"

"Yes, we'll do that," Gabe agreed, but clearly he wasn't happy.

Lily went on her way feeling miserable about how unhappy her husband was. She was certain she had told him and honestly thought he'd been listening. She found herself praying for him and not just for herself.

Lord, if I've been insensitive to Gabe's needs, help me to be more aware. And please help Gabe to see how much I want this baby, but also how desperately Ana needs You.

～

"That was good." Ana sat back with a sigh. "How was yours?"

"Delicious. I've never eaten here before."

"Oh, this is our favorite place."

Lily wondered who the "our" was but didn't ask just then.

"So do you miss Kashien?" Ana asked her.

"I miss the people mostly. We just had some exciting news, though. We might be returning to adopt a baby girl."

"From Kashien?"

"Yes. We're waiting to hear from my father anytime."

"Wow! I didn't know you could do that."

"The government rules and system of Kashien makes it one of the easier countries to adopt from."

"I hope Nick and I have children someday."

"Is that your husband?"

"No, my boyfriend. We just moved in together."

Lily had to stop herself from feeling regret over her own role in Ana's life. If the two of them had gotten together before now, would that have altered the younger woman's decision? Lily knew it was pointless to try to figure it out. After the first time they'd met, Lily had had no choice but to go home to Kashien.

"My father's real upset about it," Ana went on conversationally. "But I don't think you can really know whether you love someone unless you live with him first."

"I'm not sure I follow you," Lily said. "You're not sure if you love Nick?"

"Not enough to marry him! I mean, marriage, that's a big deal."

This was so diametrically opposed to the way Lily believed that it took a moment for her to respond. She did not want to censure this younger woman or put walls up between them, but Lily certainly did not agree. Another factor was that Ana had not invited her to comment on her situation. Lily knew she would have to go easy.

"Do you not think a couple can decide to commit to each other for life?"

"It's a pretty big step. I mean, I wouldn't buy a car without trying it out first."

"Is that a good comparison, do you think? Husbands and cars?"

"Oh, I don't know. I heard that somewhere one time and thought it was pretty funny."

Lily was reminded how young Ana was. When they had originally met in the resort gift shop, Ana had just turned 18.

"Did you and Gabe do it that way?" Ana suddenly asked. "I mean, live together?"

"No, we didn't."

"Well, maybe you didn't live together, but you didn't wait for the wedding night, did you?"

Lily could hardly believe where their conversation had gone, but she so wanted this friendship to grow.

"As a matter of fact, Ana, I was a virgin on my wedding night, and so was Gabe."

Ana's mouth hung open. "That's amazing! You must have been the last two on the planet."

"No, I don't think so. My brother is not getting married until February, and he's never been with a woman."

"Is it because you're from Kashien?"

"No, it's more about what God says is best for us. We chose to believe that."

"So you believe in God?"

"The God of the Bible, yes."

"I don't," Ana admitted without hesitation or apology as she signaled for more tea.

There were dozens of replies Lily could have offered, but she decided to let Ana lead this conversation. Only if the younger woman asked her about it would she speak on the issue of God's existence.

"I hate to eat and run," Ana continued, causing Lily to be glad she'd stayed quiet, "but I have to get to work."

"How do you like your job?"

"It's okay. The tips are good, and they wash our uniforms."

"Did you tell me where Nick works?"

"He's at the Hilton too. He's a groundskeeper."

"Do you ever get to ride together?"

"No, he's mornings and I'm afternoons." Ana looked a little crestfallen when she said this but continued, "Some days we barely see each other."

Lily didn't comment because the waitress was bringing their tab. Reaching for the bill, Lily offered to pay for the meal. Ana stared at her.

"You're awfully nice," she said quietly.

Lily smiled. "Well, you're easy to be nice to."

The younger girl shook her head in wonder.

"I think next time I'd better pay."

"You've got yourself a deal. Maybe I'll have my license, and I'll do the driving that time."

"You don't drive?"

"Not yet."

"Wow! I think I would die without my wheels."

It ended their meal on a laugh, and when Ana did drop Lily back at the resort, Lily made sure Ana had her phone number and the assurance that Lily wanted to see her again.

Chapter Thirty-Two

Gabe all but paced while he waited for his wife to return. She had been gone for only ten minutes when he realized how he'd sounded and acted. Even if he had personally known her dining companion, he wouldn't have interrupted her lunch, but it cost him to stay put and wait.

In the hours she was gone, his mind ran with all sorts of crazy notions. After all, they didn't know this woman that Lily had ridden with. What if they were in an accident? What if Lily read this woman wrong and she was not to be trusted? What if he never saw her again?

You're consumed with plans for a baby you've never met, Kapaia, and the wife you vowed your life to has needs you're ignoring. This was only one way Gabe berated himself before Lily arrived home. He was more than ready to go straight to her when the front door opened, but Celia spotted her at the same time.

"Lily!" the little girl cried and ran to hug her.

"How's my CeCe?" Lily said after she lifted her into her arms and they hugged.

"Hungry."

"You're hungry?"

"Celia," her mother called just then, "come and eat your snack."

Celia gasped with excitement and ran to the kitchen as soon as her feet touched the floor. Not until then did Lily look at her husband, who was waiting for her to be free.

"I'm sorry," Gabe said as soon as their eyes met.

"I'm sorry too."

"Why are you sorry?"

"I should have said more to you. I should have discussed it with you and made sure you knew my plans."

"Are you sure you didn't do that and I wasn't listening?"

Lily hesitated because it did seem like that to her.

"Come here," Gabe said, his hand out to take hers. Lily went up the stairs with her husband, who locked the door as soon as they were in their room.

"Tell me about Ana. Tell me about your lunch with her."

Lily came uncorked. All she and Ana had talked about and all she was feeling while they'd talked came pouring out of her.

"It's as though she doesn't know any better, Gabe. She said something about her father not liking her moving in with Nick, but she didn't elaborate. Her voice and face almost made it seem as if she felt she had no choice. It was as though this was the best she could do, so she was willing to give it a try."

"Will you be seeing her again?"

"If she calls me. She has my number and knows I want to see her, so I need to wait a little bit to see if she calls."

"We'll just pray that she does. God can bring the two of you back together."

"I think so too. I genuinely like her, Gabe, and I ache for how lost she is."

Quiet fell between the two of them for a moment before Lily glanced at the door.

"Why did we come up here and lock the door?"

Gabe smiled.

"I've been hearing for years about married couples who make up after they fight."

"Were we in a fight?"

"If I say no, are we still going to get to make up?"

Lily was still laughing when Gabe came toward her. Lily moved away, and the chase began. It was, however, short-lived. She wanted to be caught.

∿

Lily lay in her husband's arms, their heads close as he admitted his fears.

"I've worried about how you'll handle it, Lily, if we never have children, but I'm the one who's not trusting. I'm the one who wants God to answer with a yes today. I want to leave this moment for Kashien and bring that baby back and never let her go."

"It's hard to imagine why God would say no, Gabe, but raising a child is a huge undertaking. We don't want that job until God knows we're ready. After all, we've been married for only two and a half months. If we get a baby, that's fine, but most couples don't start out so soon. If it happens, we'll have to work very hard to make sure Gabe and Lily don't get put on the shelf because all they have time to do is change diapers and walk a crying baby."

"My head agrees with you, but my heart wants that baby. Even the timing seems so right. Not that I couldn't leave if it were a different time of year, but we have the money and the time, and my hopes skyrocketed on me without warning."

Lily went up on one elbow to look down into Gabe's face.

"I already told the Lord what a wonderful father you would make, and then I had to confess my arrogance. My attitude was that He didn't know that. Isn't that foolish? And in the midst of our little conversation, I remembered God's sovereignty. I can panic about the thought that you might get cancer again, but you've been there, and you're ready for that. I've seen how many children become available in Kashien. If this baby doesn't work out, there's a huge chance that another will very soon. I've been there, so I'm more relaxed.

"But all of that misses the point. God reminded me that He is in control. If you get cancer again, God will work it out for the best in us. If we can't have this baby, He has other plans for us. At the same time, if you don't get cancer, we can be grateful for health, and if He does want us to have this particular baby, He knows we're ready."

Gabe wrapped his arms around Lily and pulled her back against him. She was sweet and wise, and just now he needed her to remind him of God's power and control.

"I'll still ask," Gabe said quietly. "I'll still ask God to give us a baby, but this time I'll pray with my hands open."

Lily kissed his cheek and said, "Shall we ask right now?"

Cuddled together alone in their room, husband and wife prayed. They thanked God for new lessons every day and for His great forgiveness. They praised Him for all His works and the blessings from His hand. They prayed for Ana and Nick and about their need for Jesus Christ. And just before they finished, they asked their Savior to give them a baby in His time and to be worthy of whatever task He would place at their feet.

"Good day, Master Wang," Lily greeted the chef respectfully after she slipped in the back door of the Little Bay and found him in the kitchen.

"Good day, Mrs. Kapaia. What brings you out this morning?"

"I made something for you. Will you honor me by tasting it?"

"Thank you," Wang said graciously as he took a cookie from the offered dish. At first he took just a small bite, testing it on his tongue. From there he ate the entire cookie and stood for a moment, his eyes closed.

"I would not change a thing," he told Lily, who beamed at him.

"Thank you. Would you like to keep these?"

"I would, thank you very much. What do you hear from your father, Lily?"

"In his last letter he was doing well."

"Did he have any news for you and Gabriel?"

"Not yet," Lily said, now understanding to what he referred.

"It will come," he said calmly.

"You seem confident."

"Gabriel is a special man. He will make a special father."

Lily only smiled.

"And the wife he has chosen will bring him nothing but honor all his days."

Lily smiled shyly but didn't reply.

"Where were you one year ago, Lily?"

"Oh, let me see, a year ago I was still pretty sore from that sunburn."

"And did you think then that you would be married to Gabriel?"

"No," Lily said with soft wonder. "Not in my wildest dreams."

"And a year from now you will come and visit me and bring your child. I will ask, 'Where were you a year ago?' and you will say, 'Dreaming of the child I now have.'"

"Thank you, Wang Ho."

He bowed in respect, his face and eyes content as he watched her.

A few minutes later they said their goodbyes. Lily appreciated Wang's kind way of encouraging her, but she wasn't certain he was correct. Nevertheless, she knew Gabe would enjoy hearing what he had to say.

∼

Lily looked at the envelope addressed to her with her father's name in the return corner, her heart suddenly pounding very fast. She thought she might need to find Gabe but opted to open the missive and see what her father had to say. The air left her in a rush when his opening sentence was *Come as soon as you can.*

Lily cast about in her mind as to where Gabe was right then and remembered that he and Ashton had gone surfing. Lily walked as sedately as she could manage through the house and out onto the veranda, but as soon as her feet hit the sand, she ran as fast as she could, hoping the men would see her.

It took a little while for Gabe to see that she was not waving *at* him but *to* him, and when he got close enough to see the paper in her hand, he made a beeline for the shore.

"From your father?" he shouted as soon as the distance closed. "Yes!"

"What does he say?" Gabe kept coming as he yelled, so Lily waited until he stood dripping and panting before her.

"He says to come as soon as we can."

The yell Gabe let out as he grabbed Lily and swung her around could be heard all down the beach. Ashton landed on the shore to find his brother kissing his wife, but that didn't stop him.

"Did you get news?"

"Yes!" Gabe hugged him as well. "We're headed to Kashien!"

"I've got to tell Deanne!" Ashton said after he hugged Lily and gave her cheek a wet kiss.

Lily could only laugh before saying, "I haven't even seen Bailey and Evan, and I still need to call Jeff and your mother." All of this was said as she worked to keep her father's letter dry.

"Why don't you do all of that right after we phone the airline?"

Lily smiled up at him, and they ran like children for the house.

What followed was an adventure the likes of which Gabe had never known. He'd been to the continental United States a few times but never traveled to a foreign country. Lily was a big help as they scheduled flights, sent a swift letter back to Owen to say they were on their way, and packed as lightly as they could manage, including formula, bottled water, tiny clothing, and a folded-up diaper bag for the baby.

The family was at the airport to see them off, all of them overwhelmed with the speed in which it all came together. It was reminiscent of Lily and Gabe's wedding, and when the couple was on the plane, they felt a little like they had when their reception was over and they were alone in their car.

"We made it, Lil."

Lily smiled at him.

"I think I'll sleep the whole way there."

"Okay. I'll join you."

They did get some rest in the hours that followed, but it was a weary couple who landed in Capital City many hours later. Owen was there to meet them, and once through customs, the three walked to a hotel where they were booked for the night. Gabe and Lily were hungry, but the hour was late and all they wanted at the moment was sleep.

Owen said he would come for them in the morning and that they would see the minister of adoption at nine o'clock.

Tired as they were, neither slept well, but fatigue was of little importance when they walked into the small government office the next day. They could hear a baby crying, and Lily's heart began to pound. There were cases of couples being rejected. It would be so hard when they had come this far, but she reminded herself that God knew best.

"Sun Yang," Owen greeted the ministry head, "I wish to present my son-in-law, Gabriel Kapaia. Gabriel, this is Sun Yang. He is the head minister of foreign adoptions."

"It's a pleasure to meet you, sir," Gabe said kindly, not missing the fact that his wife's eyes were down and she said not a word.

"Mr. Walsh has filled out your papers, but there are some things he did not know. We would wish for you to complete these."

"Yes, sir."

"If you'll come this way."

Gabe was led to a table, and with Owen translating whenever needed, the forms were completed and business began.

"My son has the needed funds for this transaction," Owen said diplomatically. "But if it would be possible, while the papers are being checked, we would request to see the baby."

"Certainly." The minister bowed graciously. He was very familiar with Owen Walsh and knew him to be a fair and caring man. "I will arrange it."

"I thought the baby would be in the village," Gabe said as soon as they'd been left on their own.

"No, the adoption must take place here in Capital City, after a doctor has examined the child. And in the case of boys, they try to learn why the child is being given up."

"If you'll come through here—" the minister had returned, and a moment later they were directed to a small, windowless room with a dim light burning overhead. A nurse came in almost on their heels, a bundle in her arms. She surrendered the baby into Owen's arms because she had taken the baby from him the day before, then went out, shutting the door behind her. Owen wasted no time. He handed the baby to Lily.

Heart pounding with more emotions than she could identify, Lily shifted the blanket to find a tiny one-month-old face peeking out at her. The baby's cheeks were round and her sloe eyes as black as night. Her nose resembled a soft round button, and her eyebrows were so dark and perfect that for a moment, Lily could only stare.

"Oh, Gabe; oh, Papa." Lily was breathless with wonder. "Look at her."

Gabe couldn't manage a word. His hand came up to touch her soft little face as he marveled with his wife.

"You should wait to hold her, Gabe. It's not the custom for men here, and doing so could cause offense. You should wait until we get home."

"All right. Thank you for telling me."

Lily could wait no longer. She unfolded the blanket and inspected every square inch of the minuscule person in her arms. Judging her to be less than six pounds, the little person who tried to ball up against the cool air was utterly captivating to her. Lily didn't know if she had ever seen anything so tiny and perfect and soft. She looked as long as she dared, cooing softly down to her, and had just gotten her diapered, dressed, and rewrapped when someone knocked.

"Is everything in order, Mr. Walsh?"

"Yes, thank you. I believe we can proceed."

Things took on a surreal atmosphere for the newlyweds as they paid the minister, signed papers, and were given a medical report on their new baby daughter, as well as completely legal adoption papers. They were soon on their way to catch a bus out of the city.

Gabe sat very close to his wife and the child in her arms, still trying to believe they were parents. The bus trip to Mintsu, where they would take a wagon or cart on to Lhasa, was long, made more difficult by their attempts to make formula and measure accurately. But at last, from their place in the back of a wagon, the village where Lily was born and lived most of her life came into view.

Gabe was enchanted. His wife had told him of the way she would race with friends from the large tree in the town center, up the hill to the stone wall, and then back again, and now Gabe could see it firsthand.

"This way," Owen directed as they stepped down. Gabe remembered to let Lily follow him as he walked behind his father-in-law, and not more than three minutes later, he stepped into Owen Walsh's home. It had taken all of a very long day, but when Lily came directly to him and handed their daughter into his arms, he knew it had been worth every second.

"Sit down, Gabe," Owen directed, accurately reading the exhaustion and emotion in his face.

Gabe took a seat and did as Lily had done in the ministry office. He moved the blanket aside so he could fully see this miraculous little bundle.

Owen and Lily brought chairs close so they could look as well. Lily was the first one to speak.

"She needs a special name, Gabe."

Gabe looked up at his wife.

"She's Kashienese, I'm white, and you're half Hawaiian," Lily said. "We don't want her to forget her Kashienese heritage, but her name needs to fit into our world. What do you think?"

"I hadn't thought of it, but you're right. I'm not worried about a Hawaiian name because she'll be a Kapaia, but her first name does have to be special."

"Ling-lei is nice."

Gabe looked skeptical and apologetic all at the same time. "A Lily and a Ling-lei in the same house. I don't think we want to do that to ourselves, sweetheart."

"That's true. Do you have any ideas, Father?"

"I've been calling her Pumpkin."

This brought laughter to the room's occupants before everyone quickly fell silent, too weary to think any longer.

"She will still need a name in the morning," Owen said quietly. "Why don't we have something to eat, and you can make it an early night."

"That sounds wonderful," Lily said just as the baby began to fuss.

Gabe wrapped her snugly as Lily prepared another bottle. Owen heated some soup he'd made the day before.

They ate in quiet wonder. Owen could not stop watching his daughter with a child, and in his own home. Lily could hardly believe she was back so soon, and now a mother. Gabe was in a state of utter shock. He was in Kashien with his wife, and she was feeding their daughter! All he could think to do was cry.

He didn't break down, but the need to do so told him it was time to get some sleep.

～

Lily didn't know when anything had felt so good. It didn't matter that she was on a mat on the floor next to her bed and that Gabe was in the bed. All that mattered was that she could stretch out her aching limbs and sleep. And sleep she did, like a hibernating bear, for the next six hours.

When she heard a baby's cry in the middle of the night, it took a moment to remember where she was, but as soon as memory returned, she lit a lamp and lifted her tiny daughter from the basket she'd been sleeping in. Gabe sat up and squinted at the twosome, feeling as though he'd been run over by a truck.

"Go back to sleep," Lily told him quietly.

"Are you sure?"

"Yes. I'm fine."

Lily took the baby to the living room/kitchen area and found her father with his lantern lit, already starting a bottle.

"Thank you," she said when he handed it to her. "I'm sorry we woke you."

Owen laughed a little.

"I can sleep when you leave. It's not every day a man has his daughter and granddaughter at home. At least not this man."

Lily looked up at him.

"Did you want to feed her?"

"Yes," he agreed, a smile telling of his pleasure.

Lily enjoyed the sight and even tried to talk with her father, but things were getting fuzzy.

"Go get her bed, Lily, and put it in my room."

"Are you sure?"

"Go."

It was with a grateful heart that Lily went back to her bed on the floor. Much as she wanted to be with her baby, she desperately needed more sleep.

Lily woke slowly, the room already light, and looked up to see that she was being watched.

"Hi," Gabe said softly.

"Good morning," she said with a sleepy smile.

"Are you sore?"

"I'm fine."

"Our daughter's basket is missing. Do you know about that?"

"She's in with my father."

Gabe suddenly scooted toward the wall.

"Come on up."

Lily climbed into the single-wide bed with her husband, his chest to her back as his arms and the covers came around her.

"I've been thinking," Gabe said.

"About what?"

"Peter, Celia, and Sarah's middle names are all Hawaiian. Why don't we give our daughter a name more familiar to the United States and give her a Kashienese middle name, like Ling?"

"Oh, that's a wonderful idea, Gabe. I was trying to think of something last night after I lay down in here, but I was too tired. What names do you like?"

"Well," he said, and she could hear a smile in his voice, "I already have a Lily. I think we need a Jasmine."

Lily rolled into him so she could see his face.

"Another flower name. I would never have thought of it."

"Do you like it?"

"Jasmine Ling. Oh, it's pretty!"

"I think so."

"Shall we go tell her?"

"Yes—your father too!"

Like children on Christmas morning, they dressed and went to find their daughter, their own little Jasmine Ling Kapaia.

Chapter Thirty-Three

Oahu

"How are you?" Evan asked Bailey when he found her alone on the veranda.

Bailey looked at him as he sat down in the lounge chair next to hers. She was as in love with the man and as attracted to him as ever, but things had changed, and they'd only been married for eight years.

"Were you just looking for quiet?" Evan tried again.

"No, but if I say what I'm thinking the wrong way, I might be misunderstood."

"Well, if I don't get it the first time, tell me again."

Bailey looked at him, knowing he would listen; he always did.

"I've been thinking all this time that Ashton and Deanne took one of the cottages so they could have privacy and time alone this first year, but it's become very clear to me that it's easier for me that way too."

"Why is that?"

"Because at times it's so hard to watch Gabe and Lily interact. We've been married eight years, and we don't act the way we did at first. I would say I love you even more now, Evan, but we're not captivated with each other the way Gabe and Lily are." She looked at him, feeling terrible for having opened her mouth.

Evan reached for her hand.

"I'm glad you told me."

"You're not hurt?"

"No, because you're right. We are in a different place right now for many reasons."

"Like what?"

"Just to name two: We're eight years older than we were on our wedding day, and we now have three children."

Bailey looked frustrated.

"But that doesn't mean we aren't still fascinated by each other," Evan added, and Bailey looked back at him. "What it means is that I've gotten lazy. I think about you more than I say. I'm still as attracted to you, I still desire you, but you don't know that, so I've got to step it up a little bit."

"But it's not all your fault, Evan. I don't come to you like I used to."

"Well, then you've got to step it up too. Our relationship isn't going to look like Gabe and Lily, we have to face that, Bales, but if we've gotten too busy and too distracted to show each other how much we're in love, that's got to change."

"You're not upset with me and what I said?"

"Not in the least. But like most men, if I'm sexually satisfied, I forget to show tenderness at other times. I need you to remind me and tell me what you need."

"So your needs are being met?"

Evan looked at his wife.

"I guess it would be nice to have you pay attention to me a little more often too."

Bailey nodded but didn't say anything.

"Bailey, please keep in mind that our youngest is still a very little person, and you're nursing her. We're both going to be more tired—you the most—and I'm not sitting here disappointed in you and wishing my life away."

"Like I was doing?" Bailey said, still feeling crabby at herself and about the whole situation.

"Do you still want me, Bailey Markham, or is there someone else involved here?" Evan asked firmly.

"No—" she looked shocked—"I just want you."

"And you're who I want. As soon as Gabe and Lily arrive back with that little girl, things are going to change around here for the newlyweds. But the next time you see Gabe put his arms around Lily or look up and find their door shut, come and kiss me or hug me. I'll do the same for you. If we need those little reminders to be more affectionate, so be it!"

Bailey smiled at him.

"I like you an awful lot; do you know that, Evan Markham?"

"I do know that, but it's nice to hear."

"Have you got any room left on your chair?"

"For the woman I love? Plenty."

Bailey stood up and squeezed into the lounge chair with her husband. It wasn't built for two—and Peter could come looking for them at any moment—but for right now, they needed this closeness. They needed to remember the vows they'd made eight years earlier and be committed all over again to cherish each other in their marriage.

∼

Lhasa

On her first day home, it was very special for Lily to take her daughter and husband to the church in the village where her father was the pastor.

The service would be in Kashienese, so Lily and Gabe sat in the back so she could translate quietly for him. Before they even sang a song, however, Pastor Walsh, with great pleasure in his voice, introduced his son-in-law, welcomed his daughter back, and told the congregation that he was now a grandfather.

The group of 27 adult believers, plus their children, most of whom had greeted Lily and the baby earlier, cheered with delight over this news. Owen then asked Gabe to stand and say a few words. Gabe had not been expecting this, but he gladly came forward and spoke slowly so Owen could translate his short speech.

"Thank you for this warm welcome to your church and beautiful village. It's a delight to be here with you and finally see the village that my wife loves so well. Thank you to all of you who prayed for us and helped in any way with the adoption of our daughter. Please know that we will take her home with plans to teach her about God's saving love and to raise her to fear and serve Him with all of her heart."

Gabe returned to his seat amid respectful bows of the head from men on all sides.

"That was wonderful," Lily whispered as soon as he sat down.

"Was it appropriate?"

"Yes, very."

Gabe experienced great relief, having known some trepidation that he would unintentionally make a cultural or social blunder. However, in the next few minutes his mind was taken completely off himself. They sang several songs, but the moment Owen opened his Bible, every head in the place was up looking at Lily's father, even the women's!

"The women are looking up," he whispered to Lily, whose eyes he found looking forward as well.

"In church, during the reading of God's Word, yes. My father instituted it years ago. At first the men were against it, but Papa wanted the men and women to respect and have great awe for God's Word. He believes that if God were here speaking to us in person, He would expect all eyes to be trained on Him. We've done it this way for all of my life."

Gabe wondered when the surprises would end. Things were not as he'd expected them to be. He thought he would arrive in this village and find dozens of Owen Walshes, but that wasn't the case. As they had walked to church, he saw many men leading their families, the women and children dutifully behind, but once inside the simple wooden structure that was their church building, the men showed more care for their wives than Gabe would have expected. That Owen did not act this way with Lily made it even more of a curiosity.

At the moment, Gabe knew he needed to let Lily translate for him so he could get something out of the sermon, but he planned to ask her about his confusion as soon as he had a chance.

∼

The chance came sooner than he expected. They had just finished lunch when Owen was called away. Jasmine was sleeping in her basket, and Lily was washing a few dishes.

"I noticed it too," Lily said thoughtfully.

"So it hasn't always been that way?"

"No, but there are more elders now. For years there were only two who served with my father; now there are five. Two of them are rather young men, and I think they might be introducing some new ideas. My father is all for such changes, as long as the men can prove from Scripture that God would approve."

"Lily," Gabe asked something that had only just now occurred to him, "why didn't you marry right here in the village?"

Lily smiled.

"I read one time that when blond women go to Mexico, the men go wild. Fair women look so different and attractive to them. It's not the same way here. Kashien men love Kashien women. I'm not particularly attractive to the men here, and although many men marry just to have someone to cook for them, they at least want to find their wives tolerable to look at."

"So are you telling me that you grew up thinking yourself rather homely?"

"I don't know if I gave it much thought, Gabe, but you were the first person to ever tell me that I was somewhat appealing."

Gabe had all he could do not to gawk at her. Somewhat appealing! He found his wife downright gorgeous. Her dark-green eyes, small nose and mouth, wonderful skin, and dark straight hair were more attractive to him now than ever. Were the men here blind?

Lily laughed at his face. "Have I surprised you?"

"Tremendously."

Lily only chuckled, her face a picture of contentment.

"You don't care, do you?" Gabe suddenly realized.

"No. I didn't want anyone to notice me before I met you."

Gabe came and put his arms around her.

"I love you."

"And I love you," Lily said as she turned in his embrace, having told him the absolute truth. Gabe Kapaia was the first and only man to ever seriously catch her eye. That she caught his eye as well was something for which she would give thanks for as long as she lived.

～

"She sleeps a lot," Gabe complained as he looked down into his daughter's basket. Lily had set it on the kitchen table Monday morning. Breakfast was over, and Lily was soaking some beans for lunch.

"What did you expect?" Lily asked.

"I want to play with her."

Both Owen and Lily had a good laugh over this.

"It won't be long," Owen warned, "and you'll be wishing she would sleep more."

"You're probably right, but I wanted to get a picture of her with her eyes open, and they never are."

Gabe's wife and father-in-law were still very amused when they heard a commotion outside. Owen went to the window and then turned to Lily.

"I believe you and Jasmine are wanted outside."

Lily smiled with sudden excitement. She knew instantly what was going on, but having one for herself never once occurred to her.

"Gabe—" Owen called him to the window—"you'll want to come and watch this."

While the men stood looking outside, a circle of 11 women formed directly in front of the house. As they watched, Lily walked out, Jasmine in her arms, to stand in the midst of them.

"It's called a coorah," Owen explained. "It a village tradition and the equivalent of an American baby shower."

"A coorah?"

"Yes. It means 'new gift,' which refers to the baby who has been born."

As Gabe watched in delight, Lily faced first one woman and then another. She would walk to the woman, hand Jasmine to her and, in exchange, receive a simply wrapped baby gift. Someone had set a basket at Lily's feet, and after bowing in thanks, she would put the gift in the basket, take the baby back, and turn to the next woman.

"As she hands Jasmine to this next woman," Owen explained, "she says to her daughter, 'Jasmine Ling, please be honored to meet Mei-sun.' Mei-sun will hold Jasmine and say a few words of advice or encouragement to Lily and then admonish Lily's daughter to be obedient and bring honor to her family. Then it's repeated with the next woman."

"Wow," Gabe could only say. He couldn't believe how special this was and only wished his mother and sister could be a part of it.

"The gifts will be simple and not all new: a little shirt, a tiny hat, a wooden rattle, but almost all will have been made right here in the village."

Outwardly Gabe was speechless, but in his heart he prayed.

I know that not all days will be this sunny, Lord. There will be times when Jasmine is sick or I'm tired of being a parent, but I thank You for the blessings You keep giving. Thank You for the love being shown to us in this special act.

Help me to remember that on days when I can't see the sunshine, You're still there. Thank You that You never change, and that You died for my Jasmine as You did for Lily and me.

～

"She is perfect," Ling proclaimed of the infant in Lily's arms. The families had dinner together that night. The men were talking in the living area, and the women were at the kitchen table, the children nearby.

"Isn't she special?" Lily asked, her eyes on her daughter as well.

"This is what you always dreamed of, my friend," Ling said. "Your heart has always yearned to adopt, and now here she is."

"Today was special," Lily told Ling, her hand coming to touch the other woman's arm. "I never expected a coorah. All the things Jasmine received were so nice."

"Did you like the hat?"

Lily laughed. "I could never weave as small as you could. I was going to try before I left, but now you've done it."

"When you arrive back in Hawaii, Jasmine can wear bamboo on her head and lace on her dress, and she'll be a child of both nations."

Lily leaned to hug her.

"What would I do without you, Ling?"

"We will pray that we will never have to find out."

Ling's new baby, Daniel, fussed a little in his sister's arms, and Ling rose to take him. She began to nurse him as the women kept talking.

In the living room the men were in deep conversation about a verse in Mark 10. Gabe had been doing an intense study on the life of Christ for more than a year, and in their discussion, he showed something to Owen that he had not seen before. The older man was captivated with the new thoughts and ideas it brought about.

"Yes, I see what you're saying," Owen said as he studied verse 32. "Jesus is walking ahead of them, but His followers are amazed and fearful."

"Exactly," Gabe confirmed. "Something huge is happening here. We know the end of the story, but they were left to speculate and guess."

"It's so easy to miss the details," Lee Chen observed quietly, and Gabe was impressed with the kind way Owen spoke to him. As a man it was unusual to see kindness in this area of the world.

Interaction with women was limited, and the men seemed to be preoccupied with their reputations. For Gabe, however, the evening as a whole was enlightening. Lee Chen was loving to his wife and children, but beyond that, Gabe realized what a precious thing it was to fellowship with the body of Christ in another land and to see God's hand working across the miles.

～

It was hard to believe that they must be on their way. The time had gone so swiftly. On Tuesday, Gabe, Lily, and Jasmine had spent several hours with Lanling and the entire Sanyi family, who had cared for Jasmine when she'd been left on their doorstep. They even presented them with a gift, but there was no real way to explain how they felt.

But now Wednesday had come. After bidding the Chen family goodbye, Owen, Gabe, and his family left for Capital City. They would spend the night there so as to be more rested for the flight to Hawaii on Thursday morning.

Owen brought food to their rooms so they could have as much time alone as possible, and while Gabe and Lily ate, Owen held his granddaughter. His hands were large, and as he cradled her and Lily watched, her daughter smiled at him.

"She smiled at you!" she said, leaving her chair to come close. She watched in wonder as it happened again.

"She does often," Owen said with obvious pleasure.

"She hasn't smiled at me," Lily said, her face and tone telling them she was surprised.

"You haven't been with her for the last month," Gabe put in conversationally, not aware of how this would affect his wife.

Lily stared at her father. She had no idea he had gone and seen the baby at the Sanyis. Traditionally men had little to do with the care of babies, so such an action on her father's part had never occurred to her.

"Did you see her, Father?"

"Yes, I did, every day," he stated calmly, his eyes still on the baby.

Lily went back to her meal, asking God to help her to deal with her emotions. That Gabe knew her father had seen Jasmine every day meant they must have spoken of it. It reminded her that, to her father, she would always be a little less important.

At the moment, Lily's emotions tumbled out of control. Eating but not even tasting the food, Lily decided never to bring Jasmine back to this place where she would always be a second-class citizen.

"Lily," Gabe said quietly, having watched her face and even knowing that Owen could hear, "you need to talk to your father about this."

For a moment Lily didn't respond, but when she did look her father's way, he was watching her.

"You did not think I would visit this baby?" he asked.

"No, not in a million years," she said rather brutally.

"Why is that, Lily Cathleen?"

His voice was only slightly tight, but the use of her full name told her he was angry. Right now, Lily's anger matched his own. She came to her feet and answered with a downward slash of her hand.

"Because you're so Kashienese! And to a Kashi male, women and babies are not important. I ought to know!"

The silence that fell after this statement was horrible. No one moved or did anything for several moments. Not even the baby seemed to have a need just then.

"Lily," Owen spoke at last, his voice no longer indicating ire; indeed, he sounded rather helpless. "There are no words to describe how important you are to me. You and Jefferson are everything to me."

Lily's hands moved helplessly, her voice now coming very softly as well.

"If you could just show me, Father, or tell me once in a while." She shook her head as she worked to find the words. "I know you wanted to fit in here so you could have a ministry. And you've done that. But who better than you to show these men that according to Scripture a man is to cherish his wife and daughter. Jesus Himself gave deference to women and children, and not just the male children."

Owen's face was so calm that Lily was swamped with guilt.

"I'm sorry," she said, barely managing not to weep. "You've been so gracious to us, and now I treat your kindness with scorn. I'm sorry, Father."

Owen put Jasmine into her basket. He came to his daughter and enfolded her in his arms. Lily hadn't wanted to cry, but this was too much for her.

"I too am sorry, Lily." Owen's voice came from above her head as he hugged her slim frame. "I did think it important to be as the men of the village, but I could have been different at home. Chu Ying and Han Zhou do this with their families, even at church gatherings. I think they may have something that I have missed."

Chu and Han were the younger elders about whom Lily had spoken to Gabe. She had not had a chance to speak with them, but their wives had been part of the coorah, and they were some of the happiest women in the village.

"I'm sorry, Papa. I'm sorry," Lily said again.

"Shhh," he hushed her quietly. "We will worry about this no more. I have sinned and you have sinned, but we have forgiven each other."

Lily leaned back to look at him.

"I love you, Papa."

Owen smiled. "And I love you, Lily. Do not forget that. Keep it in your heart always."

The evening was nothing like Lily would have imagined. She sincerely regretted her outburst, but it was with total peace that Lily bid her father good night, more than happy to honor his request and deliver the baby into his room for the night.

In the morning, their time together was just as sweet at breakfast and again at the airport. Their plane was called all too soon, however, and Lily once again found herself saying goodbye and wondering when she would see this man again.

"Thank you, sir," Gabe said, shaking Owen's hand, his grip firm and smile warm.

"You're welcome." Owen smiled back, thinking that God had provided a fine husband for his Lily. "I'm praying for you, Gabriel."

"And I for you."

Owen looked to Lily then, his eyes taking in the top of her slightly bent head and then the tiny miracle in her arms. While he was looking down at her, Lily raised her eyes, knowing that it would be all right.

"Thank you, Papa," Lily said softly. "Thank you for our baby."

In a rare show of public affection, Owen's large hand came briefly to cup his daughter's cheek. Tears had come to his eyes, and he simply said, "Teach her the Way, Lily."

Lily only nodded and watched as he bent and kissed Jasmine's tiny head. As Lily turned to board with her husband, the tears came. Not as worried about protocol on the airplane, Gabe simply took Jasmine so Lily could compose herself.

It took some time. They were well into the air before her tears were dry, but when she could finally see, she looked over to see Jasmine give a huge yawn. She laughed before leaning close to Gabe's shoulder to have a better look.

"Can you believe it?" she asked, her eyes on Jasmine.

"Not quite. When we get her home and in her own little bed, I might think it's real."

Lily sighed softly, realizing she was tired. Another yawn from the smallest member of the Kapaia family told them she might be tired too. As they watched, Jasmine's little eyes closed, and with only a small whimper or two, she drifted off to sleep. Lily eventually joined her, her head still pillowed on her husband's wide shoulder.

Gabe stayed awake. He'd never given Kashien much thought before meeting Jefferson Walsh, and for many years it was just the place where Jeff had grown up. Today it meant so much more. Today Kashien held a special place in his heart, and the main reasons were snuggled against him, sound asleep.

Chapter Thirty-Four

Oahu

"Do you see them?" Deanne asked Ashton as she stood on her tiptoes to gain a glimpse of the door that led from the customs area.

"Not yet," Ashton answered, just before Carson stepped in beside them, hoping for a better view.

"There they are!" Evan was the first to see.

"Do they have the baby?" Gloria asked, her voice anxious.

"Yes!" Evan said with a laugh, and the family had all they could do to stand still.

Weary as they were, the sight of the entire family brought smiles to Gabe and Lily's faces as they swiftly moved forward, Jasmine in Gabe's arms.

"Oh, Gabe; oh, Lily."

"Oh, look at her. Isn't she beautiful?"

"She looks like a doll."

"Do you see the baby, Celia?"

"What's her name?"

Questions and comments tumbled all over each other as hugs were exchanged, tears were shed, and everyone tried at once to meet the newest member of the family. Since they were blocking the flow of traffic, they shifted off to the side a bit and continued the reunion right in the airport.

Evan's voice finally got through. "What did you name her?"

"Jasmine Ling," Gabe said as he offered her to his mother.

Gloria took the tiny person who was just starting to cry and stared down in wonder. A tear fell down her cheek as she spoke. "God gave my son a baby," she said in amazement, looking between Gabe, Jasmine, and Lily. "God gave my son a baby that I didn't think he would ever have."

It was a happy mob that finally made their way to the parking lot, where Gabe and Lily saw that the family had borrowed one of the church's 15-passenger vans for this occasion. They placed Jasmine in a car seat that had been adjusted as small as it would go for her first ride on Hawaiian soil. Gabe was glad that someone else was driving. He was so tired from the long flight and emotional trip that he just wanted to close his eyes. Lily had had a little more sleep on the plane, so she answered as many questions as she could. The only person who wasn't interested in all the facts and details was Jasmine's cousin Sarah, who was three months older.

"I've got to tell you, Lily," Bailey said when there was a lull, "you had shared with me that things could fall through, so we didn't put up any banners or balloons."

"That's fine, Bailey. I think we just want to see home the way it is."

"Did you know," Gabe began, his eyes still closed and his head back, "that in Lily's village you haul water for everything, and when the need hits, be it rain or shine, you walk 80 feet out of the house to a pit toilet?"

"Poor baby," Ashton teased him.

"Oh, I'm not complaining," Gabe clarified. "That was my way of telling my sister that all I need at home right now is a hot shower."

"I guess now isn't the time to tell you the troubles we've been having with the hot water heater, is it, Gabe?" Evan said seriously from his place behind the wheel.

Gabe's head came up, and his eyes opened to meet Evan's in the rearview mirror.

"Gotcha," the older man said with equal calm, and Gabe let his head fall back with a laugh. It was simply wonderful to be home.

⁓

"Good morning, sweetheart," Lily said softly to her baby daughter about three weeks later, her breath catching in her throat when Jasmine smiled at her for the first time. Lily had checked on her when she rose and didn't expect to find her awake, but much to her delight, those dark, almond-shaped eyes were wide open, and the moment she heard her mother's voice, she smiled.

Lily lifted Jasmine to her, and the baby just kept smiling. Distracted by the blanket touching her cheek, she lost sight of her mother for a moment, but as soon as their eyes met, she smiled again. By the time Gabe came back from the shower, Lily had coaxed smile after smile out of her and thought she might have heard a small laugh.

"Well, good morning," Gabe said as he neared the bed to kiss his wife.

"Watch this, Gabe."

Gabe was just as captivated with his daughter's smile, and his distraction with her almost made him late for work. The resort had recently opened back up, and today he had an early phone appointment.

"You'll come and see me?" he double-checked before kissing them both goodbye.

"Yes, we will. Her doctor's appointment is in two hours, and we'll come after that."

"Okay. I'll see you then."

Still in her robe, Lily gave Jasmine a bath and then walked her downstairs. She found Bailey already making breakfast.

"Can I ask a favor?"

"Certainly."

"Jasmine has an appointment this morning. I forgot that Gabe had to be out early, and I didn't get in the shower before he left."

"Just leave her, Lily. We'll be fine."

"Thank you. I'll hurry." Lily gave Sarah's little head a kiss as she passed her infant seat, but Peter and Celia were nowhere to be found.

"Where are the kids?" she asked, her hand on the door.

"Upstairs with Evan. We had a little attitude problem this morning."

Lily left the kitchen knowing she could learn a lot from Bailey and Evan. They were very good about not correcting the children in front of others, keeping the matter private, and giving the children no reason to be embarrassed in front of their aunts and uncles.

Just two days earlier, Peter had been very tired and cross at the breakfast table. Lily remembered it because it was so unlike him. Not even a minute passed before Evan and Peter were headed out of the room. When they returned, Peter's eyes were red, but his father had been gently rubbing his little head, telling Lily that all had been settled.

"I could learn a lot," the newest mother in the household was still saying to herself when she hit the bathroom door for that quick shower.

～

"How did it go?" Gabe asked as he lifted Jasmine from her stroller and kissed her tiny cheek.

"The nurses fell in love with her, even though she cried as though they were killing her—and that was only when she was being weighed."

Gabe laughed.

"You can imagine what went on when she got her shot."

Looking into her complacent little face, it was hard to believe. But Gabe had gone with Bailey one time to the doctor for Peter. If he remembered correctly, there had been many tears.

"What did the doctor have to say?"

"He said she's small, but that's to be expected. He's very happy with her overall health and says that if I want to start her on a little cereal, I can do that."

"I understand you cried," Gabe now said to his daughter before turning to Lily. "She says it's because she wanted cereal all along. Frosted Flakes."

Lily was still laughing when Mollee came to the door to tell them they had a visitor.

"She said her name was Ana Banks."

"Show her in," Gabe said immediately as Lily looked to him in excitement. Bailey had told her that Ana had called when they'd been in Kashien, but Lily had found no spare time to return the call.

"Ana!" Lily said warmly as soon as she appeared in the doorway. "Come in and meet my husband and daughter."

"You got a baby! That's great."

Introductions were made all around, and after they had talked for a time, Lily invited Ana over to the house. She declined.

"My hours have changed. I work lunches now."

"Oh, how nice for you. Do you see more of Nick?"

"Yeah," she said with a smile.

"So does that mean that you and Nick are free to join us for dinner some evening?" Gabe asked.

"Yeah," Ana said with another smile, "we might be." She'd only just said this when she took a small step toward the door.

"Jasmine and I will walk you out," Lily offered after Gabe had said his goodbyes. She put the baby back in the stroller and kissed her husband.

"You didn't tell me he was cute," Ana said as they walked from the building.

Lily laughed but changed the subject.

"So will you come to dinner sometime so I can meet Nick?"

Ana looked at her.

"If you let me buy Jasmine a gift."

"Why, Ana, that would be wonderful."

"What does she need?"

Lily had been thinking about this just that morning.

"She needs the smallest, most modest one-piece swimsuit you can imagine."

Ana smiled.

"I'll give it a try."

On impulse Lily hugged her. "Thank you for coming."

Ana didn't say anything beyond a soft goodbye, but Lily had the distinct impression that she would hear from her again.

With Jasmine fed and put down for her nap and a load of laundry started, Lily gathered her Bible and translating materials and settled in the living room to work. She hadn't had much time for that since she'd returned and wanted so much to still make it a priority.

"Hi, Lily," a small voice said. Lily looked up to see Celia coming her way. On some days she seemed to be at loose ends without Peter. Just the day before she'd had a friend over, but right now she looked in need of company.

"How are you, CeCe?"

The little girl didn't answer but sat beside Lily on the sofa and looked at her papers.

"Are you reading your Bible?" she asked.

"I am, yes. Do you know a verse from the Bible?"

"In Sunny school."

"In Sunday school? Can you tell me what it is?"

"In Sunny school."

"Is that the only place you can say it?"

"Yeah."

Lily put an arm around her and pulled her close.

"I love you, CeCe."

"I love Lily."

Lily kissed her small forehead.

"Can we swim?" the little girl asked.

"Oh, I can't, CeCe. Jasmine is sleeping, and I have to stay where I can hear her when she wakes."

"Sarah's sleeping."

She sounded so sad when she said this that it tore at Lily's heart.

"Why don't you get a game we can play?"

Celia was all for this, and in little time she was back with Chutes and Ladders. Lily played with her for the next hour, amazed at how long Celia could concentrate for a four-year-old. It crossed her mind several times that nothing would get translated at this rate, but looking into the small, trusting eyes of this special little niece, Lily was able to push the thoughts away.

∿

After lunch Celia fell asleep on the sofa by the television. In the main section of the living room, Bailey had just settled down to feed Sarah, so Lily, with Jasmine and her bottle, joined her there.

"Bailey, how can two people live in the same house and not even have time to visit?"

Bailey laughed and admitted, "I was just wondering the same thing. How are you doing?"

"Tell me something, Bailey," Lily said without answering the question. "This baby has become my whole life. Is that normal?"

"If you mean you don't have any time to yourself and she's constantly on your mind, yes, that's normal."

"And how long will it last?"

Bailey smiled. "Not being able to think of much else will go on for a time, but eventually you'll work out a schedule where you have time for you. You'll figure out that she's not going to starve if she's not fed right now, and you'll understand that no one is going to come and take her away."

"In other words, I'll learn to relax."

"Well, there's that, but it's also just gaining some experience. There's no excuse for anxiety, but even with all the help you've given me with my own gang, you're still getting used to the constant care a baby needs. Even when you're not doing something for Jasmine, you're thinking about when you'll have to. It can be very draining."

It was so lovely to have someone understand. While the babies ate, Lily picked Bailey's brain about things that had been on her mind and then tried to relax and enjoy her baby.

It was another few weeks before she realized it wasn't working. Gabe found her in the bedroom in the chair by the window. Jasmine was asleep in her bed. He approached quietly and saw in an instant that his wife had been crying.

"Hi," he said quietly after kissing her cheek and before going to sit against the wall by the window so he could see her face.

"Hello," Lily said and used another tissue. There was already a small pile on the floor beside her.

"What's up?"

"Oh, don't pay any attention to me, Gabe; I'm just feeling sorry for myself."

"Maybe if I paid some attention to you, you wouldn't feel sorry for yourself."

Lily smiled. "You're not the problem. I am."

"How is that?"

"Gabe," Lily answered testily, "do you know the last time I studied my Bible, let alone did any translating?"

Gabe waited a moment, wanting to word his encouragement well but not sure where to start. He didn't speak right away but moved farther along the wall so he could move Lily's feet until they were resting on his knees. He gently rubbed her ankles and calves, using light pressure to ease the muscles.

"Your personal Bible study needs to be a priority, Lily," he said without rebuke. "It's important. I know you agree with that, so we've got to find a way for you to have the time every day."

Lily nodded, realizing she should have talked to her husband about this a week ago, even though he was busy at work these days and often tired in the evening.

"Did you read the letter from your father?" Gabe asked.

"No, I saw the envelope but didn't have time." Lily shook her head. "Not even time to read a letter from my father." Lily just barely managed to keep from crying again.

"Come here," Gabe commanded softly, and Lily joined him on the floor. He wrapped his arms around her and continued quietly. "Have you ever seen those stress charts?" he asked, his chin resting on top of Lily's head.

"I'm not sure I know what you mean."

"They're usually done by medical groups or maybe insurance companies, but studies show something to the effect that starting a new job is fairly high on the scale. I think having a baby is always near the top. So is getting married. So now, what does Lily do? In June you moved across seven time zones, in July you got married, and in October you became a mother. In the space of five months you've hit some of the most stressful situations on the list.

"I'm not saying that God looks the other way when we're stressed. We need to be trusting and not tearing our hair out, but you have been under a lot of pressure."

"That's true, but why did you ask me if I'd read my father's letter?"

"Because he had a special note in this letter; it was to me."

Lily shifted to look into his face.

"From across the miles your father figured out that you would be trying to do it all. He told me to make sure you understand what your priorities are. He doesn't expect you to move away from Lhasa and still be a part of that church."

"Is that what you think I'm doing?"

"Not exactly, but he's not too far off."

"I need you to explain."

"In the bulletin every week is a listing of several ladies' Bible studies, but you're upset about not being able to translate."

Lily still looked at him, her expression open, so he went on.

"Your first priority is your relationship with the Lord. After that comes me, Jasmine, and then this church family. Much as I still want you to translate, Lily, I don't want you to put more time and energy into it than you do the things that are here."

"Your father already understood that. I wish I'd seen it sooner."

Lily sighed. "I hadn't thought about it in quite those terms. I just assumed I couldn't go to Bible study because Bailey doesn't go and I don't drive."

"Why don't we ask if anyone comes from our direction when we get to the Stringers' tonight?"

"So you want me to join Barb's study?"

"First of all, I want to know what you want."

"I would love to go to Bible study as long as I could take Jasmine."

"I believe they all figure out their own babysitting needs."

"Okay."

"Any other hurdles besides driving and taking Jasmine?"

"I don't think so."

"Then we'll do some asking tonight, or you can call the church office."

"I have the list in my bulletin too."

"Oh, yeah," Gabe remembered. "Mine's right here in my Bible."

While still able to hold his wife, Gabe reached for his Bible and the two studied the list he found there. Gabe did not know what each Bible study was working on, but he was able to explain to Lily who some of the leaders were. She had not met several of them.

Jasmine, completely unaware that her parents were in the room, slept on while they talked and made plans. Lily had been an early riser before having to get up in the night with a baby. They decided to try that again, even at the risk of lost sleep, in order for Lily to have that quiet time with her Savior. She was to leave the room and not worry about the baby because Gabe would be there.

"And today I'll ask Ash and Deanne if they'll take Jazz, so tonight after Bible study you and I can head out to the hot tub."

Lily smiled. "I would like that."

Even after they'd made all their plans, Gabe just wanted to hold her. It was still a miracle to him that she was his—his to cherish and take care of, his to forgive him even when he made mistakes and wasn't the best husband he could be.

Lily was feeling the same way about herself. She wished again that she had talked to Gabe about this before. She should have known that he would listen and take care of her.

～

The doorbell rang as Gabe and Lily were headed out the door for Bible study that very night. Evan, Bailey, and the kids had gone ahead, but Jasmine had spit up all over Lily and she had run to change her blouse.

"I'll get it," Gabe called as Lily's flight in the upstairs hall paused.

"Hello," Ana said when Gabe opened the door. "Is Lily home?"

"She is. Come on in."

"Is this a bad time?"

"Come on in," Gabe repeated, dodging the question. "She just ran upstairs and should be right down."

"Wow!" Ana said as she came more fully into the room. "This is even bigger than it looks from the outside."

"Yes," Gabe agreed, taking a moment to look around too. "It's pretty spacious."

"Lily said that you don't live here alone."

"No, we don't. My sister, her husband, and their three children live here as well."

"How does that work out?"

"It works well, actually. I've never known anything else, and Lily fits right in."

"You grew up here?"

"Yes. This is the house I came home to from the hospital."

Gabe found himself under Ana's speculative gaze. He was slightly relieved when he heard Lily on the stairs.

"Ana!" she said as soon as she spotted her. "I'm so glad you came."

Keeping with what she'd done last time, Lily hugged her.

"Sit down and tell me how you've been."

"So this is not a bad time?"

"As a matter of fact," Lily spoke as she led her over to the sofas and took a seat, "we were headed out the door, but I still want to talk to you. How is work?"

"It's okay."

"Are you still on days?"

"Yeah."

"And how is Nick?"

"He's okay."

Lily smiled. "Good."

"I brought Jasmine a gift," Ana said, producing a small gift bag and a card.

"Oh, thank you. Should I open it right now?"

"Sure, if you have time."

"Too bad Jasmine is sleeping in her seat," Lily said as she opened the card first and then the bag.

"Would she help with the tissue paper?" Gabe asked, and Ana seemed to think this very amusing.

Lily lifted out the gift and could only laugh in delight. Ana had done it. It was the smallest swimsuit Lily had ever seen, with red and white stripes, navy blue straps, and a blue anchor. Lily was enchanted.

"I know what we could do!" Lily had a sudden idea. "Come back tomorrow and we'll go swimming. Can you make it?"

"Not tomorrow."

"Okay," Lily said, put off for only a moment. "What day will work for you?"

Watching her, Gabe smiled. At one time she would have apologized for being presumptuous. Now she was setting all that aside to reach out.

"I'll call you after I check my work schedule," Ana said, her face as open as Lily had ever seen it. And with that, she stood. "I'd better get home."

"Thank you, Ana. I can't wait to see it on her."

Lily hugged her again, and this time Ana returned it without surprise. As they saw her to the door, they talked about everyone's plans for Thanksgiving, which was still about four weeks away, but Ana did not linger. As Gabe expected, Lily turned to him as soon as the door shut.

"Was I too pushy?"

"No. She seemed genuinely pleased."

Lily was pleased as well, and her pleasure was evident even after they arrived late to Bible study and she asked the group to please keep praying.

Chapter Thirty-Five

"Have you been stood up?" Bailey asked quietly when Lily and Jasmine arrived at the pool.

"I don't know, but on my walk out here I realized I can't be upset about this. I mean, Ana called me the day after Thanksgiving and said she would come swimming today, and now she hasn't shown up. I've done all I can do at this point, Bailey. I've got to leave it with the Lord."

"What if she's running late, and we're not in the house?"

"I put a note for her on the front door and told her to come around."

The women were quiet for a moment, and then Bailey spoke again. They talked softly because some other families were also at the pool. With their lounge chairs close, Sarah in a playpen, Jasmine asleep in her infant seat, and Celia in the shallow end of the pool, the two had some time alone.

"I want to tell you what an encouragement you've been to me, Lily."

Lily looked over at her.

"Even this thing with Ana. You reach out more than I do, and I'm trying to work on that. I've heard you and Gabe talking about women's Bible study a couple of times, and I want to tell you that wherever you decide to go, I'll go with you, so you don't need to worry about a ride."

"Bailey," Lily said gently, "where did this come from?"

"I used to go, Lily, when Peter was a baby, but when Celia came along I just got out of the habit. So you tell me which one you want to go to, and we'll do it."

Lily reached out to touch her arm.

"Thank you, Bailey. I can't tell you how excited I am to have you go with me. Do you have an interest in any particular one?"

"I had heard that Barb is doing a study about loving your husband. I think that sounds good."

"Yes, it does. The one on grace sounds good to me too, but let's go to Barb's."

"Okay. We'll probably just get a few weeks in before they break for Christmas, but let's do it. I'll call her today and ask how we get our books."

"Okay, and let's hold each other accountable on this. We're not going to let the holidays make us too busy to do our lessons or attend."

"Deal."

The two lounged in the sun and talked off and on. Bailey tried to remember if she knew anyone else who went to that study so she could tell Lily. She was able to connect some people, and that was fun.

"Are we still headed out to Christmas shop tomorrow?" Lily asked.

"I think so. Deanne is planning on it. I have only one errand to run, and we can do that on the way."

About an hour later, Evan found them still making plans and soaking up the rays while his oldest daughter frolicked with a little friend she had made.

"Lily, there was a message for you on the answering machine. Ana says she's sorry, but she can't come."

"Thanks, Evan. Did she say anything else?"

"Only that she would call you back."

Lily nodded before looking to Bailey.

"Well, at least I know."

"Do you have her number?"

"I do, yes, and I might call when she's at work so she won't feel awkward. That way I can leave a message and she'll know I'm not upset."

"That's a good way to handle it."

"I didn't erase the message, Lily, in case you wanted to hear it."

"Thanks, Evan."

Evan sat on the edge of his wife's lounge chair just then so he could tell her something. Lily was glad. She wanted a few minutes to pray and ask the Lord to help her not stand in the way for Ana.

Maybe I came on too strong, Lord. Maybe I scared her away. Help me to be bold and kind. Help me to reach out with a good balance of grace and truth.

Lily also prayed that she would leave it with the Lord and not fret. He wanted Ana to come to Him more than she did. Lily reminded herself of this for the rest of the day.

～

Gabe crawled into bed in the darkness while Lily was still over by the crib, making sure that four-month-old Jasmine was asleep. He listened in the dark as Lily came away from the crib on the other side of their bedroom and joined him in bed.

"Is she out?" he whispered.

"I think so."

Gabe cuddled close to Lily, who returned his embrace.

"You know," he whispered, his tone playful and dramatic, "we were having a good time with the lights *on*, and then someone decided she couldn't sleep unless it was *dark*."

Lily laughed softly. "Maybe we could get a soft light—one that would be very dim."

"Or maybe it's time for Miss Kapaia to move down the hall."

"It's already January, Gabe."

"What does that mean?"

"Ash and Deanne will be married one year in March. Won't they move back into the house?"

"Didn't anyone tell you that they asked for five more months?"

"No, they didn't. Can you do that? I mean, is the resort pre-pared to leave the cottage open?"

"Yes, because that takes us into our time off. But I just realized something else."

"What's that?"

Gabe didn't immediately answer.

"I think we need to have a family meeting."

"Okay. About all the moving around?"

"Yes. I'll talk to Evan and Ash about it tomorrow."

"Are you going to tell me what you're thinking?" Lily shifted slightly as she said this, but Gabe's mind was made up.

"Later," he said quietly as he brushed his lips against her cheek just a moment before finding her mouth.

"Gabe," Lily said softly between kisses, "will I always melt at your touch?"

"I hope so," he said with a smile in his voice, thinking the feeling was mutual. "I certainly hope so."

∼

Everyone but Sarah was in bed and asleep the next night when the family had their meeting. The men had discussed things that day and then talked to their wives, but everyone had a lot of questions. Bailey went first.

"Deanne, how do you feel about never living here?"

"I'm all right, Bailey. The house would be so close, and I know I'm welcome. The one who has me worried is Ash. He says it's all right, but this has been his home from birth."

"Ash?" Evan put in, even knowing what his brother-in-law would say.

"I'm fine, and I mean that. In fact, I'm excited about the pos-sibility: our own home, and a new one to boot. I feel guilty that we get it. I'm wondering if Gabe and Lily shouldn't be the ones."

"Lily and I have discussed it," Gabe said, "and her only con-cern is that you two would be all right."

"Did you realize," Evan put in, "that there's room to have a paved path all the way between both houses?"

"You've got things worked out that far?" Lily asked.

"They've been worked out for years," Gabe explained. "That area was always allotted for another house. We just haven't been to the need stage yet."

"What kind of time frame are we looking at?" Deanne asked next.

"To start building? Probably a month."

"That soon?" Deanne was surprised.

"Yes, and I wish it could be sooner. You might have to bunk in here with us for a while. Your cottage is already booked for next season."

"Would it be possible to see the plans?" Lily asked, and with that they were off. With Sarah playing in the midst of them, the six adults rolled out the original plat map that showed the grounds and room for another house.

The possibilities on the layout of the house were endless, but the placement had been settled for years.

"What do you think, Deanne?" Lily asked. "Will you like it?"

Deanne smiled. "What's not to like?"

Ashton put an arm around her. He had spoken the truth when he said he was excited. Had they come back to the big house to live, that would have been great, but this was exciting too. And in truth, the time had come. Jasmine needed Ashton's room, and since Sarah was already in with Peter and Celia, the girls would stay there and Peter would move to Lily's old room.

For the next hour they planned and talked and dreamed. Lily had made a cake that day, and they brought that out to enjoy. The plans made that evening signaled a busier time for all, but it was an evening they would long remember.

～

"Gabe," Lily called to him just two weeks after the family meeting, "come and see this."

Lily was in the hallway outside the door of Jasmine's new room. Jasmine was a baby who would cry when she had a need, but not first thing in the morning. Typically she woke up very quietly and stayed that way until someone came for her.

Right now the almost-five-month-old had spotted her mother from her crib. Her head was up as she looked through the railing, smiling in delight.

Gabe took one look and had to go get her.

"Good morning, Jasmine," he said as he kissed her cheek.

She smiled with her whole body, so delighted was she, and for a moment both parents just stood and enjoyed her.

"Is it me, or is she cute?" Lily asked.

"She's cute."

"Do you suppose we just think she's cute and wonderful because she's ours, but she isn't?" Lily asked out of curiosity.

"Honestly? Yes, we're biased because we think she's the cutest baby in the world, but I know from the way people respond when they see her that she's adorable to them too."

"Did you hear that, Jazz?" Lily asked her. "We think you're adorable."

A yawn escaped their daughter just then and caused both parents to laugh. Jasmine smiled at their smiles, and with that another day began.

～

"Lily, why are you so nice to me?" Ana asked Lily the first time they had lunch together in weeks. This time they were at the Little Bay.

"Why wouldn't I be nice to you, Ana?"

The younger woman looked away, tears in her eyes.

"Nick and I had a big fight this morning." Ana looked back at Lily, her eyes showing betrayal. "We live together. We're supposed to be falling in love. Why can't he treat me with as much kindness as you do?"

"Maybe he's being as kind to you as he knows how to be."

"What do you mean?"

"Ana, I'm not naturally a nice person. I've had to go through great changes not to be selfish."

"How did you do that?"

Lily Kapaia was not ashamed of the gospel, but she hated clichés and religious platitudes. Nevertheless, there was only one answer she could give Ana.

"I trusted God's Son, Jesus Christ, to change me."

Ana stared at her.

"A woman just moved in next door to us. She's so nice, and she goes to that Christian church up the road. Is that what you are? A Christian?"

"Yes, Ana. I'm a follower of Jesus Christ."

"Why did you never tell me?"

"Because the first time we had lunch, you said you didn't believe in God. Why would I try to force Him on you?"

"But you kept being nice. You kept wanting to be my friend."

"That's true. I still want to be your friend."

"So you did want to tell me about it?"

Lily smiled. "More that I can say, but only because I care, Ana. I'm not convinced that you're all that happy, and I know what peace I have in Christ. I wanted to share that with you."

"What church do you go to?"

"The one up the road."

"Oh, man!" Ana said, her hands coming to her eyes. "I don't think I'm ready for this."

Lily sat very quietly, and when Ana looked up, she admitted, "I hated church when I was a kid. My dad made me go."

"Why did you hate it, Ana?"

Lily shook her head quietly when she heard the answer, but Ana caught it.

"Are you saying your church is different?"

"I do think my church is different, Ana, but that's not what I would try to introduce you to. You need to come face-to-face with the Jesus of the Bible. If you came to our church, you would have a chance to learn about Him. That might be where your journey begins—by coming to church with me—but at some point you need to face your own mortality and consider eternity."

No one had ever talked to Ana Banks like this. She felt upset and excited all at the same time. At the moment, however, upset won out.

"I'll think about what you've said, Lily, but I'm not a bad person. Why would God—if there is a God—want to punish me?"

Lily crushed a napkin in her palm and set it between them.

"If this was a ball of clay, Ana, and you were going to make something out of it, maybe a cup or a small bowl, would you allow the clay to tell you what to do?"

Ana looked down at the balled-up napkin and then back at Lily. She didn't speak. Lily picked up the napkin and started to work it with her fingers, managing a decent impression of working with a lump of clay.

"Maybe you would start molding this clay, thinking, 'I'll make a small sugar bowl with this clay. I'll put it on my table to hold sugar.' But while you're working and forming the bowl, the clay speaks up and tells you to cut it out. If that were to actually happen, you would be stunned."

"And you're saying that we're all mouthy lumps of clay?"

"The Bible says we are lumps of clay, Ana, and that God created us. The Bible also says that we all sin, so don't ever plan to stand before God and say you are not a bad person. You might be able to convince yourself, but don't bother with Him."

"So why did He make us this way, if we're so awful?"

"He made us to love and serve Him."

"What gives Him the right?"

Lily picked up the napkin.

"The clay has no say in the matter."

"But He could have made us perfect."

"But He did, Ana," Lily said gently, seeing that the other woman was truly listening. "Remember Adam and Eve and the fruit? They sinned in the garden. Man chose to go astray, but God still loved us, so He provided a way back to Him through His Son. Now we don't have to be lost. Now we don't have to remain in our sin. We can be saved in Christ Jesus."

"How do you do that?"

"As my husband would say, you get on the same page with God. You agree that you're the problem and He's the answer. You believe that Jesus came to die for you and that He can save you from your sins. But I must warn you, Ana, you don't go into this with a motive of your own. God doesn't want just part of your heart. He wants it all.

"It's a life of joy and peace—not always easy and not always fun—but once God saves us, He lives inside us and helps us to live for Him. I've known great heartache as a child of God, sometimes because of my own sin and sometimes from outside circumstances. But I wouldn't go a day on this earth without the saving love of Jesus Christ in my life, and that's not even mentioning eternity."

Ana felt frightened—more frightened than she ever had in her life. She was used to being strong and taking care of herself, but what chance did she stand against this God that Lily described?

"Are you still going to be my friend if I need to think about this some more?" Ana finally asked.

"Yes. Are you still going to be my friend if I keep talking to you about it?"

Ana smiled. "Yes, but tell me something, Lily. You believe a lot of people aren't Christians then, don't you?"

"I'm afraid so."

Ana's face said what was in her heart.

"Sounds arrogant, doesn't it?" Lily picked up the napkin. "The only problem with someone telling me that I'm arrogant is that I'm in the same boat they are. I'm a sinner who didn't deserve the love I was shown, but the door didn't close when God rescued me, Ana. Anyone who believes will be received, and I can give you verses from the Bible that underscore everything I've said."

Almost as if the mentioning of the Bible was more than she could take, Ana retreated from Lily. Lily, immediately aware of the situation, changed the subject, telling Ana she needed to come and see Jasmine in her suit.

"Did it fit?"

"It's a tiny bit big, but when you weigh as little as Jazz does, that's to be expected."

"Is that what you call her—Jazz?"

"Sometimes."

"That's cute."

Lily wanted to ask if Ana thought she would ever have children, but she didn't wish to be misunderstood. It was wrong of Ana to be living with Nick before they married. The issue did not need to be compounded by adding children.

But more than that, Lily knew she'd already given Ana a lot to think about. She couldn't lie to make her feel better, but she'd said enough for one day. Lily didn't wait for Ana to find a reason to leave, but was in fact the first one to gather her purse.

Lily exited in the fashion Ana usually did, telling the younger woman to call when she had time. Lily left without looking back, but she would have been pleased to know that Ana ordered another soda and sat alone for a time.

Chapter Thirty-Six

Still in the apartment, Jeff and Annika Walsh had Gabe, Lily, and Jasmine to dinner about six weeks after they were married. Jasmine, more than six months old and the apple of her uncle's eye, was now sitting up with only the occasional tip-over. Jeff didn't care in the least if he made a fool of himself. He lay down on his stomach the moment Lily put Jasmine on a blanket in the middle of the living room floor and proceeded to do anything that would make her laugh.

"Look at the bear, Jazz," Jeff encouraged her, as he wiggled a small stuffed bear in front of her.

"Where did that come from?" Lily asked.

"Jeff has been bringing toys home from the grocery store when we shop," Annika filled in, a smile in her voice. "He says Jasmine needs toys of her own at our place."

"Yes, she does," Jeff confirmed. "And I've been meaning to ask you two when you're going to go away for the weekend so we can have her."

"Well, now," Gabe said with a smile for his wife, "that's an offer we can't resist."

Lily agreed with him. It would be very fun, but her mind was mostly on the thought that Jeff and Annika needed a baby of their own. Annika came to Barb's Bible study with Lily and Bailey, and the three of them were having some of the most wonderful female fellowship they had enjoyed in years.

Lily felt herself running ahead of the Lord and stopped to pray. *For all I know, You don't have children planned for Jeff and Annika, Lord. I'm so sure I know what's right. Help me to remember that You're in charge and don't need my help.*

"That's a serious face," Gabe said quietly, coming to sit very close to her.

"I was being stern with myself."

"Dinner's ready," Annika said as she put a casserole on the table and began to fill glasses with iced tea.

Gabe's look told his wife he would check with her later.

"Come along, Miss Jasmine," Jeff said as he plucked her off the floor.

"I can hold her, Jeff," Lily offered.

"You don't have to," he said with a smile walking to the kitchen table to put the baby in a little seat that hooked on the edge of the table.

"I've seen those," Gabe said, going over to inspect.

"Will it hold her?" Lily asked, a little uncertain as to how it was staying on.

"Yes, come and see."

The baby seat inspected and the aromas of the meal rising up to meet them, the four sat down to eat.

"We got a letter from Father yesterday," Jeff commented.

"We got one Tuesday," Lily said. "And do you know what I realized? His seventy-fifth birthday is coming up. We need to do something special."

"Such as?"

"Well, I was in the Christian bookstore a few weeks ago and found at least three books that Father would love. One was a Bible dictionary, very updated from his own. I didn't think about taking him in there when he was here for our wedding, but I know he would enjoy some new books."

"And how long will those take to arrive?" Gabe asked.

"At least three weeks, so we'd probably better get going on ordering them."

"Your father is a remarkable man," Annika commented quietly, her face thoughtful. "And very brave."

"What made you think of that?" Jeff asked.

"Oh, just thinking about his life. He had a burden for the people of Kashien, and he went so they could hear of Christ. I know he hasn't always done the right thing, but I still admire him."

"And he's changing," Gabe said. "I can sense in his letters a softening. Even with the little time I've known him, I can see a change. Not an easy thing to do at his age."

Lily had had her eyes on Jasmine, and she now said, "We need to add pictures of all of us, and the latest ones of Jasmine, when we send his birthday box."

"We have film in the camera," Annika said. "We could start tonight."

"It's a plan," Gabe said as he reached for another roll.

Leaving the dishes for later, Annika went for the camera as soon as dinner was over.

～

As was the tradition in Hawaii for a baby's first birthday, a luau was planned. Jasmine Ling Kapaia's birthday luau would be September 7, 2001, the day after she turned one year old. The absolute delight of her parents, who had just started their time off, she would be the guest of honor at this grand affair with family and friends attending.

The cove was not large enough to accommodate all of the people who had been invited, so the luau was set up in the area they used for the guests. But before the main meal began, tours of Ashton and Deanne's almost-completed house were conducted. They would be moving into the three-bedroom home in just two weeks, and things were coming together quickly.

All in all the evening was a delight. Jasmine received various gifts, and when she wasn't attempting to walk in the sand, she was passed from person to person the entire evening. She suffered the attention with grace, but her head was laid against her Uncle Evan's shoulder when the evening ended, and he carried her away from the barbecue pit.

"Well, you charmed everyone who attended," Evan said to Jasmine as he led the pilgrimage back inside. They had just seen the last guest off.

She smiled at him, and his heart melted. Indeed, she was as dear to him as though she were his own.

"Where is Sarah?" Evan always asked this question of his niece because it was so fun to watch her look around. At one year old and 15 months, respectively, there were times when the cousins didn't know that other people existed. But when they found each other, it was great fun to watch.

"Go night-night, Jazz," her father now said to her from another chair, and Jasmine smiled as she laid her head down on Evan's chest.

Gloria and Carson had not seen this before, and they melted.

"Come and see Grandma, Jasmine," Gloria coaxed her. "Come and let Grandma hold you."

Evan put her down, and she toddled her way over. Jeff, who was more delighted than ever whenever his only niece walked, took a moment to kiss her before letting her move on her way. Celia held her little hand and led her to Gloria.

Watching in quiet fatigue, Lily wondered if there was a baby who was loved more. But as she sat there she realized that the best way to show love to a child was to obey God. It was easy to lose sight of the important and buy a child gifts and fancy toys. But a heart that could show true love to a child would be a heart that understood what a great God it served, a heart that took obedience seriously.

"That's a serious face," Gabe said quietly when he sat down beside her.

"I was just thinking."

"Want to share?"

Lily looked at him. "I'm not sure I can get the words out right now."

Gabe needed no other explanation. He took his wife's hand and sat with the family, enjoying this special time. He had only to look in God's Word to understand the kind of God it was who saved him. But if ever he needed a reminder, he need only look at the faces in this room. Peter and even Celia had come to a saving knowledge of Jesus Christ. Now just Sarah and Jasmine needed to follow. Indeed, God had been very good to them.

～

Gabe took the block from Jasmine's tiny hand and thanked her as though it were a diamond. She was working hard on sharing these days, and her parents were reinforcing this whenever they could.

Jasmine had just handed her father another block when Lily came in the room. In her hand was a letter, and she looked stunned.

"What's up?" Gabe asked as Jasmine spotted her mother and walked over to attack her legs.

Lily sat down.

"It's a letter from my father."

"Is he all right?"

Lily looked at Gabe a moment before speaking.

"He says there's another baby. When he wrote this, he had just learned of her. She was five days old on the day he wrote."

It was slow in coming, but Gabe's mouth stretched until it was a full-blown smile. Watching him, Lily's own mouth opened a little.

"Gabe, what are you thinking?"

"Have you remembered that the church just gave us a gift for our *baby fund*?"

"Yes," Lily answered tentatively.

"And did I tell you that we got a letter from Mom and Carson yesterday?"

"No."

Jasmine had now worked her way into her mother's lap and was snuggling against her in a most adorable fashion, but Lily's eyes were wholly on Gabe.

"Mom didn't have much to say," Gabe went on with great pleasure. "But she included a check to add to our fund, and she said that Carson had been praying that we would have a chance to adopt again."

"Gabe, Jazz is only 14 months old," Lily felt a need to remind her spouse, even as her heart was losing ground. "And we just started the busy season."

"Nevertheless, there's a baby in Kashien who needs a home. What better place than here?"

Lily tried not to smile at his tone or face, but it wasn't working. She didn't know how they would all survive this. But as sure as Gabe Kapaia was smiling at her, Lily knew she was headed back to Kashien to adopt another baby.

Epilogue

More than Five Years Later
Capital City, Kashien

For the first time Owen did not meet Gabe and Lily as they came out of customs. Another first for the adopting couple was that they didn't come alone. Six-and-a-half-year-old Jasmine was old enough to understand about keeping her eyes down, and five-year-old Cathleen was doing very well too. But three-year-old Alison had no such qualms. Having slept on the plane, she was now ready to take in everything and smile at whoever looked her way. Her parents had nowhere near as much energy, but they knew the routine, and it wasn't long before they were walking into the hotel.

Gabe handled all arrangements and ushered his family to the room, hoping their plan would come together as neatly as it had in the letters to his father-in-law. He opened the door and smiled when he saw him. Owen Walsh had just stood up from his place in the chair, a smile coming to his face as both Jasmine and Cathleen ran to him.

This was the reason they didn't meet in the airport. Lily had done nothing but talk about her father for months, and the children would not have understood why they couldn't hug him and greet him the moment he came into view. The hotel allowed them the privacy needed to do this.

Lily came next, Alison in her arms, and the reunion was complete. For a time Owen gave all his attention to the little girls. He looked at their new shoes and told them about the country they had been born in and what an honor it was to have them back. They showed him the drawings they had done, the ones their mother had tucked into a side pocket in the suitcase, and generally had a wonderful time.

As they had in the past, Owen and Gabe went for food and brought it back to the hotel so they could relax in this foreign culture. Once the girls were busy with their meal, the adults had time to talk.

"How are Jefferson, Annika, Jenna, and Gregory?"

"Doing great. Annika is still a little queasy with her latest pregnancy, but she sent new pictures for you."

"I'll look forward to seeing them."

"Jeff wants to know if you have electricity in the village yet," Gabe put in. "He wants to set you up with e-mail."

Owen only smiled and asked about the church family. Gabe explained the changes they'd gone through, some painful, but that many people had grown stronger.

"How is Ana?" Owen wished to know next. The two had never met, but Lily had written of her often.

"Out of my life at the moment," Lily said with regret. "Not too long ago I was thinking about how long ago we'd met, before Jazz was born. She still comes in and out of my life, desperately seeking but not wanting the answers I give her. I think I told you that she and Nick got married last summer."

"Yes, you wrote of that."

"We went to the wedding, and they seemed genuinely pleased to have us there," Gabe put in. "But Ana doesn't return Lily's calls very often. They still go to lunch once in a while, but there's a part of Ana that still holds us all at arm's length."

"Maybe they will have children," Owen commented.

"Maybe."

"If they do," he continued, "it will be hard for them, but it might help. Often having children causes one to face his own mortality."

The children had needs that interrupted the adults, so for a time conversation stopped, but soon after dinner, Lily had a surprise for her father.

"Okay, girls, line up for me."

Gabe and Owen both smiled as Alison lined up very proudly, her dark eyes filled with delight. Her older sisters exchanged a smile as they watched her and then looked to their mother.

"Go ahead."

The girls looked at their grandfather and recited the Twenty-Third Psalm in Kashienese. Owen, now more than 80 years old, sat with tears in his eyes as he listened to them.

The verses were said word perfectly, but Lily wasn't through with her surprise.

"Go ahead, Papa, talk to them in Kashi. Ask them anything."

To his utter amazement, the girls understood him and answered him in beautifully accented Kashienese. Lily had said that she would be keeping on top of their Kashienese studies, but he had no idea. And since this was the first time for any of them to return to the land of their birth, Owen was amazed.

But as special as the evening was, Lily and Gabe needed sleep. They would be headed to the public minister's office in the morning, and it was time to make an early night of it.

～

"It's going to be much the same," Owen said, having forgotten that he'd already told them. "But there will be a few extra papers."

Gabe and Lily took this all in, keeping the girls very quiet, and for the fourth time they were shown to a small room, and a baby was handed to Owen. The moment the door was shut, the baby—a boy this time—was given into Lily's arms.

"A boy," she said in quiet wonder and turned to see Gabe's face. He didn't speak. At the moment he was only capable of staring at the fourth miraculous child God had given into their care.

What followed was a repeat of many years past, only this time it was made with three other children in tow. Gabe had no choice but to be seen attending the children when their needs arose while Lily held the new baby. When Lhasa came into view, the adults knew complete relief.

The girls were all put to bed, and Owen gave little Brandon Chen a bottle. Tired as Gabe and Lily were, they both decided to take a short walk. Lily took Gabe to her favorite tree, and the two watched the sun fall from the sky.

When it was dark enough not to be seen, Gabe put his arms around his wife from the back. Her waist was still small, and her stomach flat. With his palm he covered it.

"Do you ever ache to have a baby here?" Gabe whispered in her ear.

Lily laughed. "Gabriel, we got Jazz when we'd been married three months. When would I have time to ache for that?"

Gabe laughed with her and hugged her close.

"How many more do you think, Lily? How many more children will God give us from this village?"

"I don't know, but I want to be ready, Gabe. I didn't know what a mother's heart could experience. Jasmine was so special, but you know I had my doubts about coming for Cathleen. Now I can't imagine life without any of them, even this tiny baby boy whom I just met."

Gabe turned Lily in his embrace, his back to the tree and Lily close against him.

"We'll keep praying, Lil. We'll pray for the people of this village, that they would all turn to Him. But we'll still keep asking God to strengthen us for each new little person He sends our way."

"And for each other," Lily added, "for our marriage, so that when they're all gone, we'll still be strong in Him."

"Either way I win," Gabe said, looking down into her face.

"How's that?"

"Whether or not the children are home, or grown and gone, you'll still be mine."

A soft laugh filled with utter contentment escaped Lily, just before Gabe's lips came down to meet hers.

Books by Lori Wick

A Place Called Home Series
A Place Called Home
A Song for Silas
The Long Road Home
A Gathering of Memories

The Californians
Whatever Tomorrow Brings
As Time Goes By
Sean Donovan
Donovan's Daughter

Kensington Chronicles
The Hawk and the Jewel
Wings of the Morning
Who Brings Forth the Wind
The Knight and the Dove

Rocky Mountain Memories
Where the Wild Rose Blooms
Whispers of Moonlight
To Know Her by Name
Promise Me Tomorrow

The Yellow Rose Trilogy
Every Little Thing About You
A Texas Sky
City Girl

English Garden Series
The Proposal
The Rescue
The Visitor
The Pursuit

The Tucker Mills Trilogy
Moonlight on the Millpond
Just Above a Whisper
Leave a Candle Burning

Big Sky Dreams
Cassidy
Sabrina
Jessie

Contemporary Fiction
Sophie's Heart
Pretense
The Princess
Bamboo & Lace
Every Storm
White Chocolate Moments

To learn more about books by Harvest House Publishers
or to read sample chapters, log on to our website:

www.harvesthousepublishers.com

HARVEST HOUSE PUBLISHERS

EUGENE, OREGON